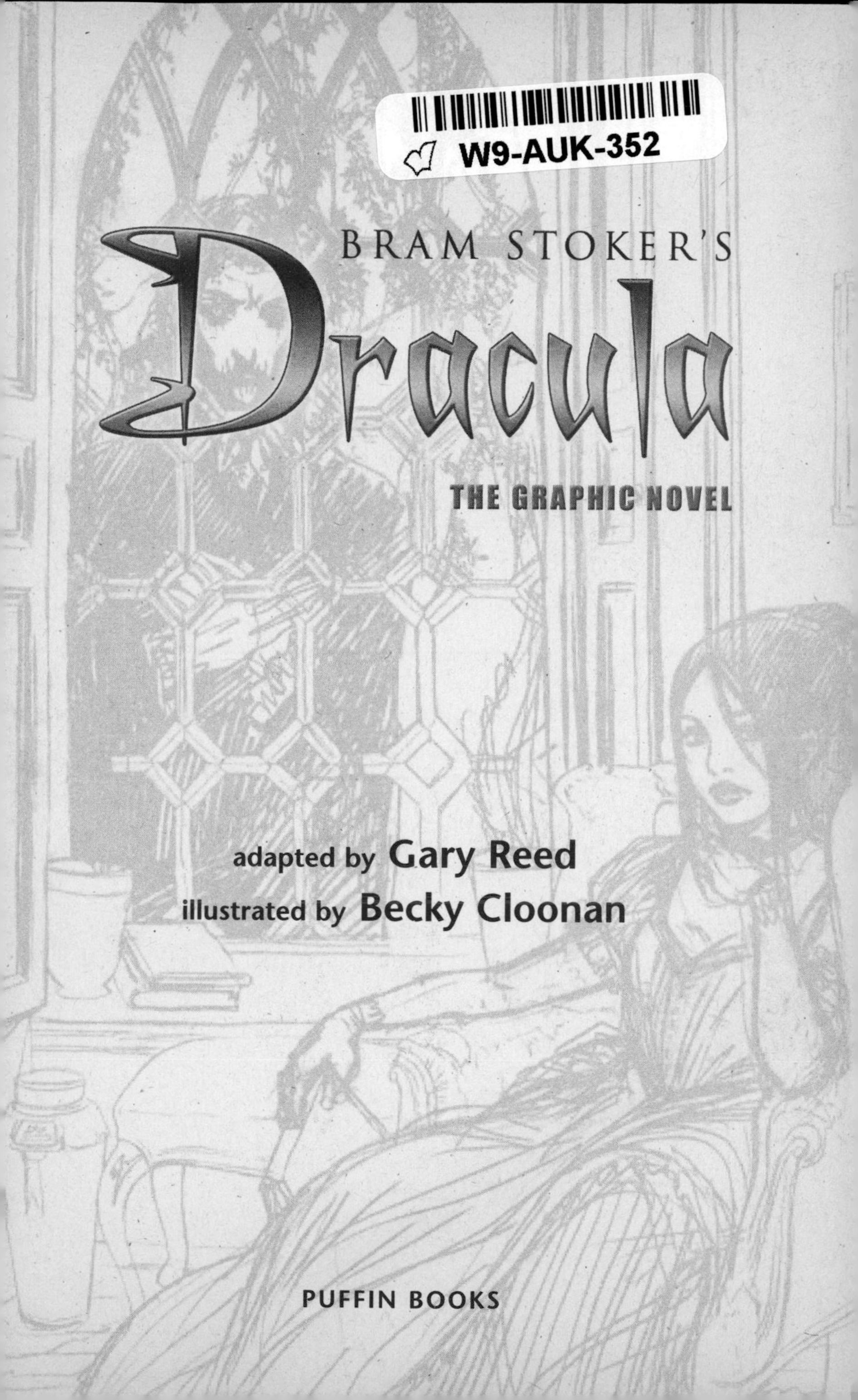

BRAM STOKER'S

Dracula

THE GRAPHIC NOVEL

adapted by **Gary Reed**
illustrated by **Becky Cloonan**

PUFFIN BOOKS

PUFFIN BOOKS
Published by the Penguin Group
Penguin Young Readers Group,
345 Hudson Street, New York, NY 10014 U.S.A.
Penguin Group (Canada), 90 Eglinton Avenue East, Suite 700,
Toronto, Ontario, Canada M4P 2Y3 (a division of Pearson Penguin Canada Inc.)
Penguin Books Ltd, 80 Strand, London WC2R 0RL, England
Penguin Ireland, 25 St. Stephen's Green, Dublin 2, Ireland
(a division of Penguin Books Ltd)
Penguin Group (Australia), 250 Camberwell Road, Camberwell, Victoria 3124, Australia (a division of Pearson Australia Group Pty Ltd)
Penguin Books India Pvt Ltd, 11 Community Centre, Panchsheel Park,
New Delhi – 110 017, India
Penguin Group (NZ), Cnr Airborne and Rosedale Roads, Albany, Auckland 1310,
New Zealand (a division of Pearson New Zealand Ltd)
Penguin Books (South Africa) (Pty) Ltd, 24 Sturdee Avenue, Rosebank,
Johannesburg 2196, South Africa

Registered Offices: Penguin Books Ltd, 80 Strand, London WC2R 0RL, England

First published by Puffin Books, a division of Penguin Young Readers Group, 2006

10 9 8 7 6 5 4 3 2 1

Copyright © Byron Preiss Visual Publications, 2006
All rights reserved

A Byron Preiss Book
Byron Preiss Visual Publications
24 West 25th Street, New York, NY 10010

Adapted by Gary Reed
Illustrated by Becky Cloonan
Cover art by Dennis Calero
Lettering by Ryan Yount, Matt Postawa, Raul Carvajal
Series Editor: Dwight Jon Zimmerman
Series Assistant Editor: April Isaacs
Interior design by Matt Postawa, Raul Carvajal, Gilda Hannah, and Brandon Diaz
Cover design by Matt Postawa

Puffin Books ISBN: 0-14-240572-8

Printed in the United States of America

Except in the United States of America, this book is sold subject to the
condition that it shall not, by way of trade or otherwise, be lent, re-sold, hired
out, or otherwise circulated without the publisher's prior consent in any form of
binding or cover other than that in which it is published and without a similar
condition including this condition being imposed on the subsequent purchaser.

The publisher does not have any control over and does not assume any
responsibility for author or third-party Web sites or their content.

BRAM STOKER'S

Dracula

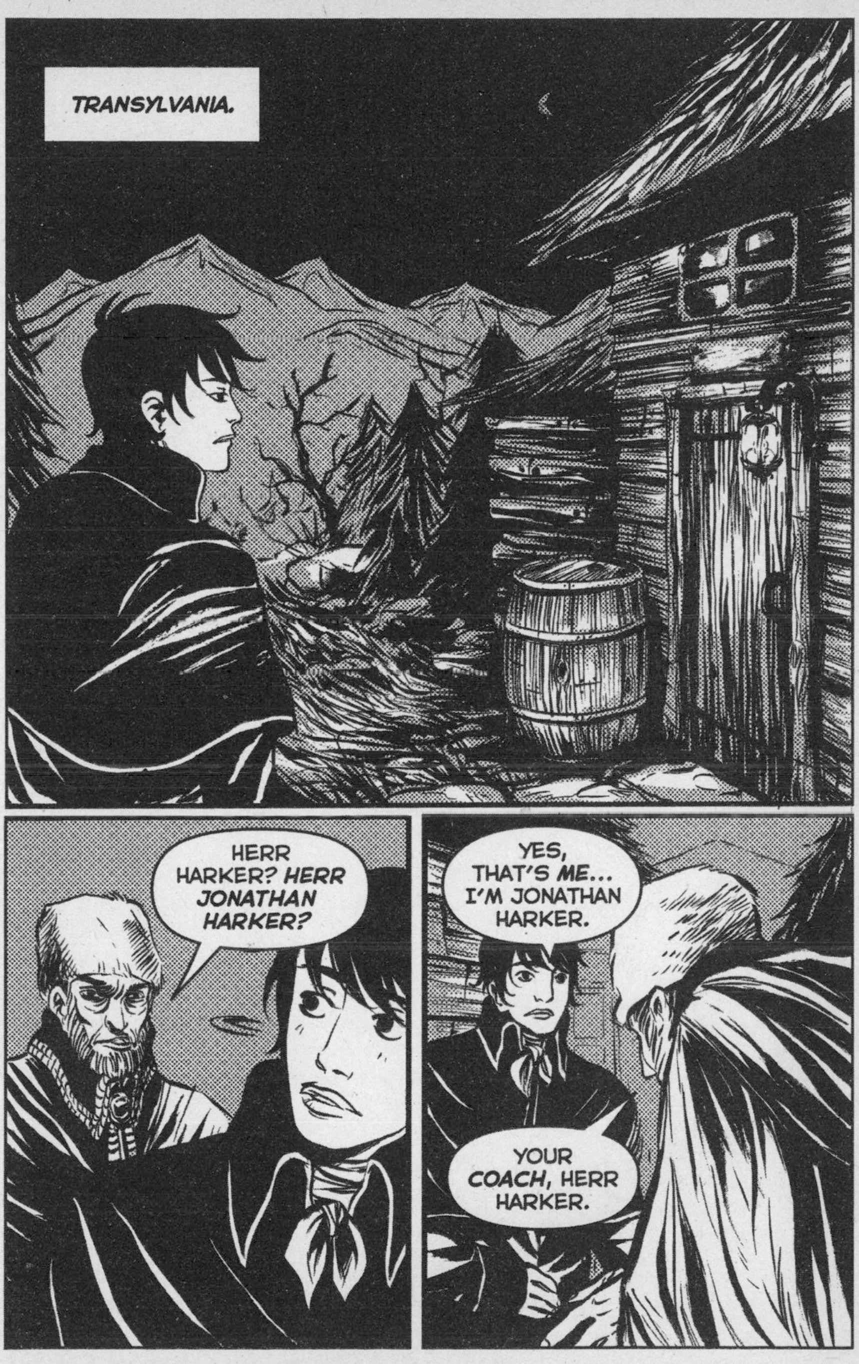
TRANSYLVANIA.
HERR HARKER? *HERR JONATHAN HARKER?*
YES, THAT'S *ME*... I'M JONATHAN HARKER.
YOUR *COACH*, HERR HARKER.

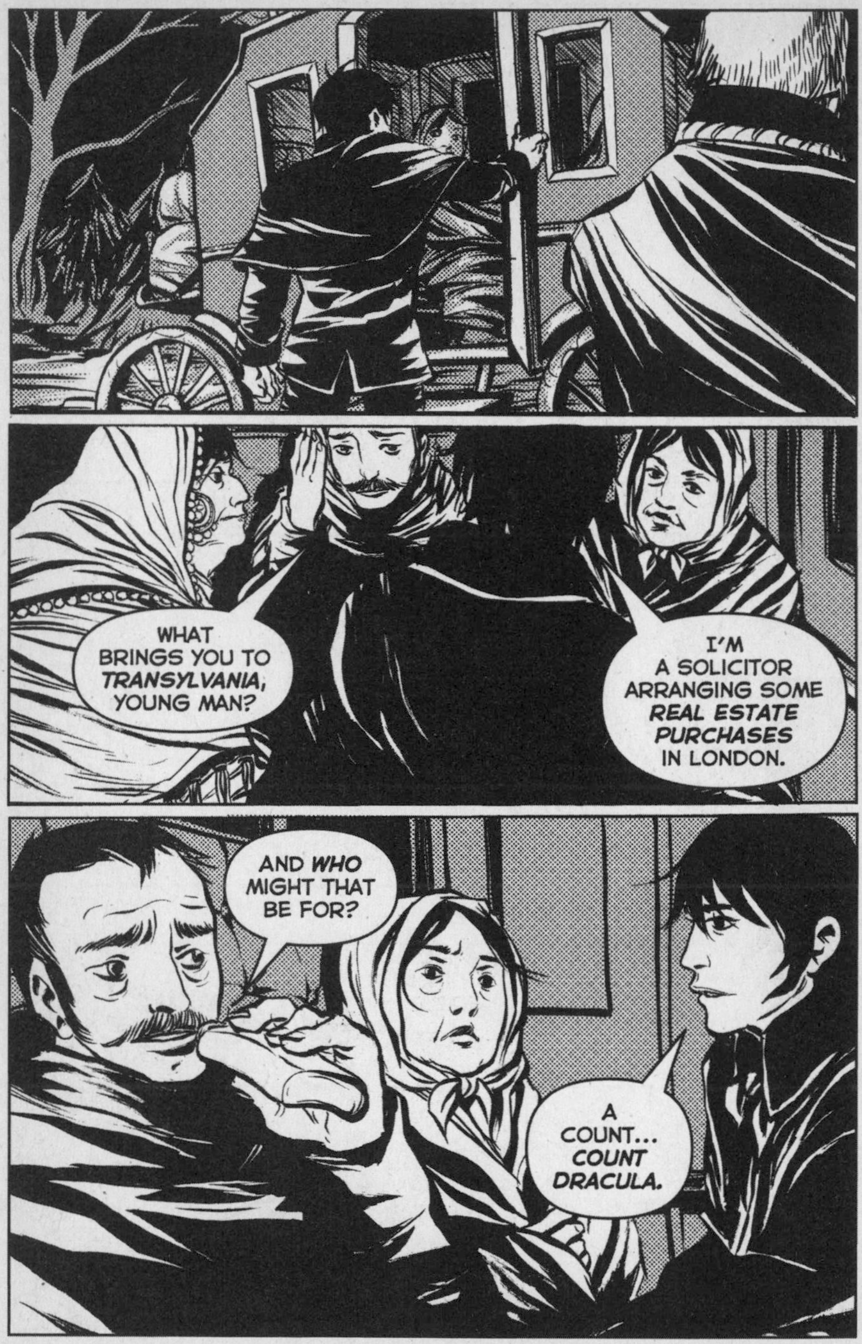
WHAT BRINGS YOU TO TRANSYLVANIA, YOUNG MAN?
I'M A SOLICITOR ARRANGING SOME REAL ESTATE PURCHASES IN LONDON.
AND WHO MIGHT THAT BE FOR?
A COUNT... COUNT DRACULA.

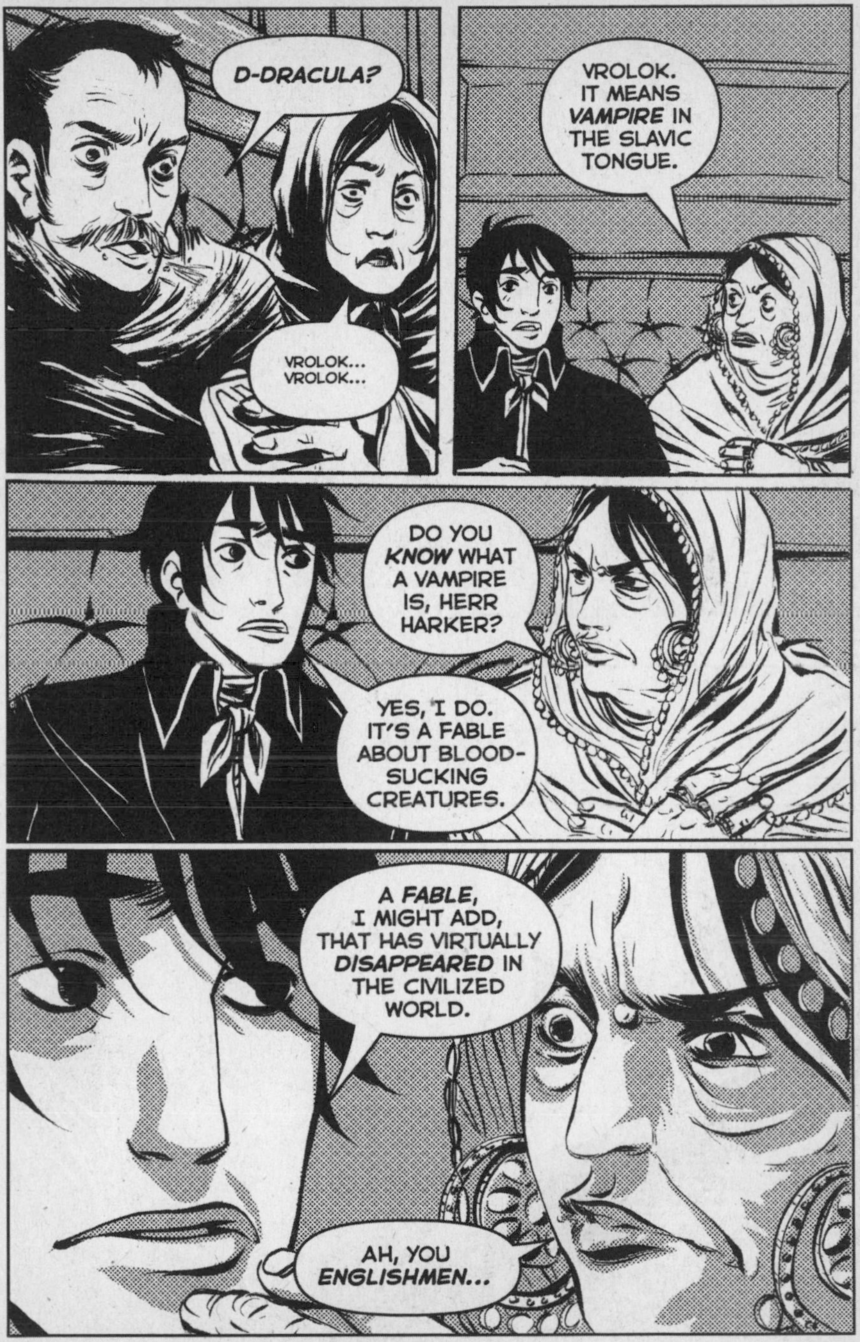
D-DRACULA?
VROLOK... VROLOK...
VROLOK. IT MEANS VAMPIRE IN THE SLAVIC TONGUE.
DO YOU KNOW WHAT A VAMPIRE IS, HERR HARKER?
YES, I DO. IT'S A FABLE ABOUT BLOOD-SUCKING CREATURES.
A FABLE, I MIGHT ADD, THAT HAS VIRTUALLY DISAPPEARED IN THE CIVILIZED WORLD.
AH, YOU ENGLISHMEN...

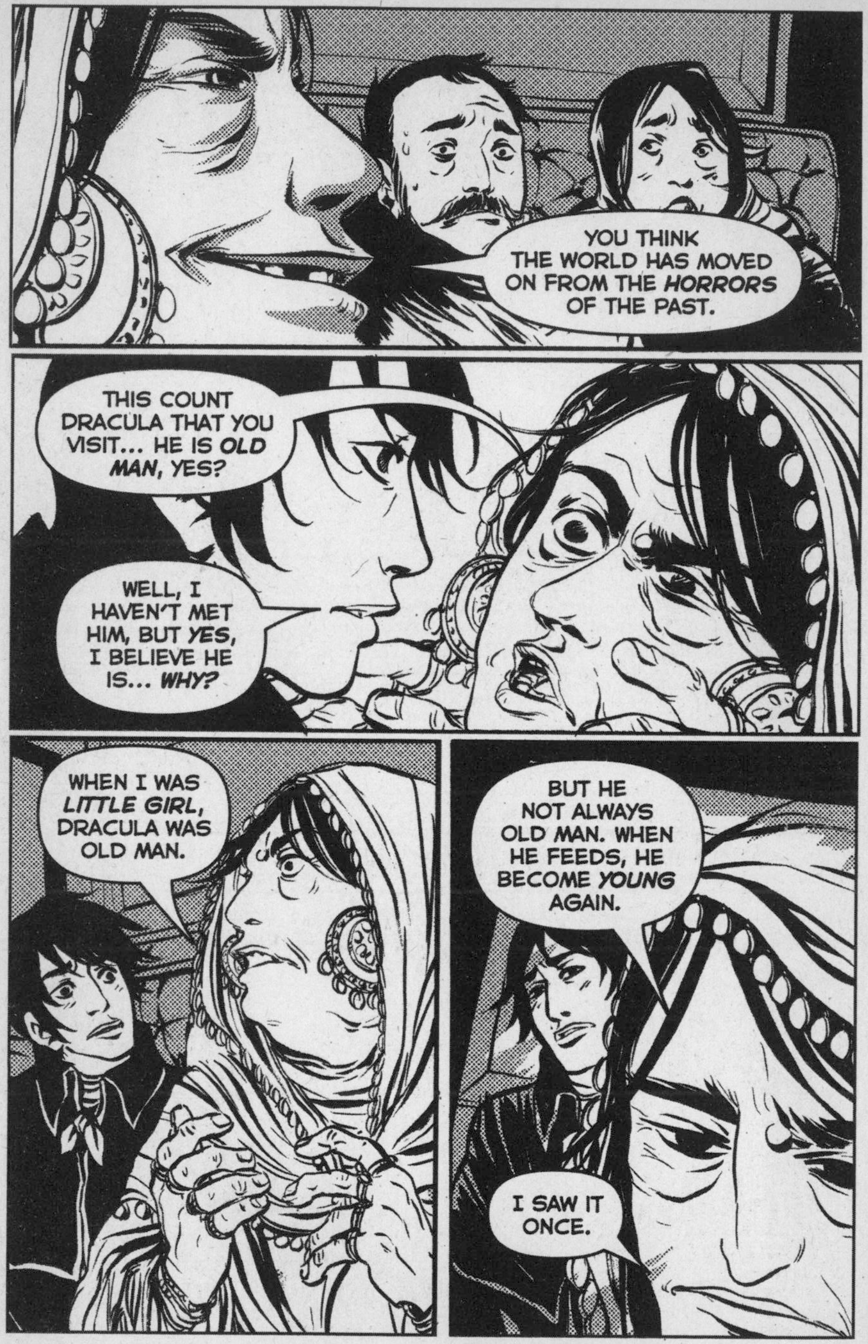
YOU THINK THE WORLD HAS MOVED ON FROM THE *HORRORS* OF THE PAST.
THIS COUNT DRACULA THAT YOU VISIT... HE IS *OLD MAN*, YES?
WELL, I HAVEN'T MET HIM, BUT *YES*, I BELIEVE HE IS... *WHY?*
WHEN I WAS *LITTLE GIRL*, DRACULA WAS OLD MAN.
BUT HE NOT ALWAYS OLD MAN. WHEN HE FEEDS, HE BECOME *YOUNG* AGAIN.
I SAW IT ONCE.

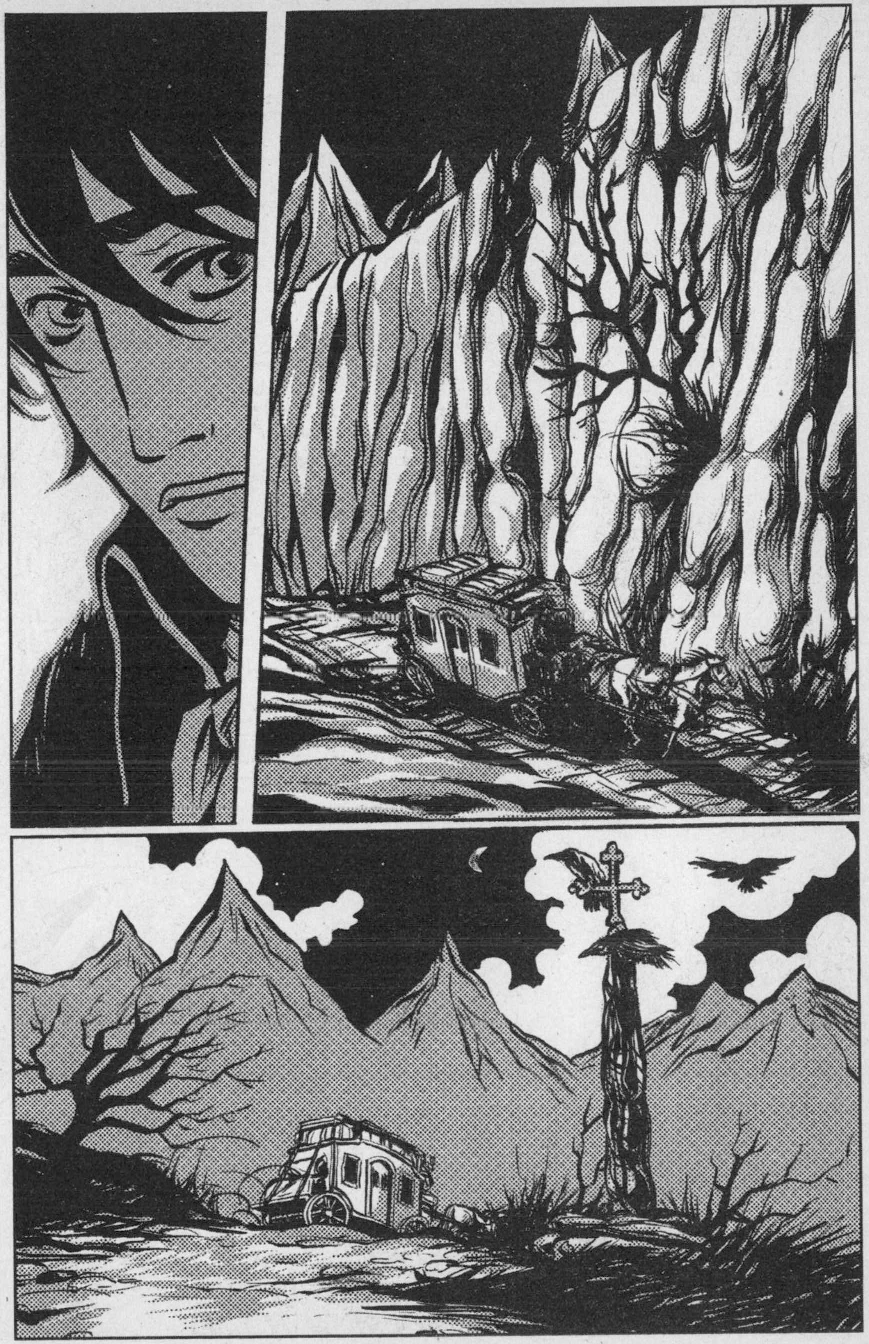

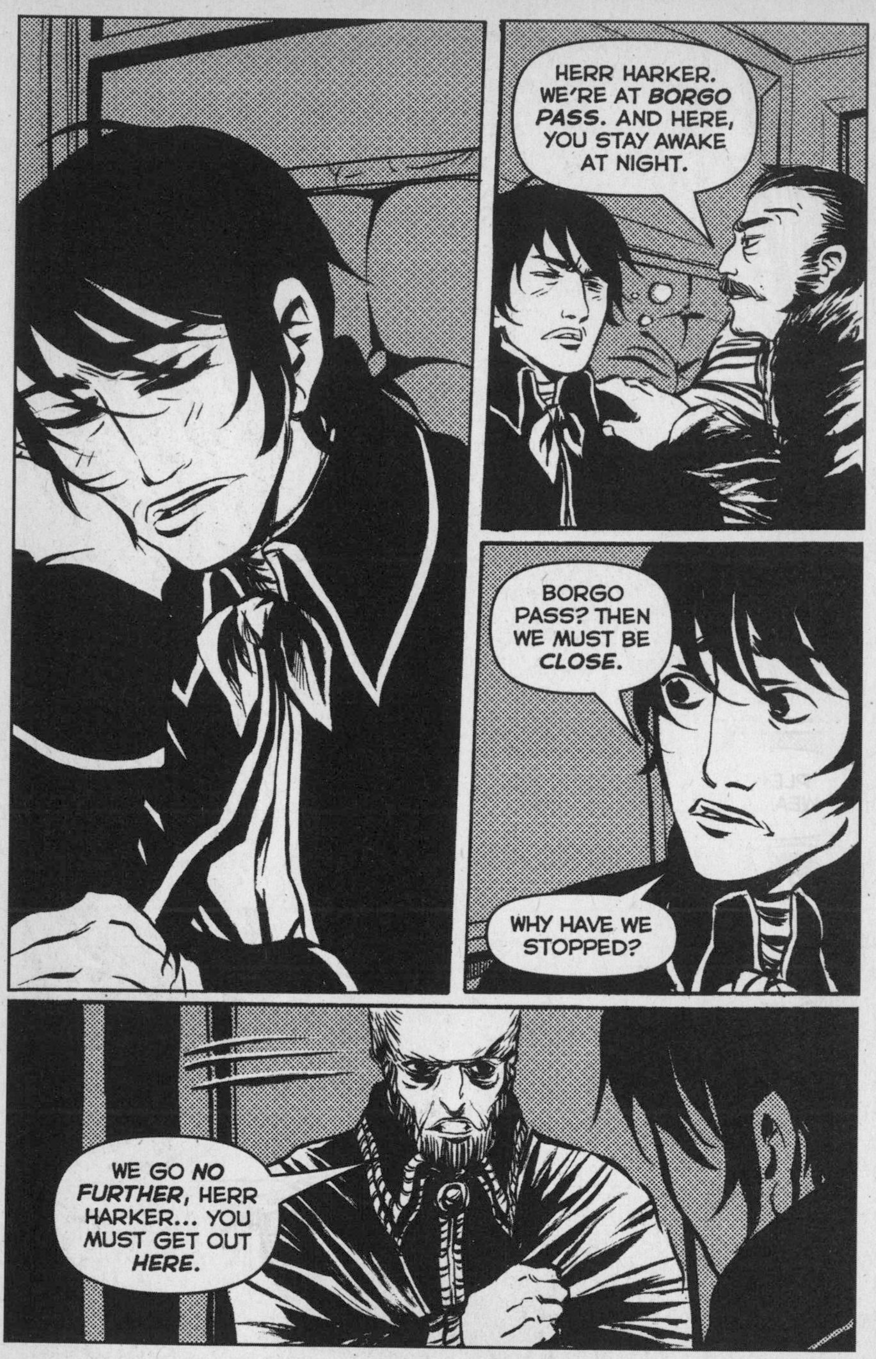
HERR HARKER. WE'RE AT BORGO PASS. AND HERE, YOU STAY AWAKE AT NIGHT.
BORGO PASS? THEN WE MUST BE CLOSE.
WHY HAVE WE STOPPED?
WE GO NO FURTHER, HERR HARKER... YOU MUST GET OUT HERE.

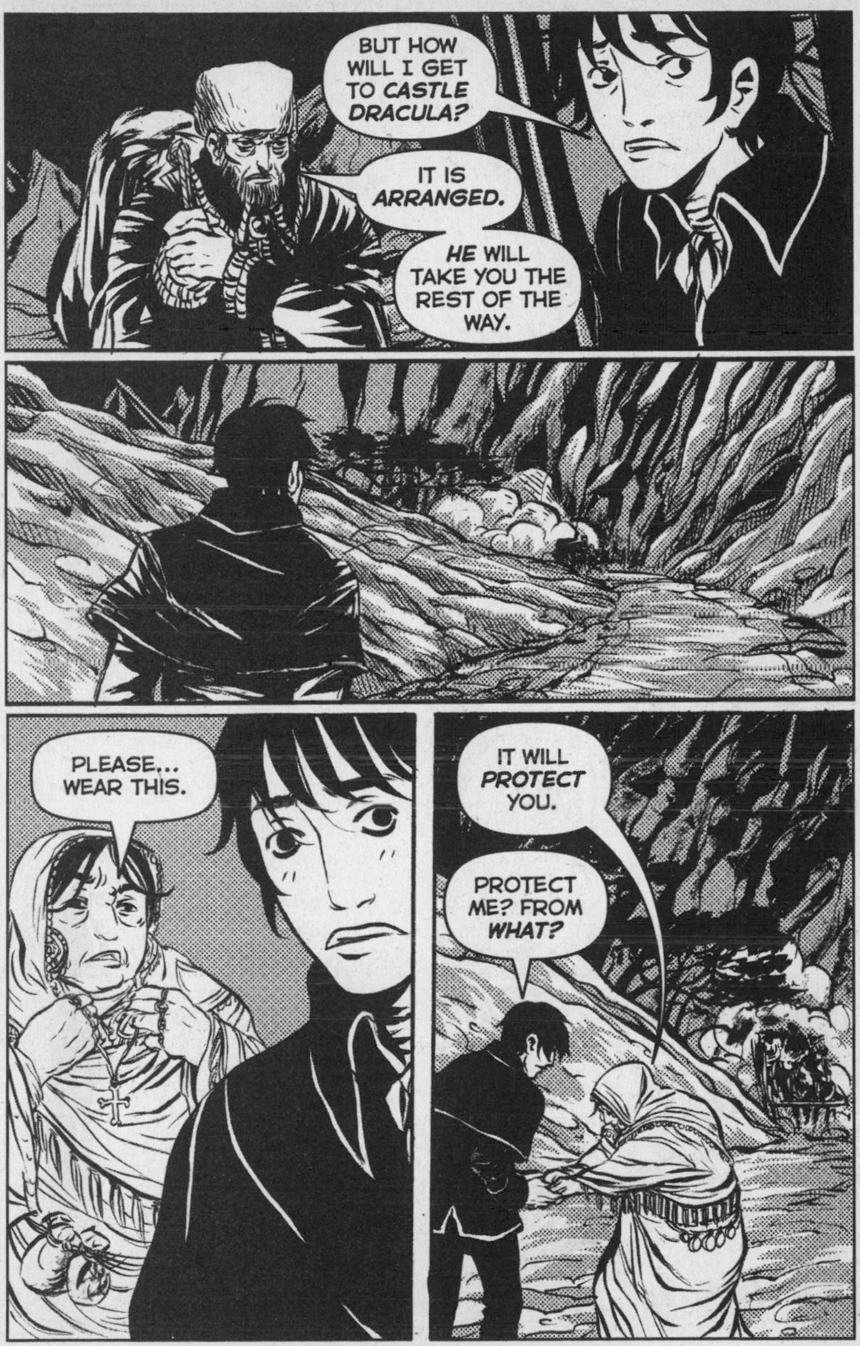
BUT HOW WILL I GET TO CASTLE DRACULA?
IT IS ARRANGED.
HE WILL TAKE YOU THE REST OF THE WAY.
PLEASE... WEAR THIS.
IT WILL PROTECT YOU.
PROTECT ME? FROM WHAT?

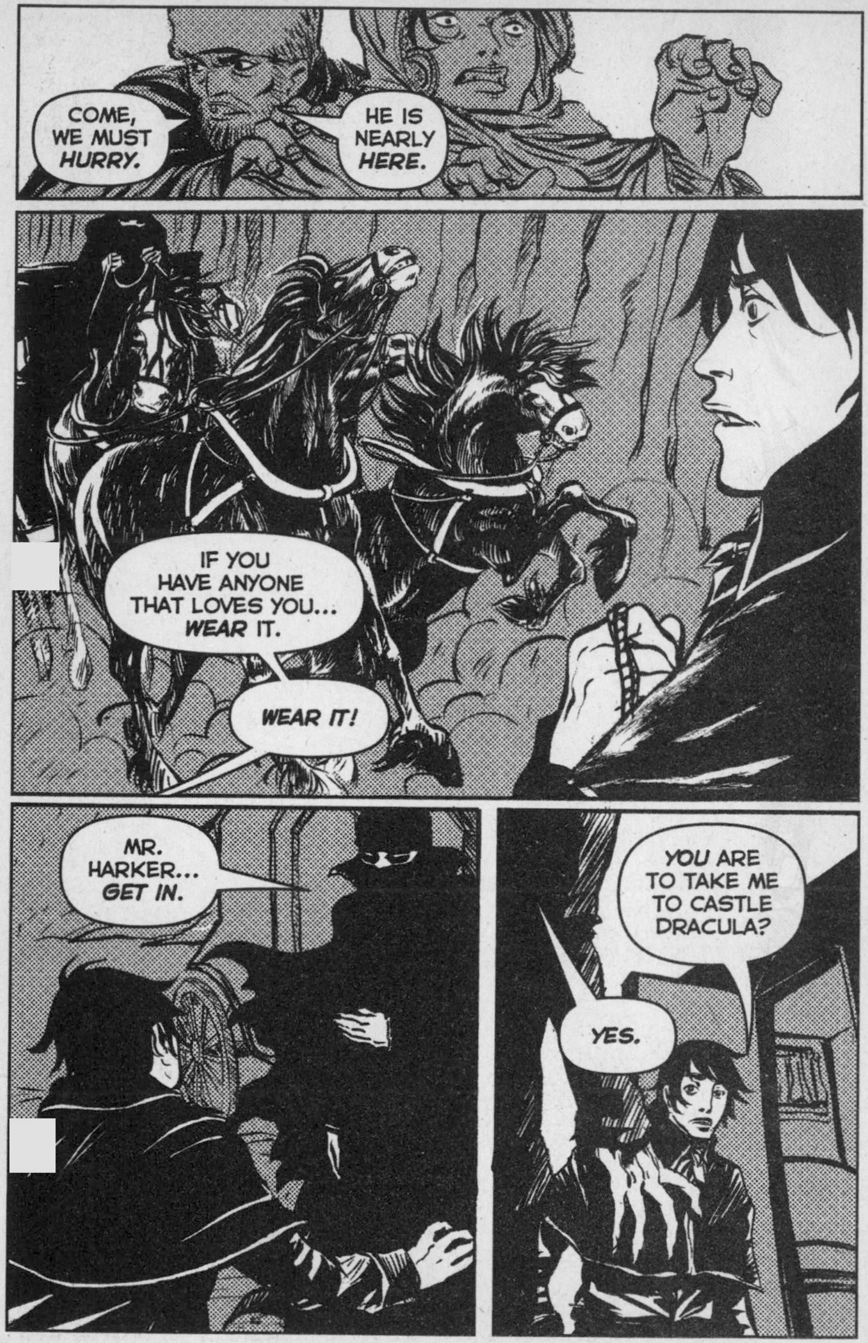
COME, WE MUST HURRY.
HE IS NEARLY HERE.
IF YOU HAVE ANYONE THAT LOVES YOU... WEAR IT.
WEAR IT!
MR. HARKER... GET IN.
YOU ARE TO TAKE ME TO CASTLE DRACULA?
YES.

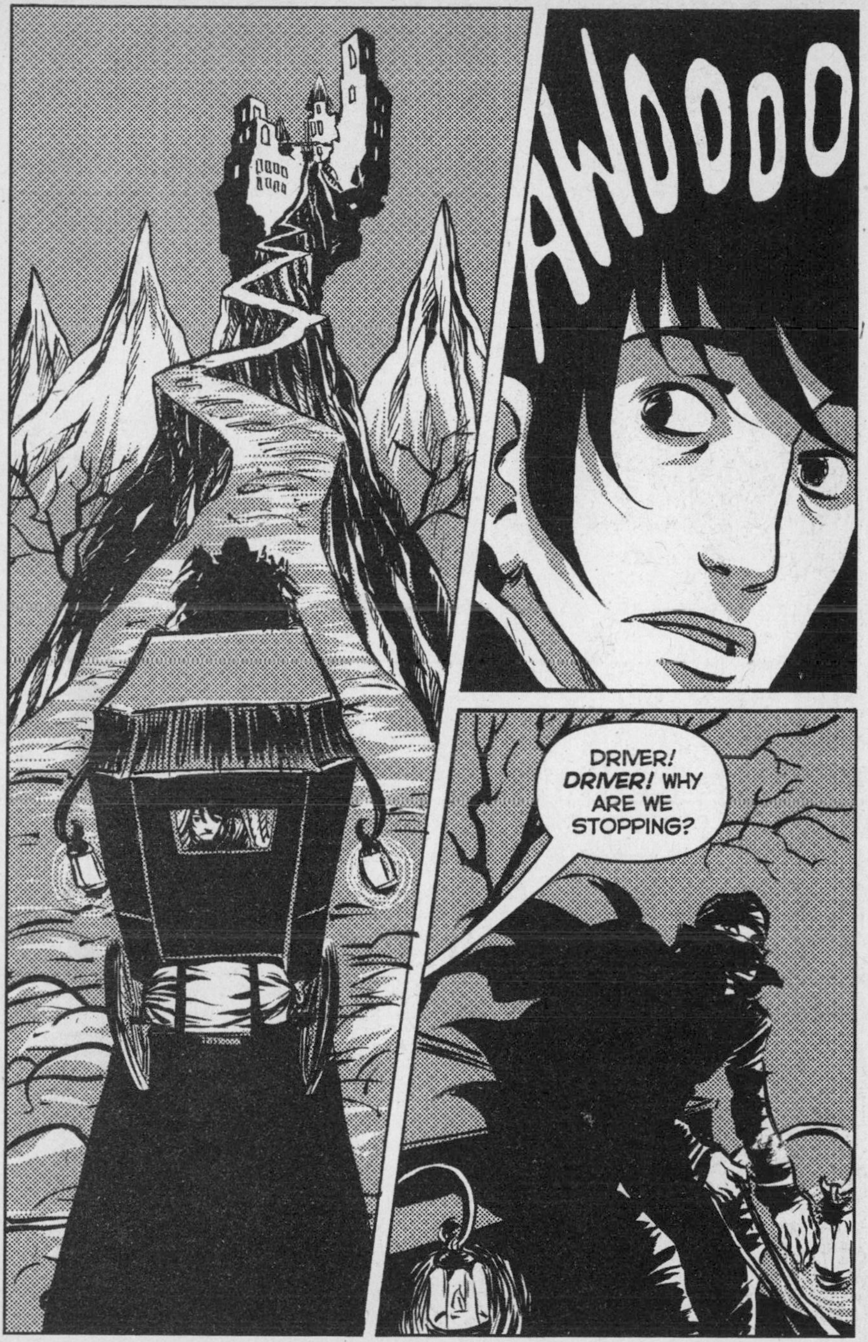
AWOOOO
DRIVER! DRIVER! WHY ARE WE STOPPING?

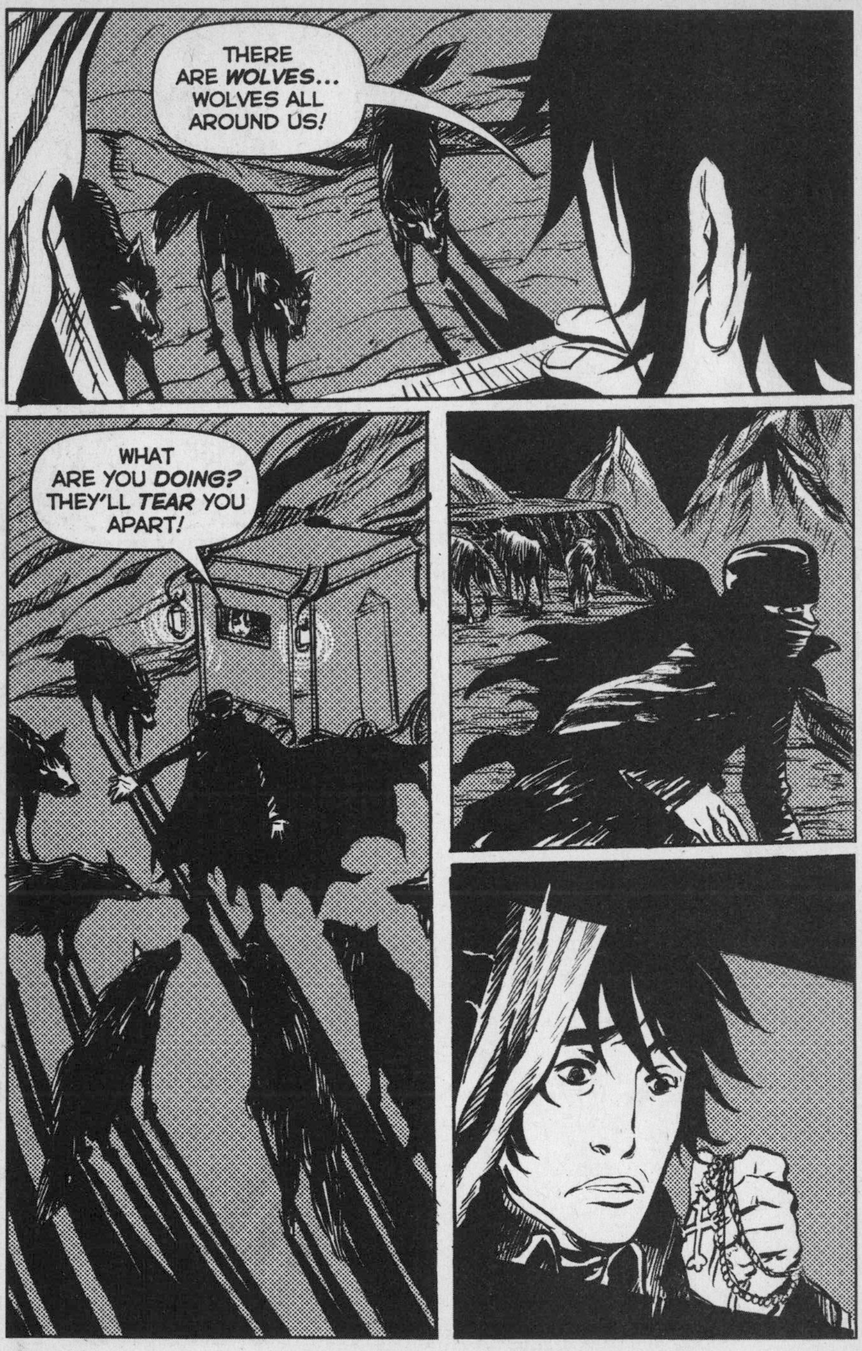
THERE ARE WOLVES... WOLVES ALL AROUND US!
WHAT ARE YOU DOING? THEY'LL TEAR YOU APART!

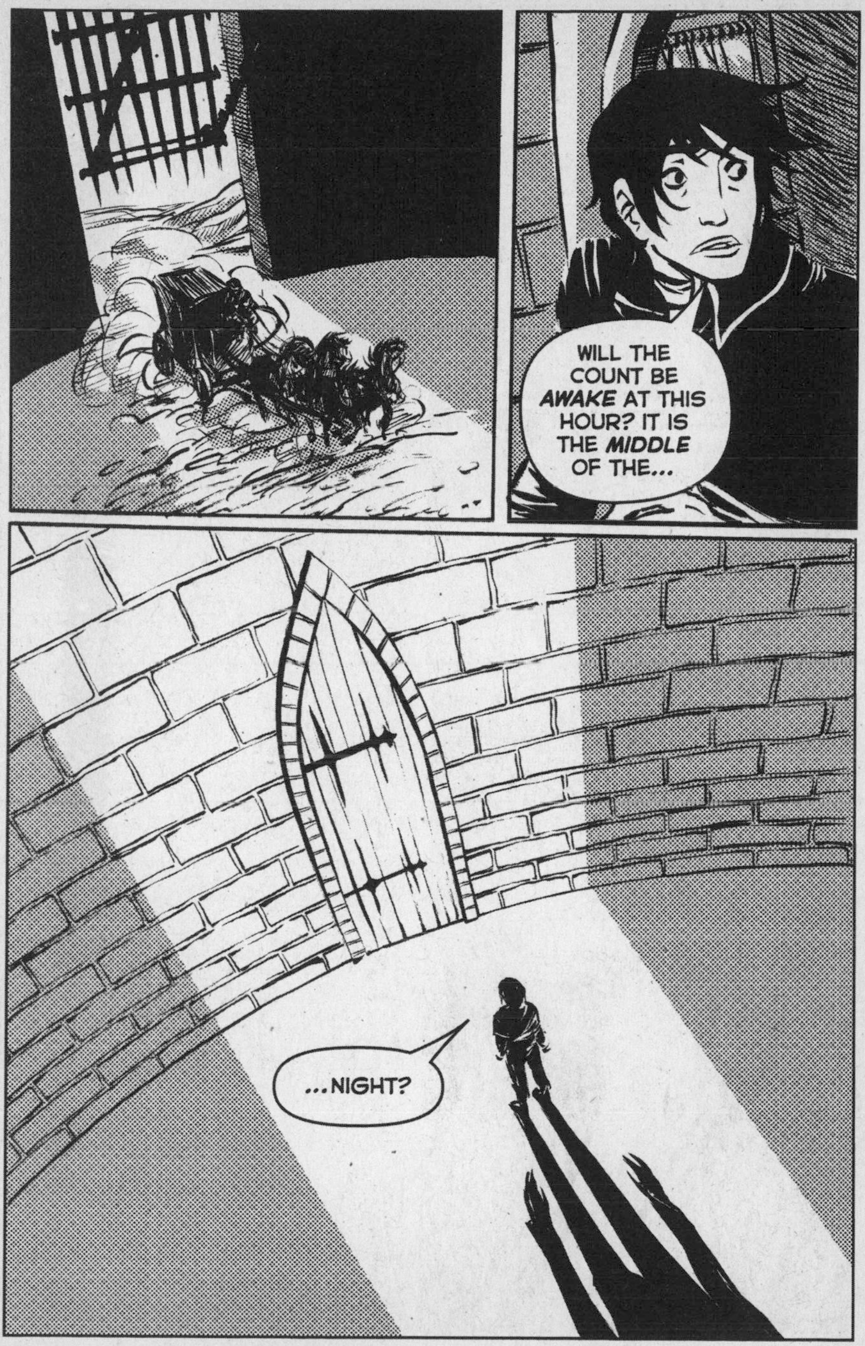
WILL THE COUNT BE *AWAKE* AT THIS HOUR? IT IS THE *MIDDLE* OF THE...
...NIGHT?

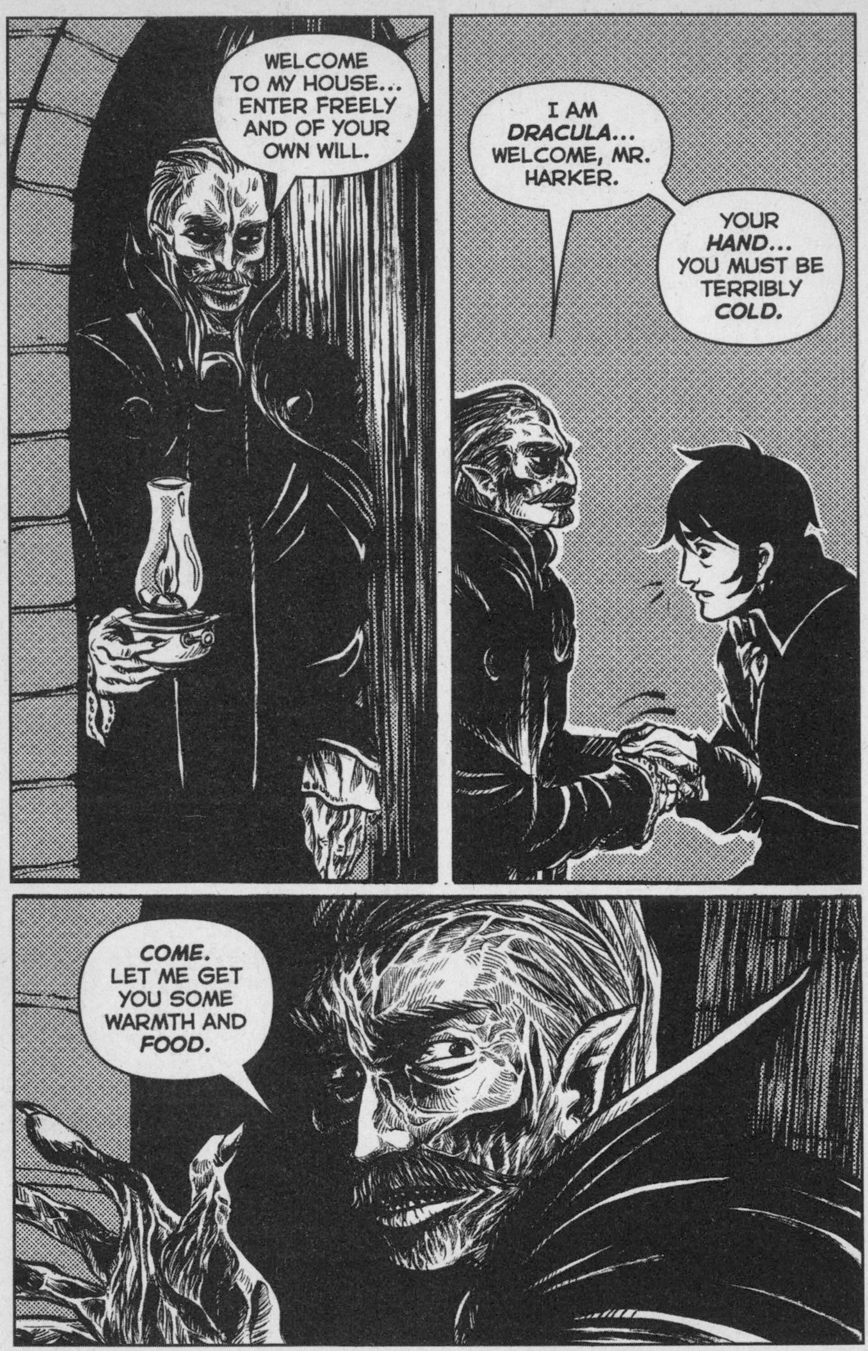
WELCOME TO MY HOUSE... ENTER FREELY AND OF YOUR OWN WILL.
I AM DRACULA... WELCOME, MR. HARKER.
YOUR HAND... YOU MUST BE TERRIBLY COLD.
COME. LET ME GET YOU SOME WARMTH AND FOOD.

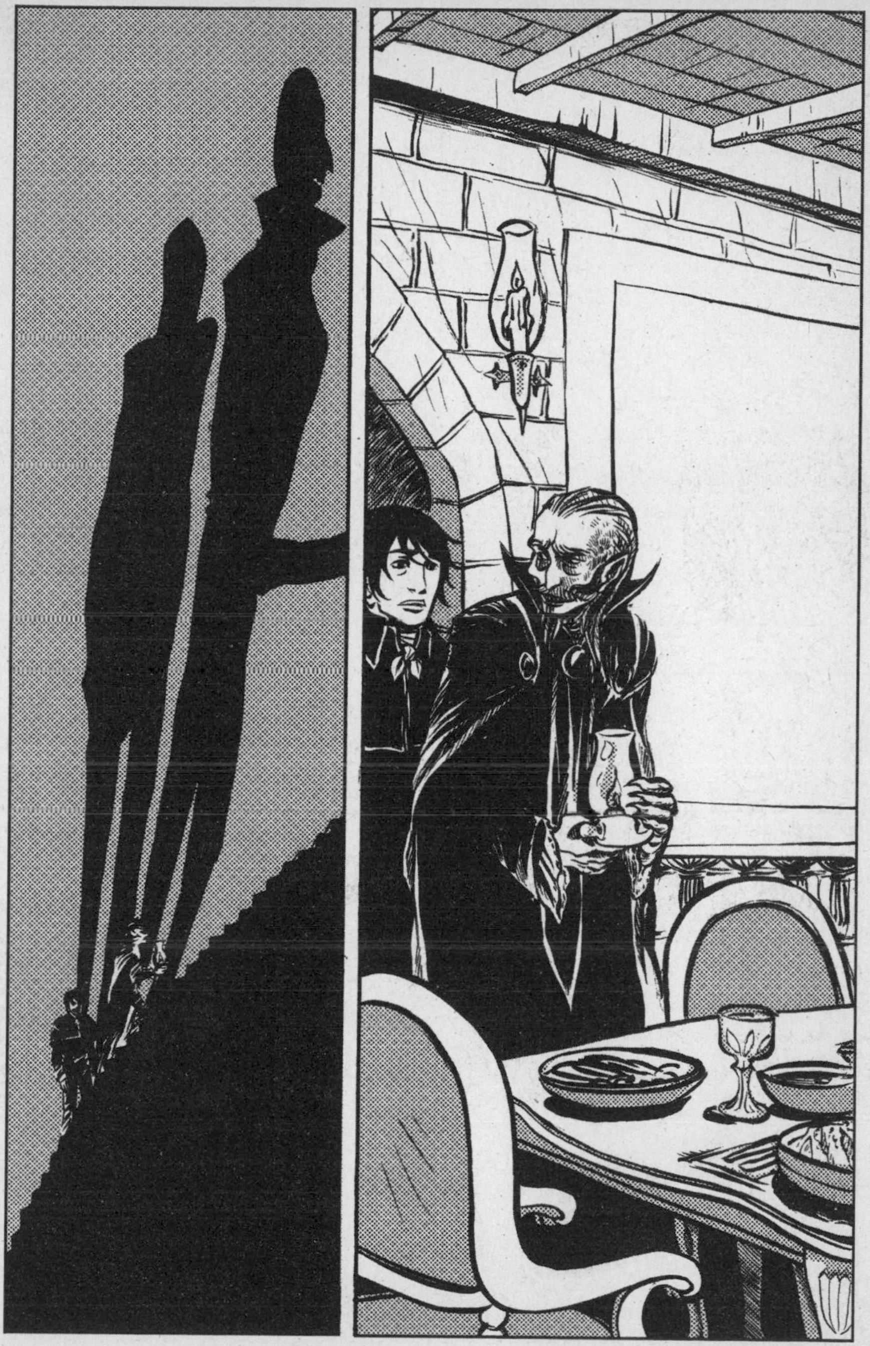

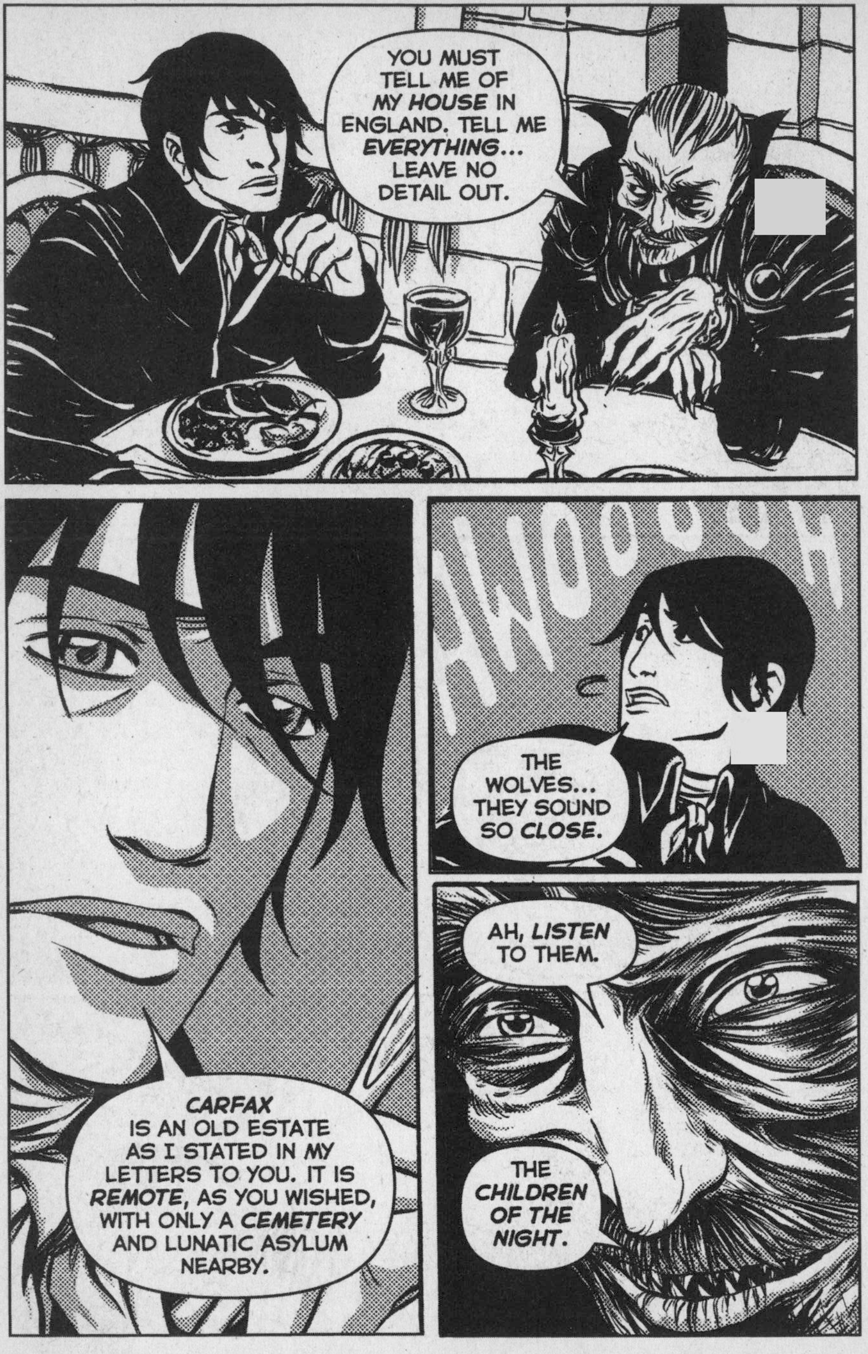
YOU MUST TELL ME OF MY HOUSE IN ENGLAND. TELL ME EVERYTHING... LEAVE NO DETAIL OUT.
CARFAX IS AN OLD ESTATE AS I STATED IN MY LETTERS TO YOU. IT IS REMOTE, AS YOU WISHED, WITH ONLY A CEMETERY AND LUNATIC ASYLUM NEARBY.
AWOOOOOH
THE WOLVES... THEY SOUND SO CLOSE.
AH, LISTEN TO THEM.
THE CHILDREN OF THE NIGHT.

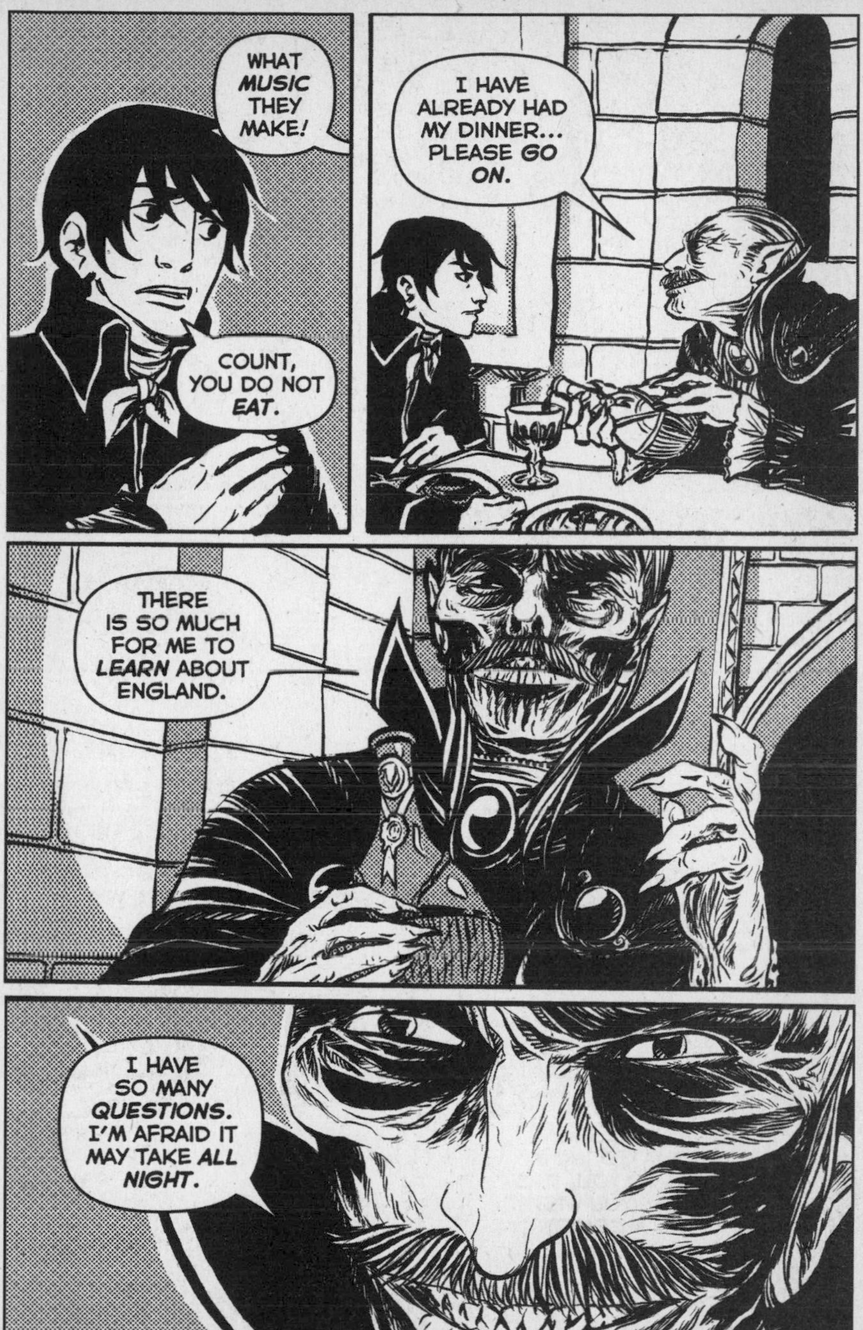
WHAT MUSIC THEY MAKE!
COUNT, YOU DO NOT EAT.
I HAVE ALREADY HAD MY DINNER... PLEASE GO ON.
THERE IS SO MUCH FOR ME TO LEARN ABOUT ENGLAND.
I HAVE SO MANY QUESTIONS. I'M AFRAID IT MAY TAKE ALL NIGHT.

My dearest Mina,

I cannot tell you how strange this land is, and how there is a sense of dread hanging over me while I am at Castle Dracula. Transylvania is a dark and old place and the Count is a very unusual man.

The first days here have been the same. During the day, the Count is not to be seen. But at night, there is a feast prepared and I sit and eat while the Count asks me questions about England. We stay up all night talking, but as soon as daylight comes he is quick to leave.

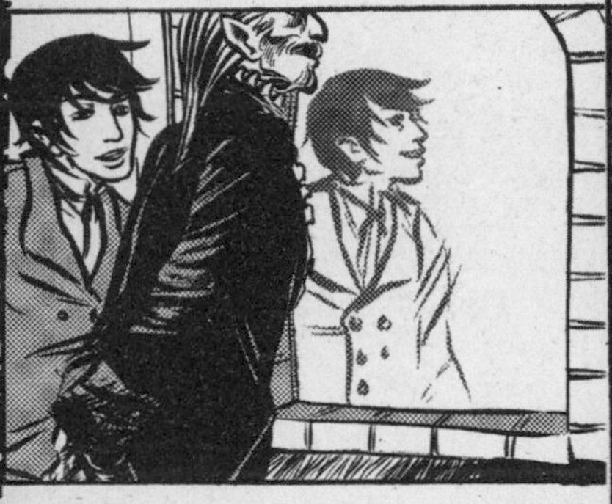

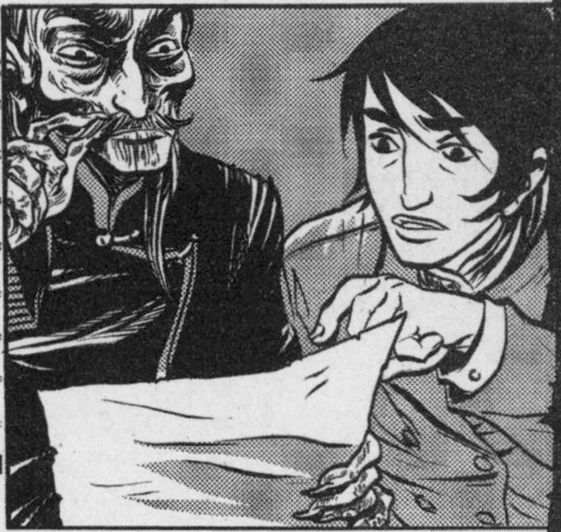

It is also odd that I have not seen him eat, drink, or even smoke.

The castle here is old. Most of the rooms are locked and there is dust everywhere. I have not seen a soul outside of the Count anywhere, yet the food is always prepared.

I am keeping a journal of my experiences on this trip. I can't wait until I can share them with you.

Your husband-to-be,

Jonathan

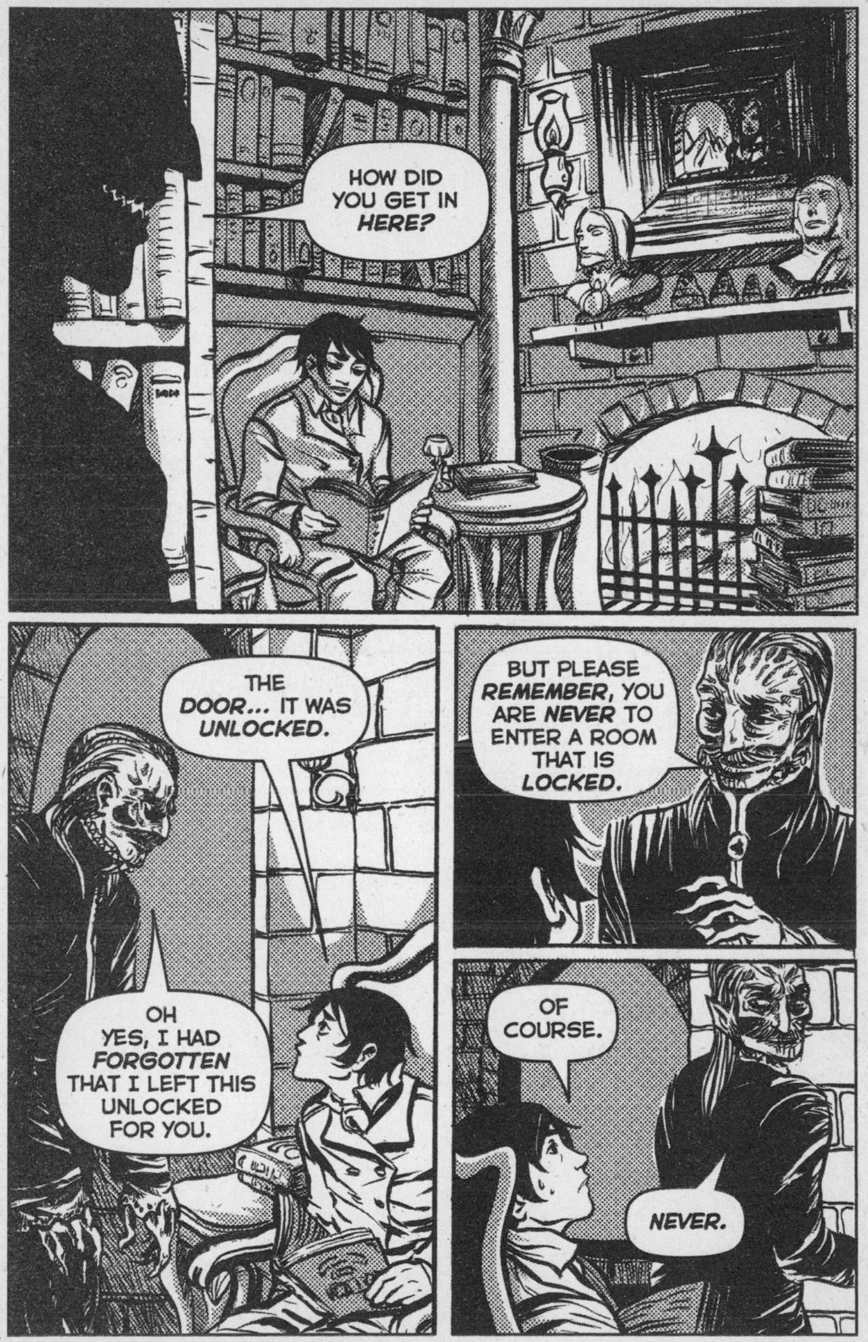
HOW DID YOU GET IN *HERE?*
THE *DOOR...* IT WAS *UNLOCKED.*
OH YES, I HAD *FORGOTTEN* THAT I LEFT THIS UNLOCKED FOR YOU.
BUT PLEASE *REMEMBER,* YOU ARE *NEVER* TO ENTER A ROOM THAT IS *LOCKED.*
OF COURSE.
NEVER.

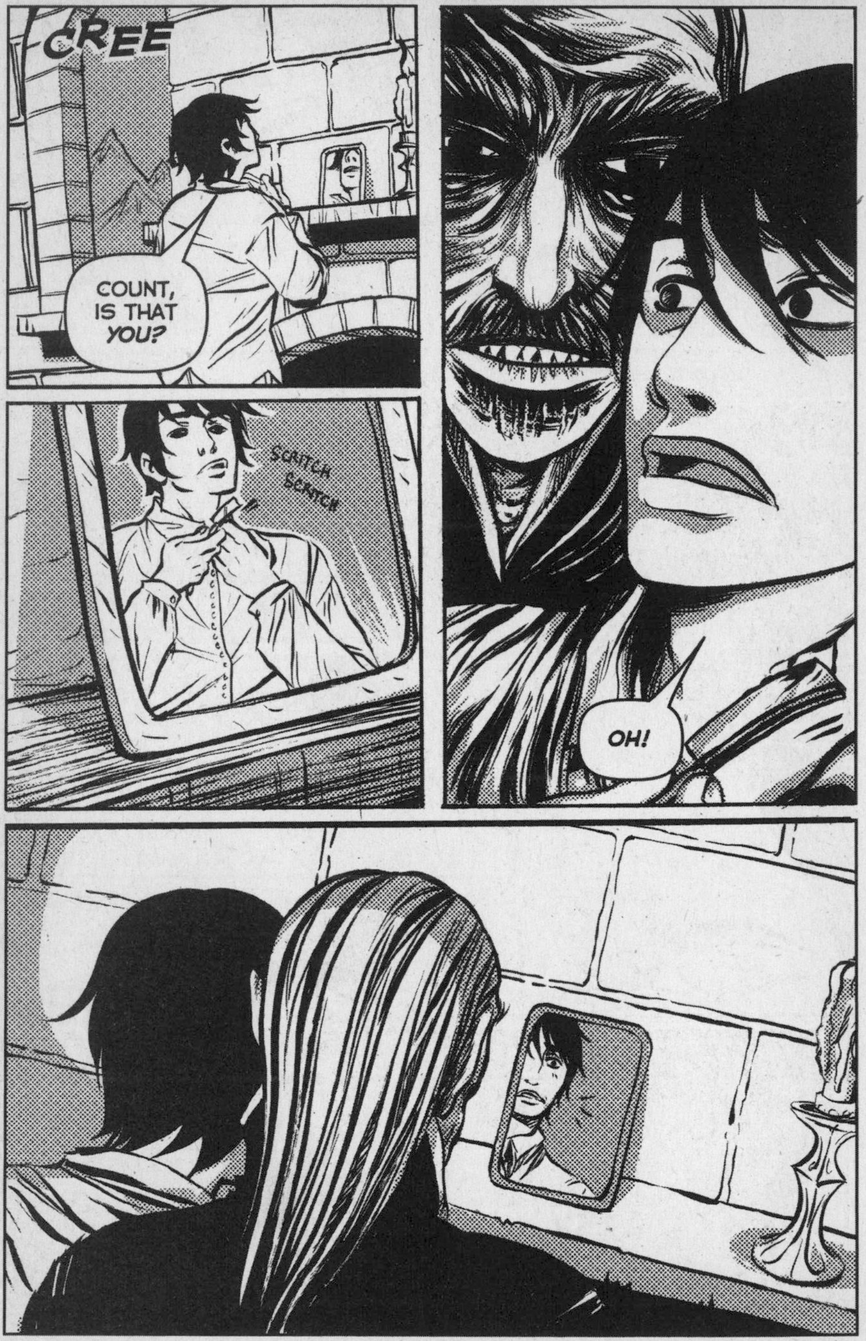
CREE
COUNT, IS THAT YOU?
SCRITCH SCRITCH
OH!

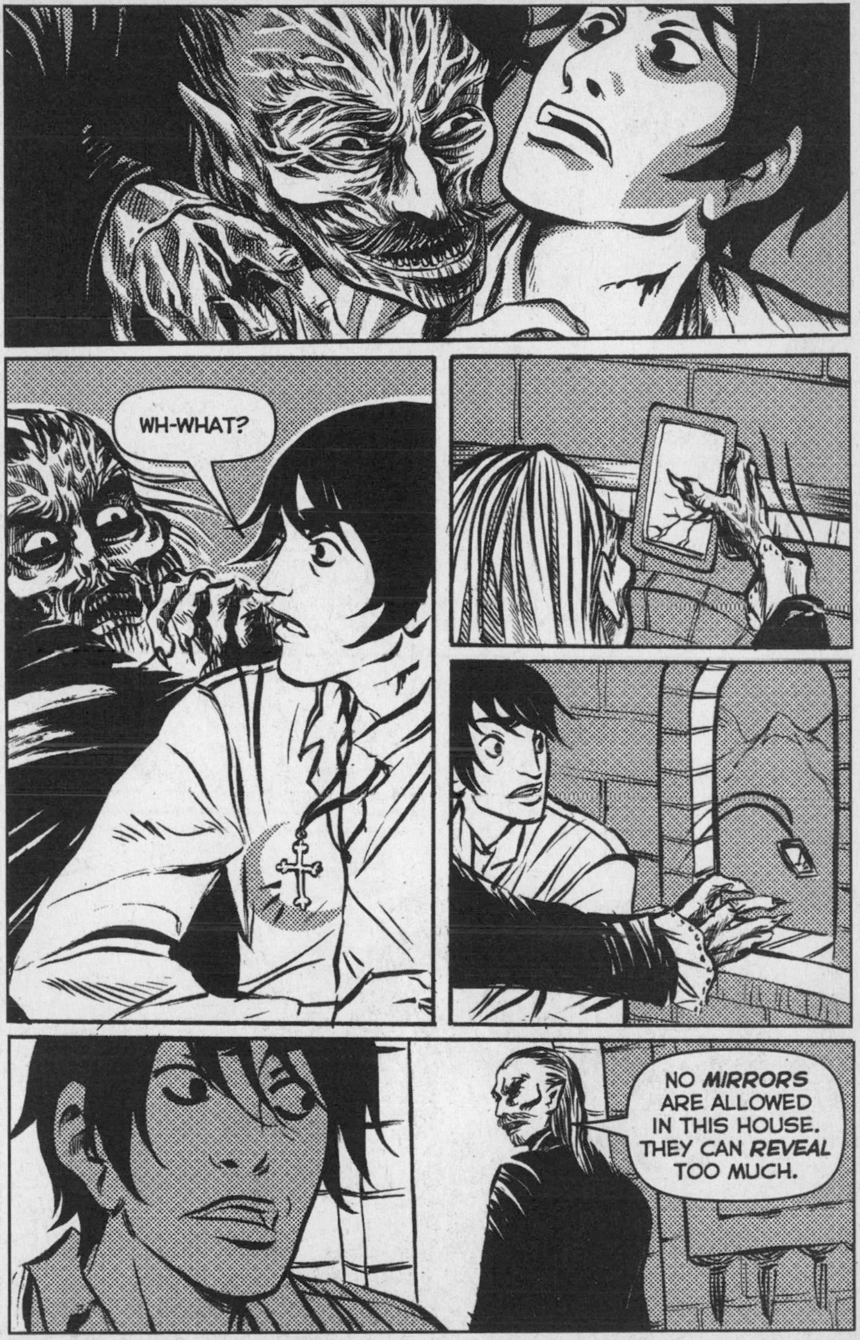
WH-WHAT?
NO *MIRRORS* ARE ALLOWED IN THIS HOUSE. THEY CAN *REVEAL* TOO MUCH.

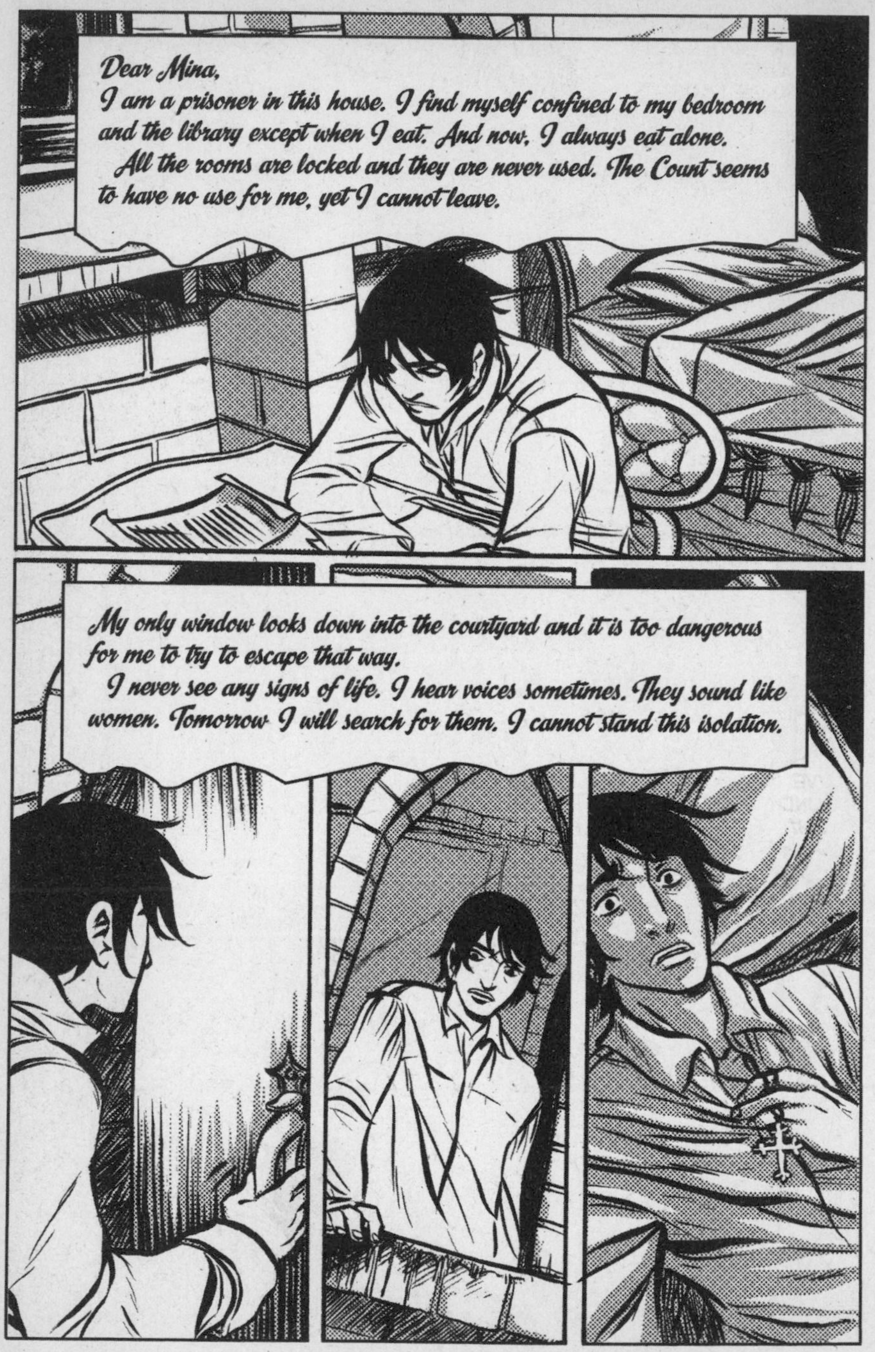
Dear Mina,
I am a prisoner in this house. I find myself confined to my bedroom and the library except when I eat. And now, I always eat alone.
All the rooms are locked and they are never used. The Count seems to have no use for me, yet I cannot leave.
My only window looks down into the courtyard and it is too dangerous for me to try to escape that way.
I never see any signs of life. I hear voices sometimes. They sound like women. Tomorrow I will search for them. I cannot stand this isolation.

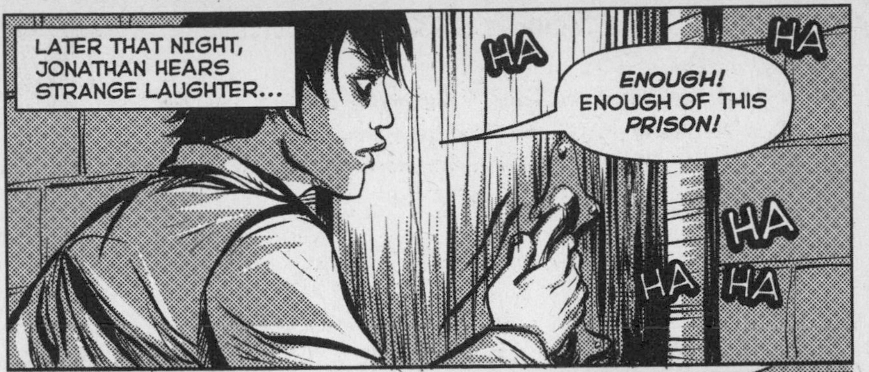
LATER THAT NIGHT, JONATHAN HEARS STRANGE LAUGHTER...
HA
HA
ENOUGH! ENOUGH OF THIS PRISON!
HA
HA
HA

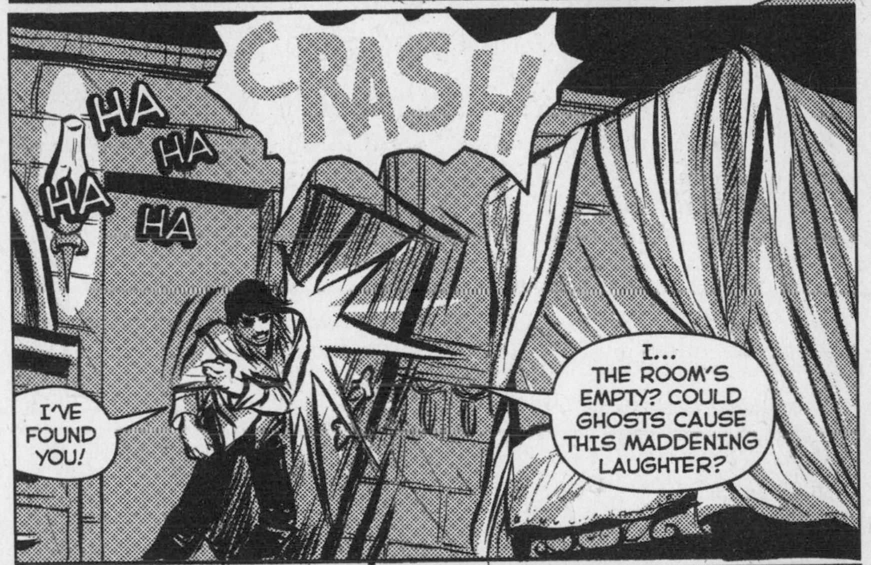
CRASH
HA
HA
HA
HA
I'VE FOUND YOU!
I... THE ROOM'S EMPTY? COULD GHOSTS CAUSE THIS MADDENING LAUGHTER?

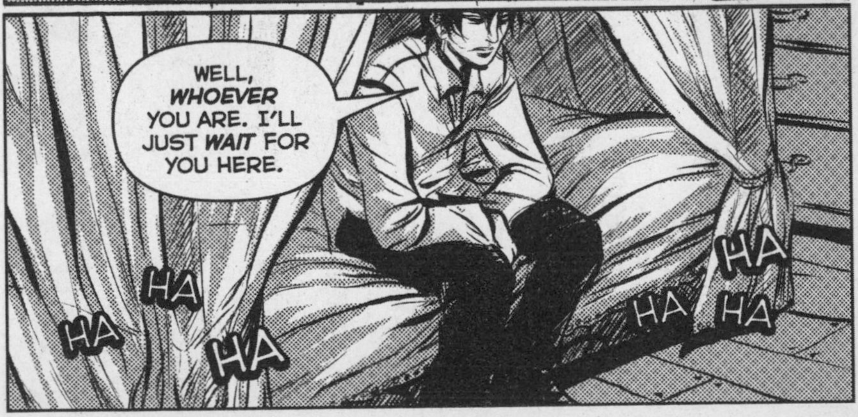
WELL, WHOEVER YOU ARE. I'LL JUST WAIT FOR YOU HERE.
HA
HA
HA
HA
HA
HA

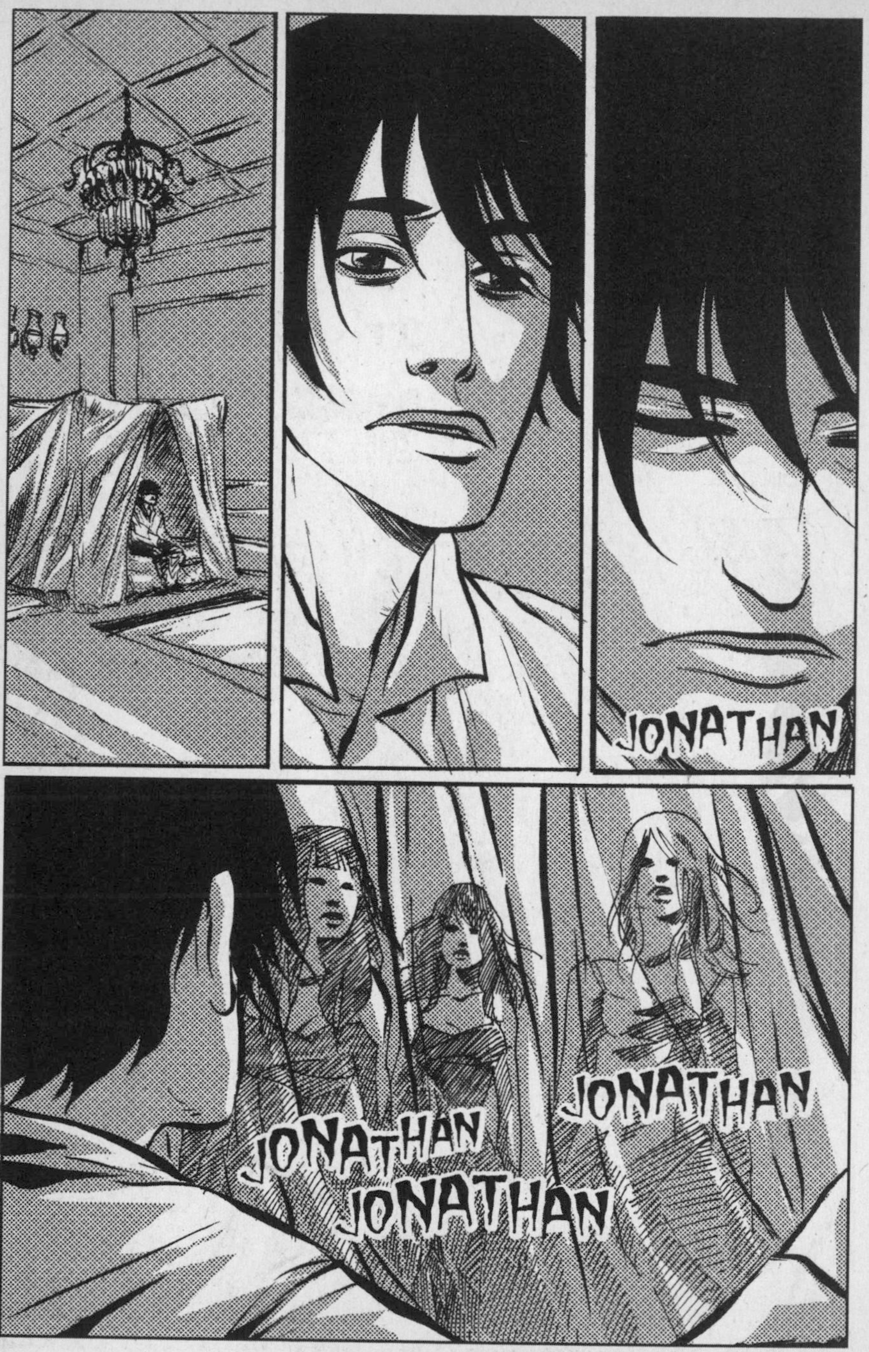
JONATHAN
JONATHAN
JONATHAN
JONATHAN

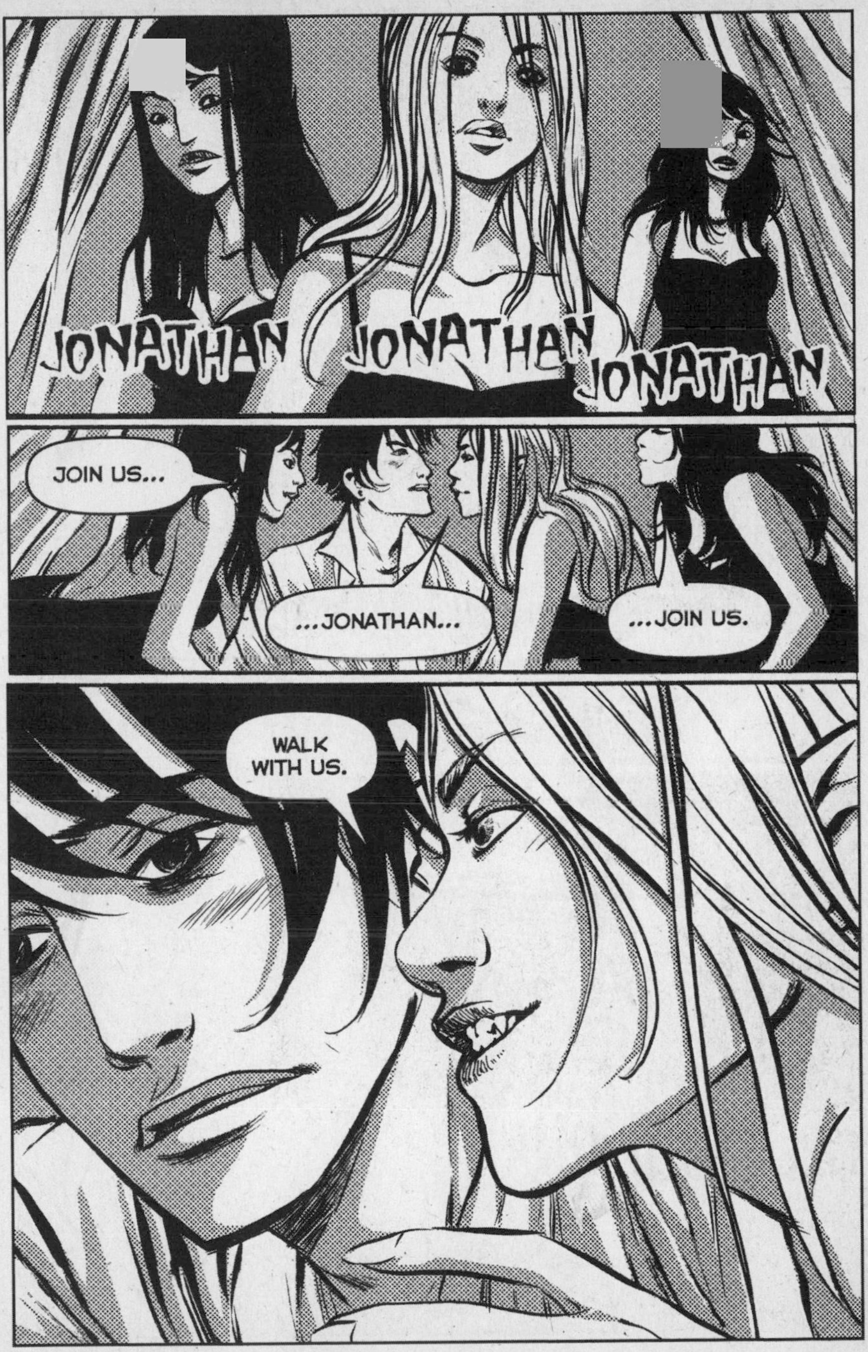
JONATHAN
JONATHAN
JONATHAN
JOIN US...
...JONATHAN...
...JOIN US.
WALK WITH US.

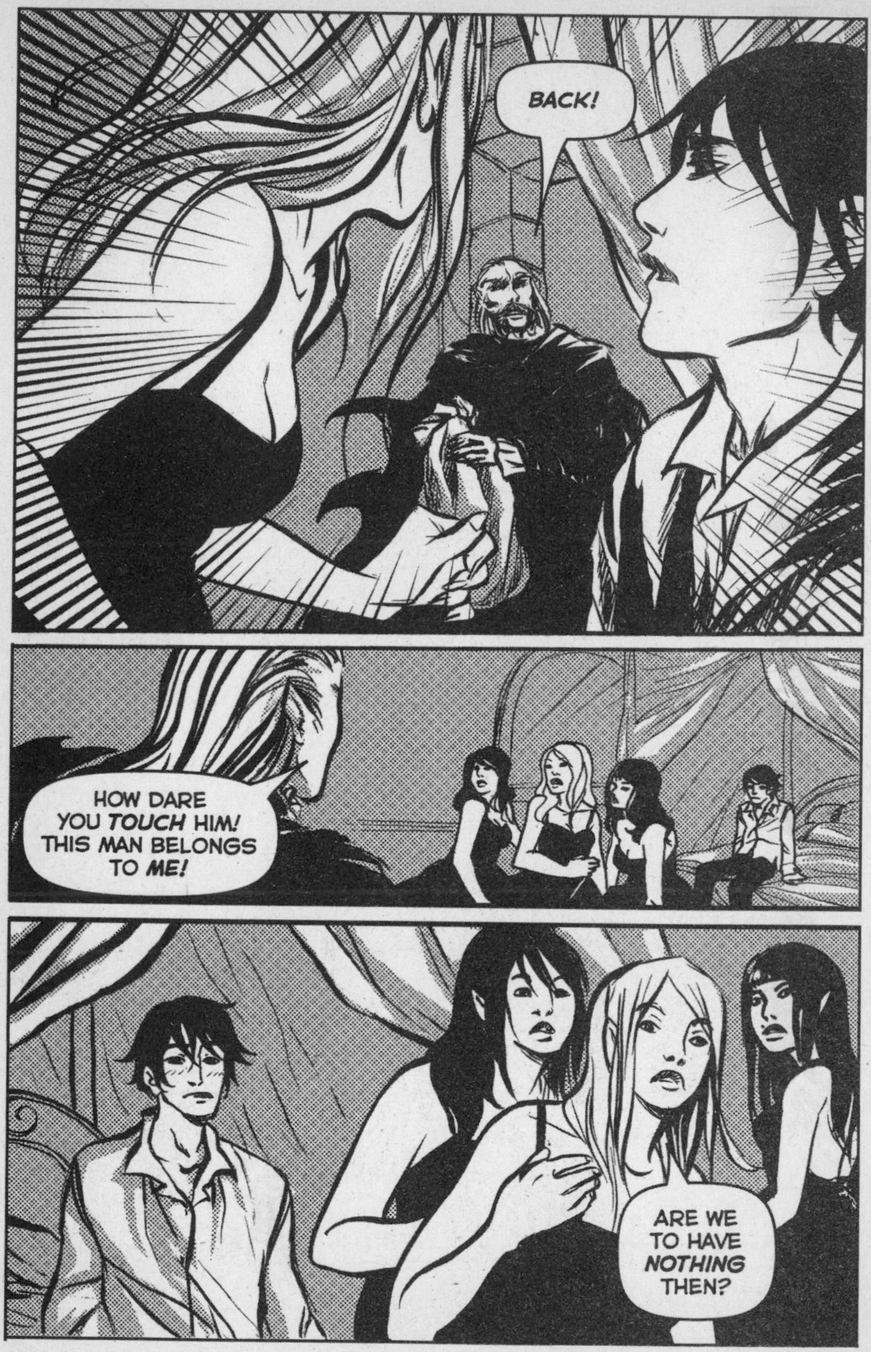
BACK!
HOW DARE YOU TOUCH HIM! THIS MAN BELONGS TO ME!
ARE WE TO HAVE NOTHING THEN?

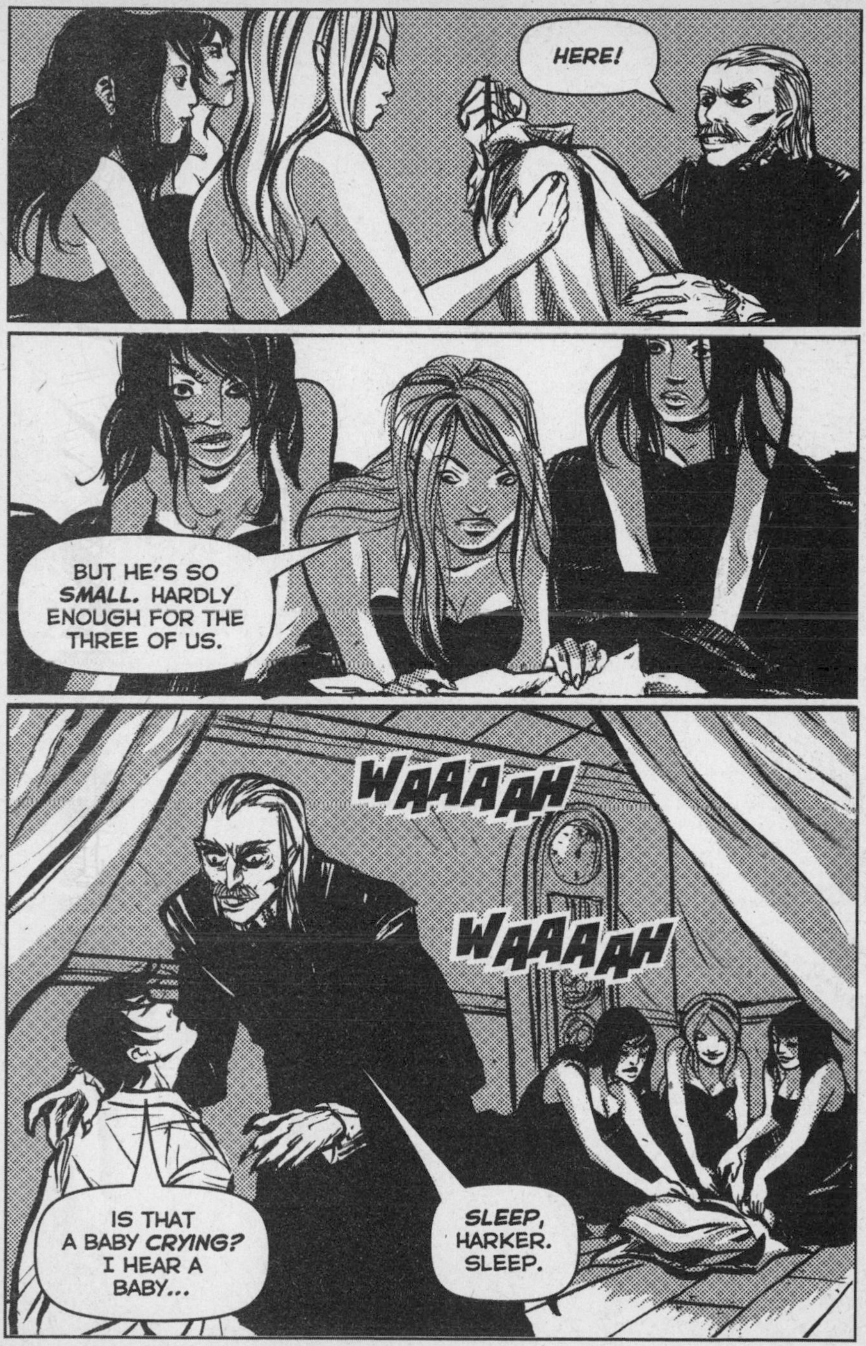
HERE!
BUT HE'S SO SMALL. HARDLY ENOUGH FOR THE THREE OF US.
WAAAAH
WAAAAH
IS THAT A BABY CRYING? I HEAR A BABY...
SLEEP, HARKER. SLEEP.

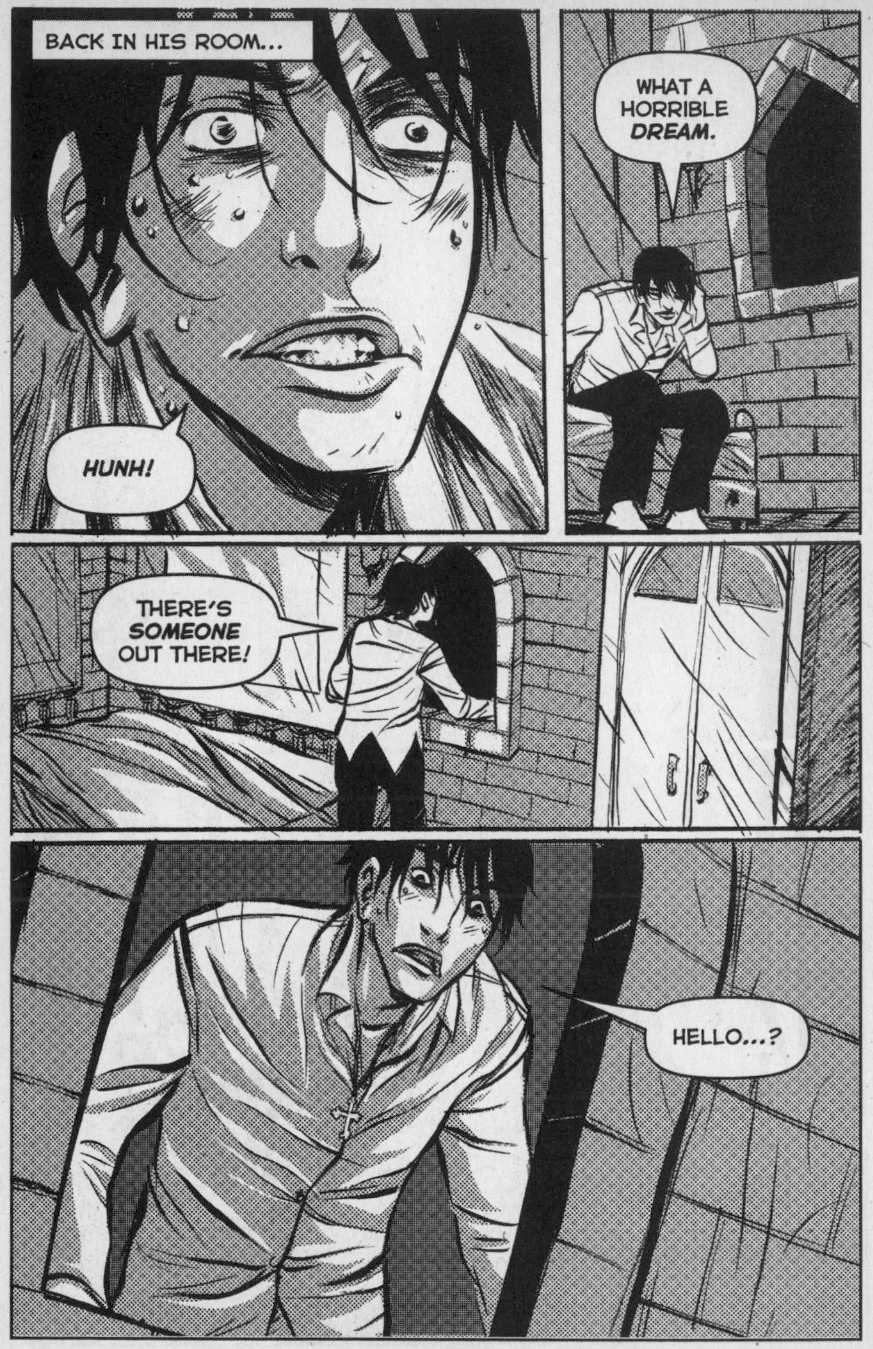
BACK IN HIS ROOM...
HUNH!
WHAT A HORRIBLE DREAM.
THERE'S SOMEONE OUT THERE!
HELLO...?

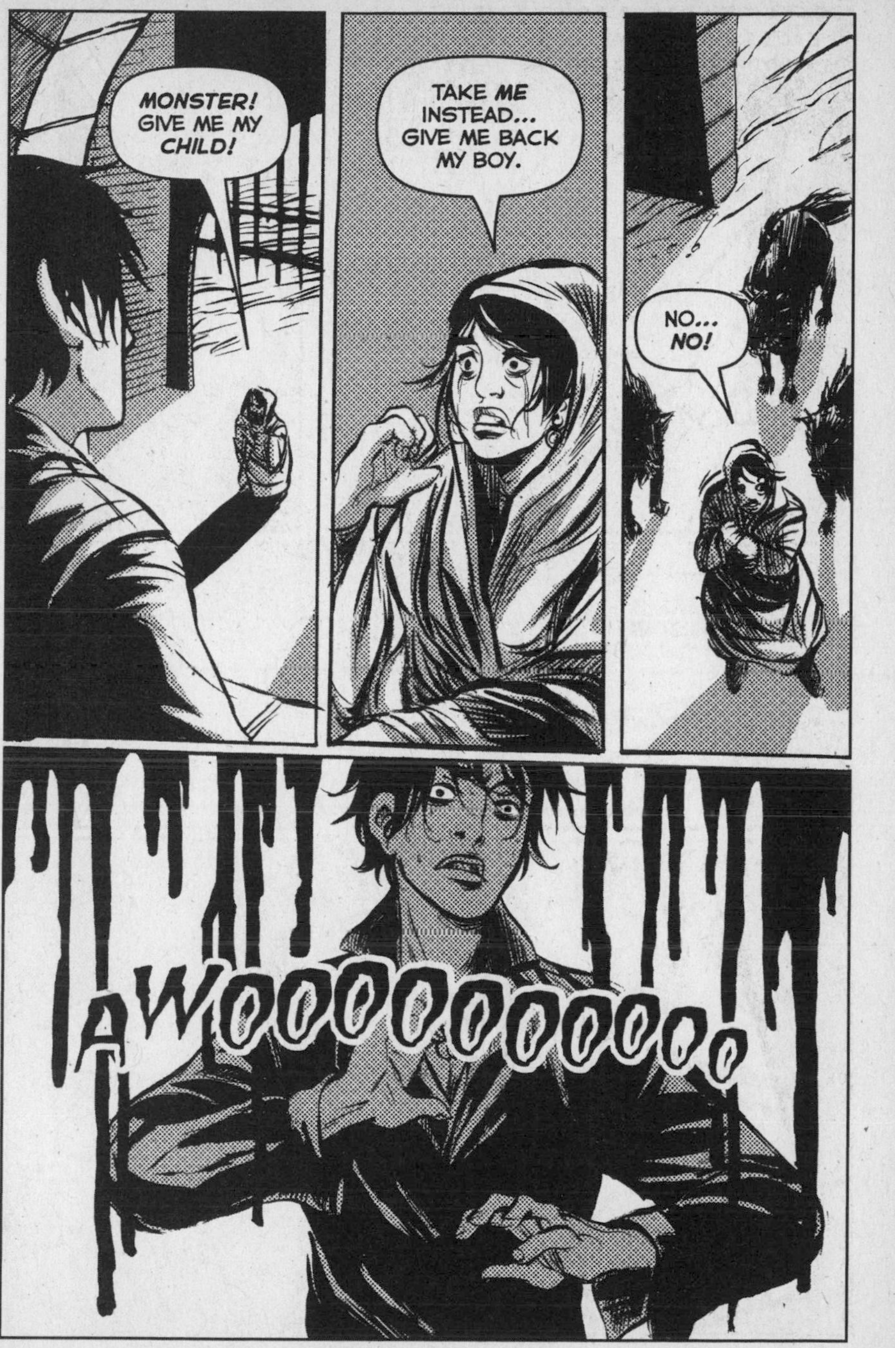
MONSTER! GIVE ME MY CHILD!
TAKE ME INSTEAD... GIVE ME BACK MY BOY.
NO... NO!
AWOOOOOOOOOOO!

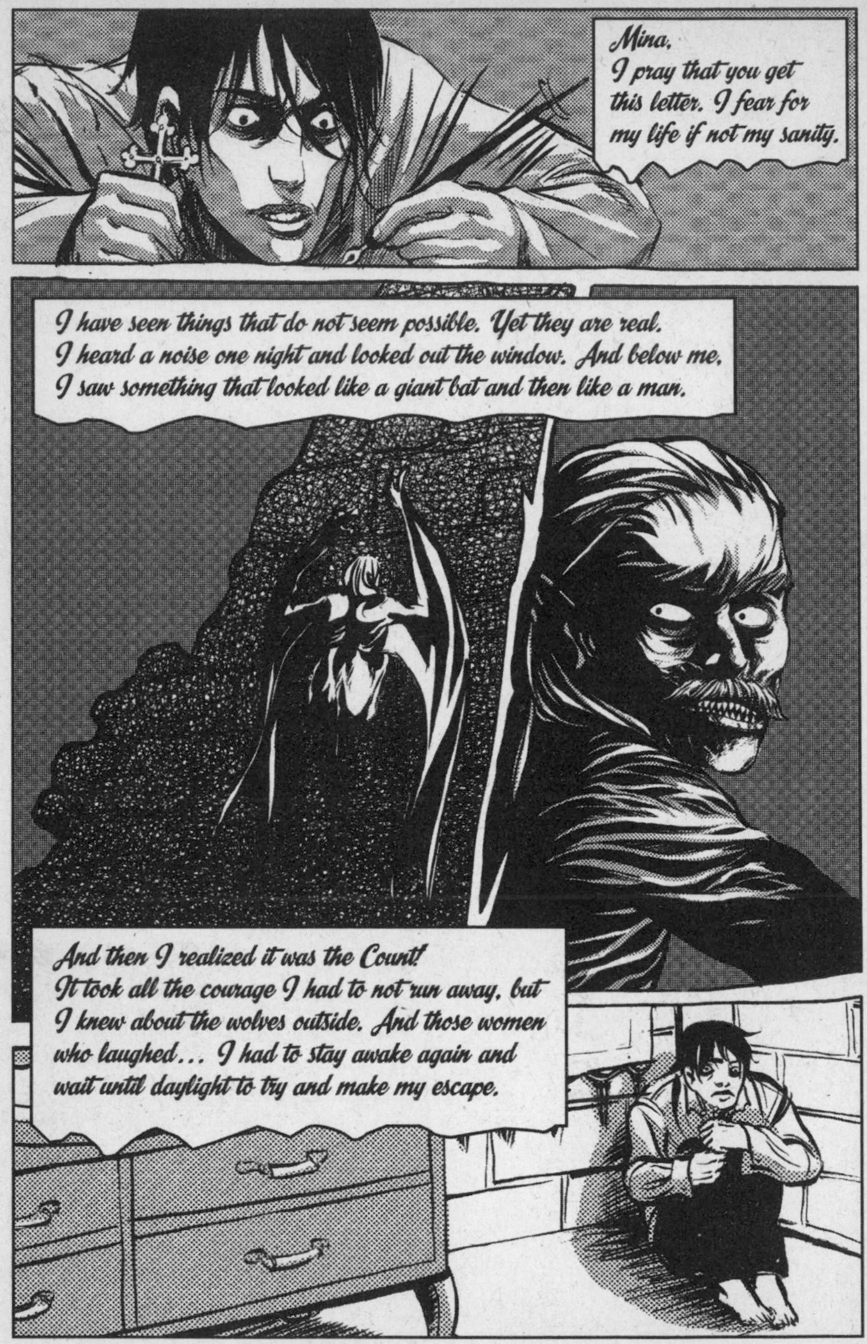
Mina,
I pray that you get this letter. I fear for my life if not my sanity.
I have seen things that do not seem possible. Yet they are real.
I heard a noise one night and looked out the window. And below me,
I saw something that looked like a giant bat and then like a man.
And then I realized it was the Count!
It took all the courage I had to not run away, but I knew about the wolves outside. And those women who laughed... I had to stay awake again and wait until daylight to try and make my escape.

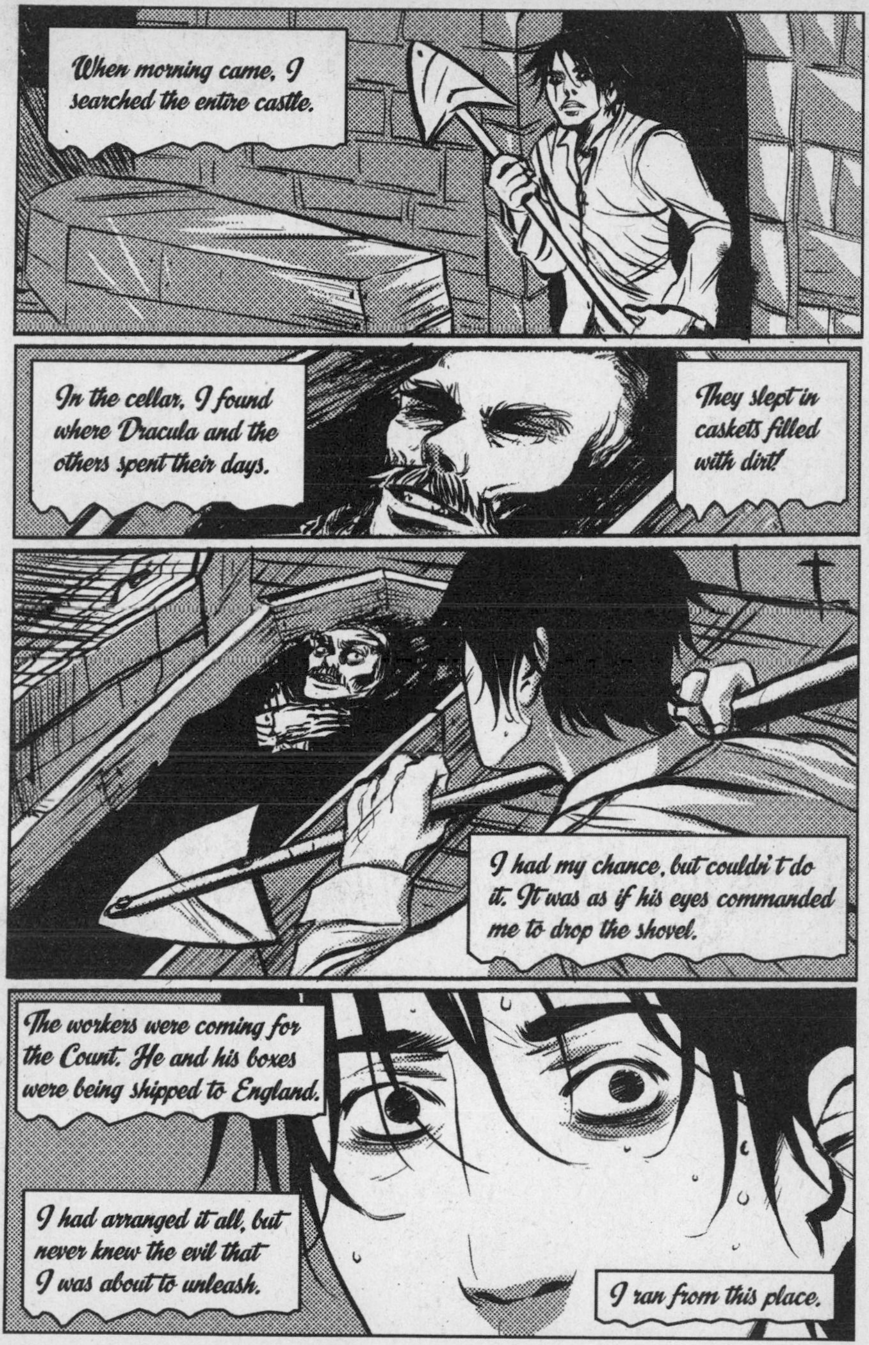
When morning came, I searched the entire castle.
In the cellar, I found where Dracula and the others spent their days.
They slept in caskets filled with dirt!
I had my chance, but couldn't do it. It was as if his eyes commanded me to drop the shovel.
The workers were coming for the Count. He and his boxes were being shipped to England.
I had arranged it all, but never knew the evil that I was about to unleash.
I ran from this place.

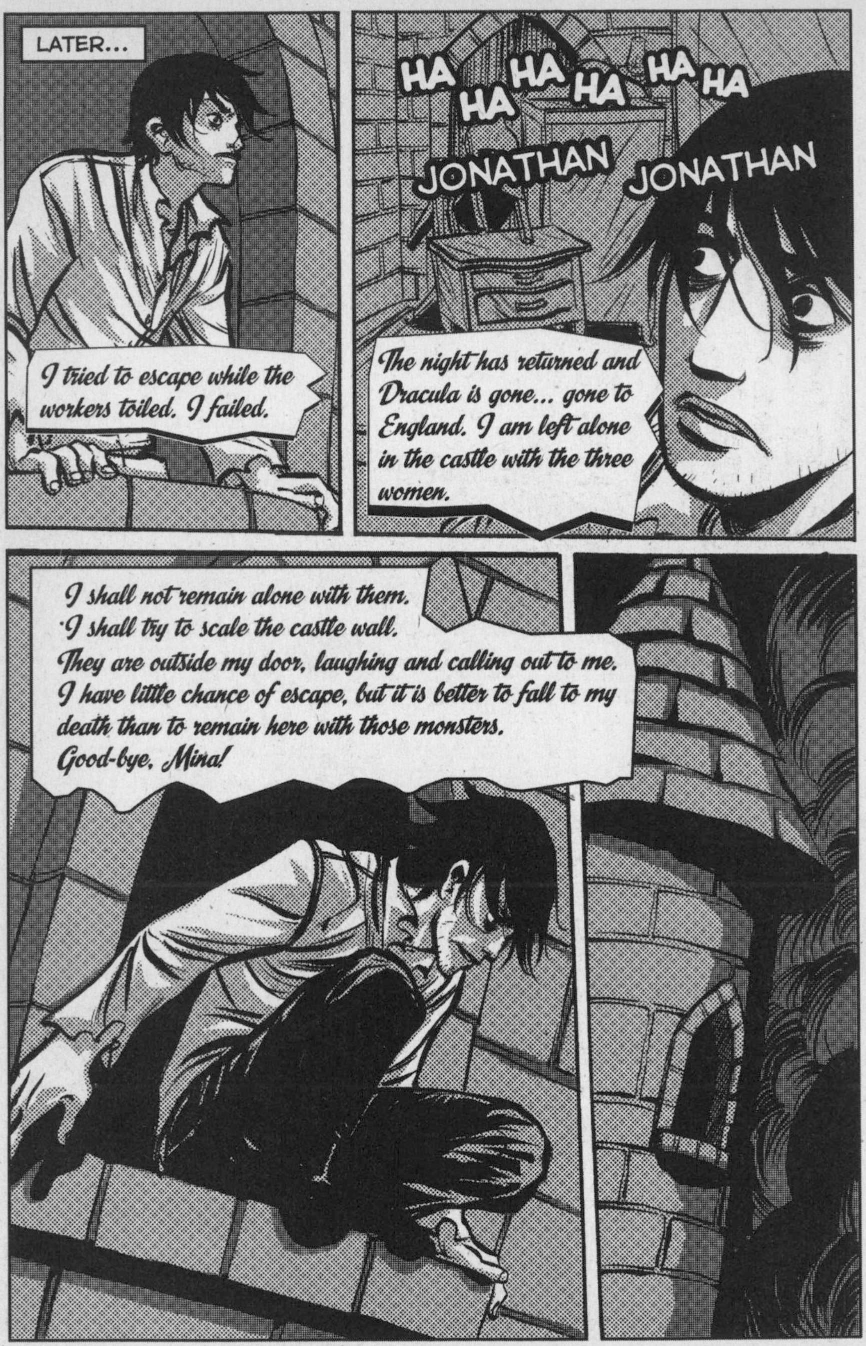
LATER...
I tried to escape while the workers toiled. I failed.
HA HA HA HA HA HA
JONATHAN JONATHAN
The night has returned and Dracula is gone... gone to England. I am left alone in the castle with the three women.
I shall not remain alone with them.
I shall try to scale the castle wall.
They are outside my door, laughing and calling out to me.
I have little chance of escape, but it is better to fall to my death than to remain here with those monsters.
Good-bye, Mina!

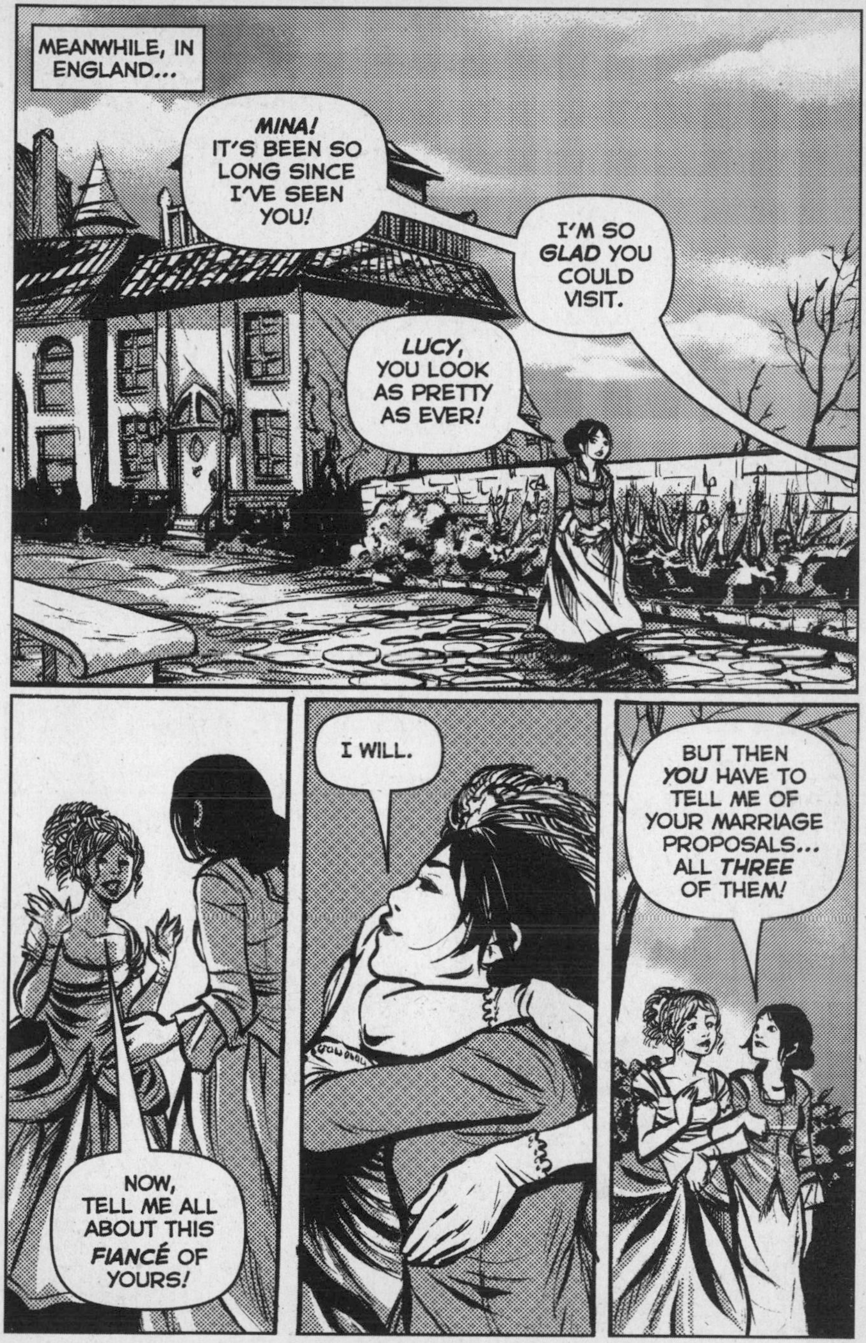
MEANWHILE, IN ENGLAND...
MINA! IT'S BEEN SO LONG SINCE I'VE SEEN YOU!
I'M SO GLAD YOU COULD VISIT.
LUCY, YOU LOOK AS PRETTY AS EVER!
NOW, TELL ME ALL ABOUT THIS FIANCÉ OF YOURS!
I WILL.
BUT THEN YOU HAVE TO TELL ME OF YOUR MARRIAGE PROPOSALS... ALL THREE OF THEM!

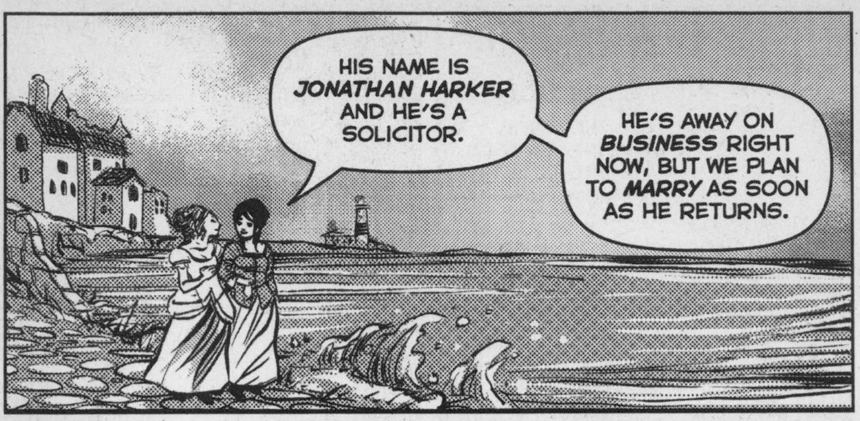
HIS NAME IS JONATHAN HARKER AND HE'S A SOLICITOR.
HE'S AWAY ON BUSINESS RIGHT NOW, BUT WE PLAN TO MARRY AS SOON AS HE RETURNS.

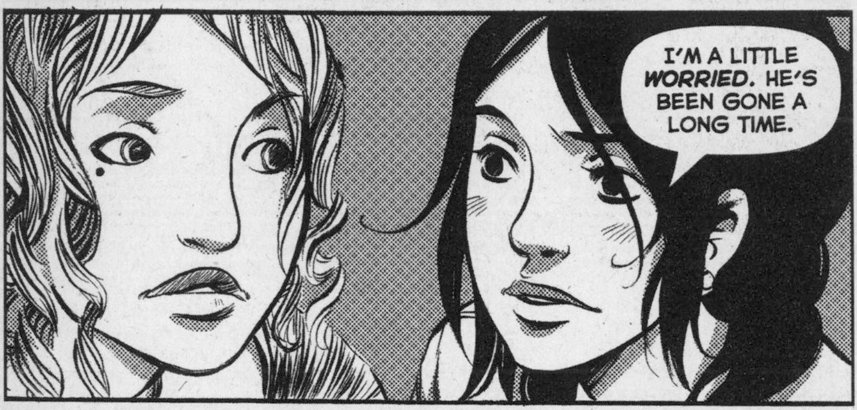
I'M A LITTLE WORRIED. HE'S BEEN GONE A LONG TIME.

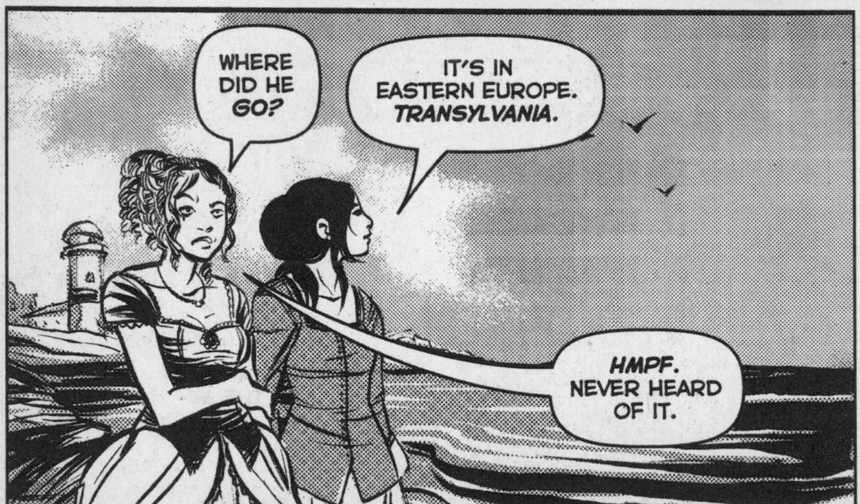
WHERE DID HE GO?
IT'S IN EASTERN EUROPE. TRANSYLVANIA.
HMPF. NEVER HEARD OF IT.

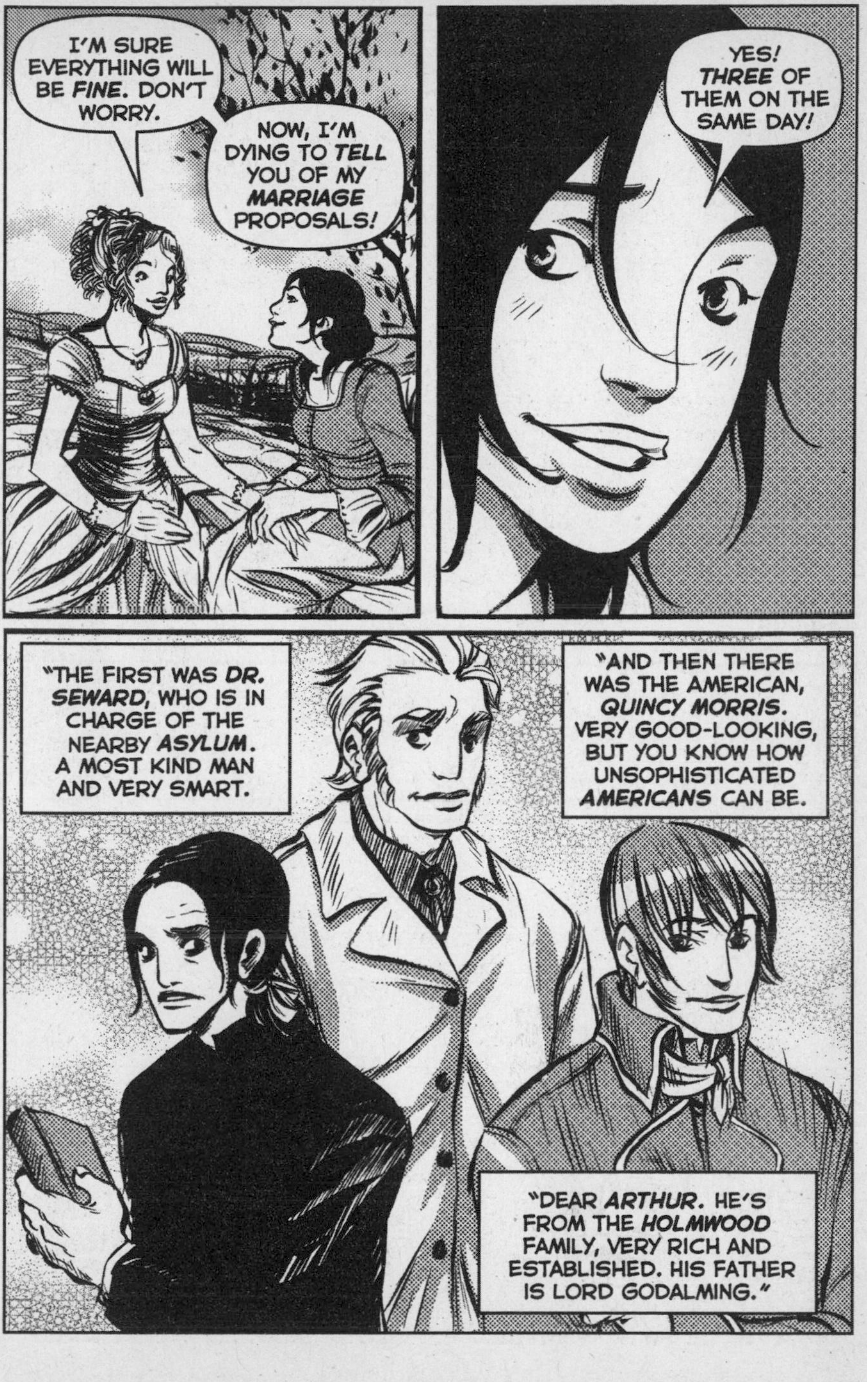
I'M SURE EVERYTHING WILL BE FINE. DON'T WORRY.
NOW, I'M DYING TO TELL YOU OF MY MARRIAGE PROPOSALS!
YES! THREE OF THEM ON THE SAME DAY!
"THE FIRST WAS DR. SEWARD, WHO IS IN CHARGE OF THE NEARBY ASYLUM. A MOST KIND MAN AND VERY SMART.
"AND THEN THERE WAS THE AMERICAN, QUINCY MORRIS. VERY GOOD-LOOKING, BUT YOU KNOW HOW UNSOPHISTICATED AMERICANS CAN BE.
"DEAR ARTHUR. HE'S FROM THE HOLMWOOD FAMILY, VERY RICH AND ESTABLISHED. HIS FATHER IS LORD GODALMING."

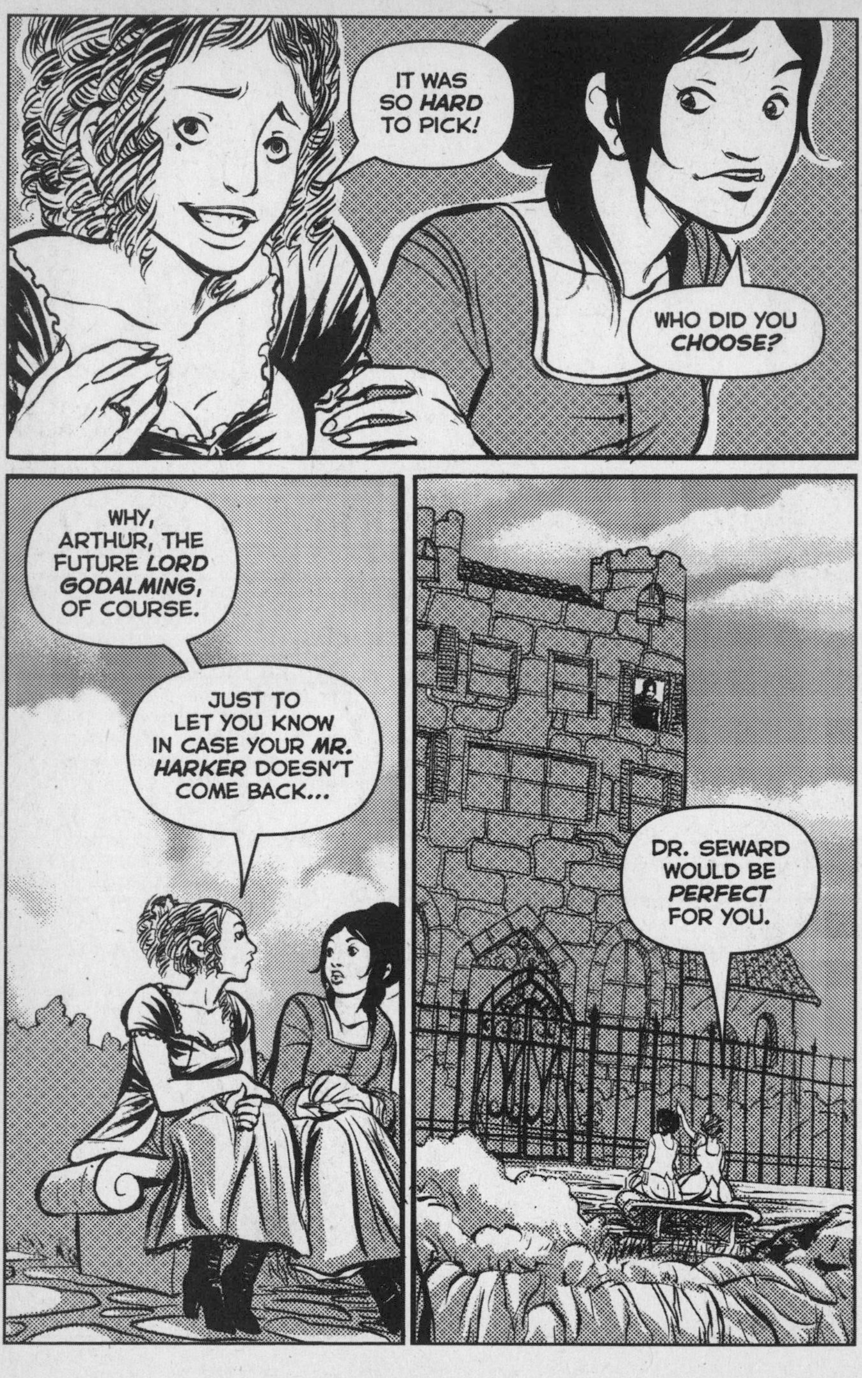
IT WAS SO *HARD* TO PICK!
WHO DID YOU *CHOOSE?*
WHY, ARTHUR, THE FUTURE *LORD GODALMING*, OF COURSE.
JUST TO LET YOU KNOW IN CASE YOUR *MR. HARKER* DOESN'T COME BACK...
DR. SEWARD WOULD BE *PERFECT* FOR YOU.

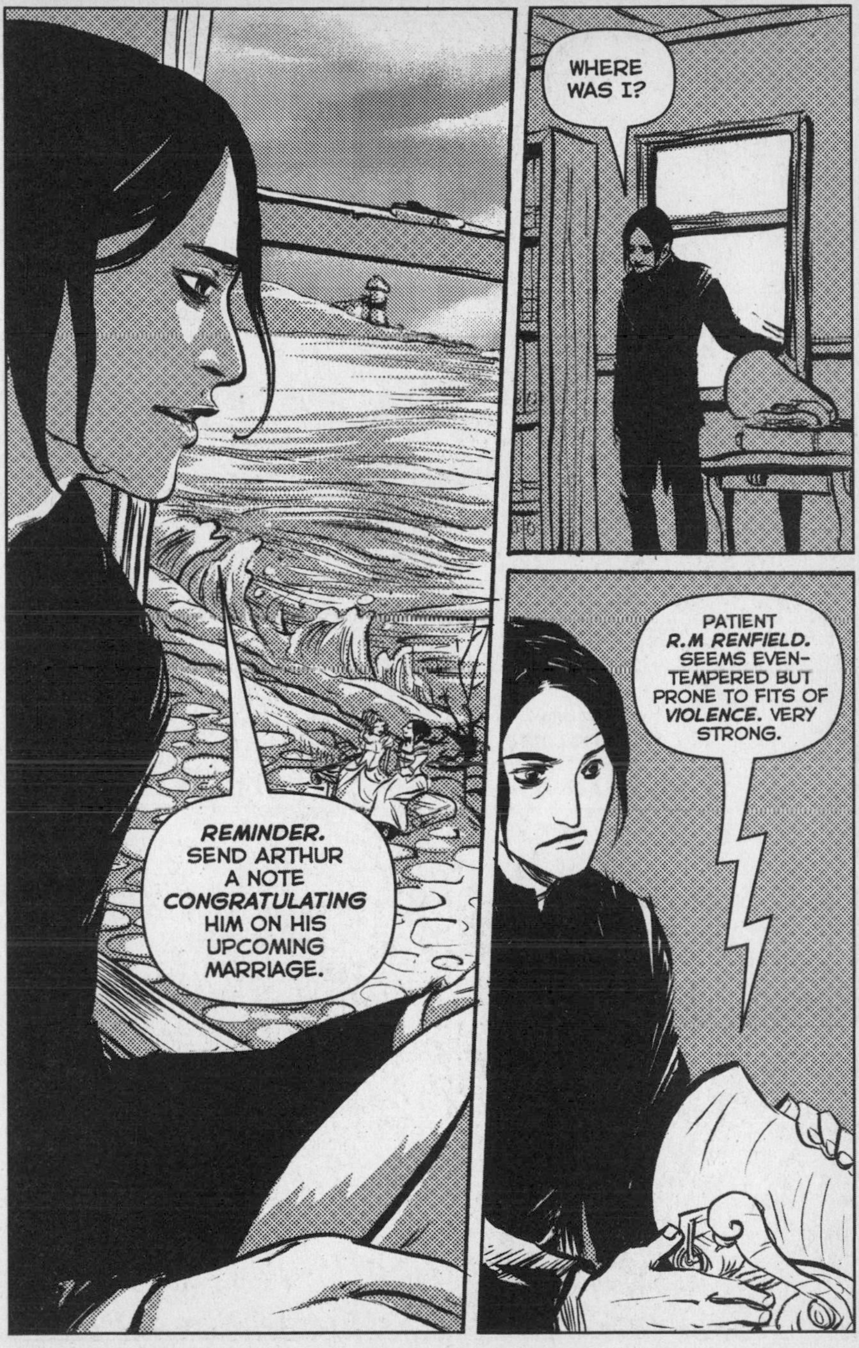
REMINDER. SEND ARTHUR A NOTE CONGRATULATING HIM ON HIS UPCOMING MARRIAGE.
WHERE WAS I?
PATIENT R.M RENFIELD. SEEMS EVEN-TEMPERED BUT PRONE TO FITS OF VIOLENCE. VERY STRONG.

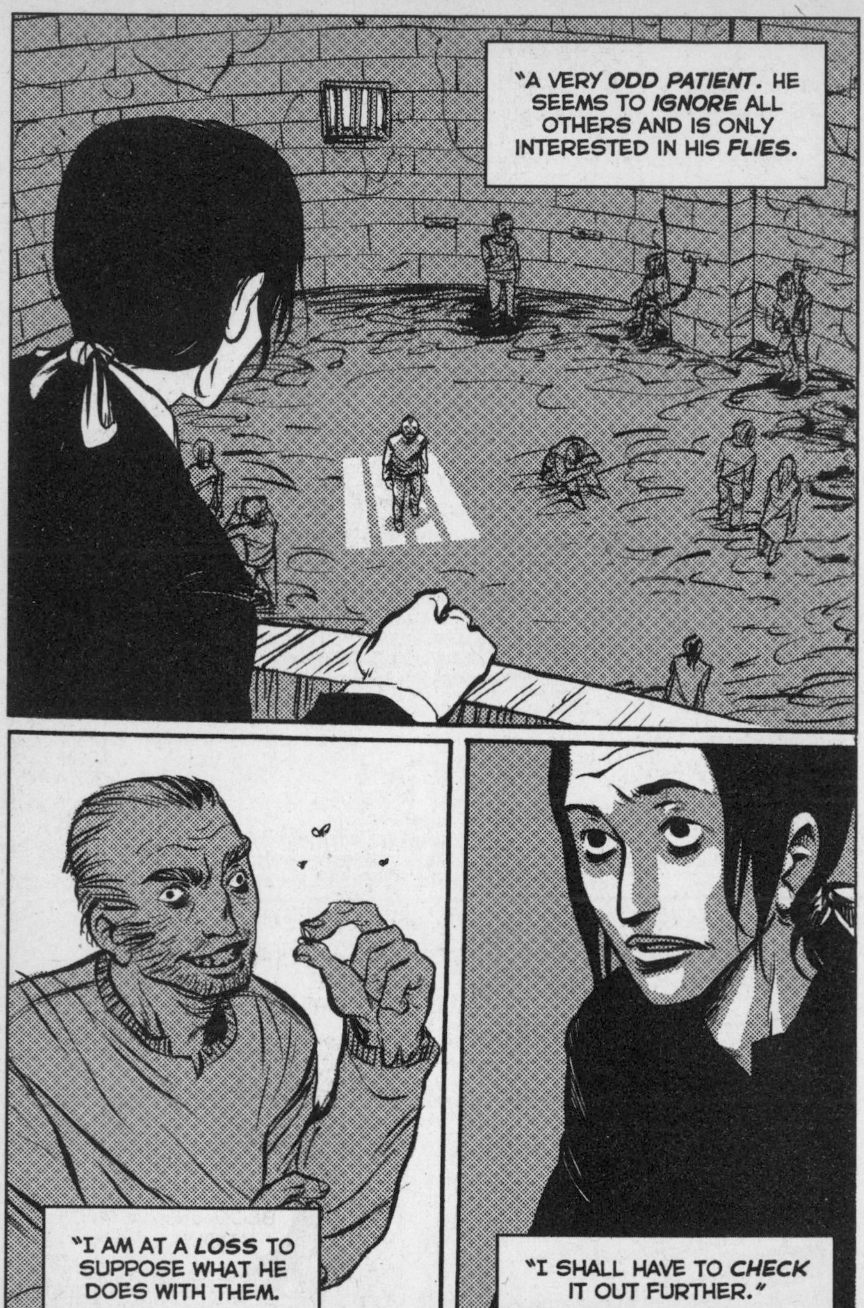
"A VERY ODD PATIENT. HE SEEMS TO IGNORE ALL OTHERS AND IS ONLY INTERESTED IN HIS FLIES.
"I AM AT A LOSS TO SUPPOSE WHAT HE DOES WITH THEM.
"I SHALL HAVE TO CHECK IT OUT FURTHER."

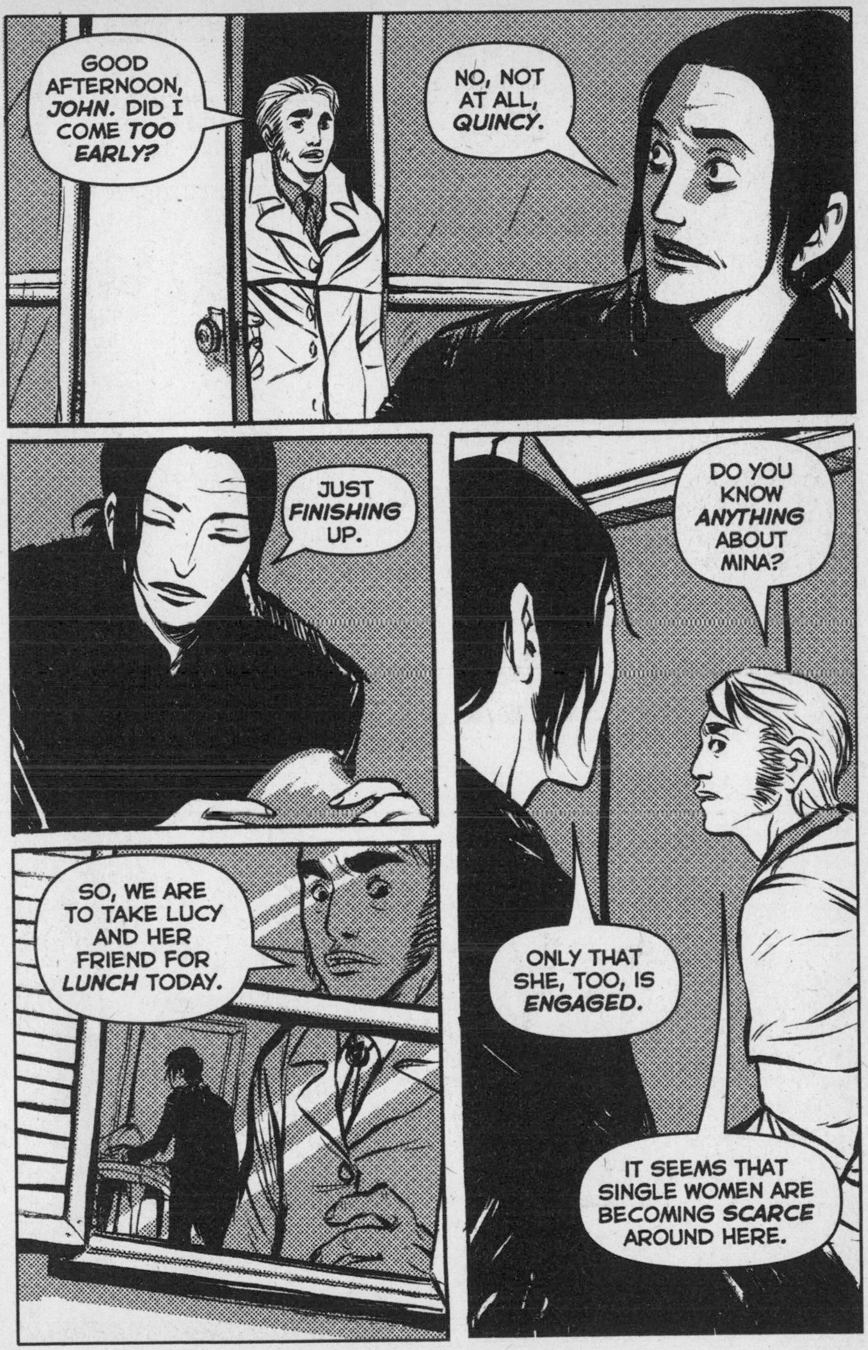
GOOD AFTERNOON, JOHN. DID I COME TOO EARLY?
NO, NOT AT ALL, QUINCY.
JUST FINISHING UP.
SO, WE ARE TO TAKE LUCY AND HER FRIEND FOR LUNCH TODAY.
DO YOU KNOW ANYTHING ABOUT MINA?
ONLY THAT SHE, TOO, IS ENGAGED.
IT SEEMS THAT SINGLE WOMEN ARE BECOMING SCARCE AROUND HERE.

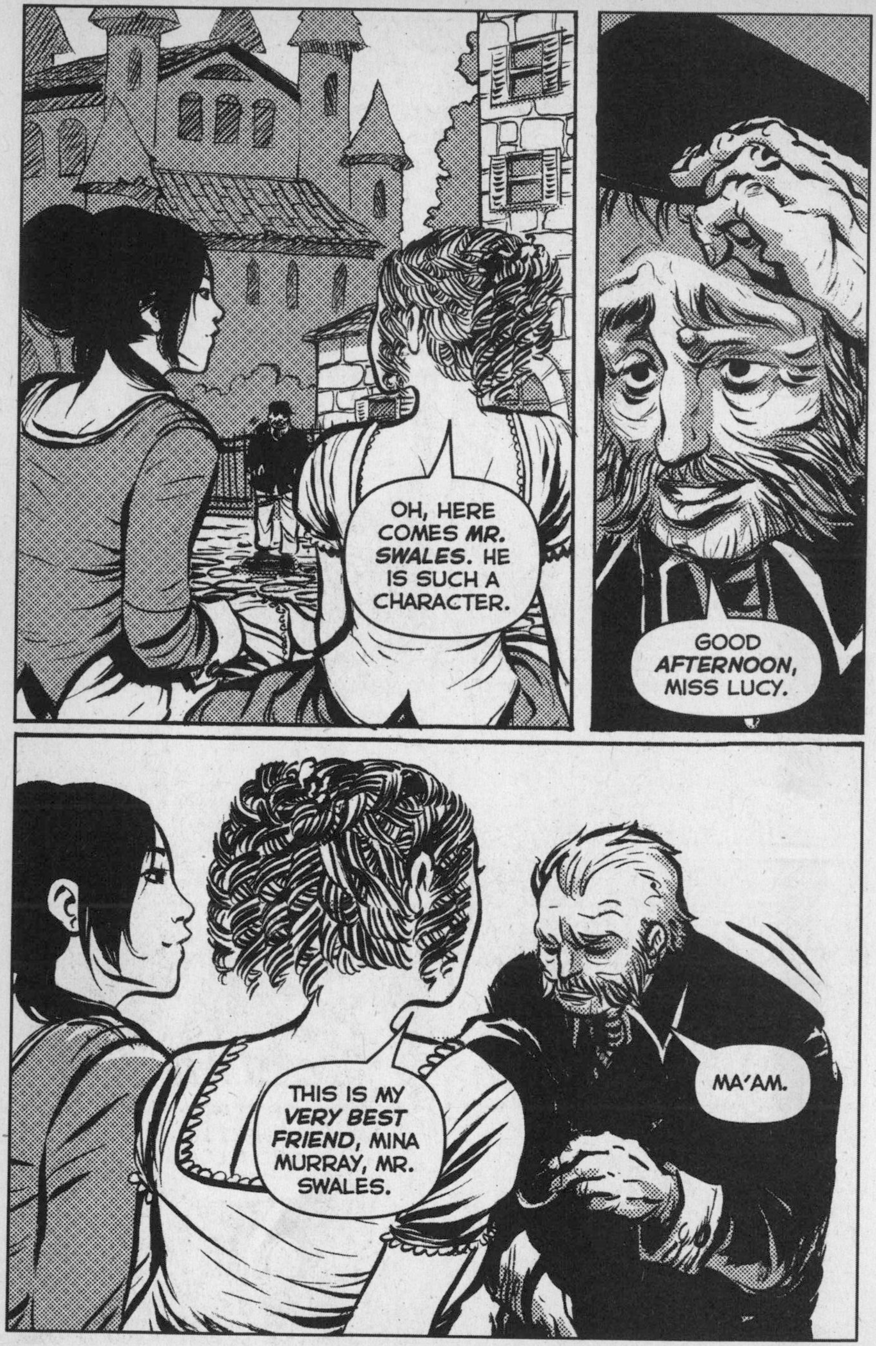
OH, HERE COMES MR. SWALES. HE IS SUCH A CHARACTER.
GOOD AFTERNOON, MISS LUCY.
THIS IS MY VERY BEST FRIEND, MINA MURRAY, MR. SWALES.
MA'AM.

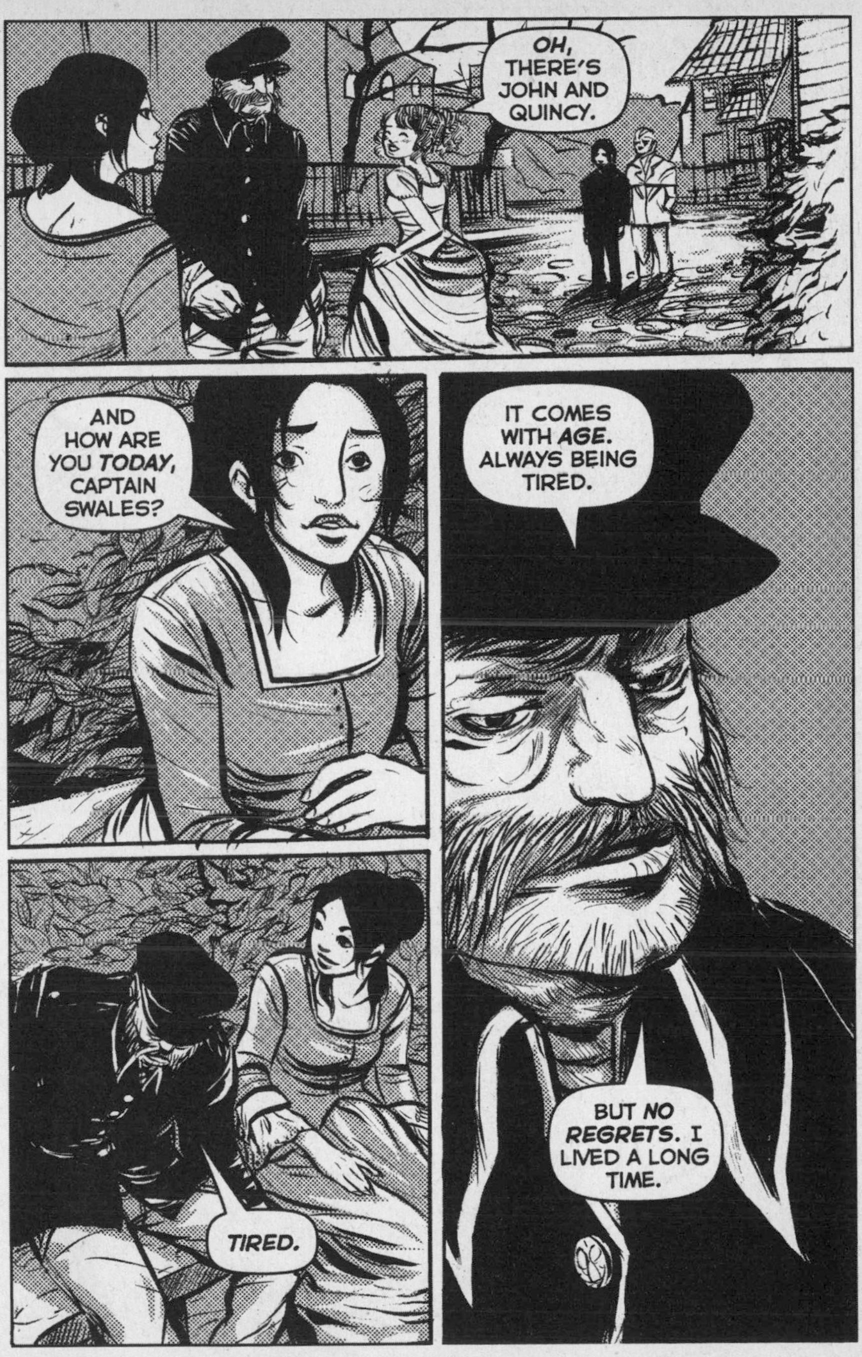
OH, THERE'S JOHN AND QUINCY.
AND HOW ARE YOU TODAY, CAPTAIN SWALES?
IT COMES WITH AGE. ALWAYS BEING TIRED.
TIRED.
BUT NO REGRETS. I LIVED A LONG TIME.

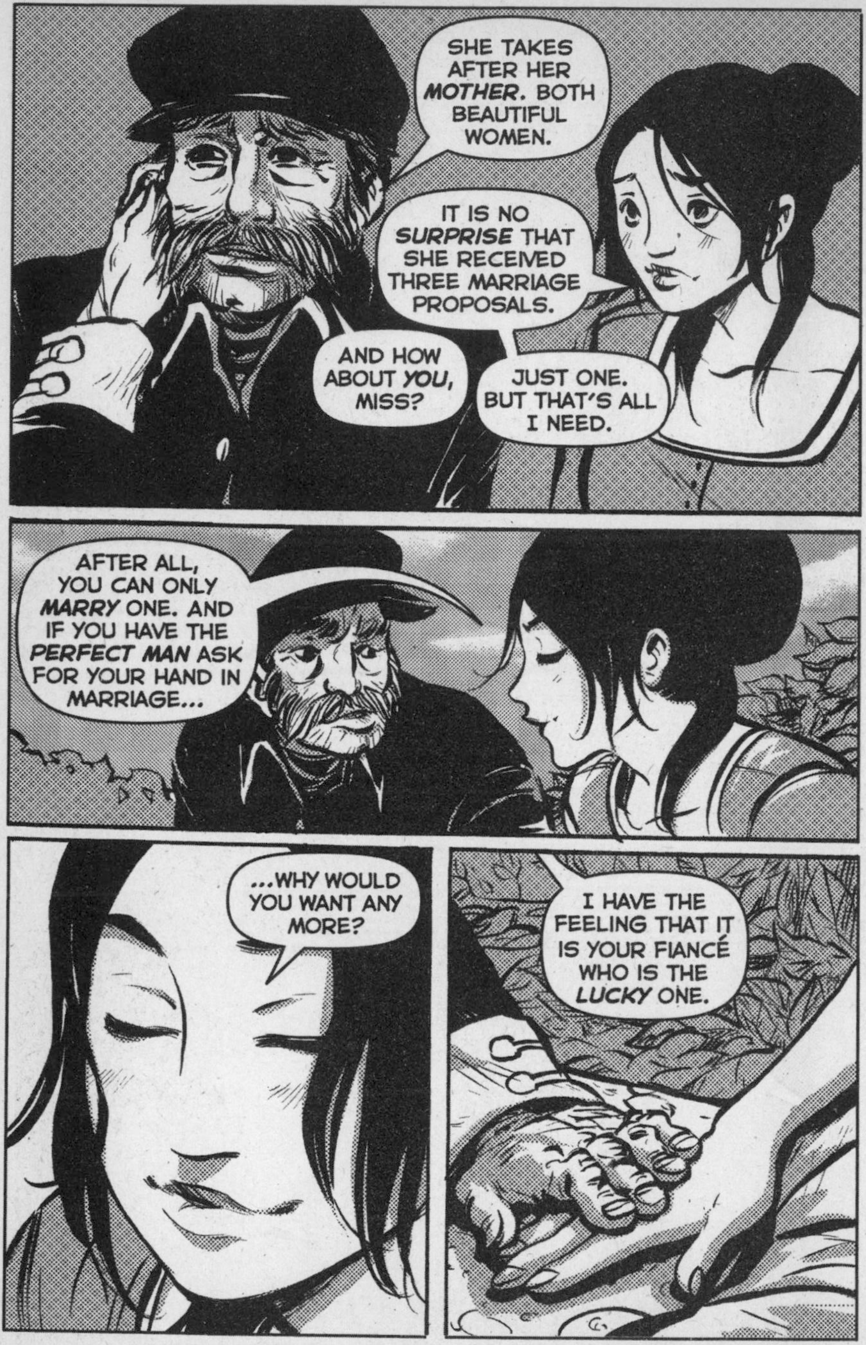
SHE TAKES AFTER HER *MOTHER.* BOTH BEAUTIFUL WOMEN.
IT IS NO *SURPRISE* THAT SHE RECEIVED THREE MARRIAGE PROPOSALS.
AND HOW ABOUT *YOU,* MISS?
JUST ONE. BUT THAT'S ALL I NEED.
AFTER ALL, YOU CAN ONLY *MARRY* ONE. AND IF YOU HAVE THE *PERFECT MAN* ASK FOR YOUR HAND IN MARRIAGE...
...WHY WOULD YOU WANT ANY MORE?
I HAVE THE FEELING THAT IT IS YOUR FIANCÉ WHO IS THE *LUCKY* ONE.

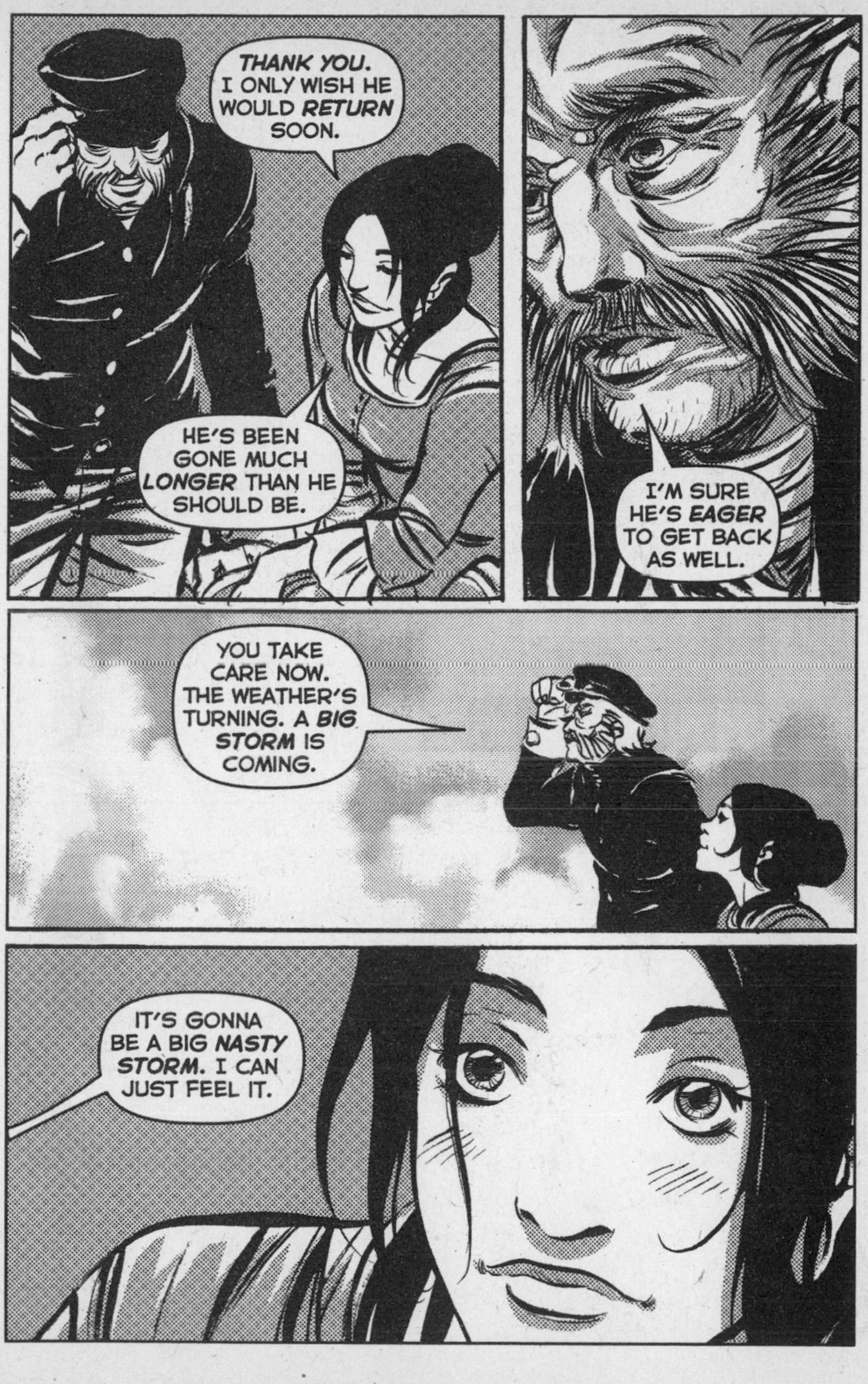
THANK YOU. I ONLY WISH HE WOULD RETURN SOON.
HE'S BEEN GONE MUCH LONGER THAN HE SHOULD BE.
I'M SURE HE'S EAGER TO GET BACK AS WELL.
YOU TAKE CARE NOW. THE WEATHER'S TURNING. A BIG STORM IS COMING.
IT'S GONNA BE A BIG NASTY STORM. I CAN JUST FEEL IT.

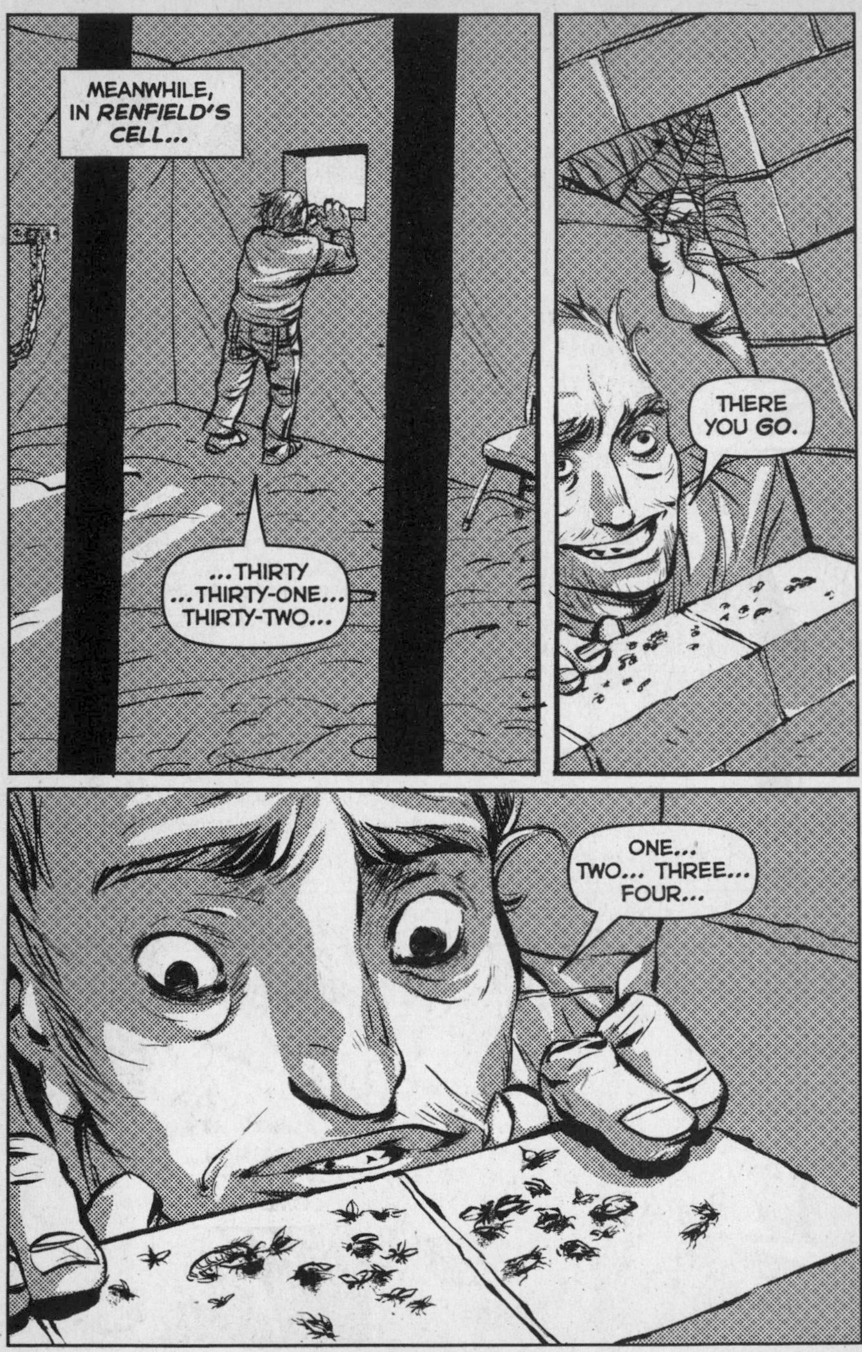
MEANWHILE, IN RENFIELD'S CELL...
...THIRTY ...THIRTY-ONE... THIRTY-TWO...
THERE YOU GO.
ONE... TWO... THREE... FOUR...

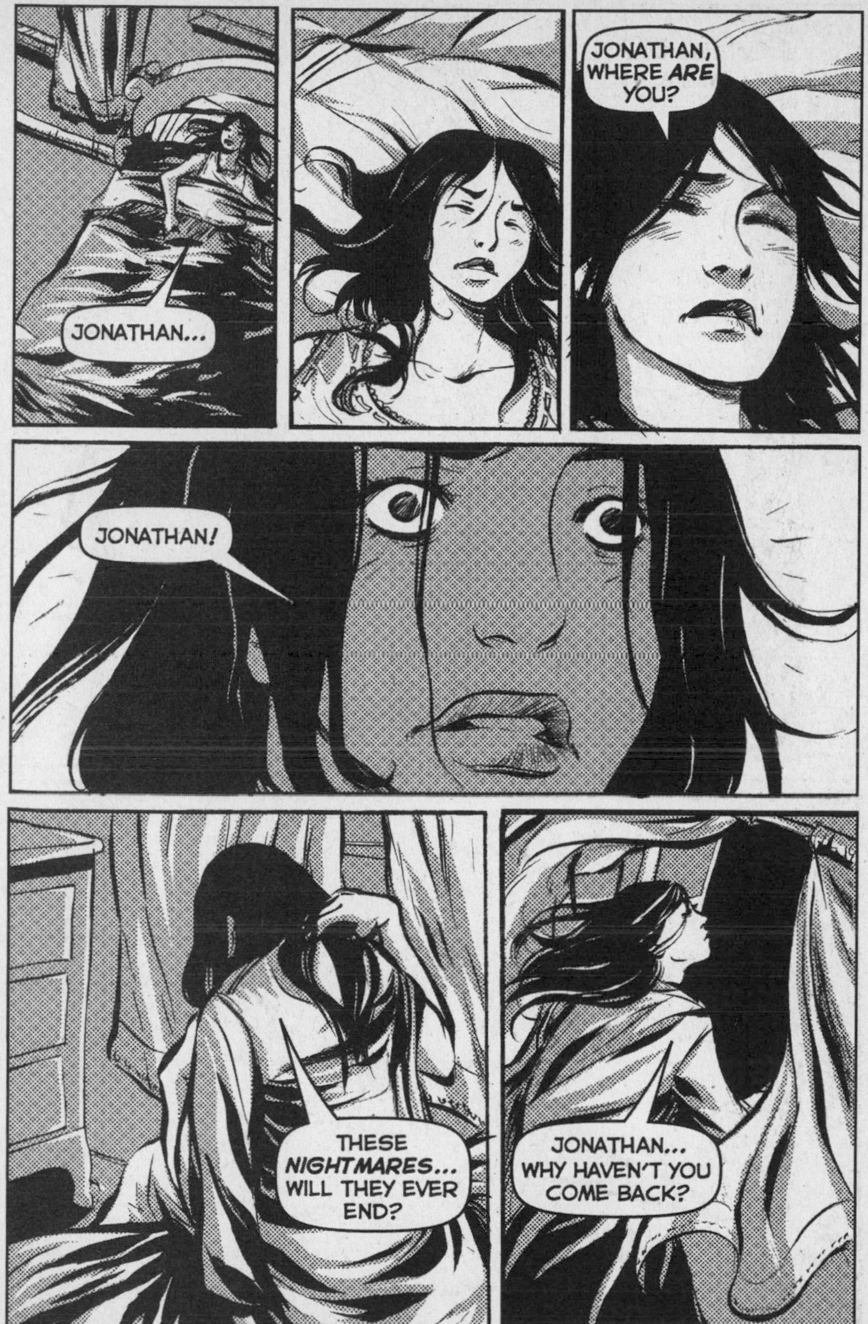
JONATHAN...
JONATHAN, WHERE ARE YOU?
JONATHAN!
THESE NIGHTMARES... WILL THEY EVER END?
JONATHAN... WHY HAVEN'T YOU COME BACK?

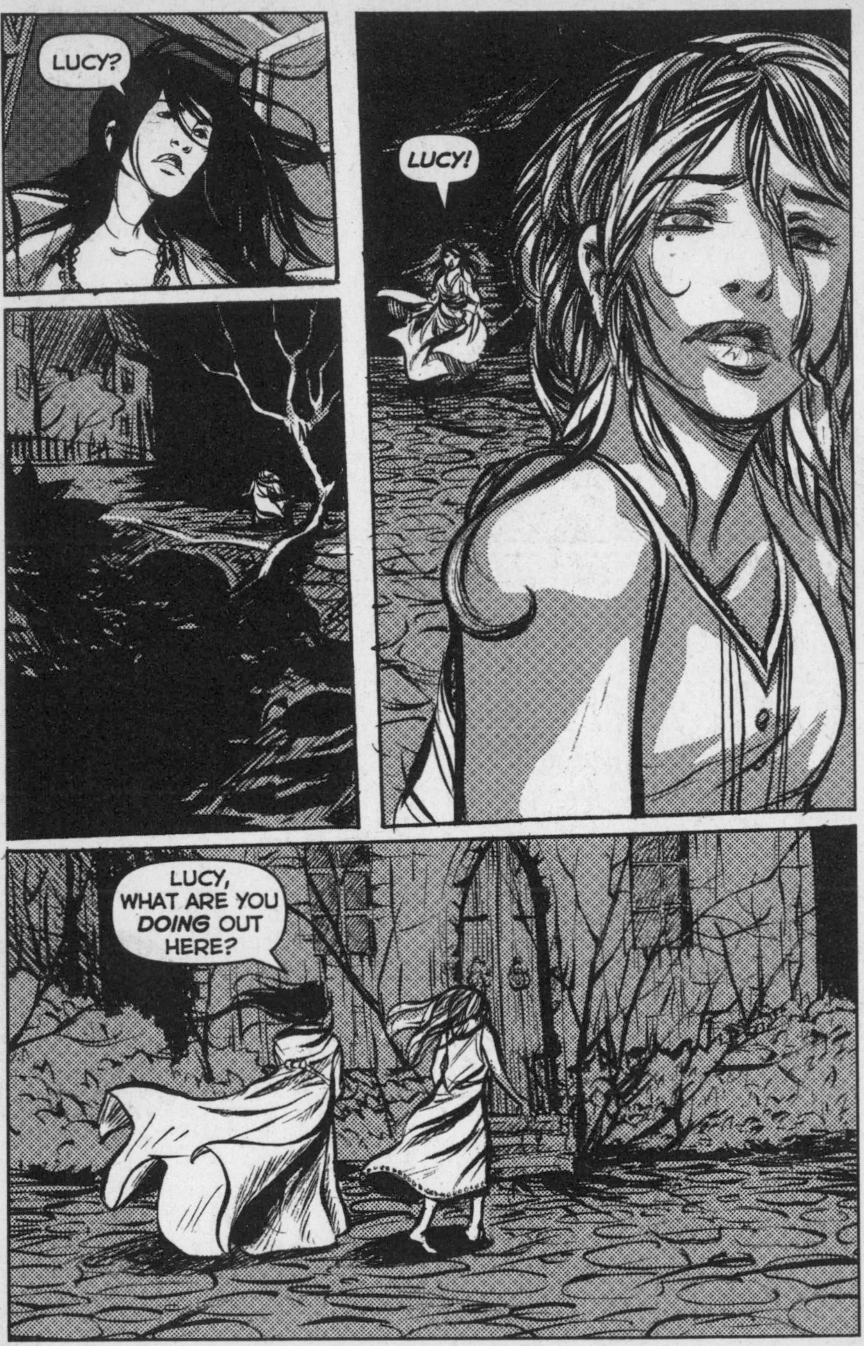
LUCY?
LUCY!
LUCY, WHAT ARE YOU *DOING* OUT HERE?

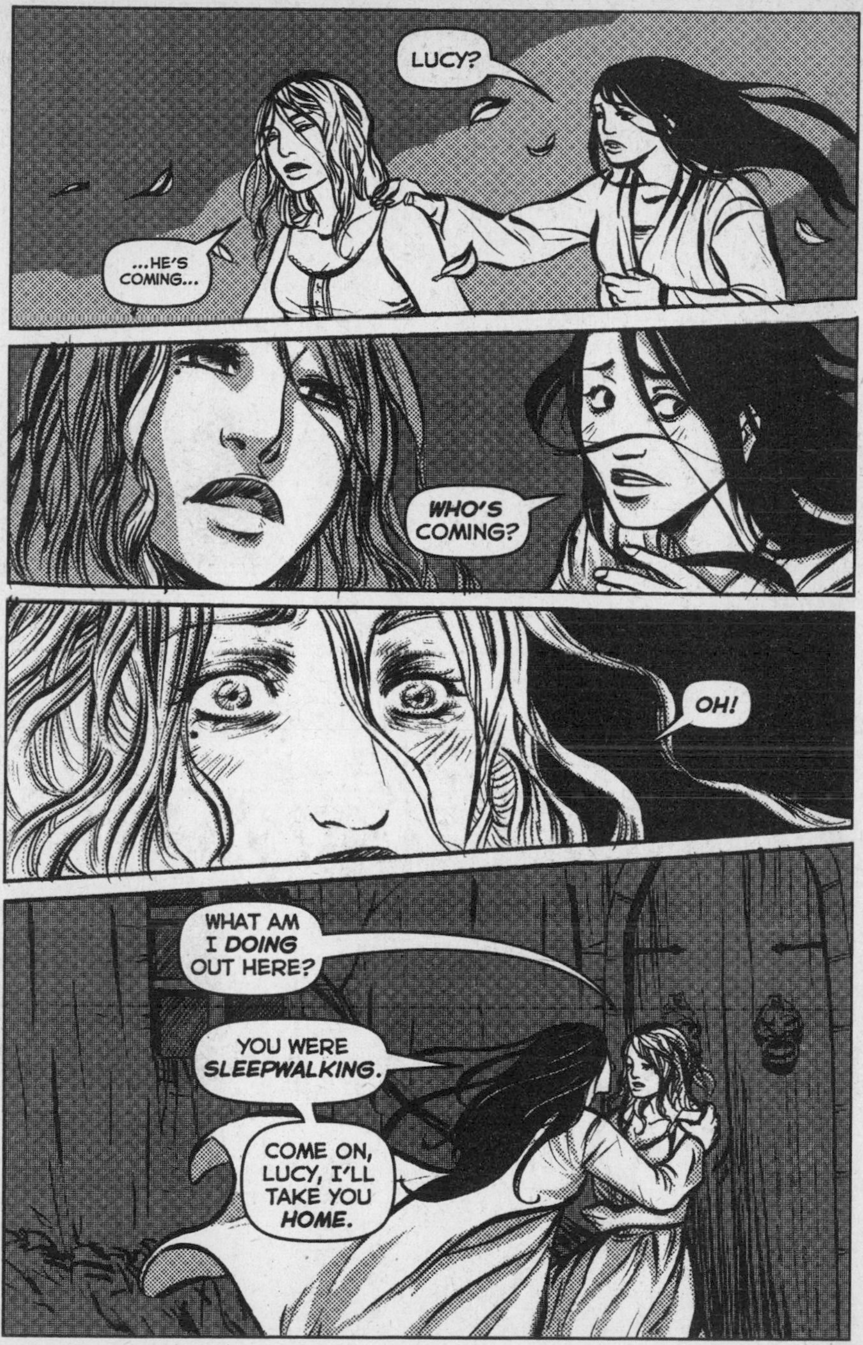
LUCY?
...HE'S COMING...
WHO'S COMING?
OH!
WHAT AM I DOING OUT HERE?
YOU WERE SLEEPWALKING.
COME ON, LUCY, I'LL TAKE YOU HOME.

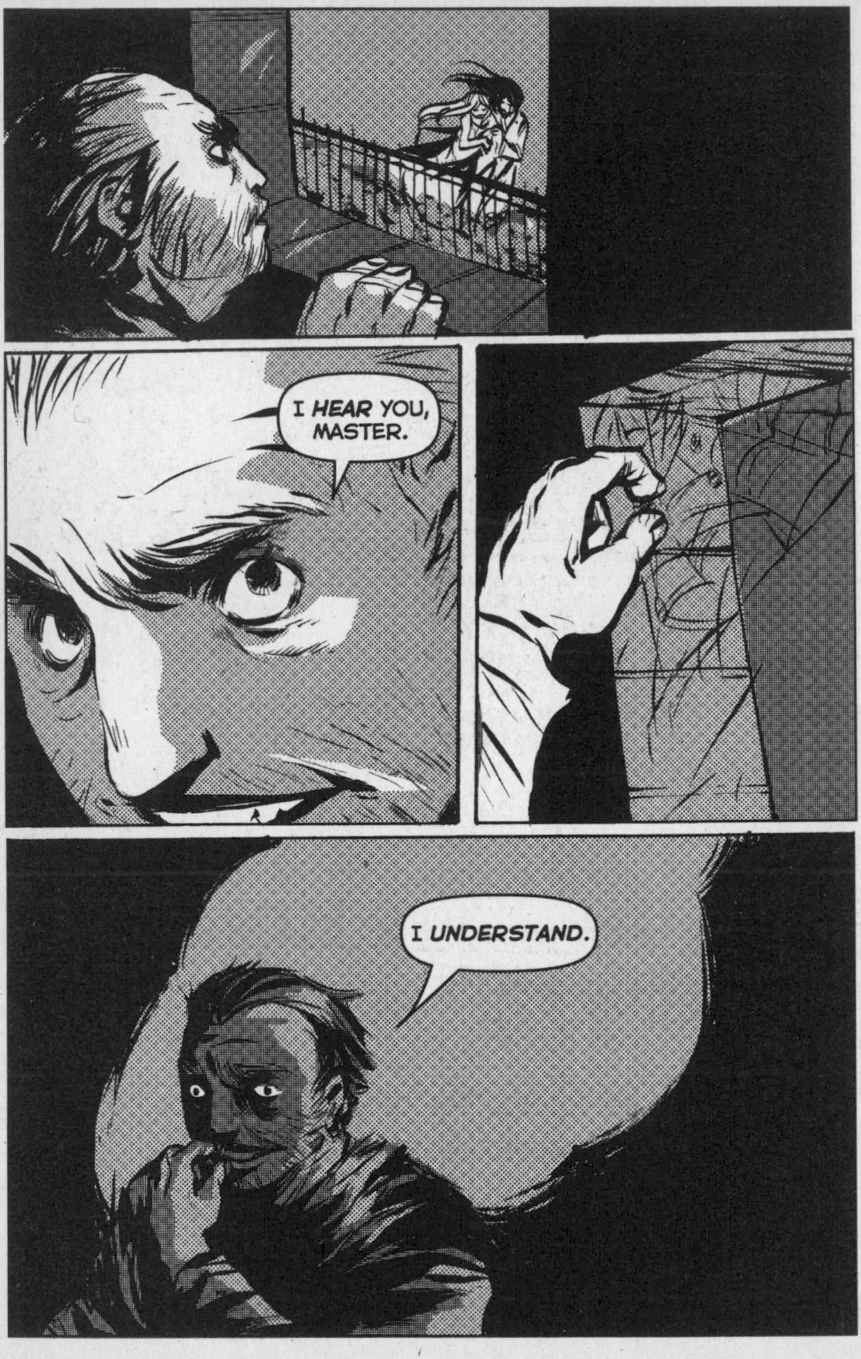
I HEAR YOU, MASTER.
I UNDERSTAND.

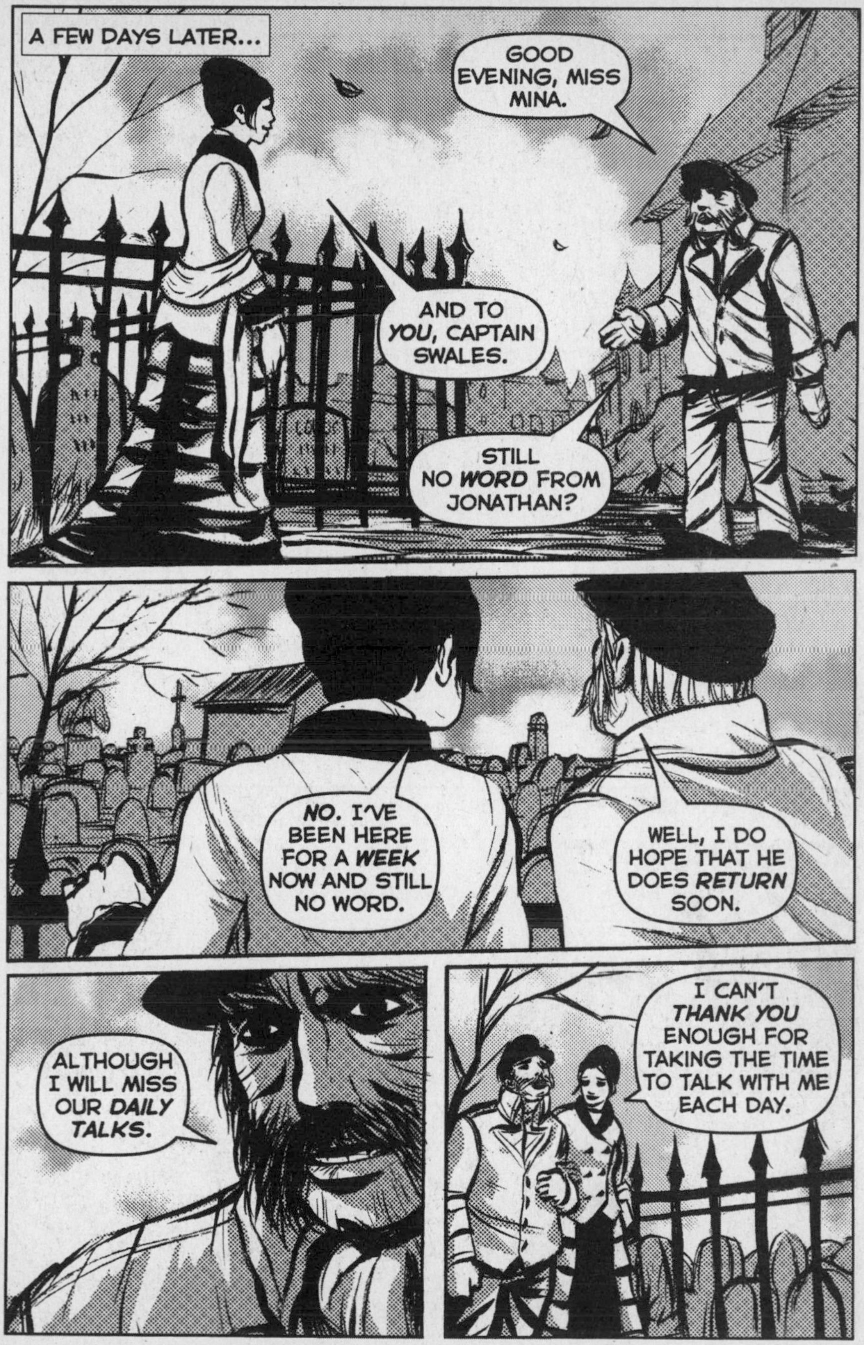

A FEW DAYS LATER...
GOOD EVENING, MISS MINA.
AND TO YOU, CAPTAIN SWALES.
STILL NO WORD FROM JONATHAN?
NO. I'VE BEEN HERE FOR A WEEK NOW AND STILL NO WORD.
WELL, I DO HOPE THAT HE DOES RETURN SOON.
ALTHOUGH I WILL MISS OUR DAILY TALKS.
I CAN'T THANK YOU ENOUGH FOR TAKING THE TIME TO TALK WITH ME EACH DAY.

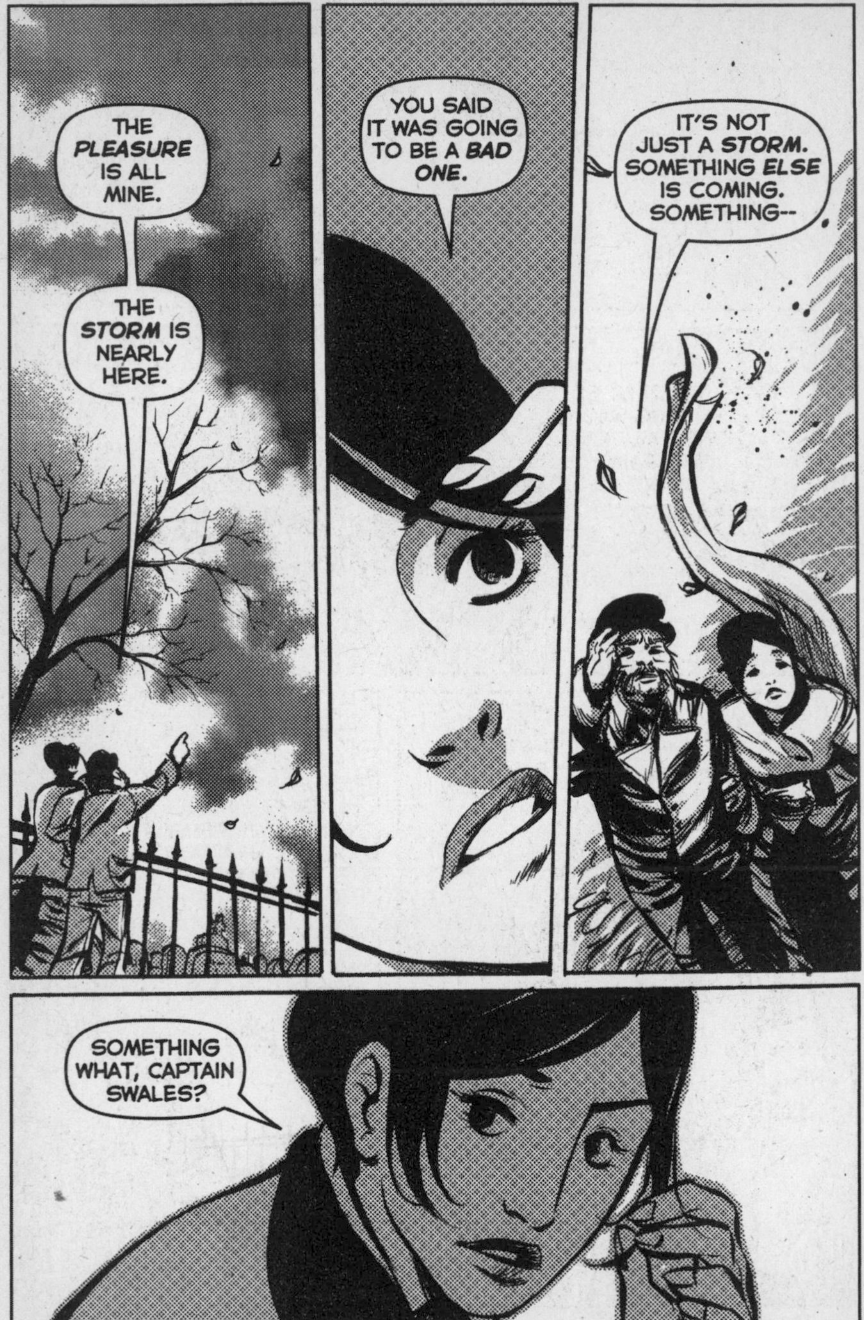
THE *PLEASURE* IS ALL MINE.
THE *STORM* IS NEARLY HERE.
YOU SAID IT WAS GOING TO BE A *BAD ONE.*
IT'S NOT JUST A *STORM.* SOMETHING *ELSE* IS COMING. SOMETHING--
SOMETHING WHAT, CAPTAIN SWALES?

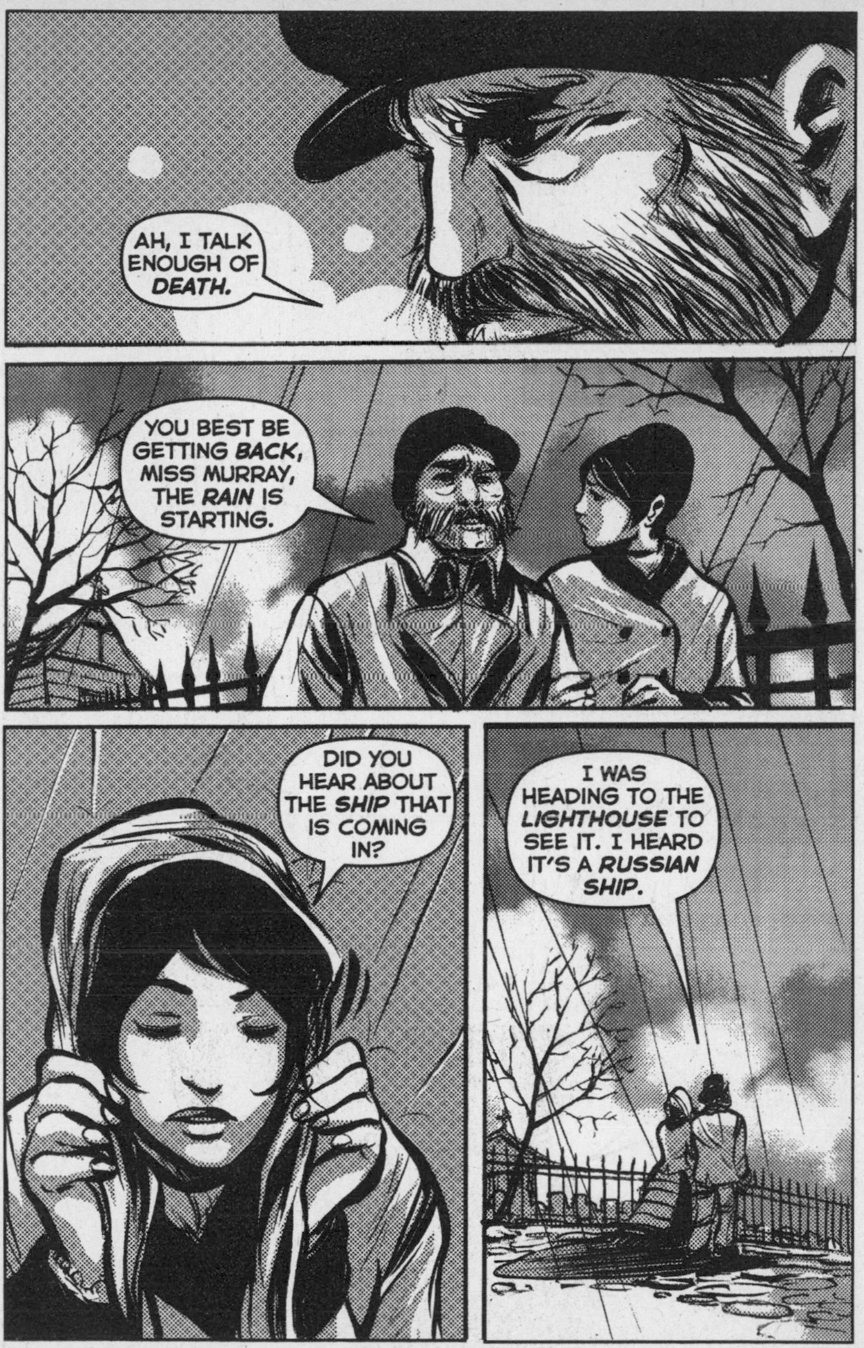
AH, I TALK ENOUGH OF DEATH.
YOU BEST BE GETTING BACK, MISS MURRAY, THE RAIN IS STARTING.
DID YOU HEAR ABOUT THE SHIP THAT IS COMING IN?
I WAS HEADING TO THE LIGHTHOUSE TO SEE IT. I HEARD IT'S A RUSSIAN SHIP.

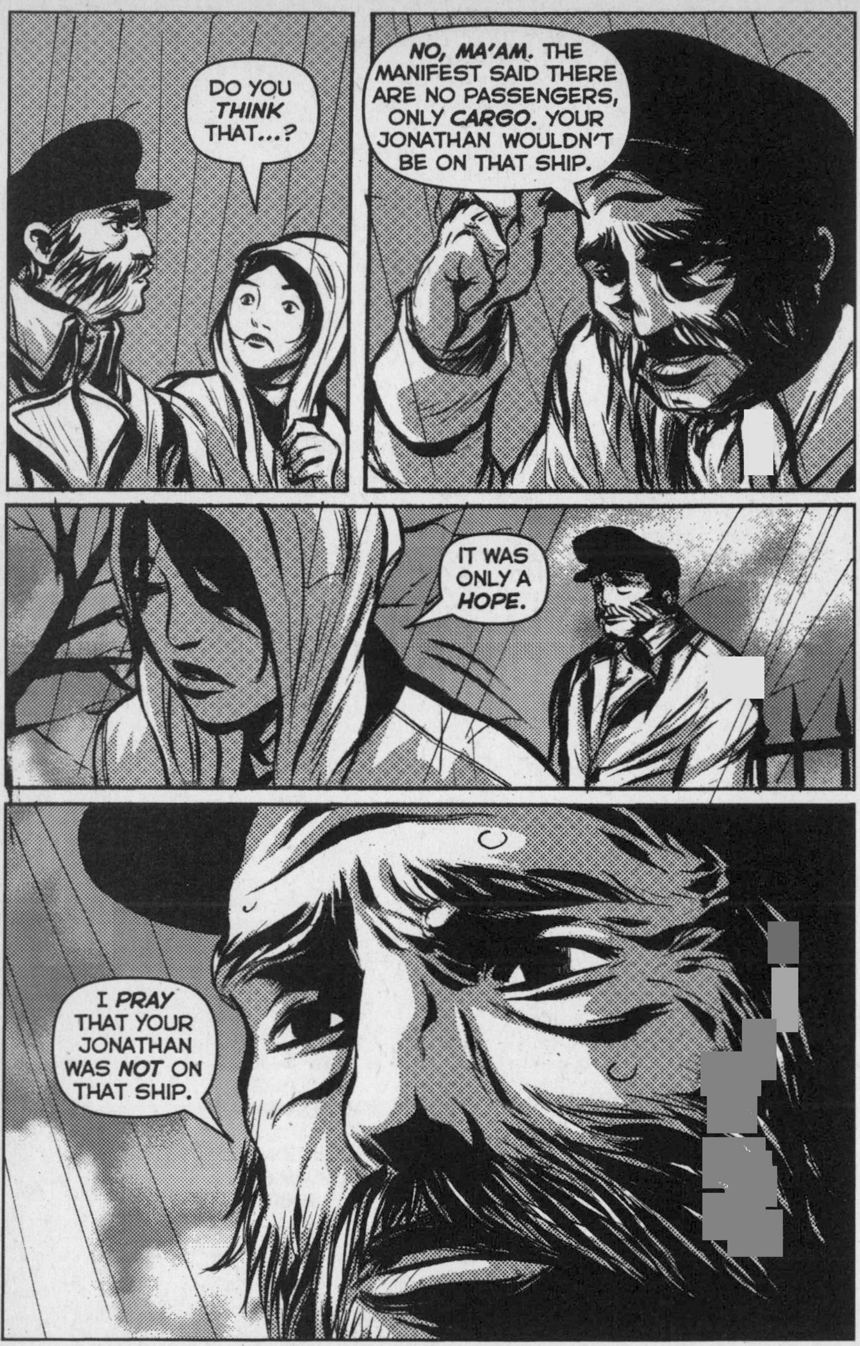
DO YOU THINK THAT...?
NO, MA'AM. THE MANIFEST SAID THERE ARE NO PASSENGERS, ONLY CARGO. YOUR JONATHAN WOULDN'T BE ON THAT SHIP.
IT WAS ONLY A HOPE.
I PRAY THAT YOUR JONATHAN WAS NOT ON THAT SHIP.

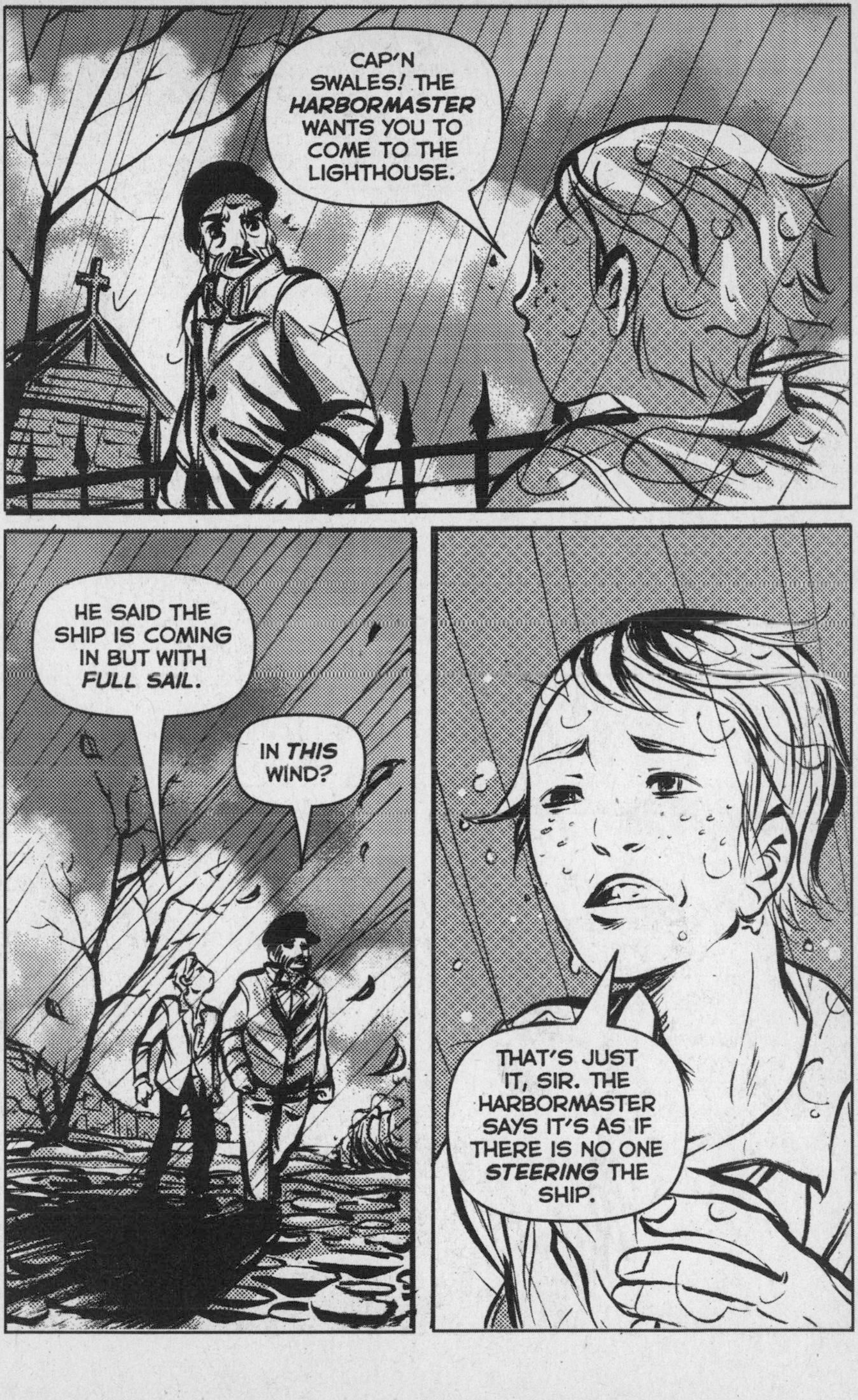
CAP'N SWALES! THE *HARBORMASTER* WANTS YOU TO COME TO THE LIGHTHOUSE.
HE SAID THE SHIP IS COMING IN BUT WITH *FULL SAIL*.
IN *THIS* WIND?
THAT'S JUST IT, SIR. THE HARBORMASTER SAYS IT'S AS IF THERE IS NO ONE *STEERING* THE SHIP.

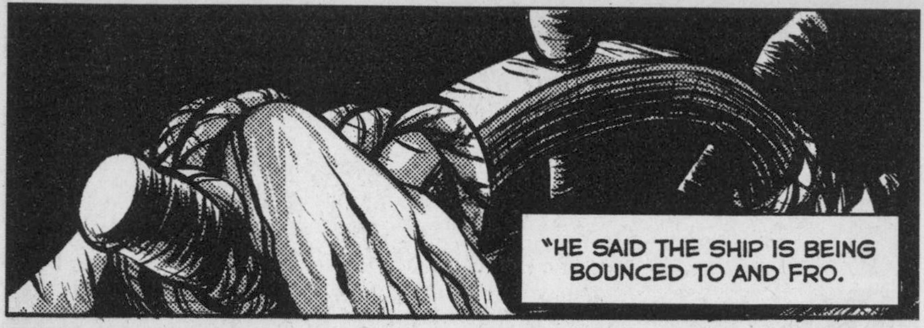
"HE SAID THE SHIP IS BEING BOUNCED TO AND FRO.

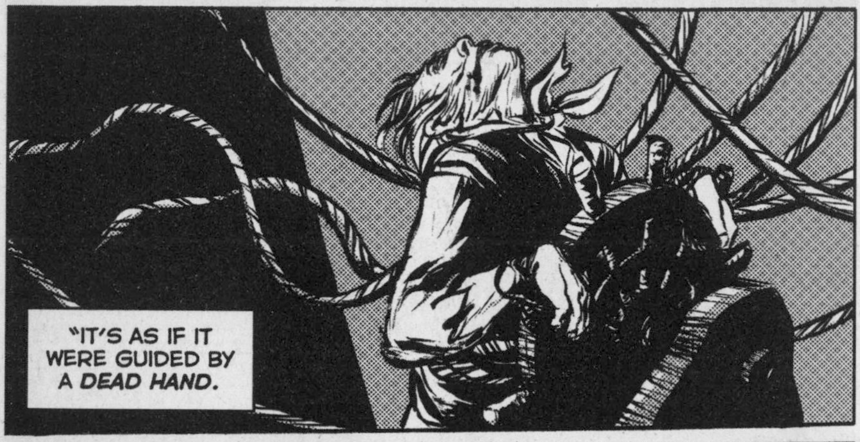
"IT'S AS IF IT WERE GUIDED BY A *DEAD HAND*.

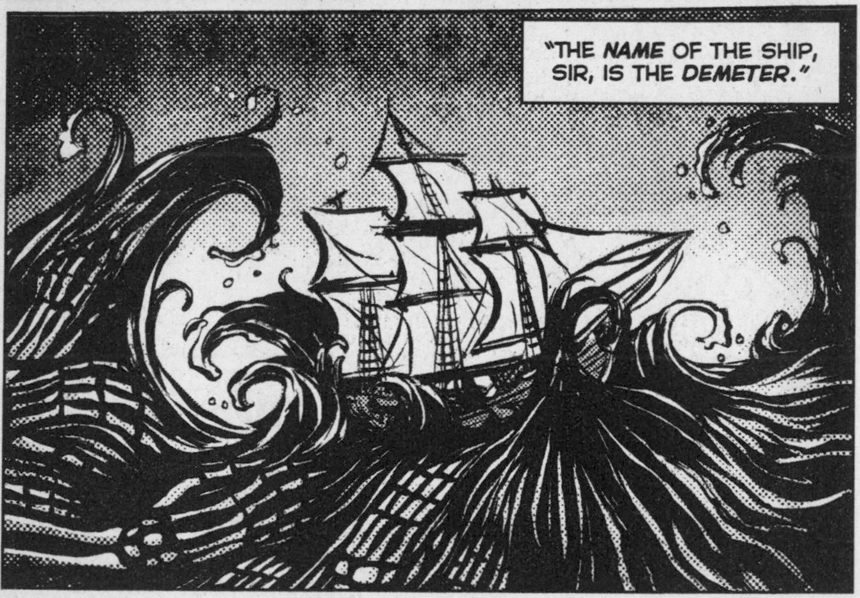
"THE *NAME* OF THE SHIP, SIR, IS THE *DEMETER*."

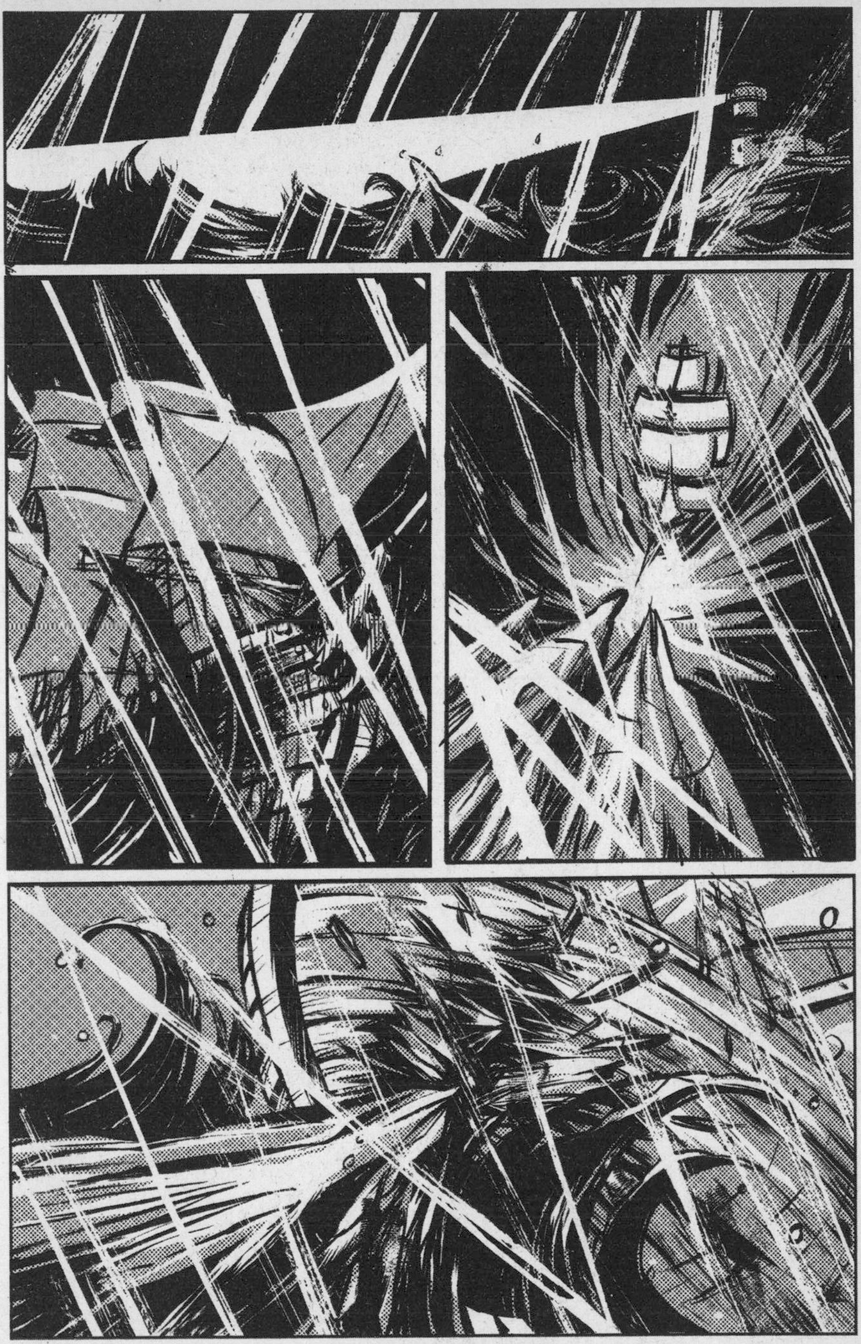

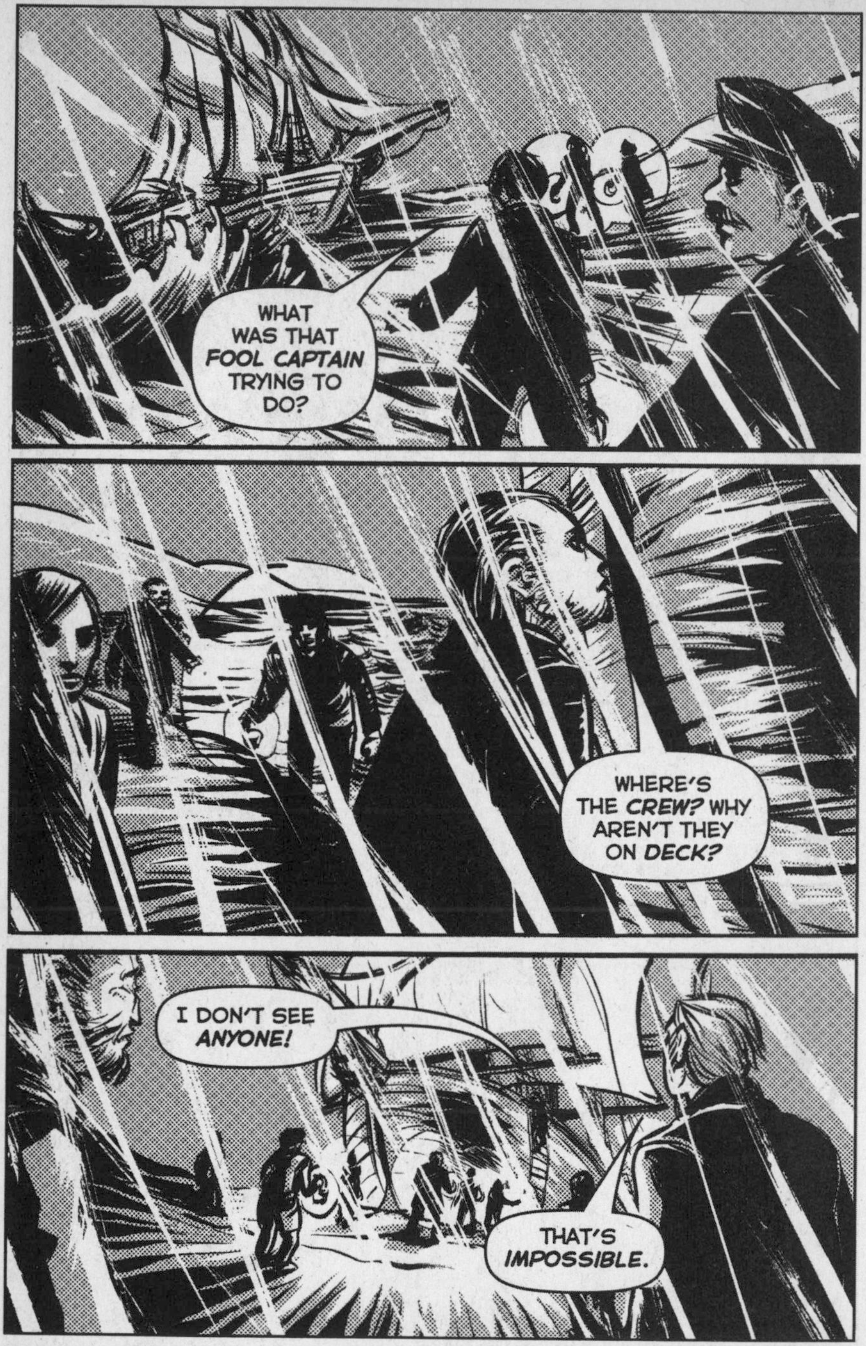
WHAT WAS THAT FOOL CAPTAIN TRYING TO DO?
WHERE'S THE CREW? WHY AREN'T THEY ON DECK?
I DON'T SEE ANYONE!
THAT'S IMPOSSIBLE.

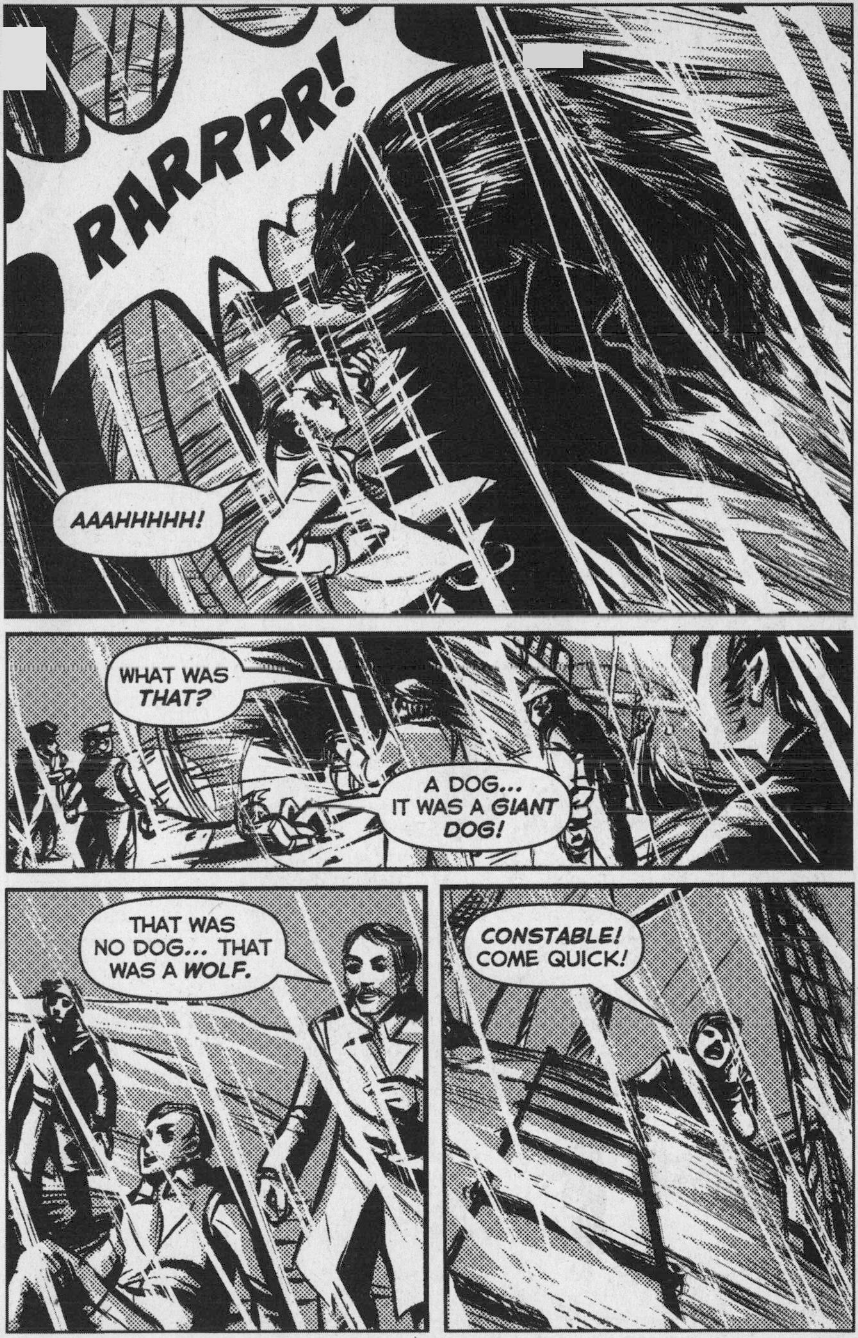
RARRRR!
AAAHHHHH!
WHAT WAS THAT?
A DOG... IT WAS A GIANT DOG!
THAT WAS NO DOG... THAT WAS A WOLF.
CONSTABLE! COME QUICK!

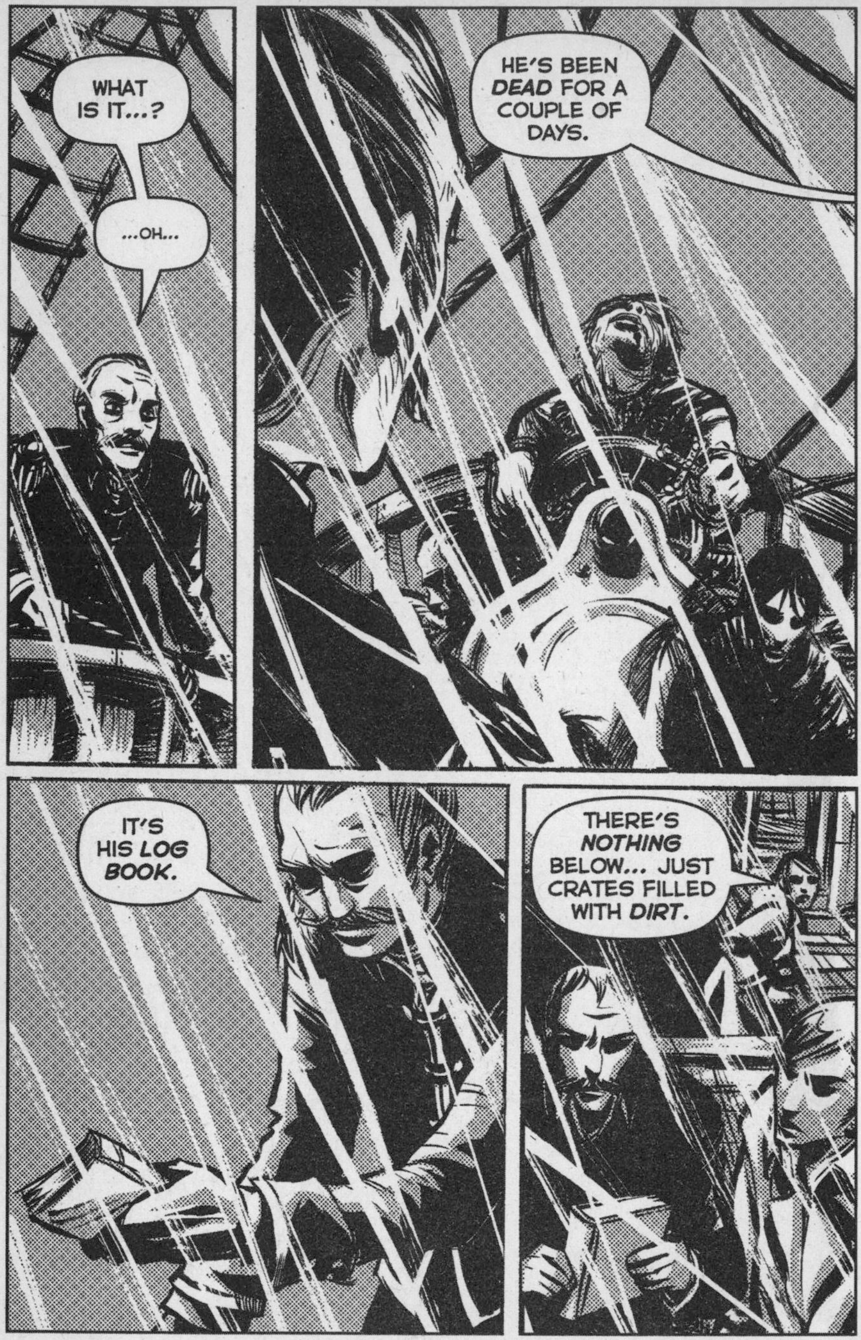
WHAT IS IT...?
...OH...
HE'S BEEN DEAD FOR A COUPLE OF DAYS.
IT'S HIS LOG BOOK.
THERE'S NOTHING BELOW... JUST CRATES FILLED WITH DIRT.

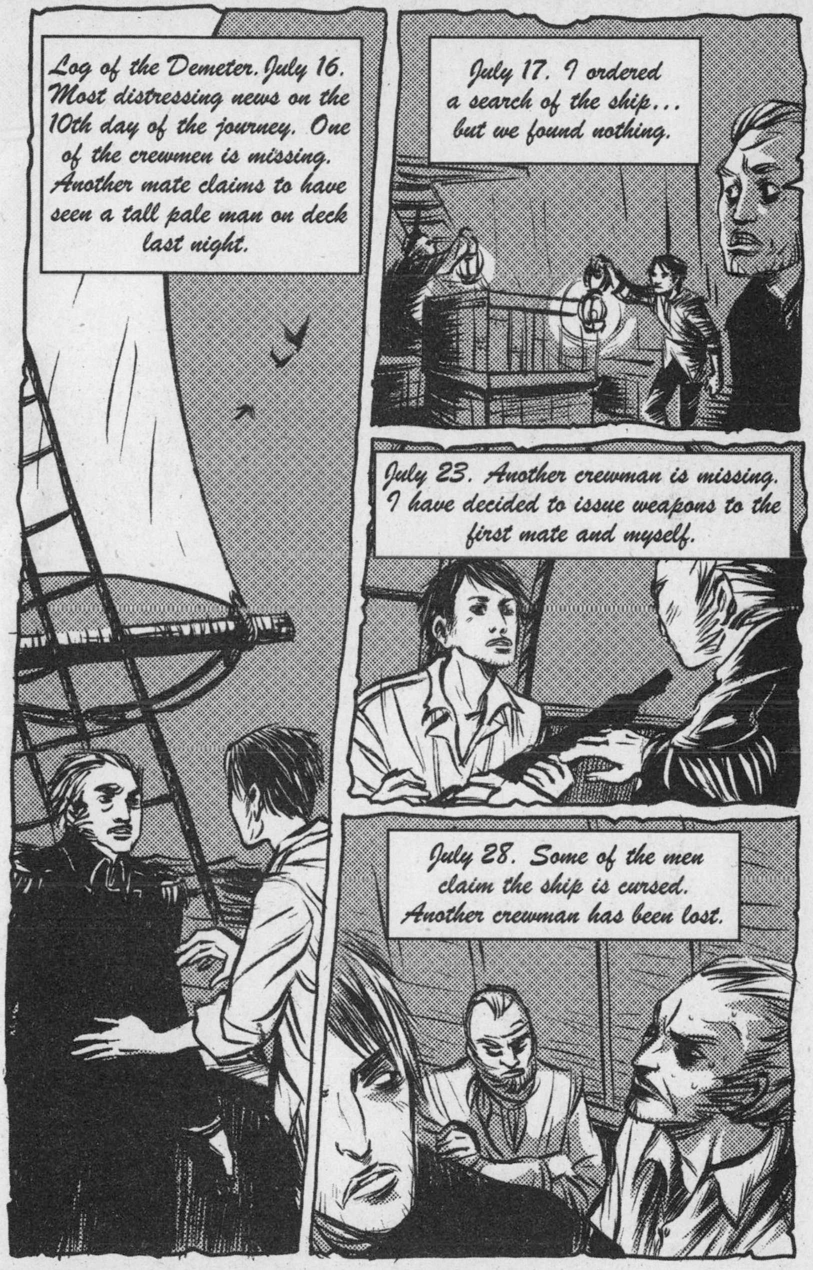
Log of the Demeter. July 16. Most distressing news on the 10th day of the journey. One of the crewmen is missing. Another mate claims to have seen a tall pale man on deck last night.
July 17. I ordered a search of the ship... but we found nothing.
July 23. Another crewman is missing. I have decided to issue weapons to the first mate and myself.
July 28. Some of the men claim the ship is cursed. Another crewman has been lost.

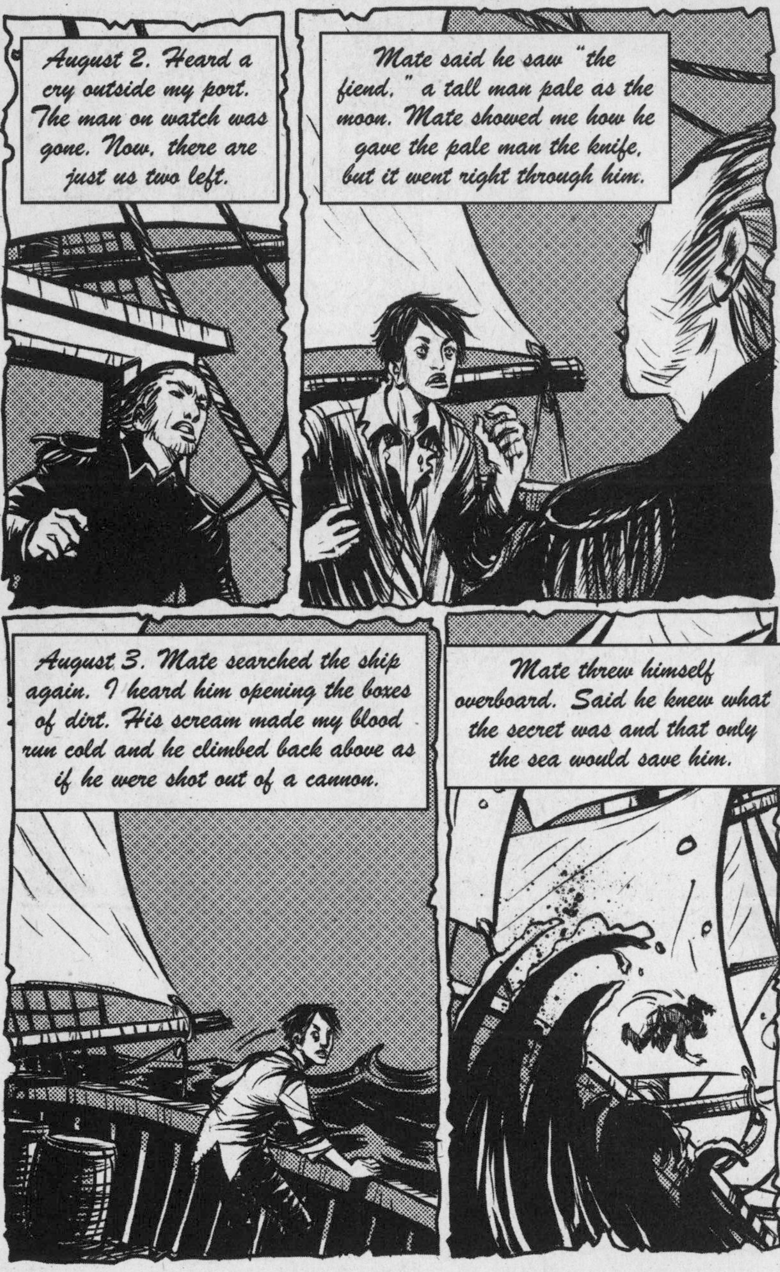
August 2. Heard a cry outside my port. The man on watch was gone. Now, there are just us two left.
Mate said he saw "the fiend," a tall man pale as the moon. Mate showed me how he gave the pale man the knife, but it went right through him.
August 3. Mate searched the ship again. I heard him opening the boxes of dirt. His scream made my blood run cold and he climbed back above as if he were shot out of a cannon.
Mate threw himself overboard. Said he knew what the secret was and that only the sea would save him.

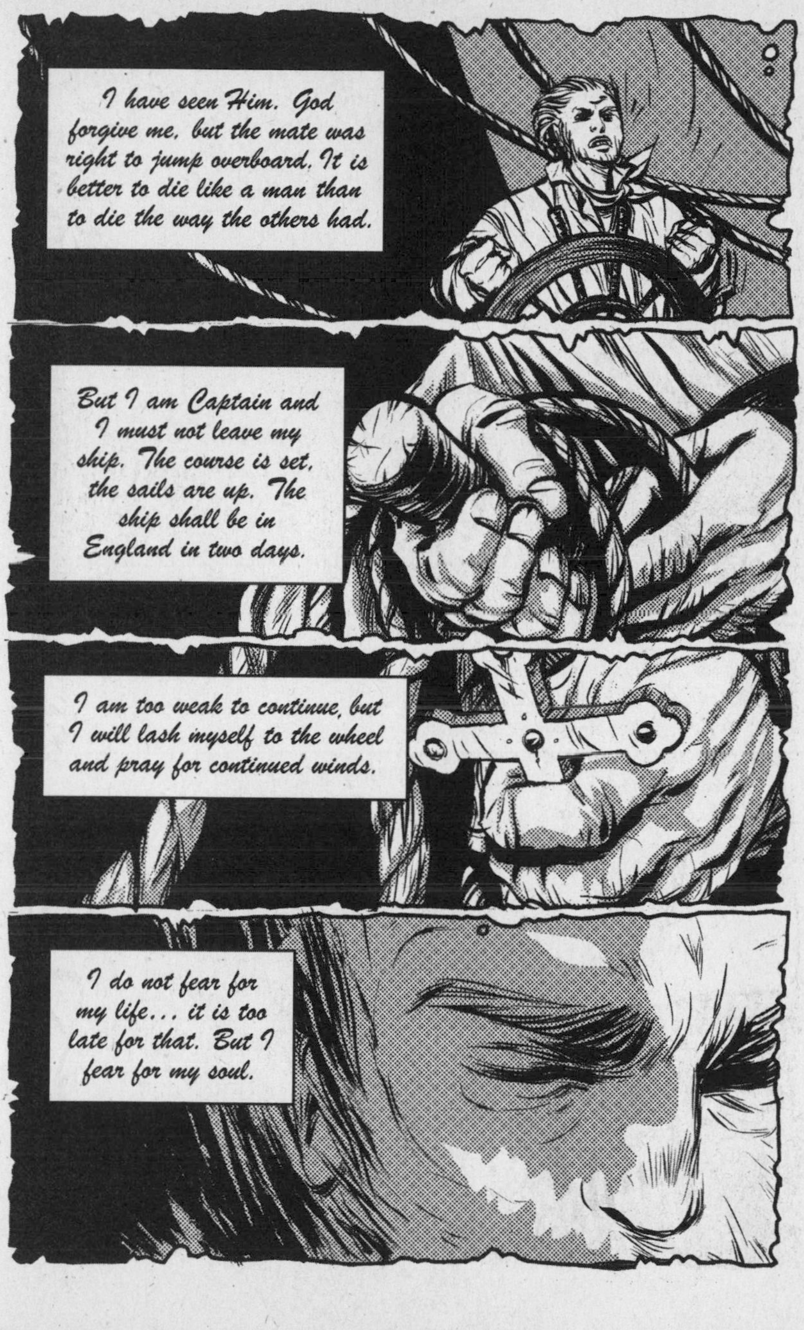
I have seen Him. God forgive me, but the mate was right to jump overboard. It is better to die like a man than to die the way the others had.
But I am Captain and I must not leave my ship. The course is set, the sails are up. The ship shall be in England in two days.
I am too weak to continue, but I will lash myself to the wheel and pray for continued winds.
I do not fear for my life... it is too late for that. But I fear for my soul.

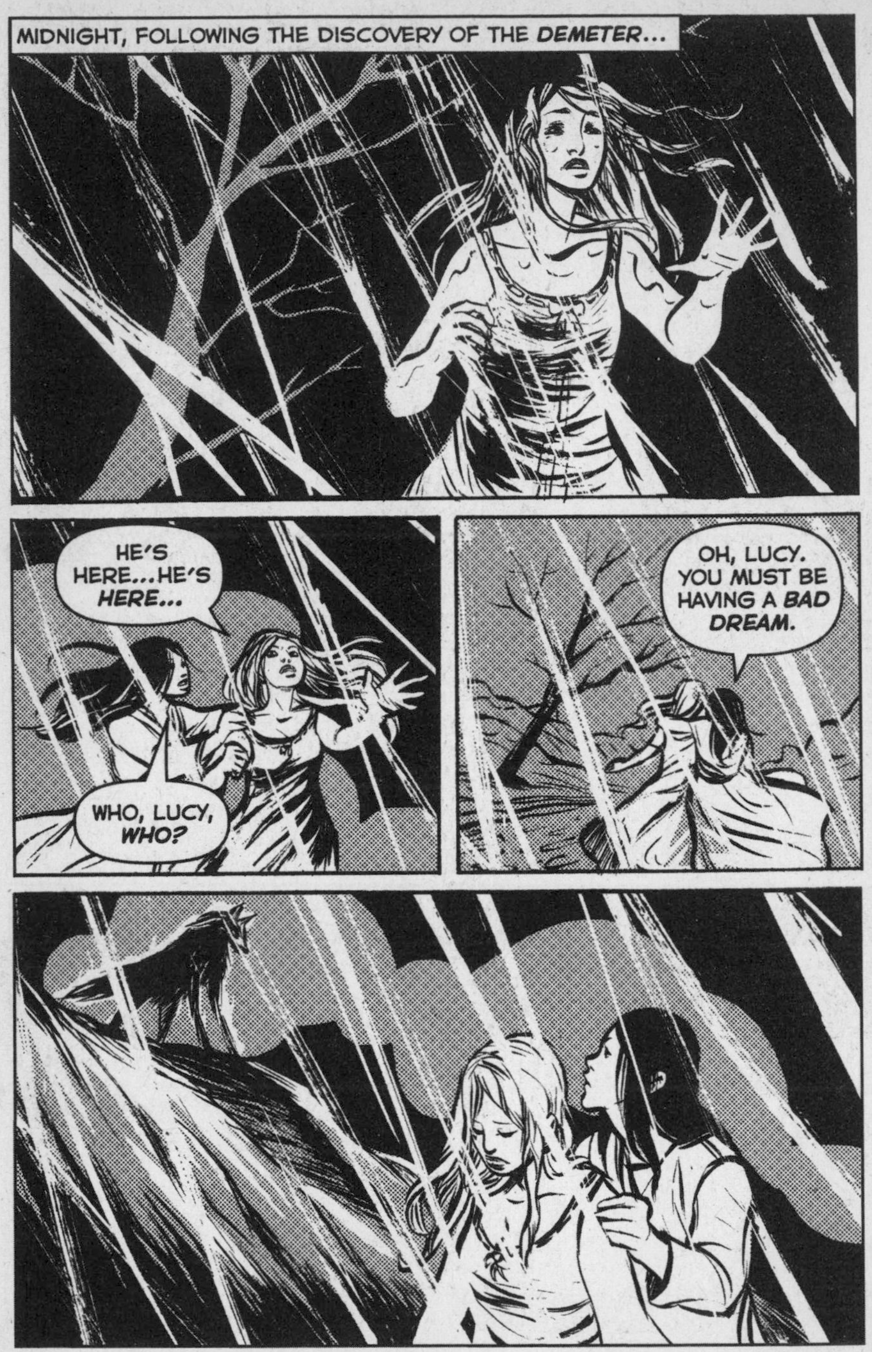
MIDNIGHT, FOLLOWING THE DISCOVERY OF THE *DEMETER*...
HE'S HERE...HE'S *HERE*...
WHO, LUCY, *WHO?*
OH, LUCY. YOU MUST BE HAVING A *BAD DREAM*.

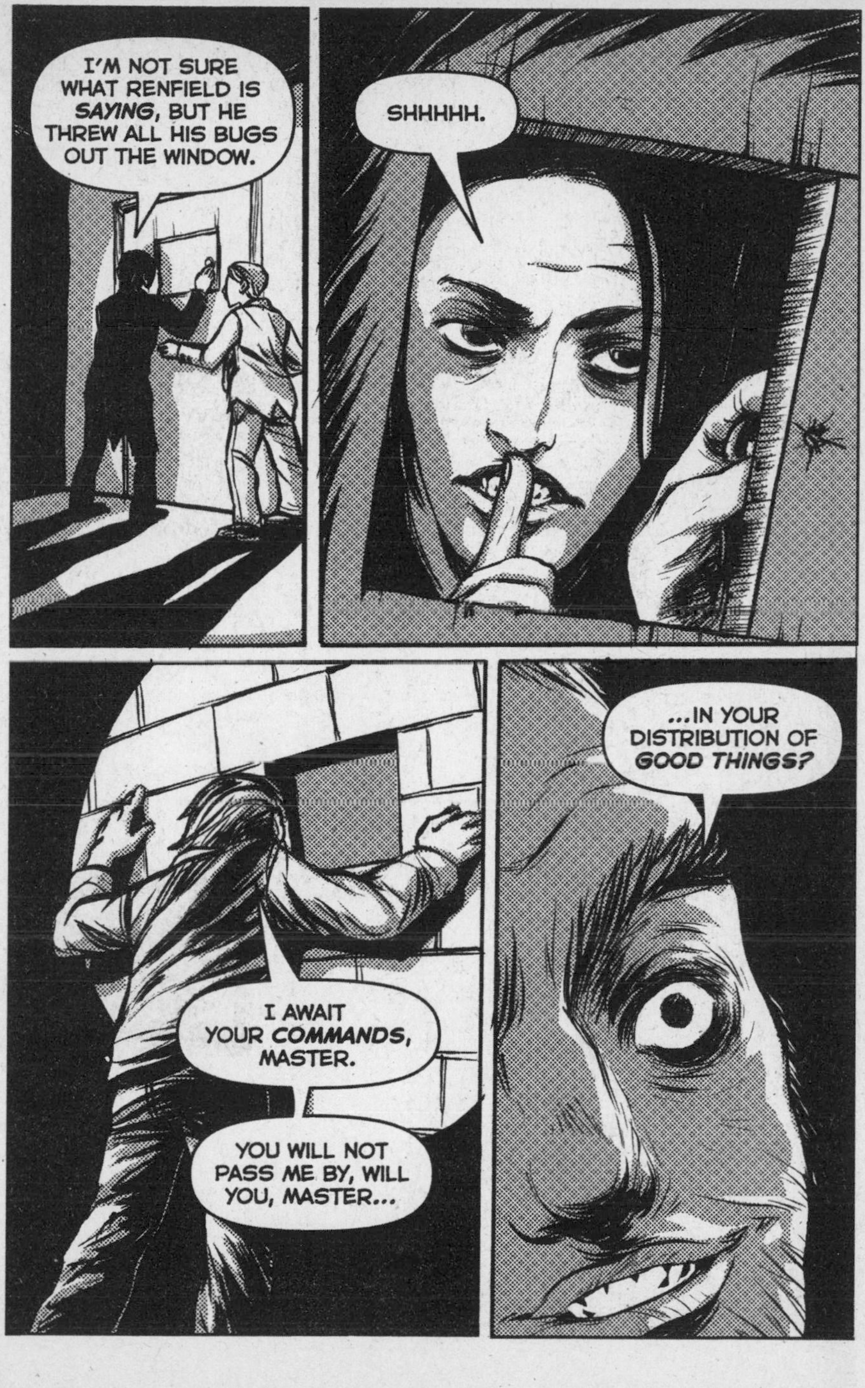
I'M NOT SURE WHAT RENFIELD IS SAYING, BUT HE THREW ALL HIS BUGS OUT THE WINDOW.
SHHHHH.
I AWAIT YOUR COMMANDS, MASTER.
YOU WILL NOT PASS ME BY, WILL YOU, MASTER...
...IN YOUR DISTRIBUTION OF GOOD THINGS?

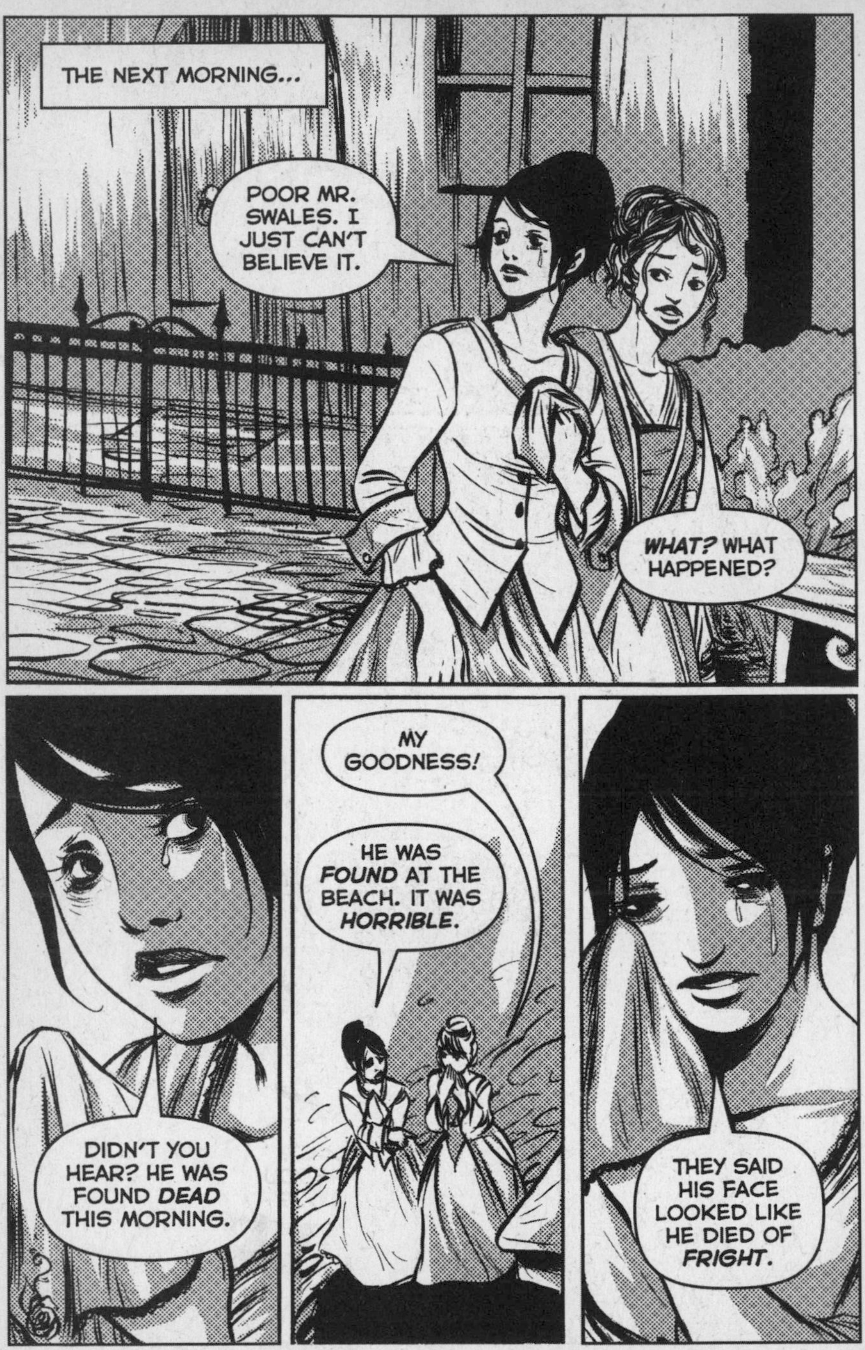
THE NEXT MORNING...
POOR MR. SWALES. I JUST CAN'T BELIEVE IT.
WHAT? WHAT HAPPENED?
DIDN'T YOU HEAR? HE WAS FOUND DEAD THIS MORNING.
MY GOODNESS!
HE WAS FOUND AT THE BEACH. IT WAS HORRIBLE.
THEY SAID HIS FACE LOOKED LIKE HE DIED OF FRIGHT.

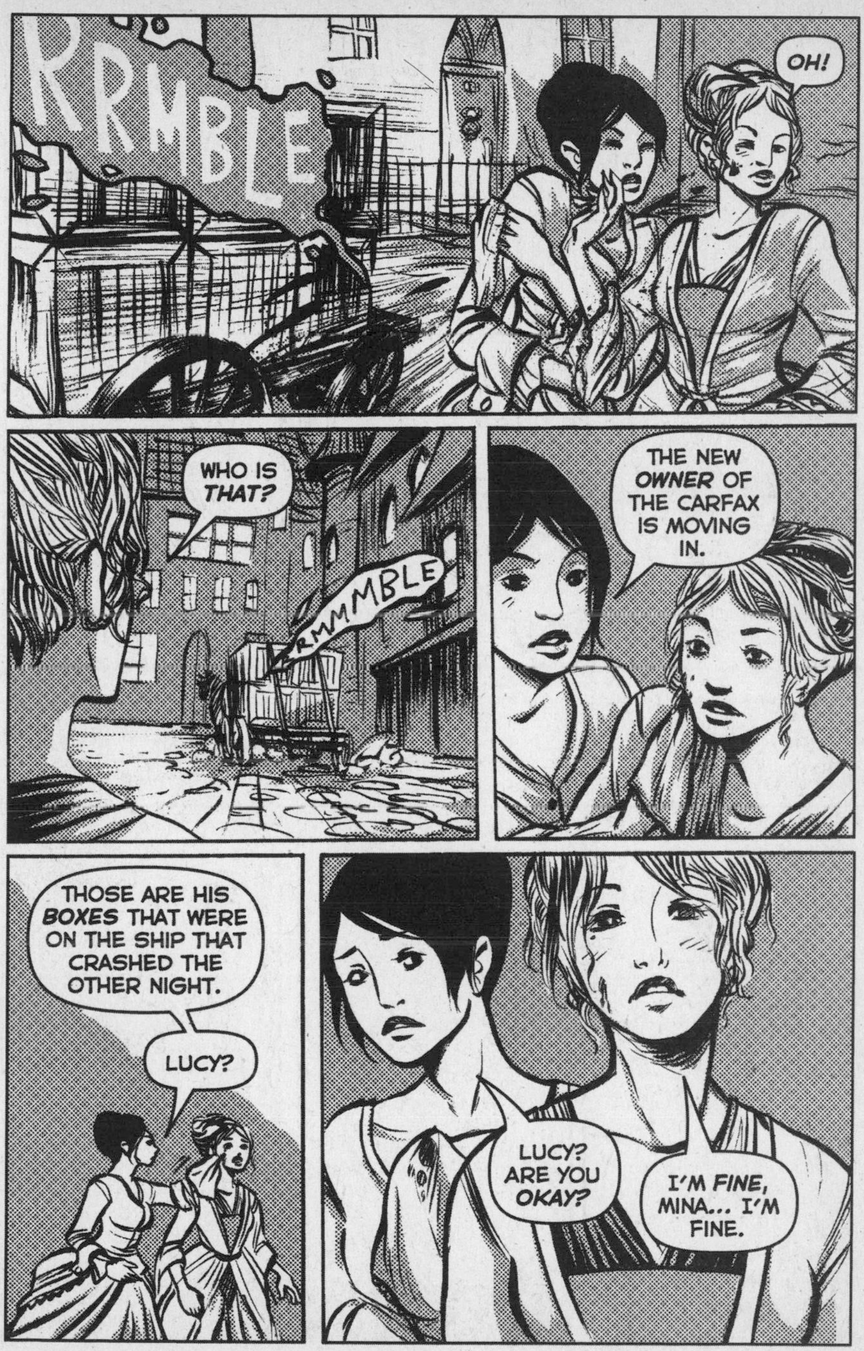
RRMBLE
OH!
WHO IS THAT?
RMMMBLE
THE NEW OWNER OF THE CARFAX IS MOVING IN.
THOSE ARE HIS BOXES THAT WERE ON THE SHIP THAT CRASHED THE OTHER NIGHT.
LUCY?
LUCY? ARE YOU OKAY?
I'M FINE, MINA... I'M FINE.

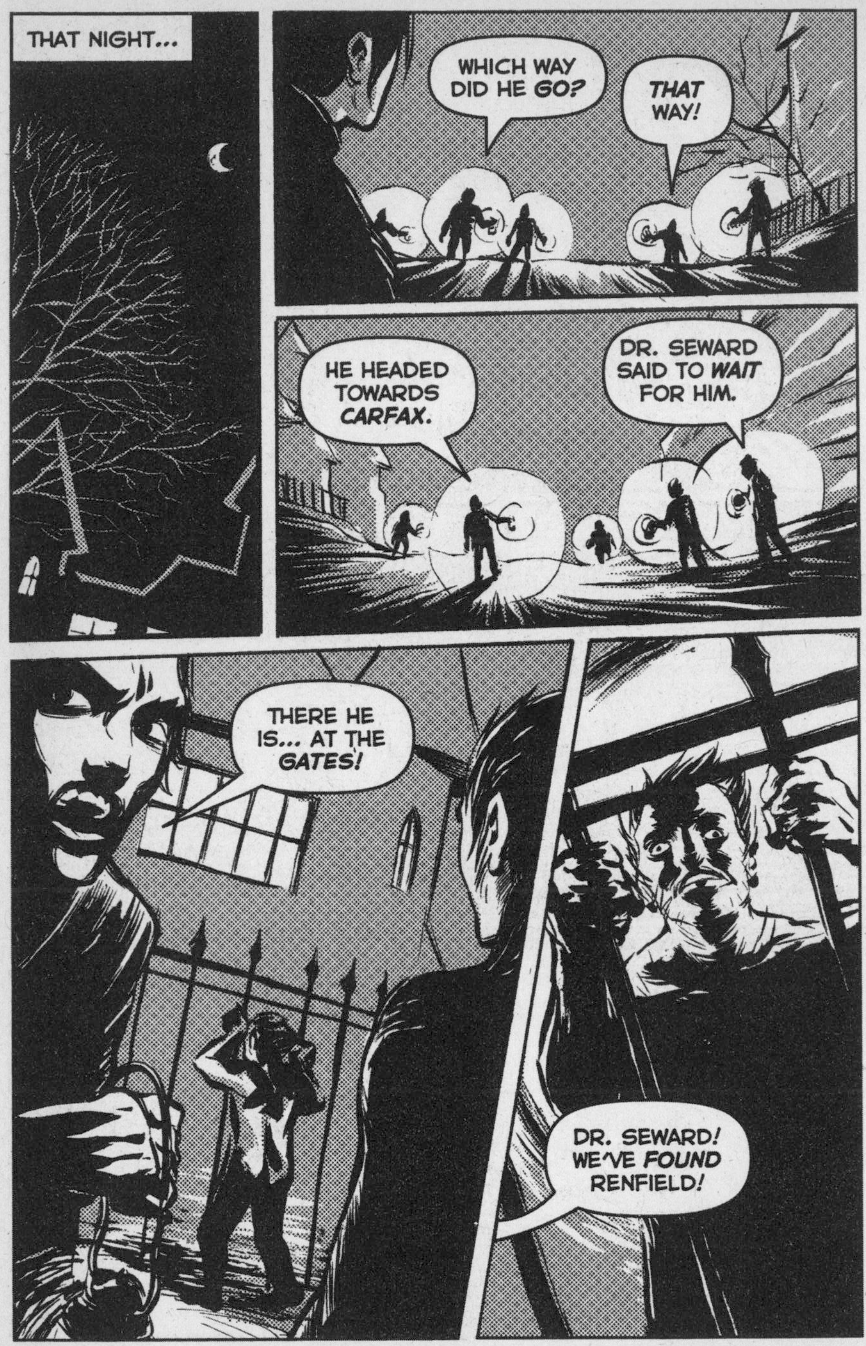
THAT NIGHT...
WHICH WAY DID HE GO?
THAT WAY!
HE HEADED TOWARDS CARFAX.
DR. SEWARD SAID TO WAIT FOR HIM.
THERE HE IS... AT THE GATES!
DR. SEWARD! WE'VE FOUND RENFIELD!

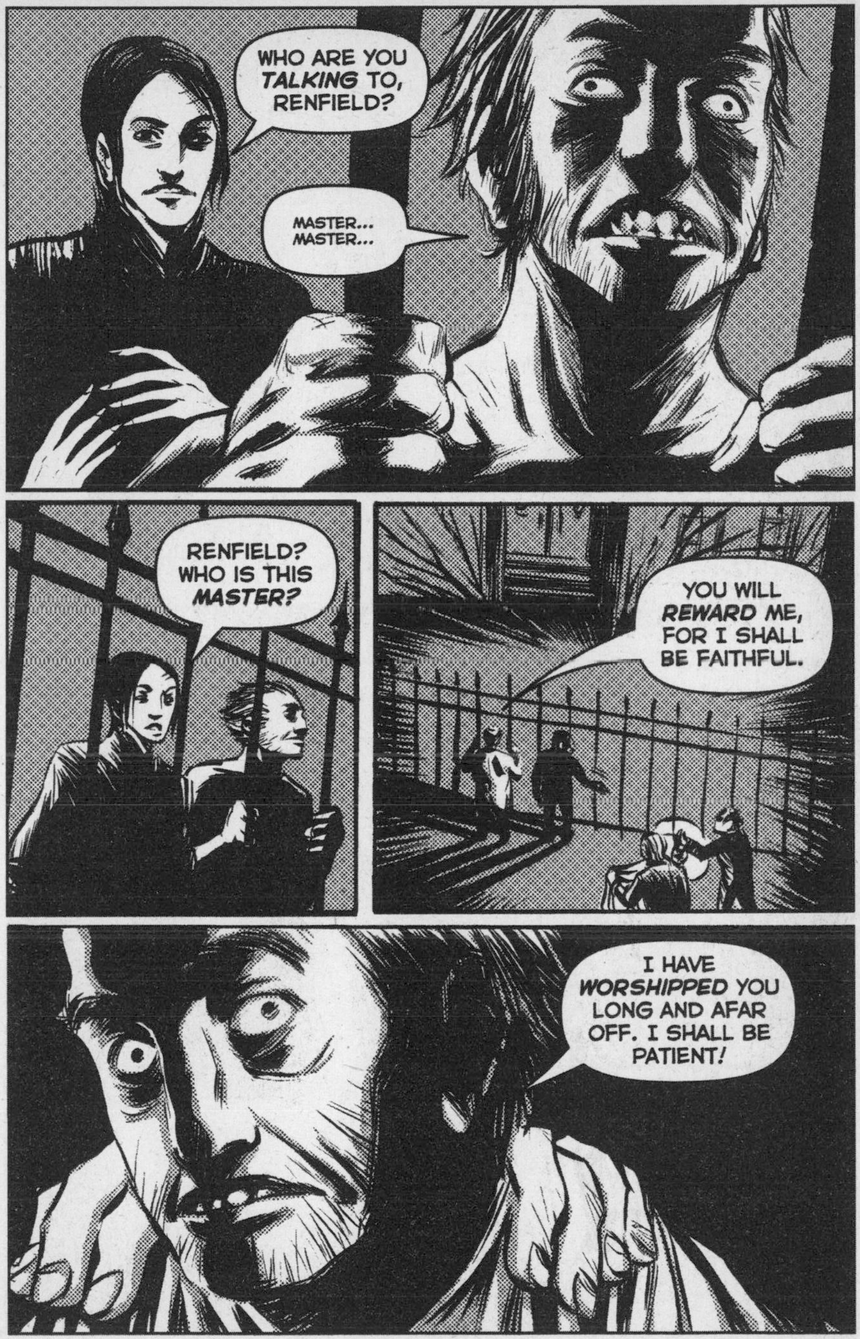

WHO ARE YOU TALKING TO, RENFIELD?
MASTER... MASTER...
RENFIELD? WHO IS THIS MASTER?
YOU WILL REWARD ME, FOR I SHALL BE FAITHFUL.
I HAVE WORSHIPPED YOU LONG AND AFAR OFF. I SHALL BE PATIENT!

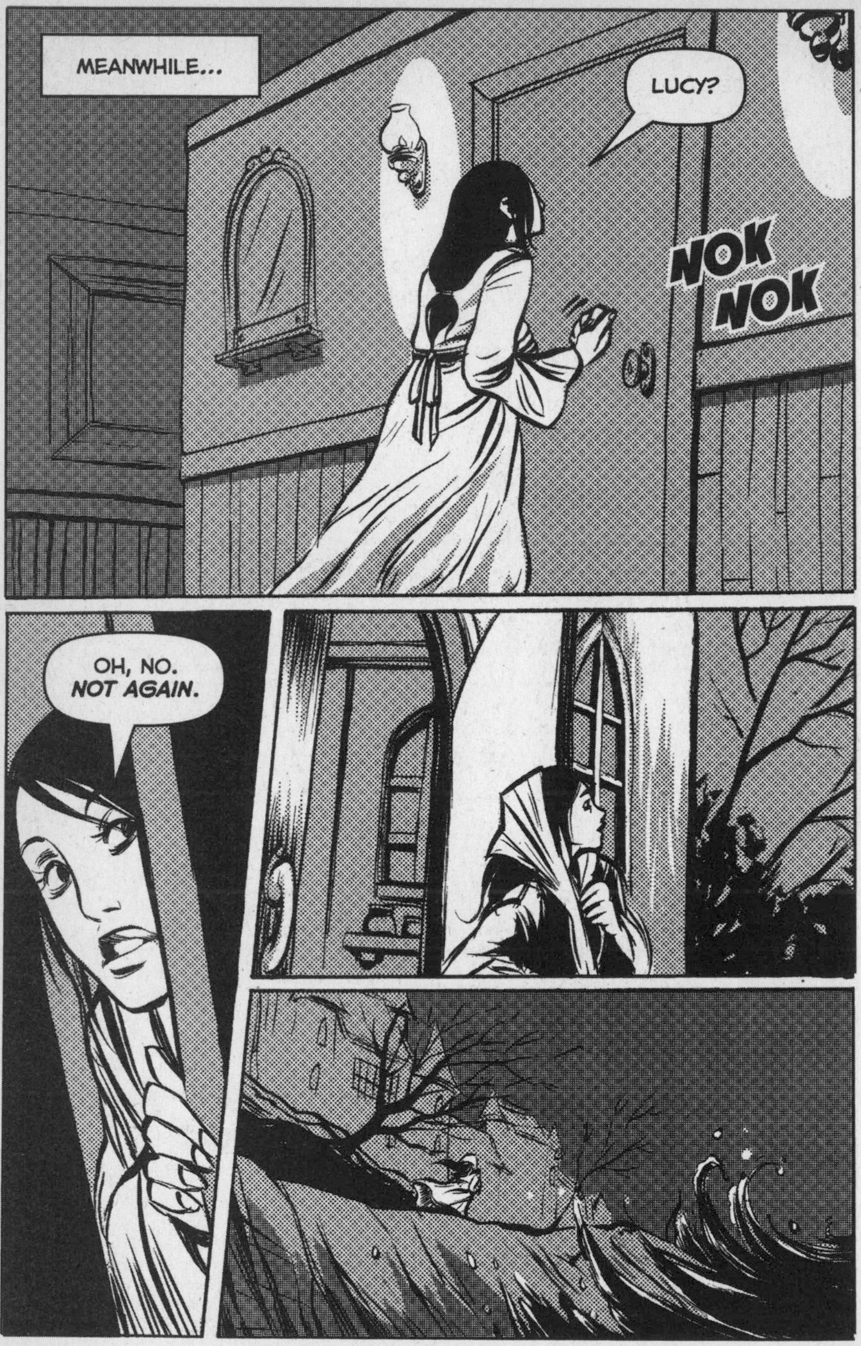
MEANWHILE...
LUCY?
NOK NOK
OH, NO. NOT AGAIN.

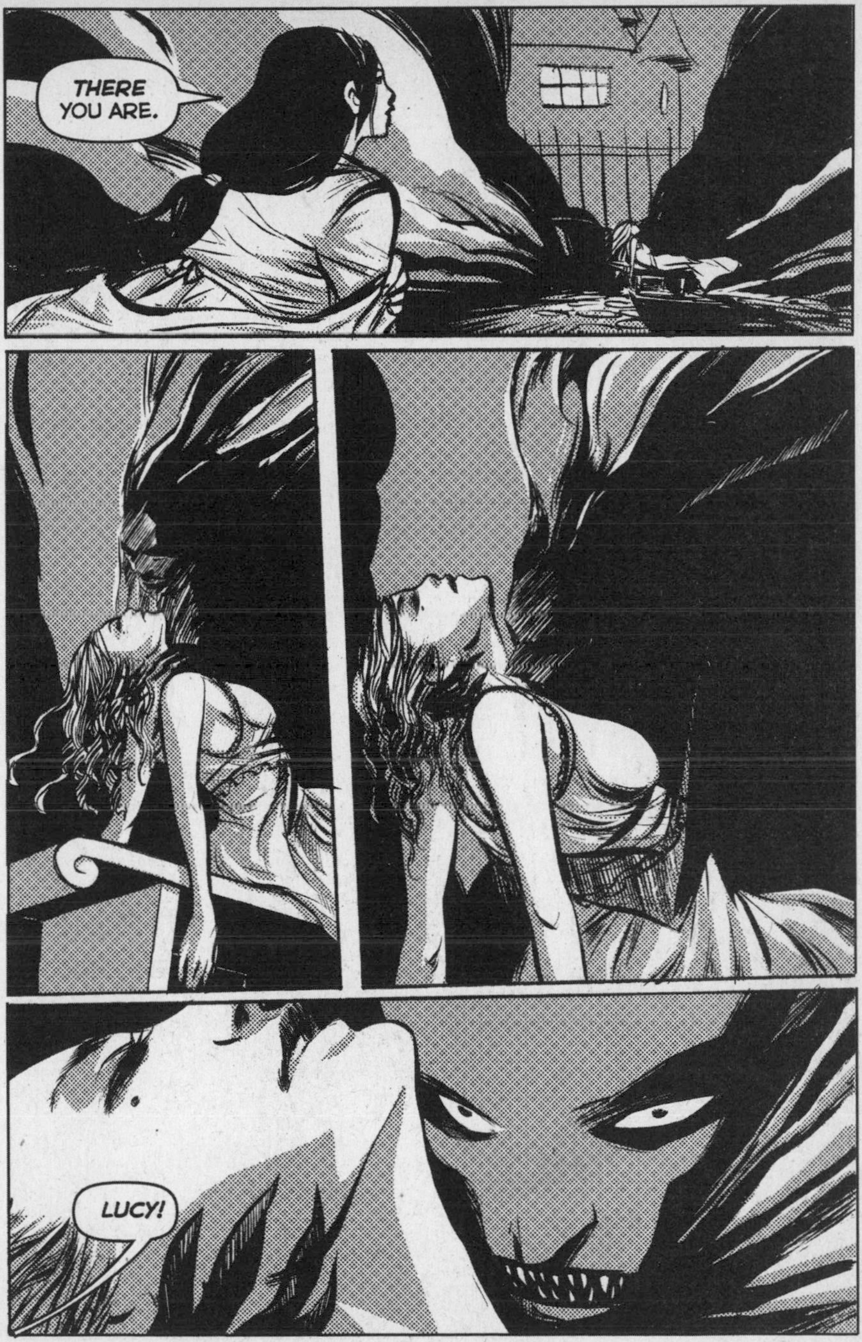
THERE YOU ARE.
LUCY!

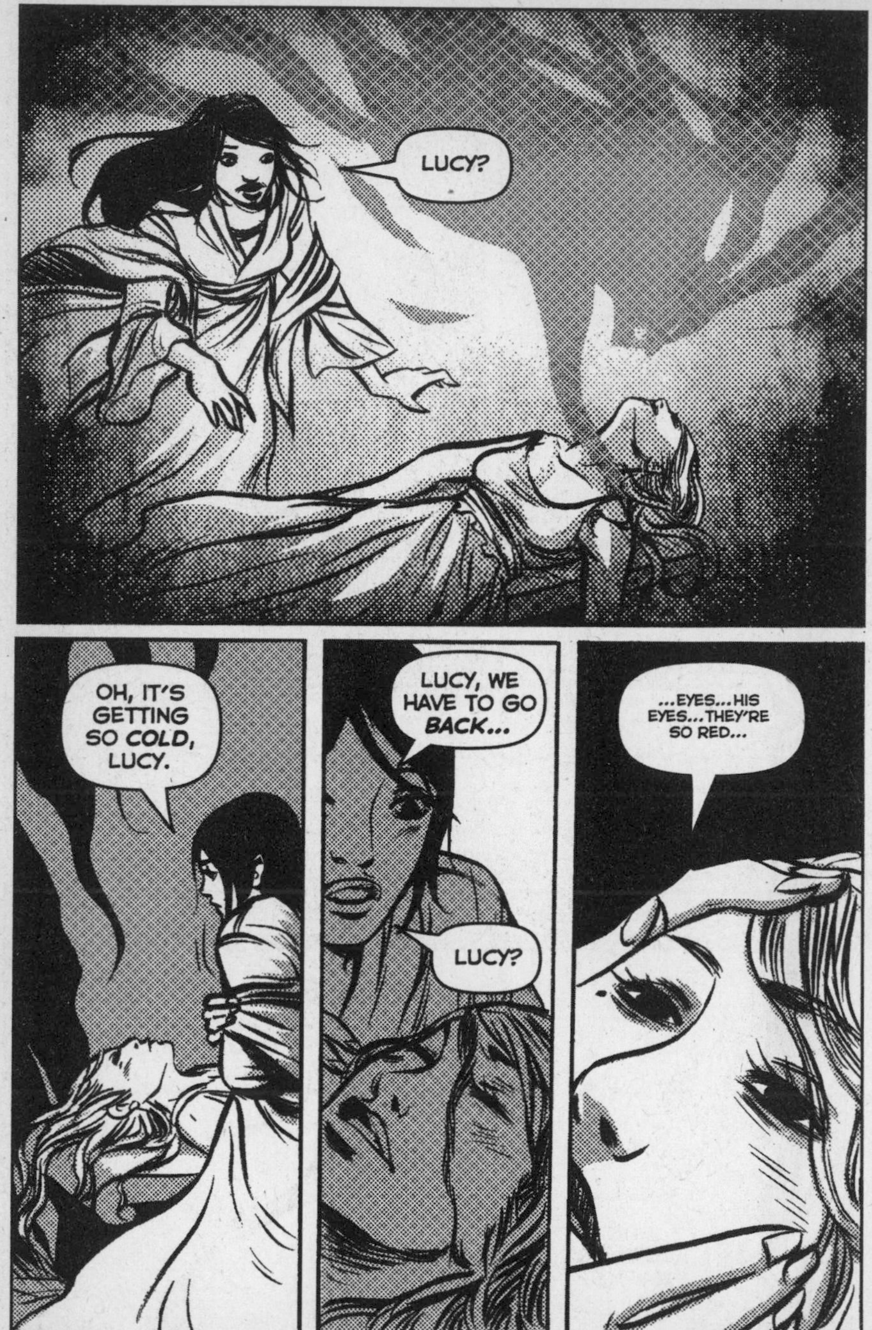
LUCY?
OH, IT'S GETTING SO COLD, LUCY.
LUCY, WE HAVE TO GO BACK...
LUCY?
...EYES...HIS EYES...THEY'RE SO RED...

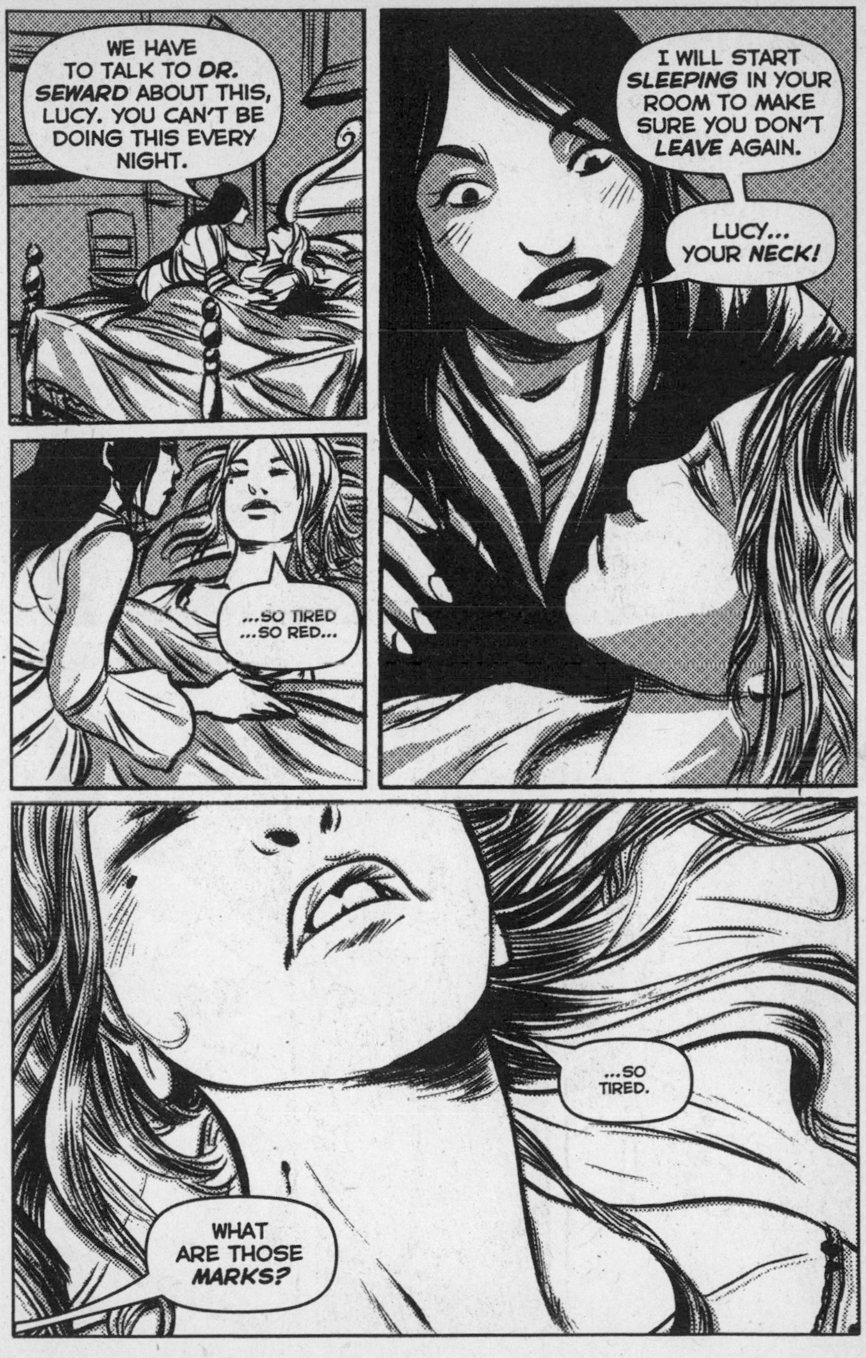
WE HAVE TO TALK TO DR. SEWARD ABOUT THIS, LUCY. YOU CAN'T BE DOING THIS EVERY NIGHT.
I WILL START SLEEPING IN YOUR ROOM TO MAKE SURE YOU DON'T LEAVE AGAIN.
LUCY... YOUR NECK!
...SO TIRED ...SO RED...
...SO TIRED.
WHAT ARE THOSE MARKS?

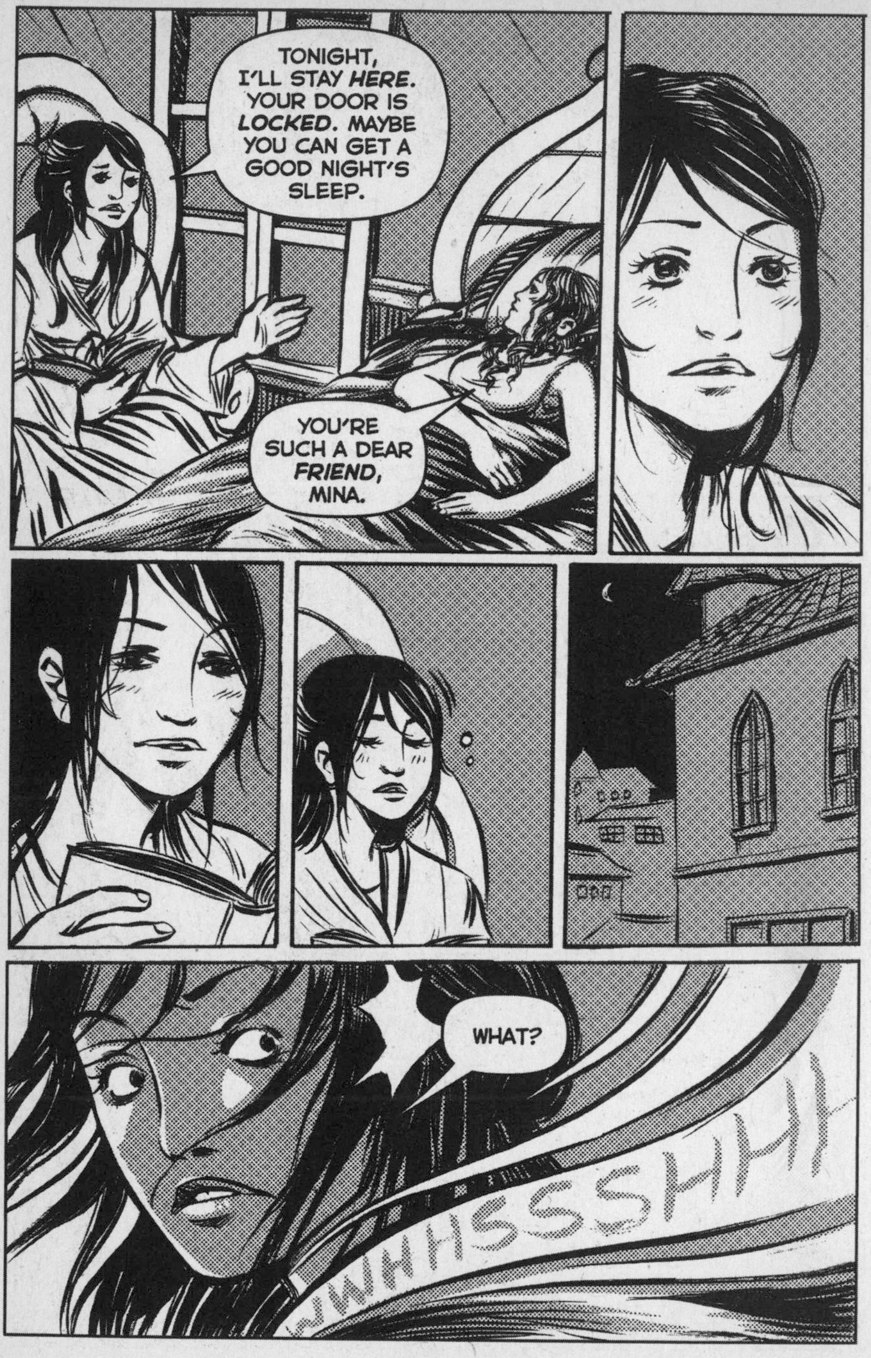
TONIGHT, I'LL STAY *HERE*. YOUR DOOR IS *LOCKED*. MAYBE YOU CAN GET A GOOD NIGHT'S SLEEP.
YOU'RE SUCH A DEAR *FRIEND*, MINA.
WHAT?
WWHHSSSSHH

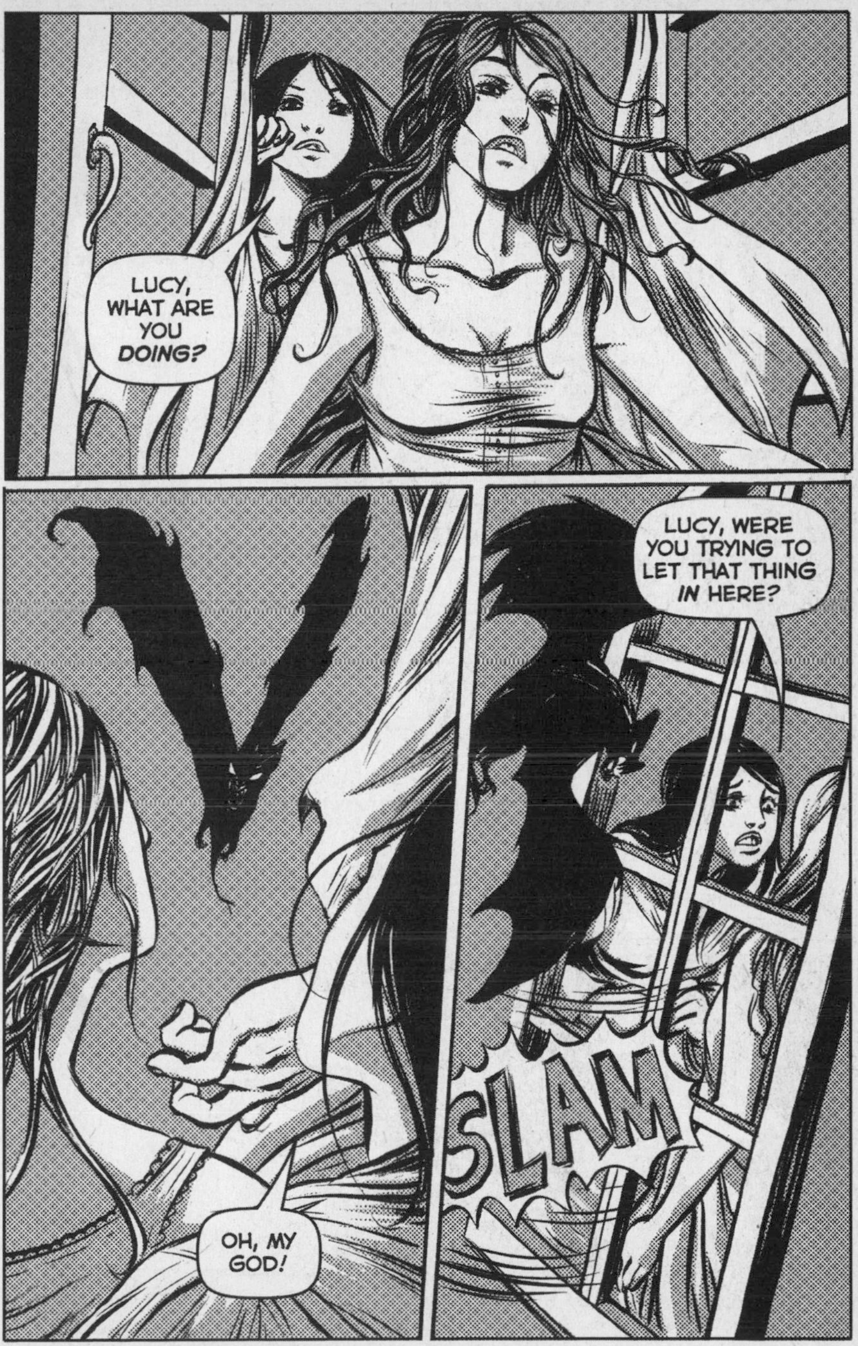
LUCY, WHAT ARE YOU *DOING?*
OH, MY GOD!
LUCY, WERE YOU TRYING TO LET THAT THING *IN* HERE?
SLAM

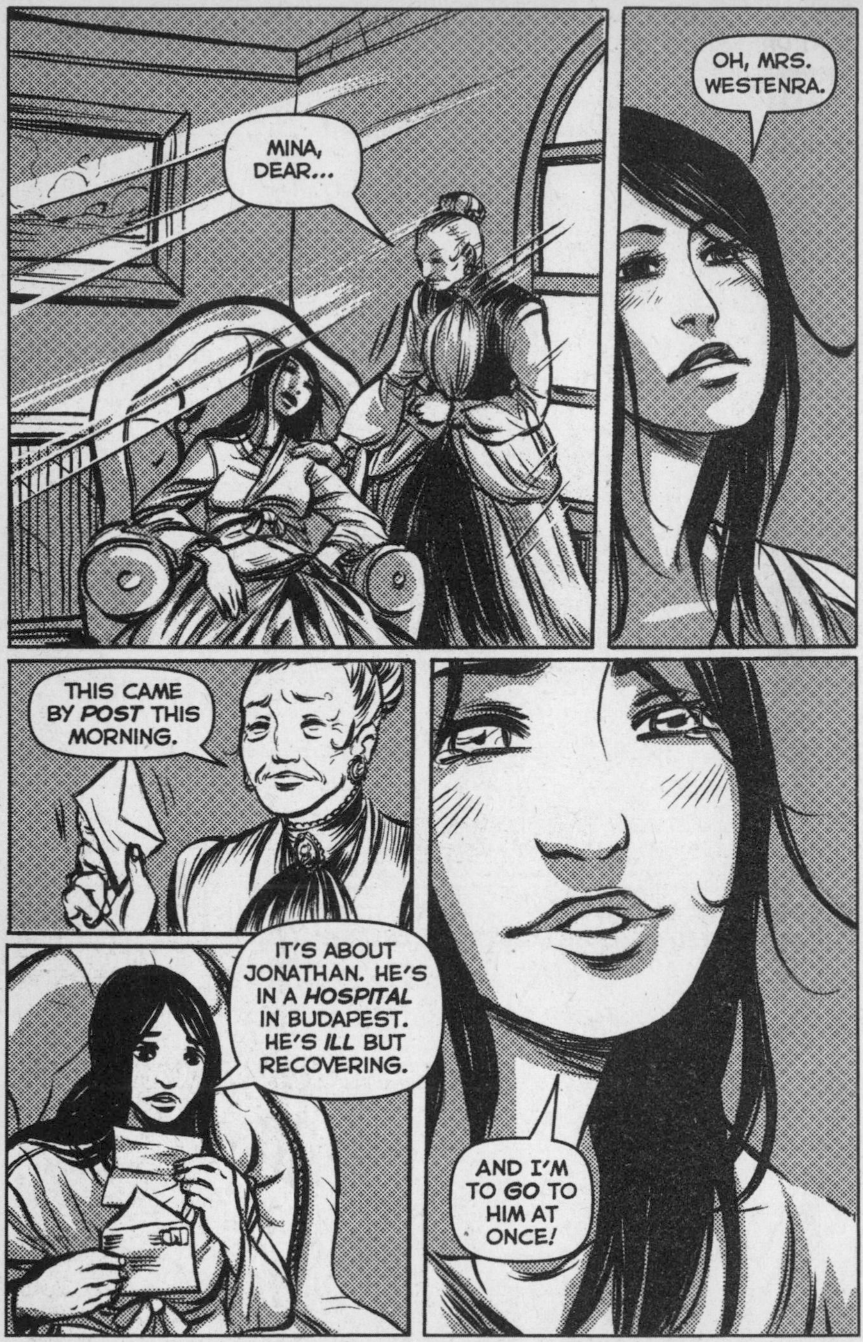
MINA, DEAR...
OH, MRS. WESTENRA.
THIS CAME BY POST THIS MORNING.
IT'S ABOUT JONATHAN. HE'S IN A HOSPITAL IN BUDAPEST. HE'S ILL BUT RECOVERING.
AND I'M TO GO TO HIM AT ONCE!

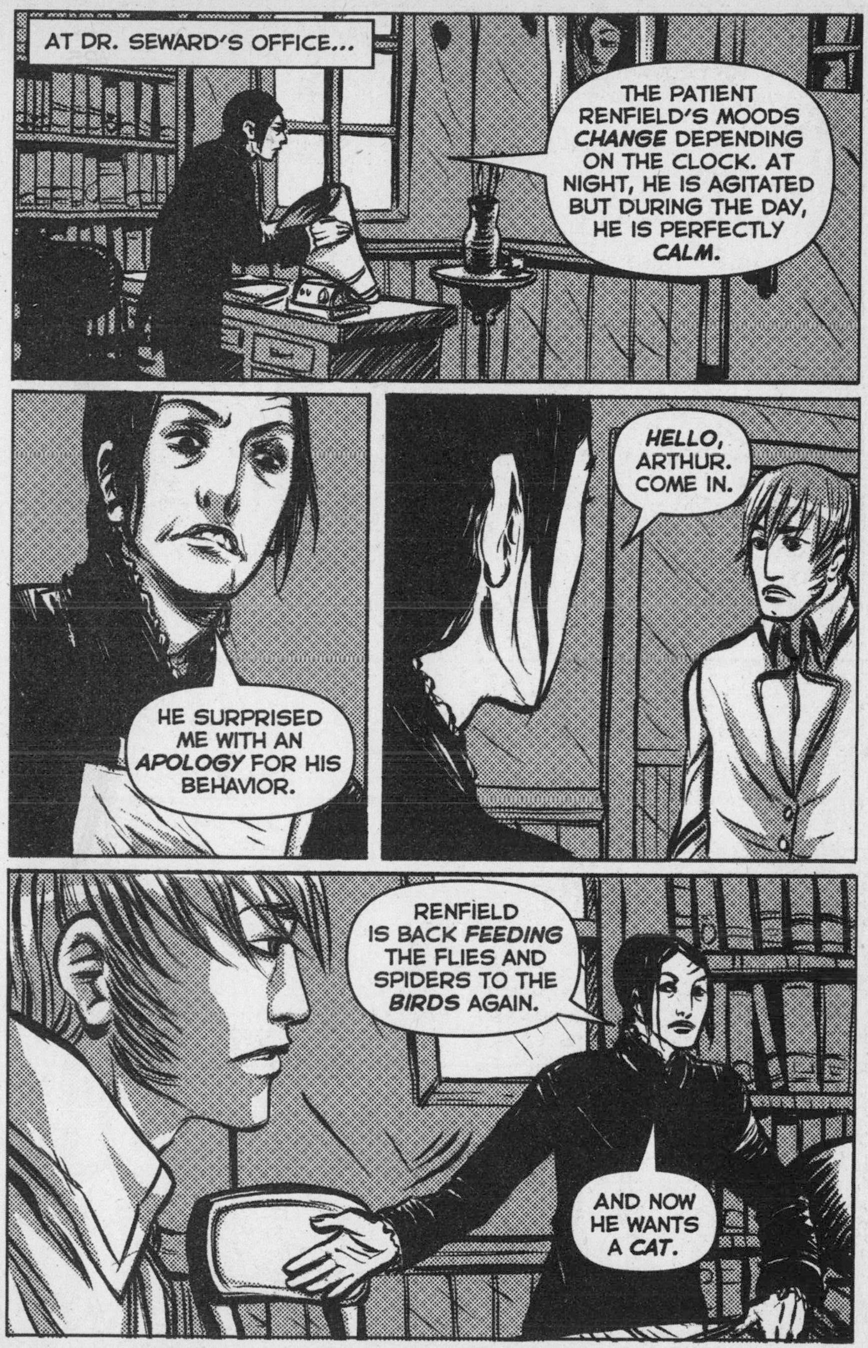
AT DR. SEWARD'S OFFICE...
THE PATIENT RENFIELD'S MOODS CHANGE DEPENDING ON THE CLOCK. AT NIGHT, HE IS AGITATED BUT DURING THE DAY, HE IS PERFECTLY CALM.
HE SURPRISED ME WITH AN APOLOGY FOR HIS BEHAVIOR.
HELLO, ARTHUR. COME IN.
RENFIELD IS BACK FEEDING THE FLIES AND SPIDERS TO THE BIRDS AGAIN.
AND NOW HE WANTS A CAT.

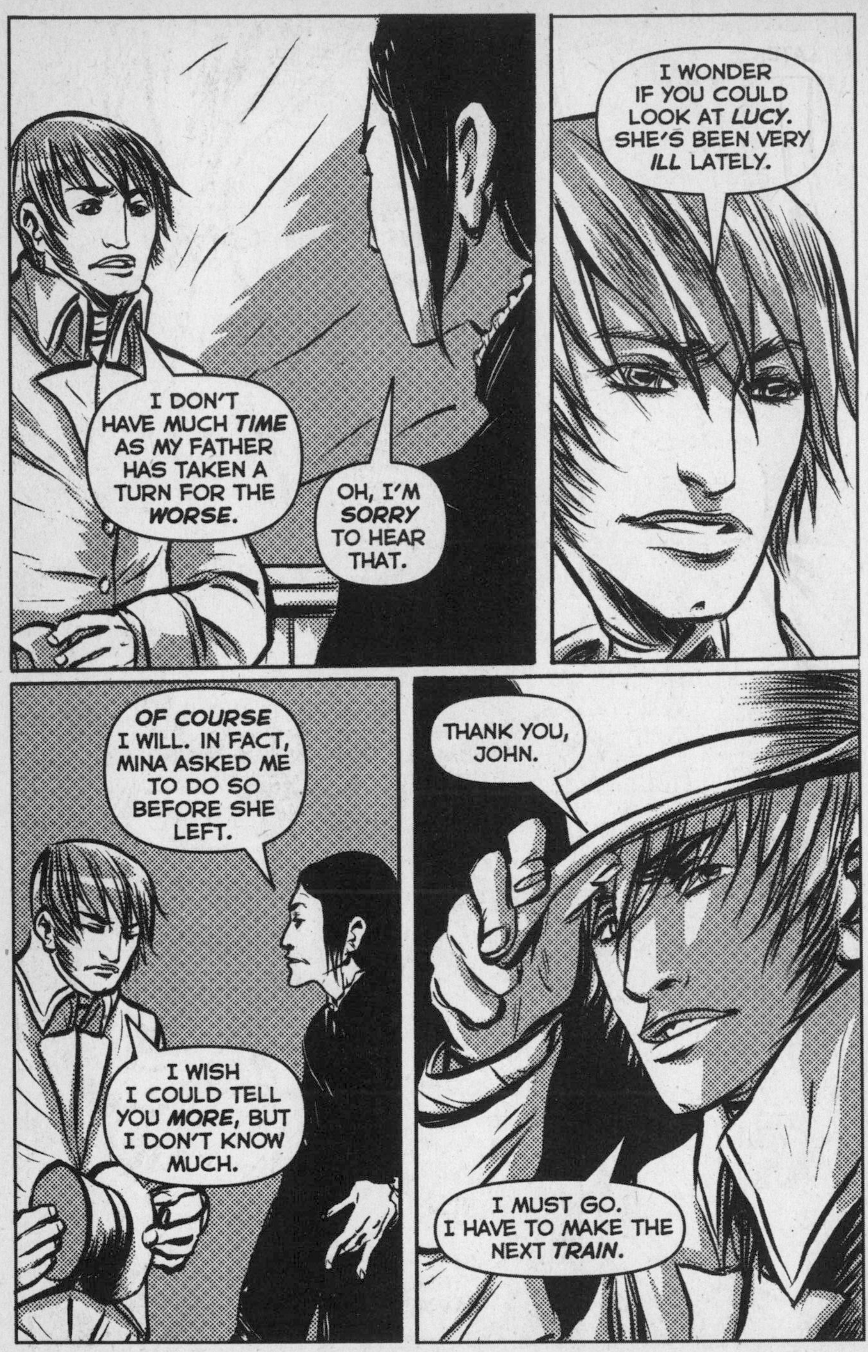
I DON'T HAVE MUCH TIME AS MY FATHER HAS TAKEN A TURN FOR THE WORSE.
OH, I'M SORRY TO HEAR THAT.
I WONDER IF YOU COULD LOOK AT LUCY. SHE'S BEEN VERY ILL LATELY.
OF COURSE I WILL. IN FACT, MINA ASKED ME TO DO SO BEFORE SHE LEFT.
I WISH I COULD TELL YOU MORE, BUT I DON'T KNOW MUCH.
THANK YOU, JOHN.
I MUST GO. I HAVE TO MAKE THE NEXT TRAIN.

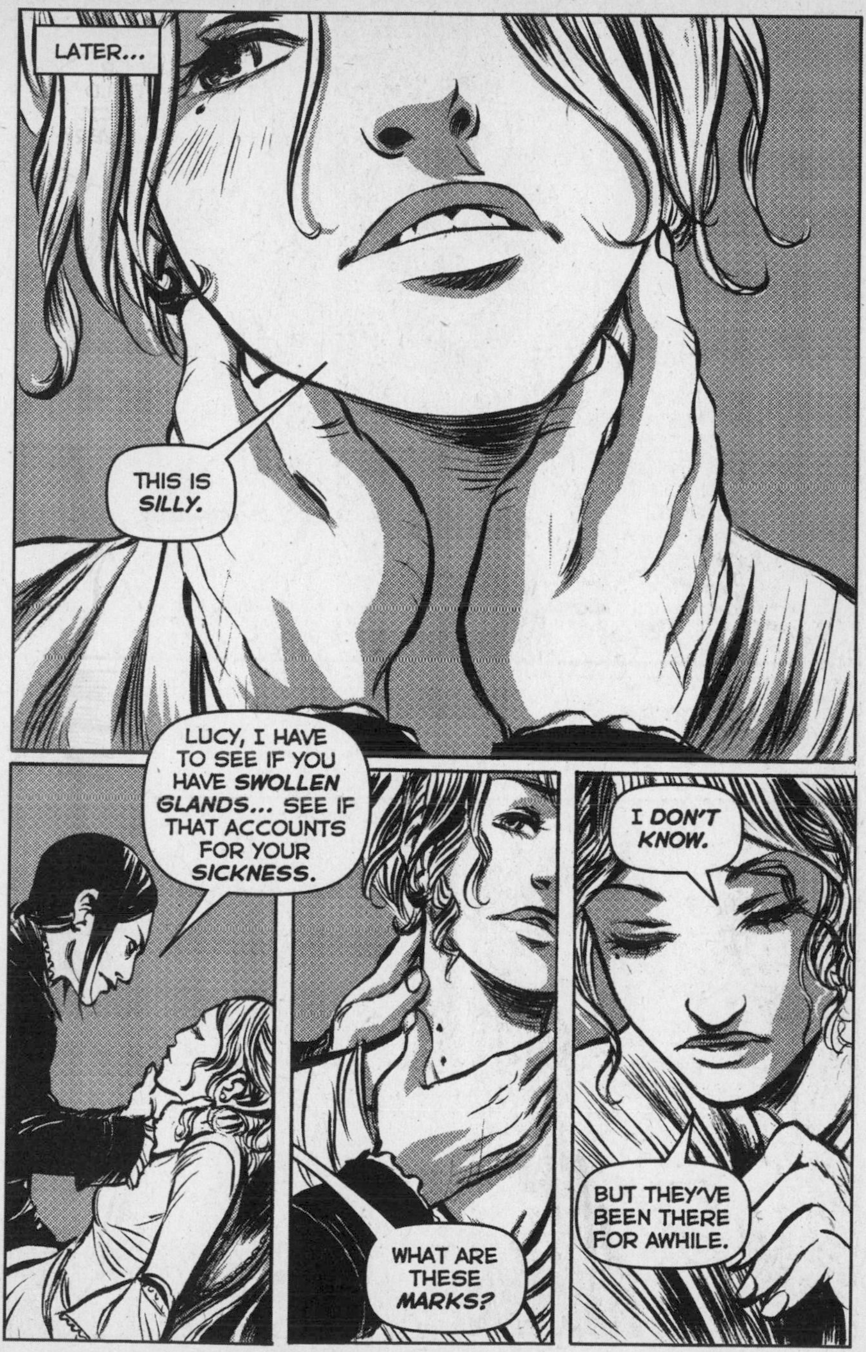
LATER...
THIS IS SILLY.
LUCY, I HAVE TO SEE IF YOU HAVE SWOLLEN GLANDS... SEE IF THAT ACCOUNTS FOR YOUR SICKNESS.
WHAT ARE THESE MARKS?
I DON'T KNOW.
BUT THEY'VE BEEN THERE FOR AWHILE.

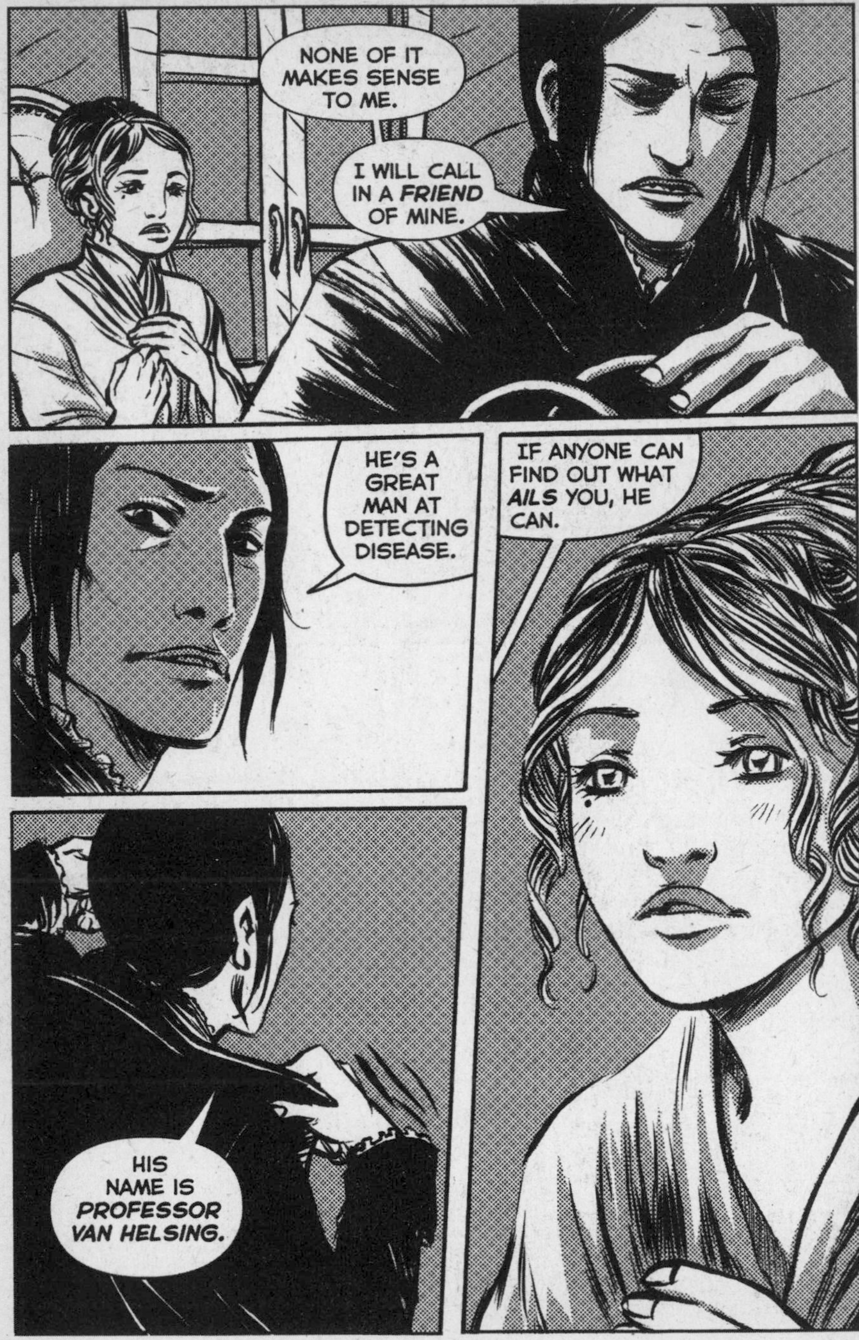
NONE OF IT MAKES SENSE TO ME.
I WILL CALL IN A *FRIEND* OF MINE.
HE'S A GREAT MAN AT DETECTING DISEASE.
IF ANYONE CAN FIND OUT WHAT *AILS* YOU, HE CAN.
HIS NAME IS *PROFESSOR VAN HELSING.*

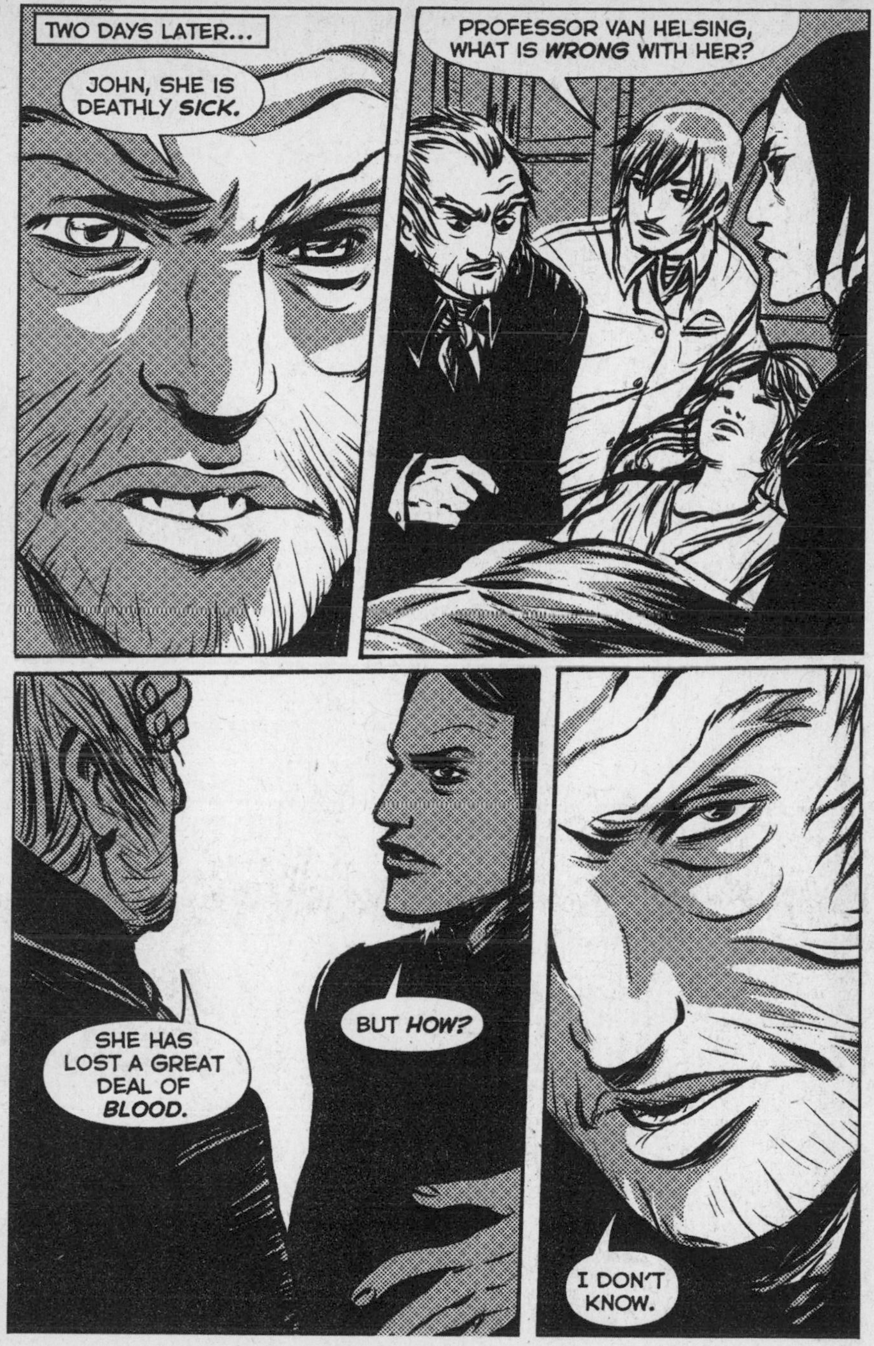
TWO DAYS LATER...
JOHN, SHE IS DEATHLY SICK.
PROFESSOR VAN HELSING, WHAT IS WRONG WITH HER?
SHE HAS LOST A GREAT DEAL OF BLOOD.
BUT HOW?
I DON'T KNOW.

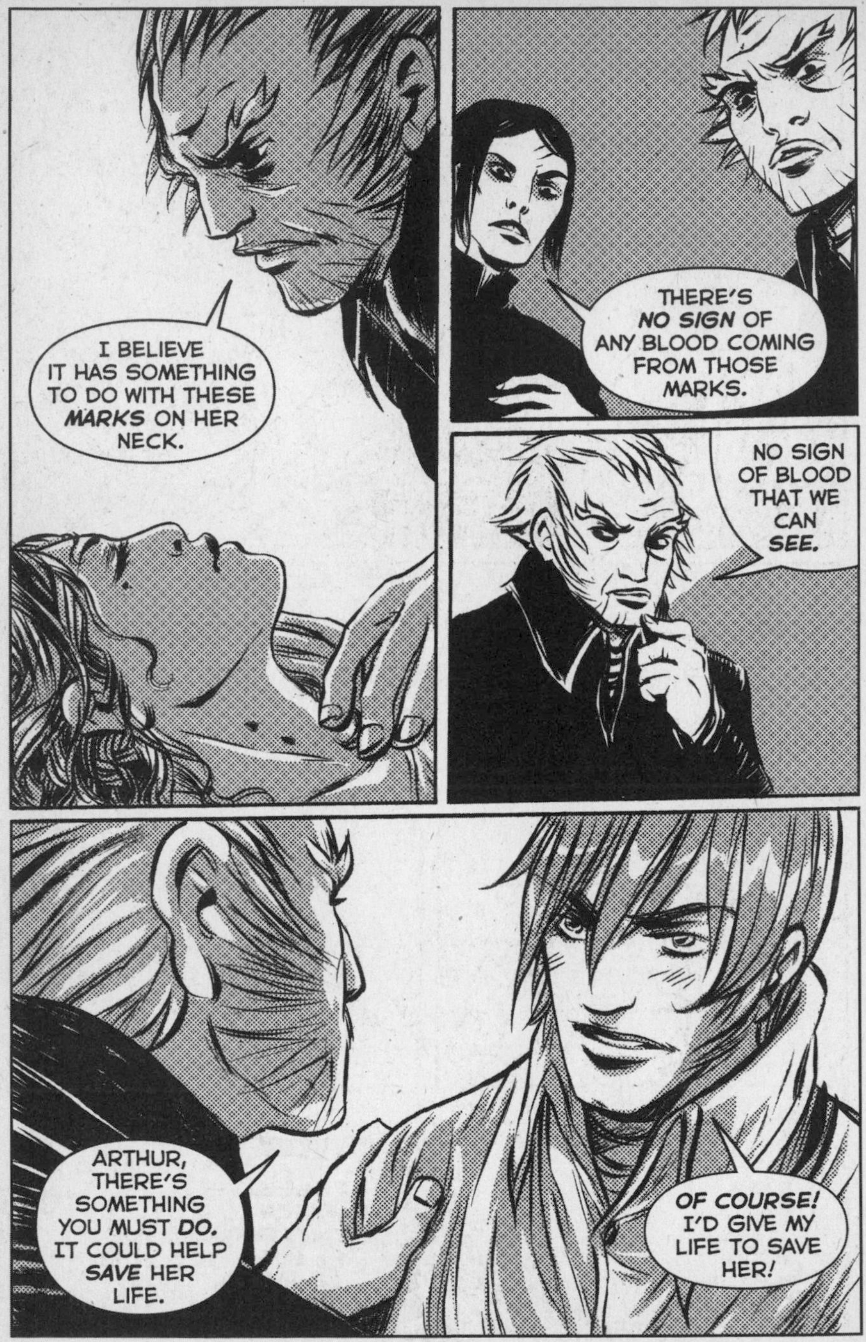
I BELIEVE IT HAS SOMETHING TO DO WITH THESE MARKS ON HER NECK.
THERE'S NO SIGN OF ANY BLOOD COMING FROM THOSE MARKS.
NO SIGN OF BLOOD THAT WE CAN SEE.
ARTHUR, THERE'S SOMETHING YOU MUST DO. IT COULD HELP SAVE HER LIFE.
OF COURSE! I'D GIVE MY LIFE TO SAVE HER!

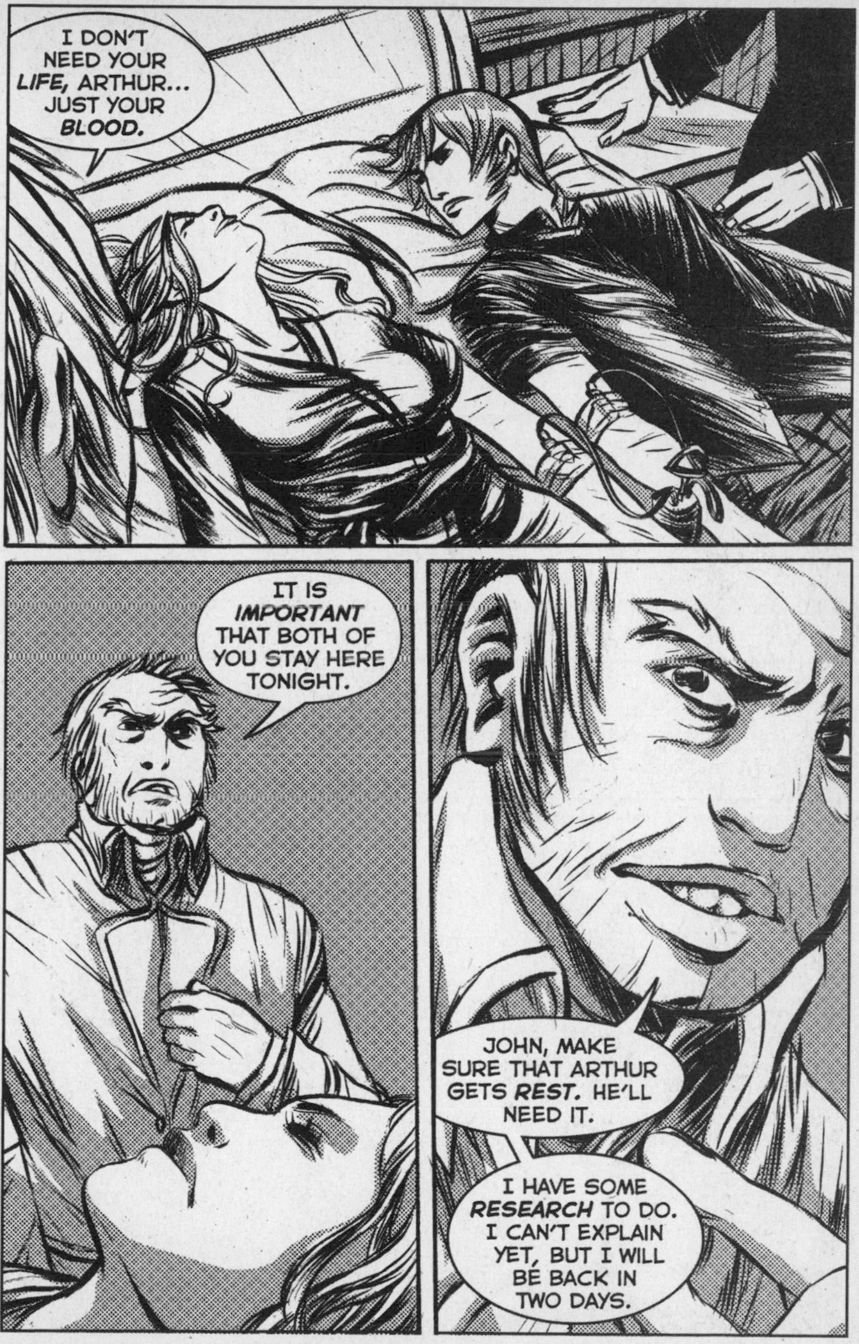
I DON'T NEED YOUR LIFE, ARTHUR... JUST YOUR BLOOD.
IT IS IMPORTANT THAT BOTH OF YOU STAY HERE TONIGHT.
JOHN, MAKE SURE THAT ARTHUR GETS REST. HE'LL NEED IT.
I HAVE SOME RESEARCH TO DO. I CAN'T EXPLAIN YET, BUT I WILL BE BACK IN TWO DAYS.

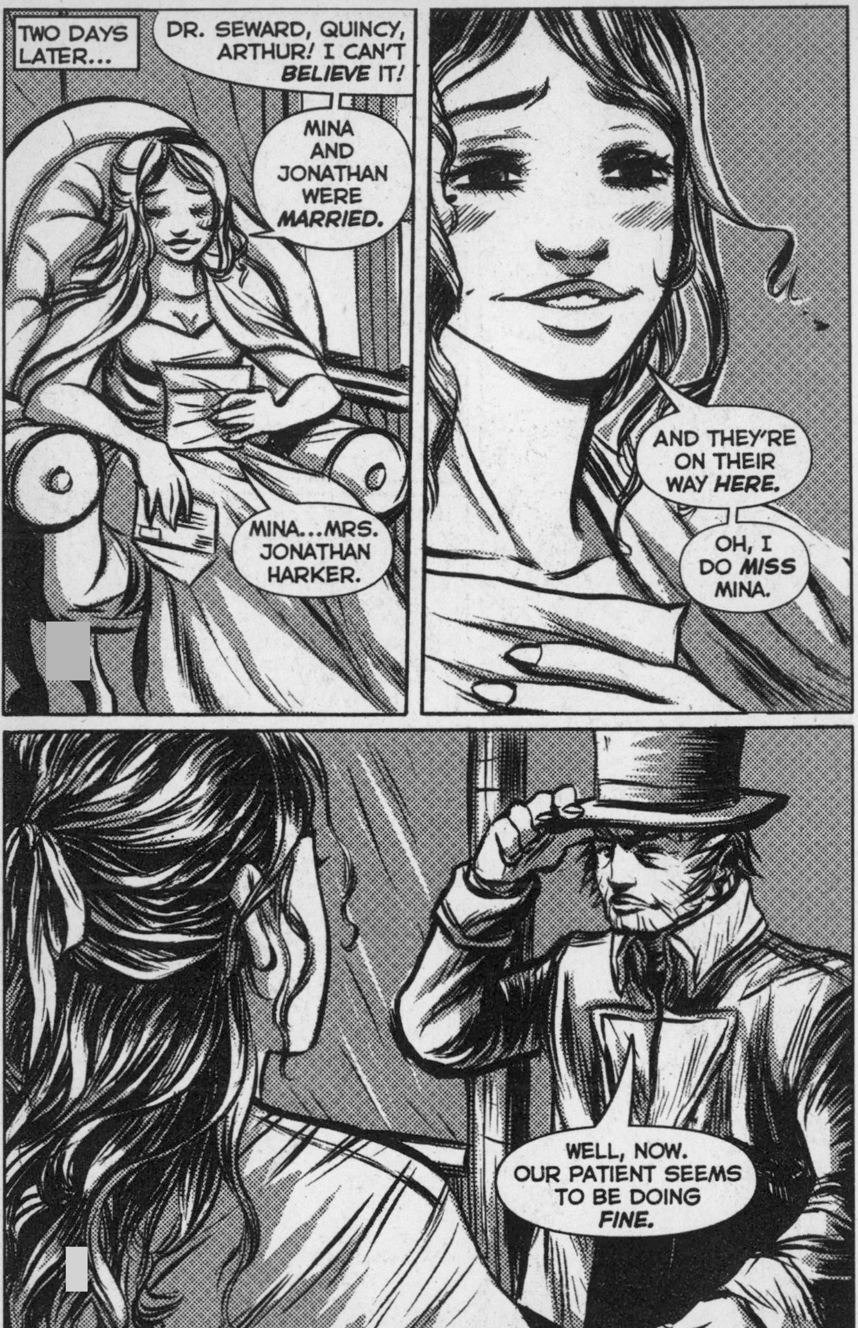
TWO DAYS LATER...
DR. SEWARD, QUINCY, ARTHUR! I CAN'T BELIEVE IT!
MINA AND JONATHAN WERE MARRIED.
MINA...MRS. JONATHAN HARKER.
AND THEY'RE ON THEIR WAY HERE.
OH, I DO MISS MINA.
WELL, NOW. OUR PATIENT SEEMS TO BE DOING FINE.

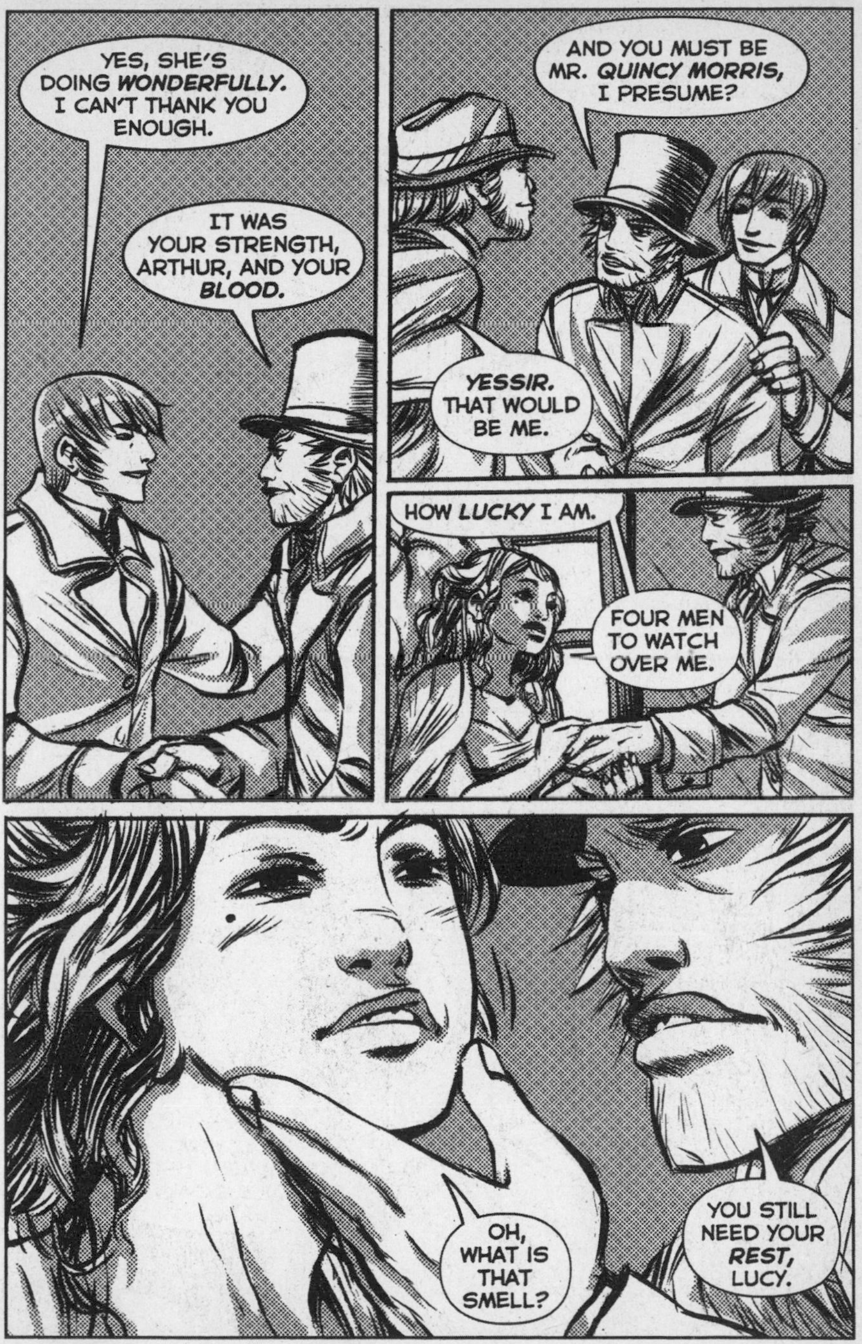
YES, SHE'S DOING WONDERFULLY. I CAN'T THANK YOU ENOUGH.
IT WAS YOUR STRENGTH, ARTHUR, AND YOUR BLOOD.
AND YOU MUST BE MR. QUINCY MORRIS, I PRESUME?
YESSIR. THAT WOULD BE ME.
HOW LUCKY I AM.
FOUR MEN TO WATCH OVER ME.
OH, WHAT IS THAT SMELL?
YOU STILL NEED YOUR REST, LUCY.

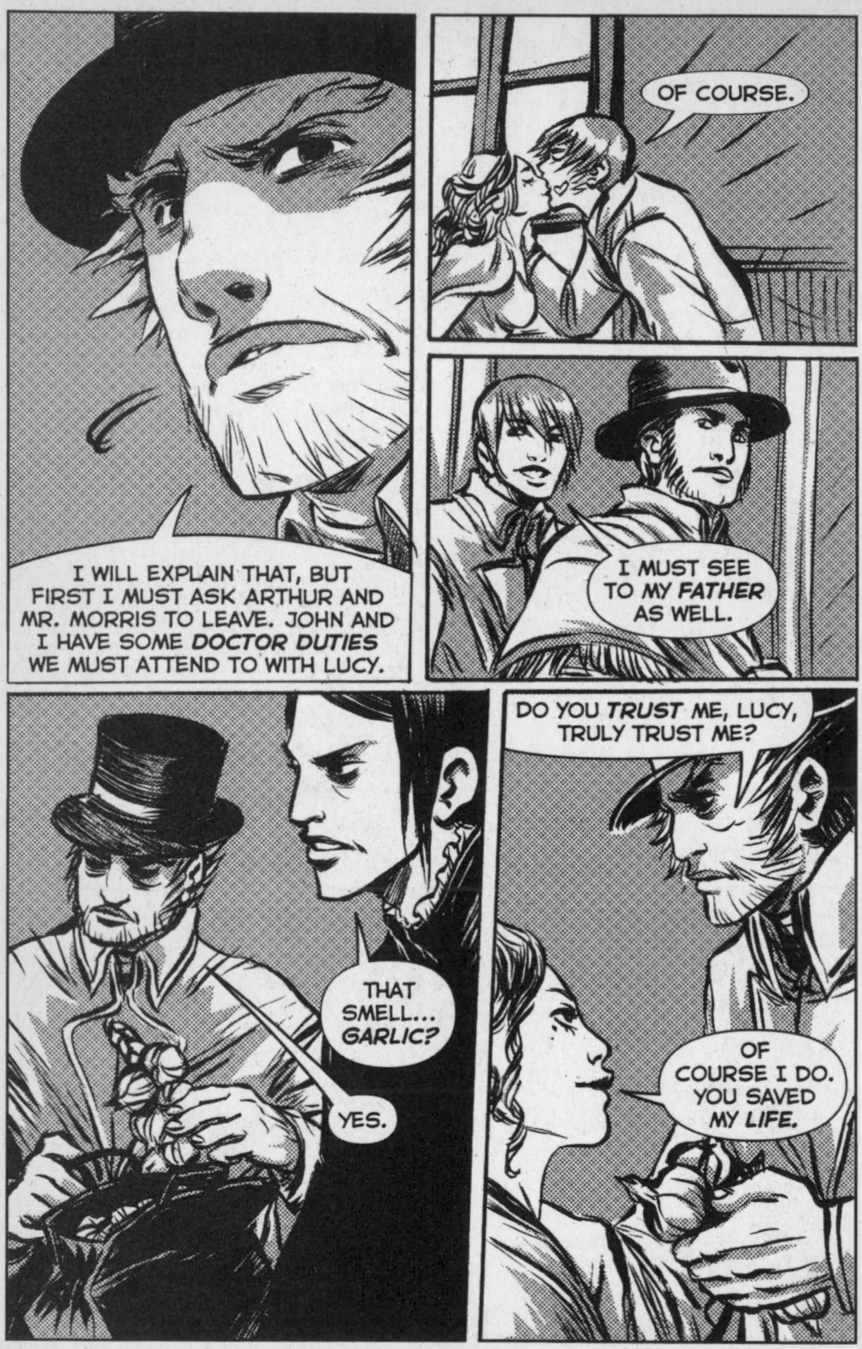
I WILL EXPLAIN THAT, BUT FIRST I MUST ASK ARTHUR AND MR. MORRIS TO LEAVE. JOHN AND I HAVE SOME *DOCTOR DUTIES* WE MUST ATTEND TO WITH LUCY.
OF COURSE.
I MUST SEE TO *MY FATHER* AS WELL.
THAT SMELL... *GARLIC?*
YES.
DO YOU *TRUST* ME, LUCY, TRULY TRUST ME?
OF COURSE I DO. YOU SAVED *MY LIFE.*

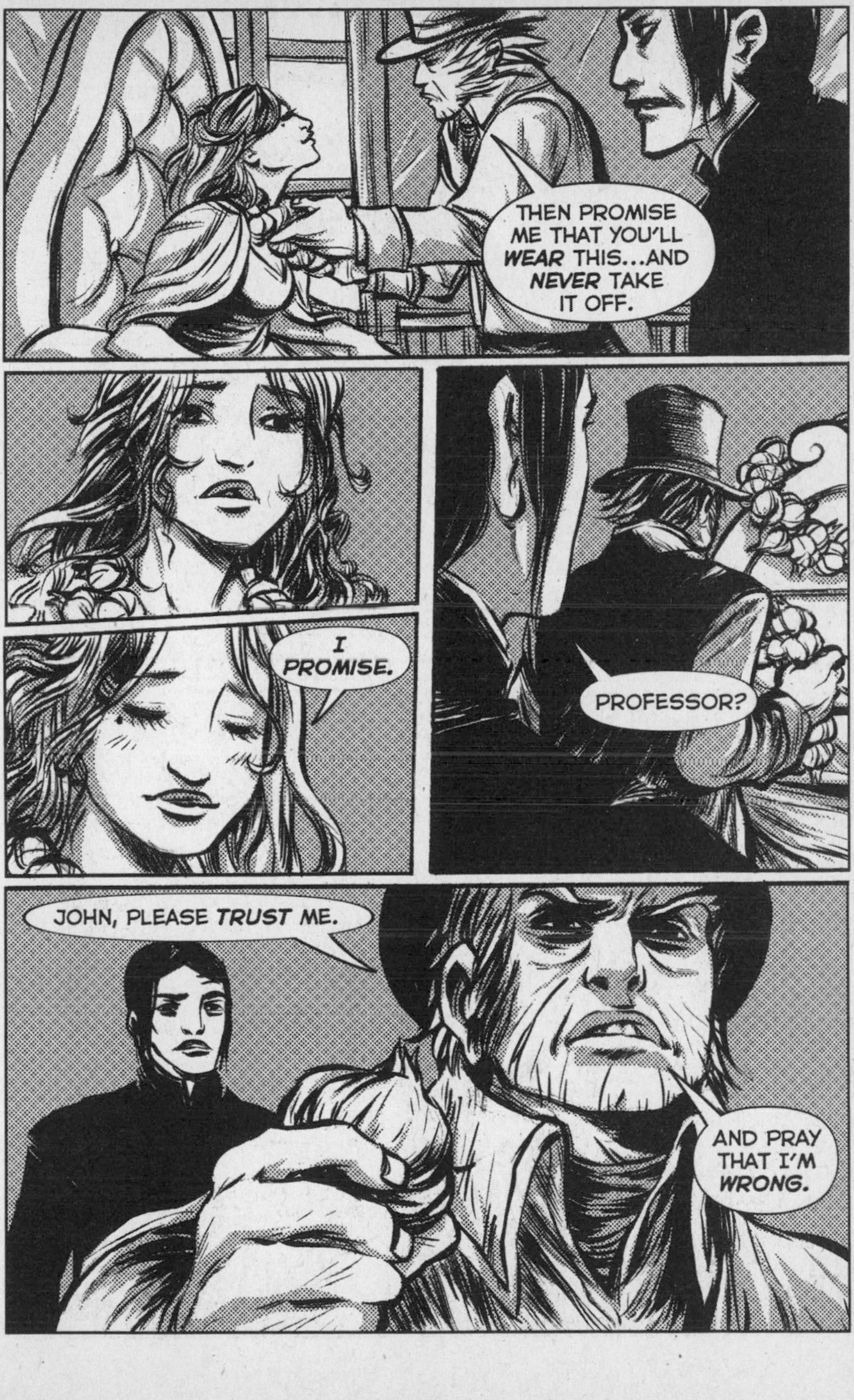
THEN PROMISE ME THAT YOU'LL WEAR THIS...AND NEVER TAKE IT OFF.
I PROMISE.
PROFESSOR?
JOHN, PLEASE TRUST ME.
AND PRAY THAT I'M WRONG.

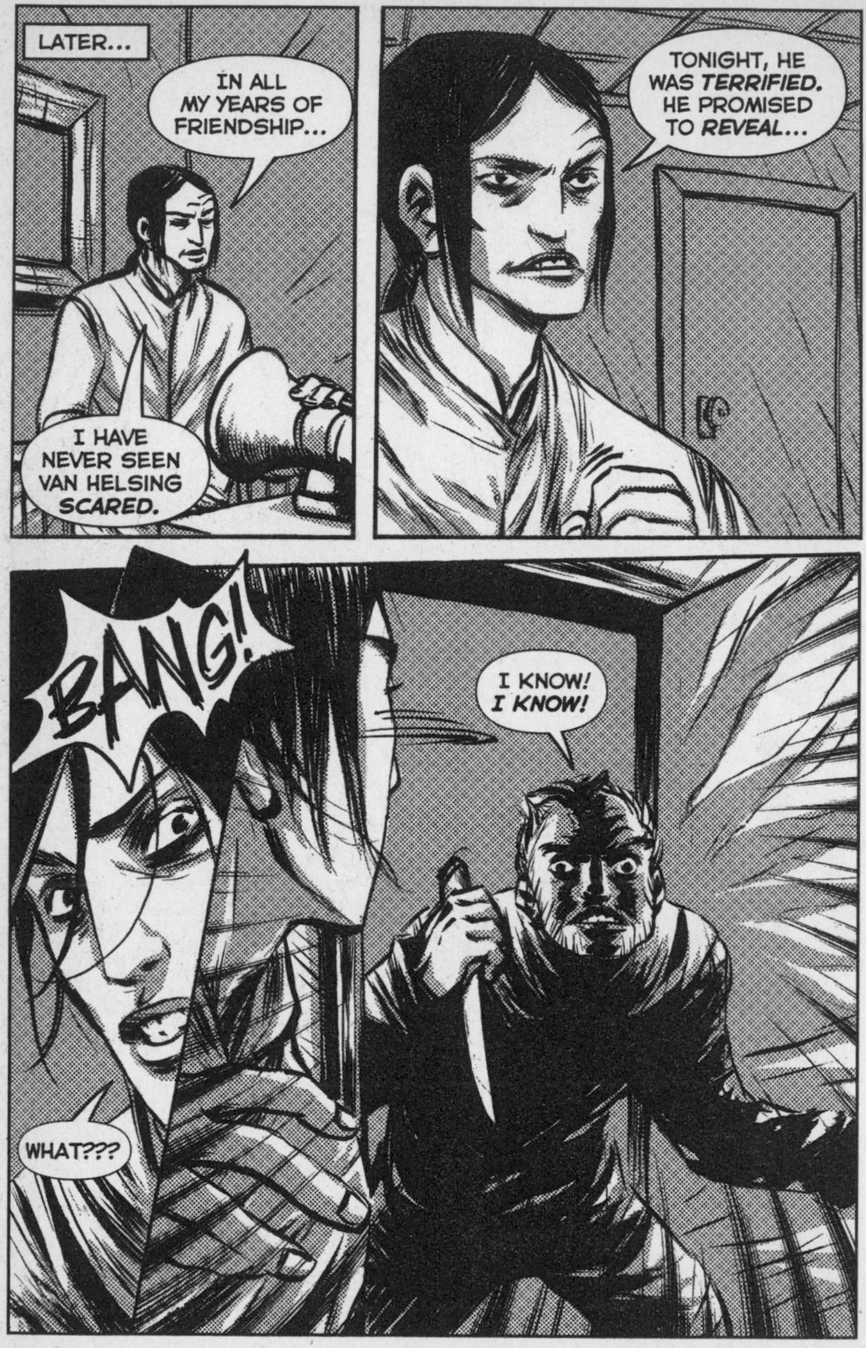
LATER...
IN ALL MY YEARS OF FRIENDSHIP...
I HAVE NEVER SEEN VAN HELSING SCARED.
TONIGHT, HE WAS TERRIFIED. HE PROMISED TO REVEAL...
BANG!!
I KNOW! I KNOW!
WHAT???

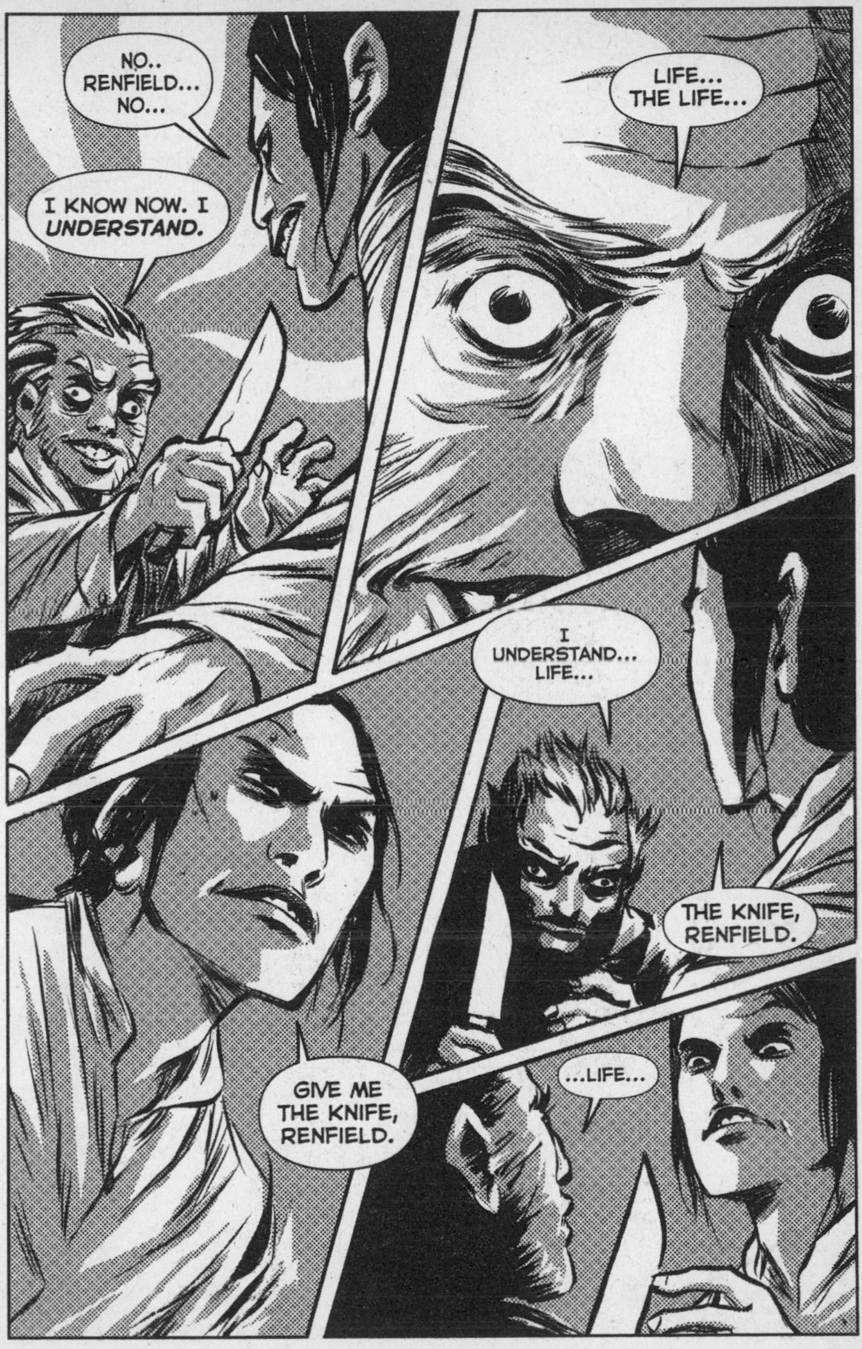
NO.. RENFIELD... NO...
I KNOW NOW. I *UNDERSTAND.*
LIFE... THE LIFE...
I UNDERSTAND... LIFE...
THE KNIFE, RENFIELD.
GIVE ME THE KNIFE, RENFIELD.
...LIFE...

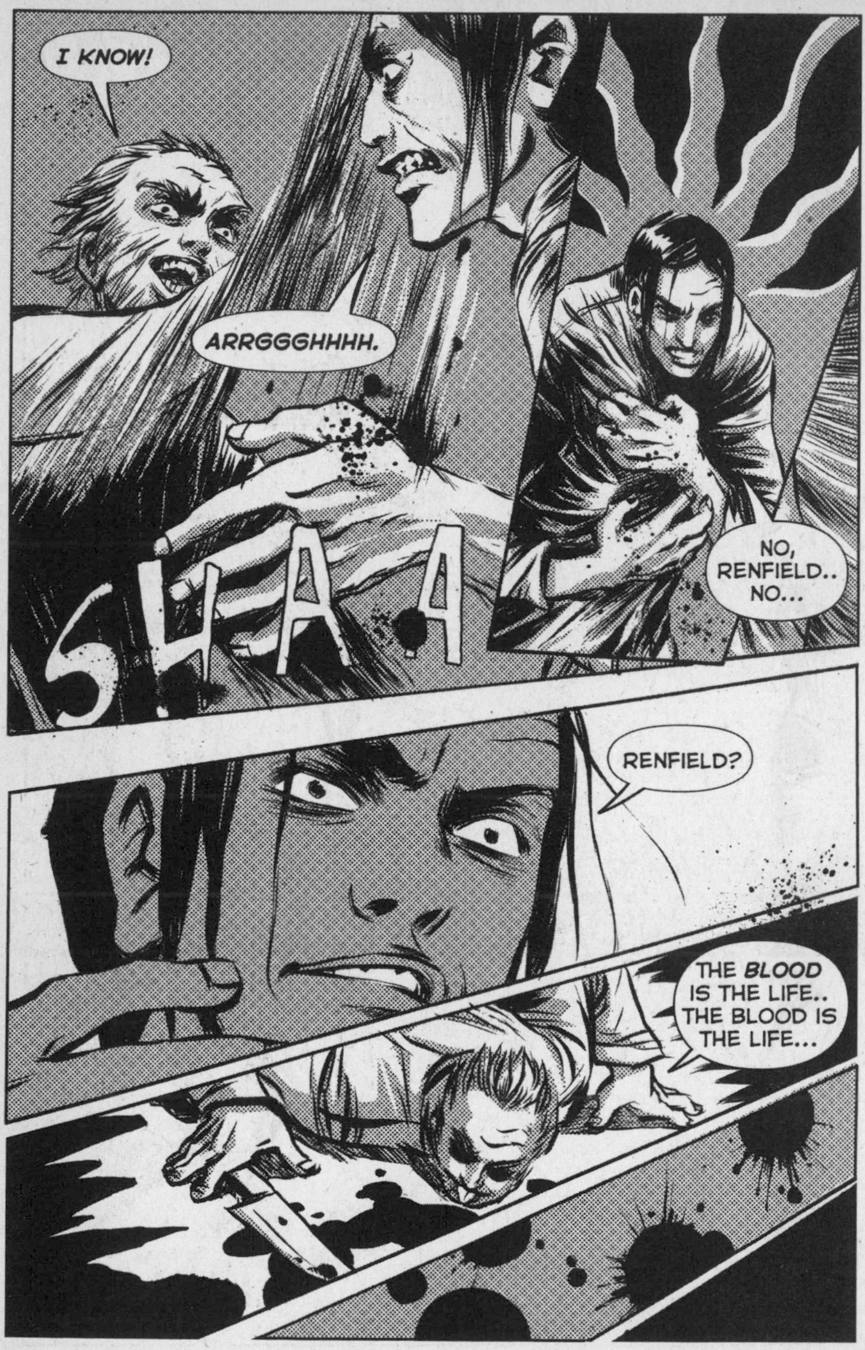
I KNOW!
ARRGGGHHHH.
SHAA
NO, RENFIELD.. NO...
RENFIELD?
THE BLOOD IS THE LIFE.. THE BLOOD IS THE LIFE...

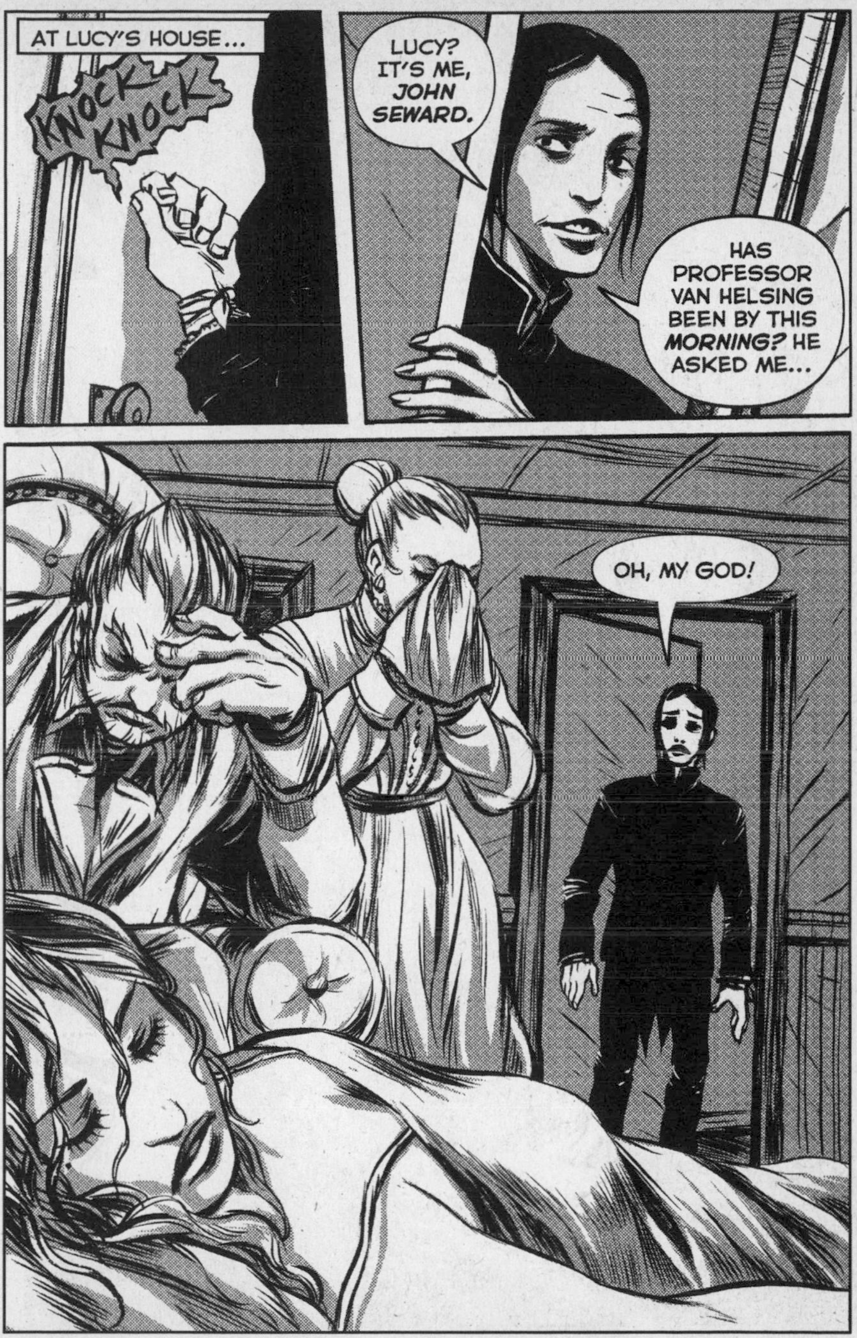
AT LUCY'S HOUSE...
KNOCK KNOCK
LUCY? IT'S ME, *JOHN SEWARD.*
HAS PROFESSOR VAN HELSING BEEN BY THIS *MORNING?* HE ASKED ME...
OH, MY GOD!

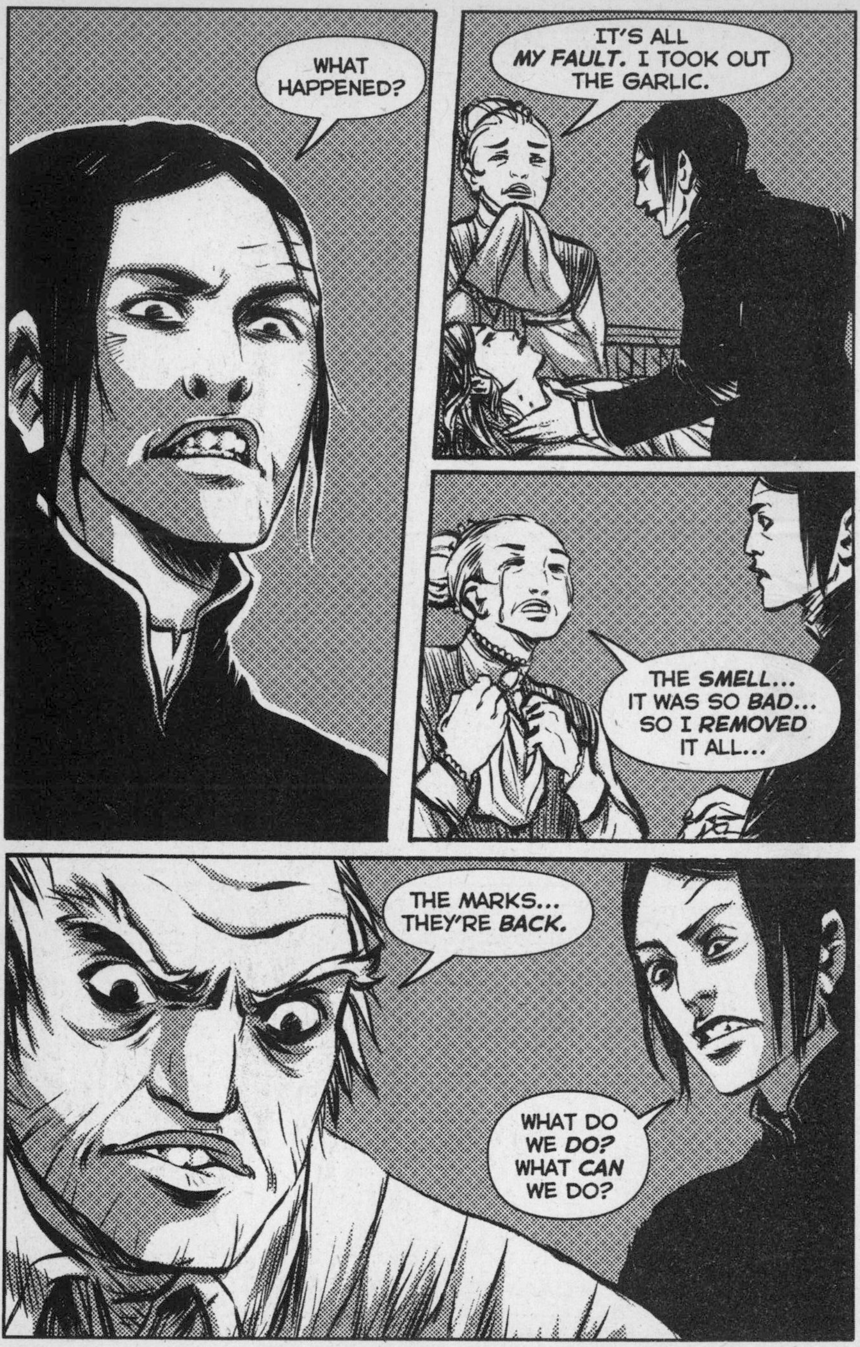
WHAT HAPPENED?
IT'S ALL *MY FAULT.* I TOOK OUT THE GARLIC.
THE *SMELL*... IT WAS SO *BAD*... SO I *REMOVED* IT ALL...
THE MARKS... THEY'RE *BACK.*
WHAT DO WE *DO?* WHAT *CAN* WE DO?

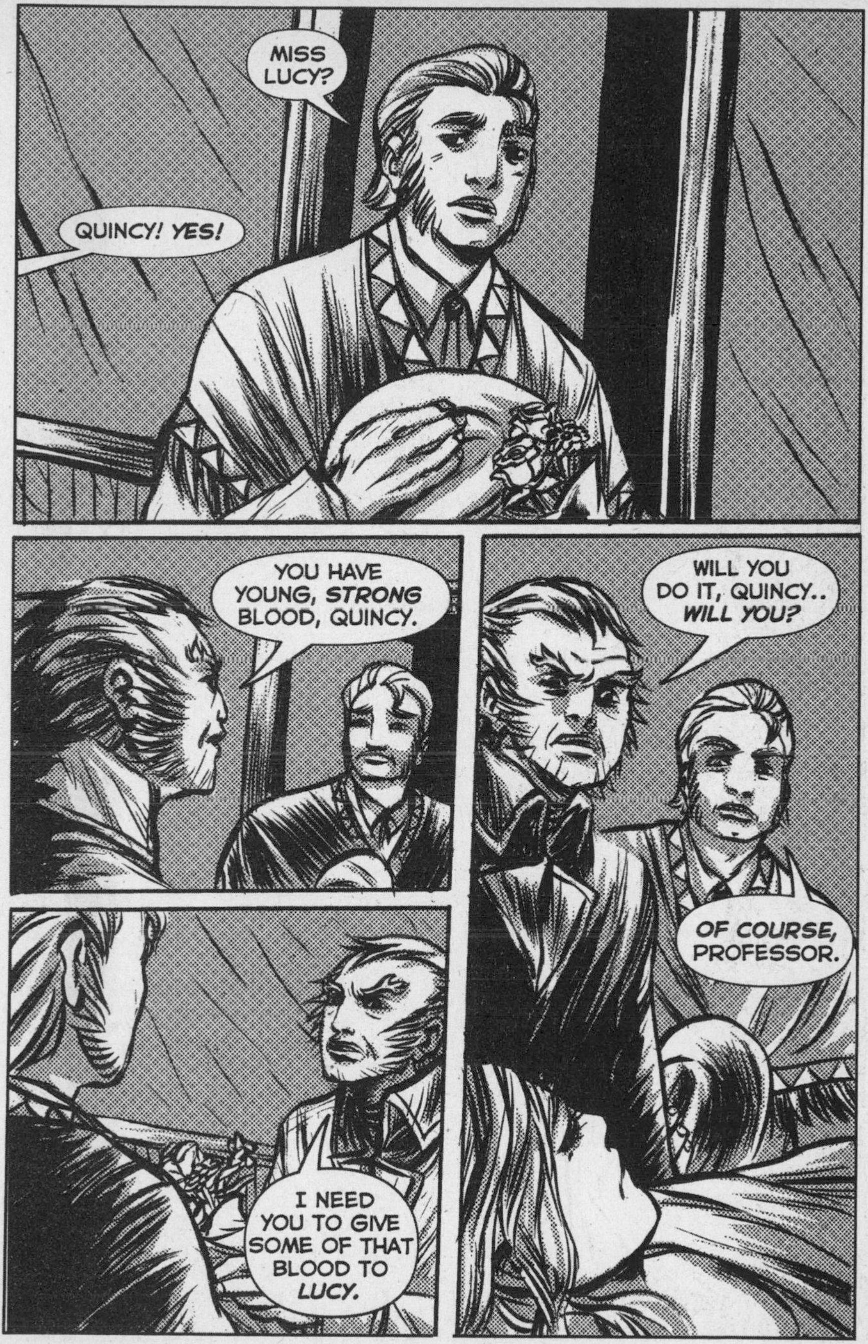
MISS LUCY?
QUINCY! YES!
YOU HAVE YOUNG, STRONG BLOOD, QUINCY.
I NEED YOU TO GIVE SOME OF THAT BLOOD TO LUCY.
WILL YOU DO IT, QUINCY.. WILL YOU?
OF COURSE, PROFESSOR.

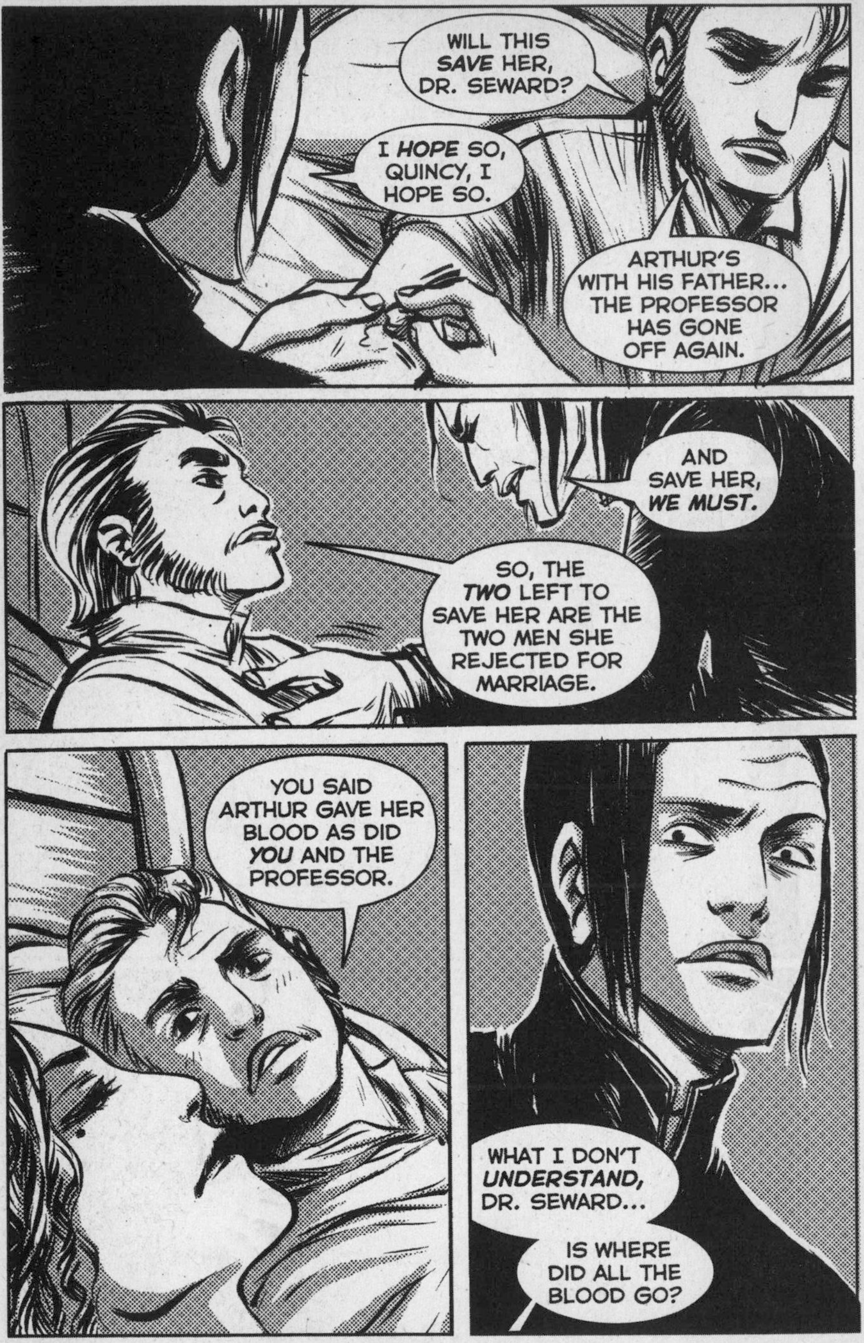
WILL THIS SAVE HER, DR. SEWARD?
I HOPE SO, QUINCY, I HOPE SO.
ARTHUR'S WITH HIS FATHER... THE PROFESSOR HAS GONE OFF AGAIN.
AND SAVE HER, WE MUST.
SO, THE TWO LEFT TO SAVE HER ARE THE TWO MEN SHE REJECTED FOR MARRIAGE.
YOU SAID ARTHUR GAVE HER BLOOD AS DID YOU AND THE PROFESSOR.
WHAT I DON'T UNDERSTAND, DR. SEWARD...
IS WHERE DID ALL THE BLOOD GO?

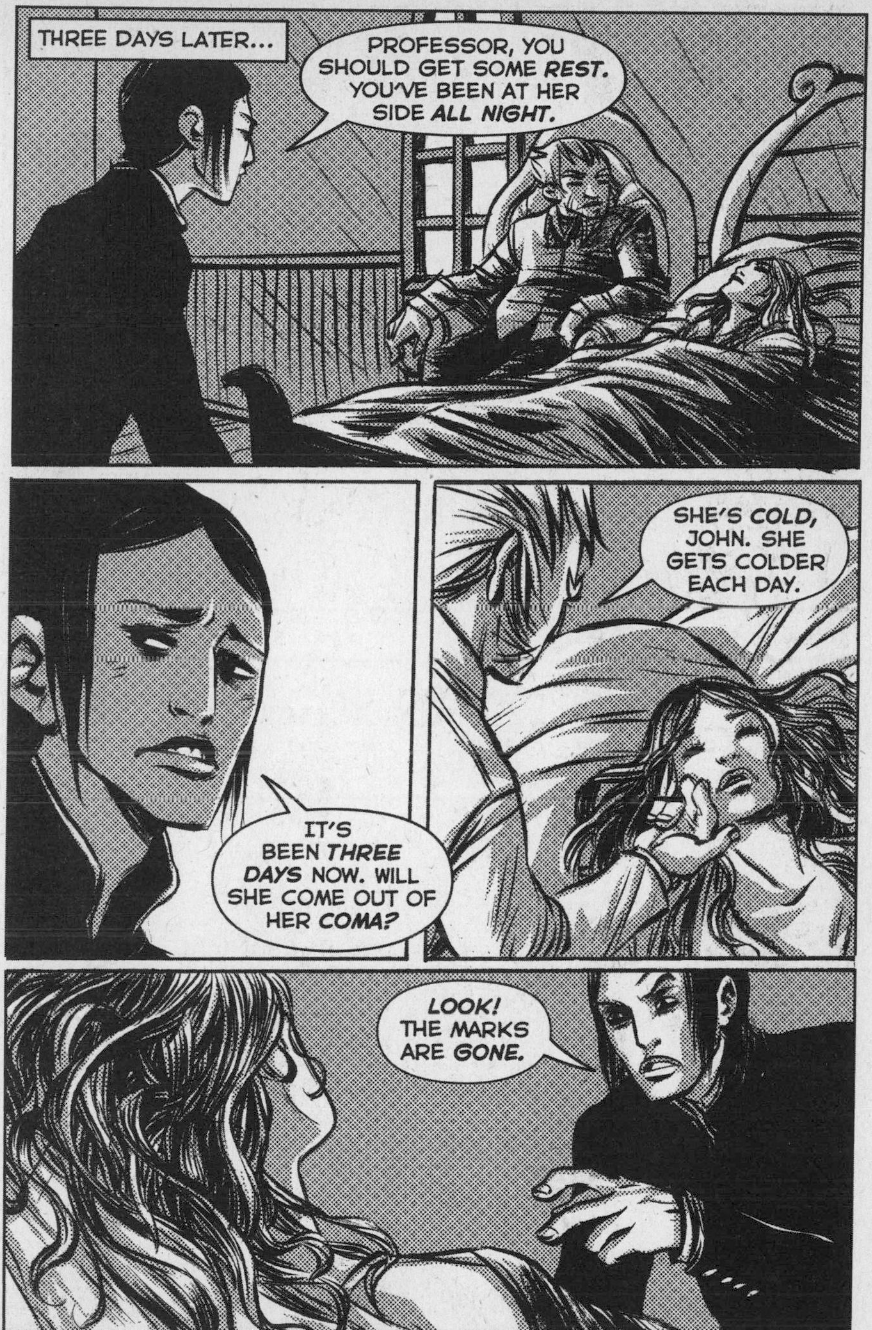

THREE DAYS LATER...
PROFESSOR, YOU SHOULD GET SOME REST. YOU'VE BEEN AT HER SIDE ALL NIGHT.
IT'S BEEN THREE DAYS NOW. WILL SHE COME OUT OF HER COMA?
SHE'S COLD, JOHN. SHE GETS COLDER EACH DAY.
LOOK! THE MARKS ARE GONE.

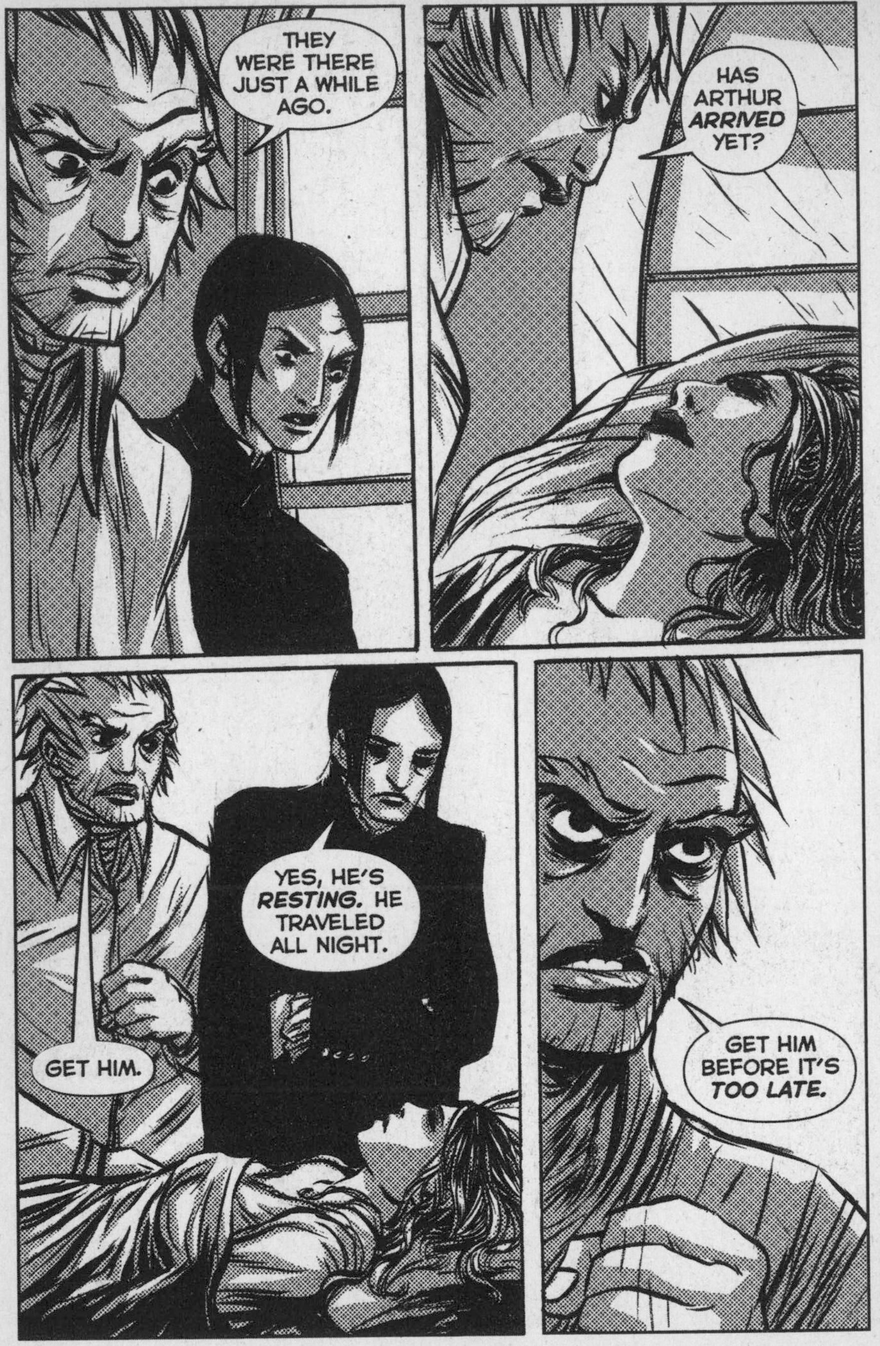
THEY WERE THERE JUST A WHILE AGO.
HAS ARTHUR ARRIVED YET?
YES, HE'S RESTING. HE TRAVELED ALL NIGHT.
GET HIM.
GET HIM BEFORE IT'S TOO LATE.

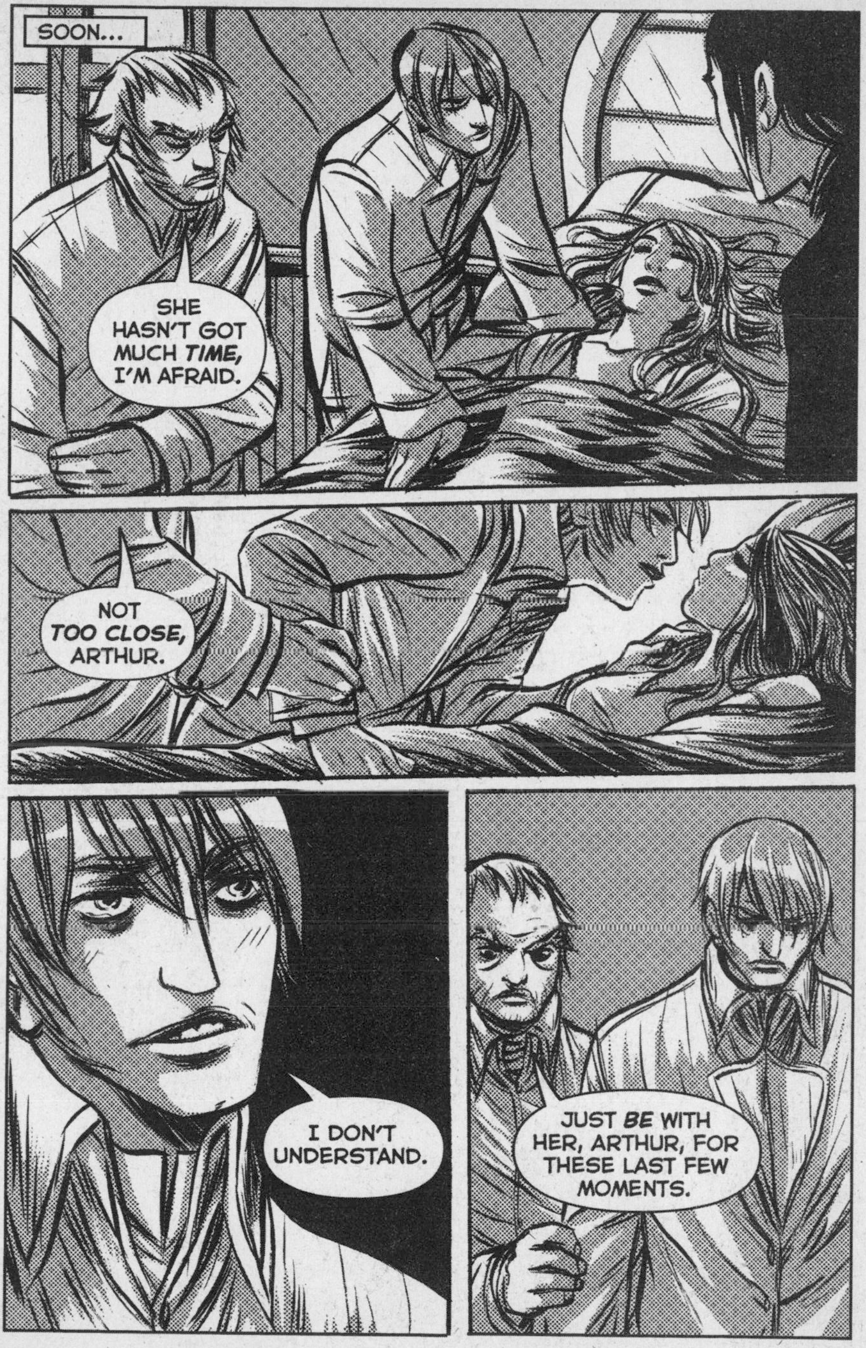
SOON...
SHE HASN'T GOT MUCH *TIME,* I'M AFRAID.
NOT *TOO CLOSE,* ARTHUR.
I DON'T UNDERSTAND.
JUST *BE* WITH HER, ARTHUR, FOR THESE LAST FEW MOMENTS.

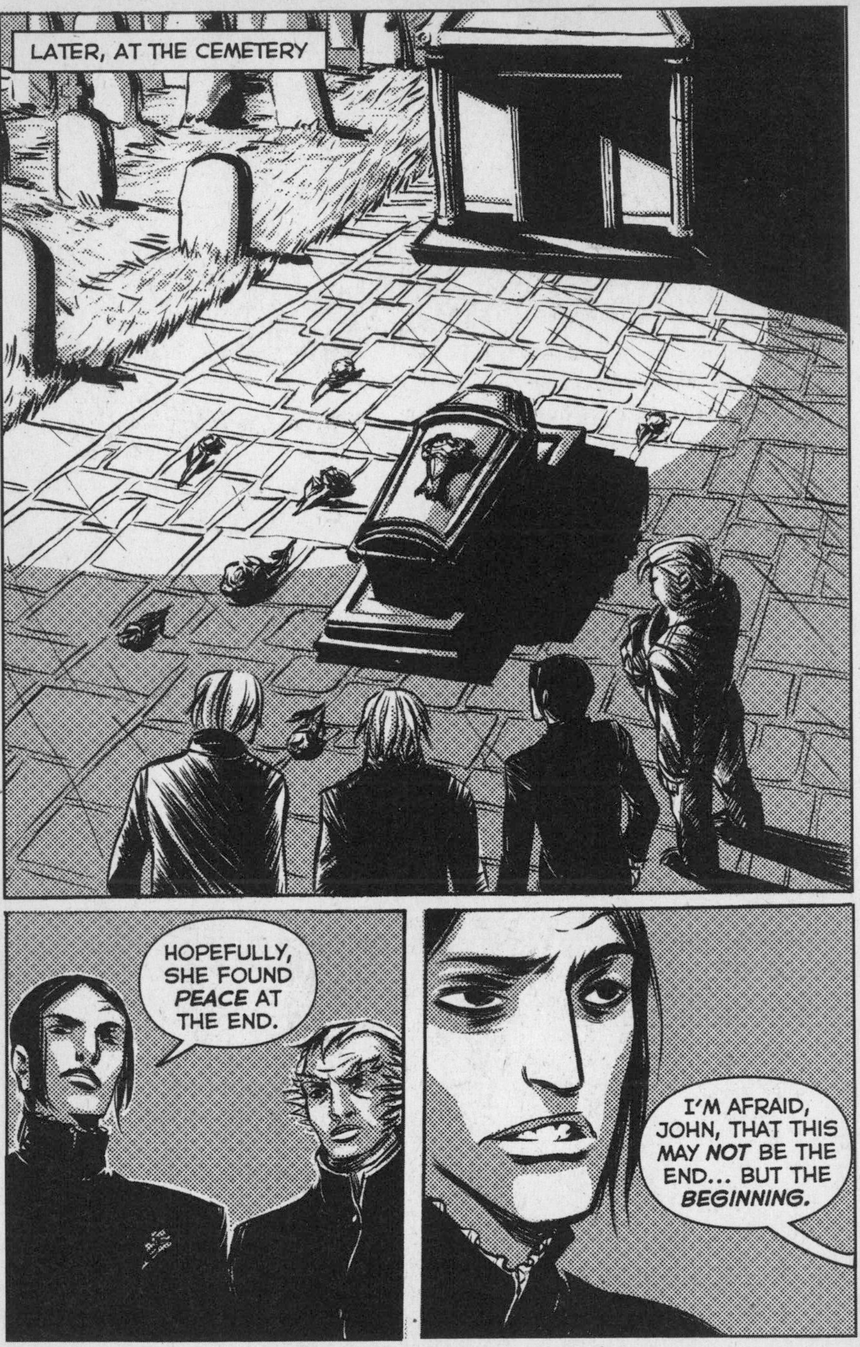
LATER, AT THE CEMETERY
HOPEFULLY, SHE FOUND *PEACE* AT THE END.
I'M AFRAID, JOHN, THAT THIS MAY *NOT* BE THE END... BUT THE *BEGINNING.*

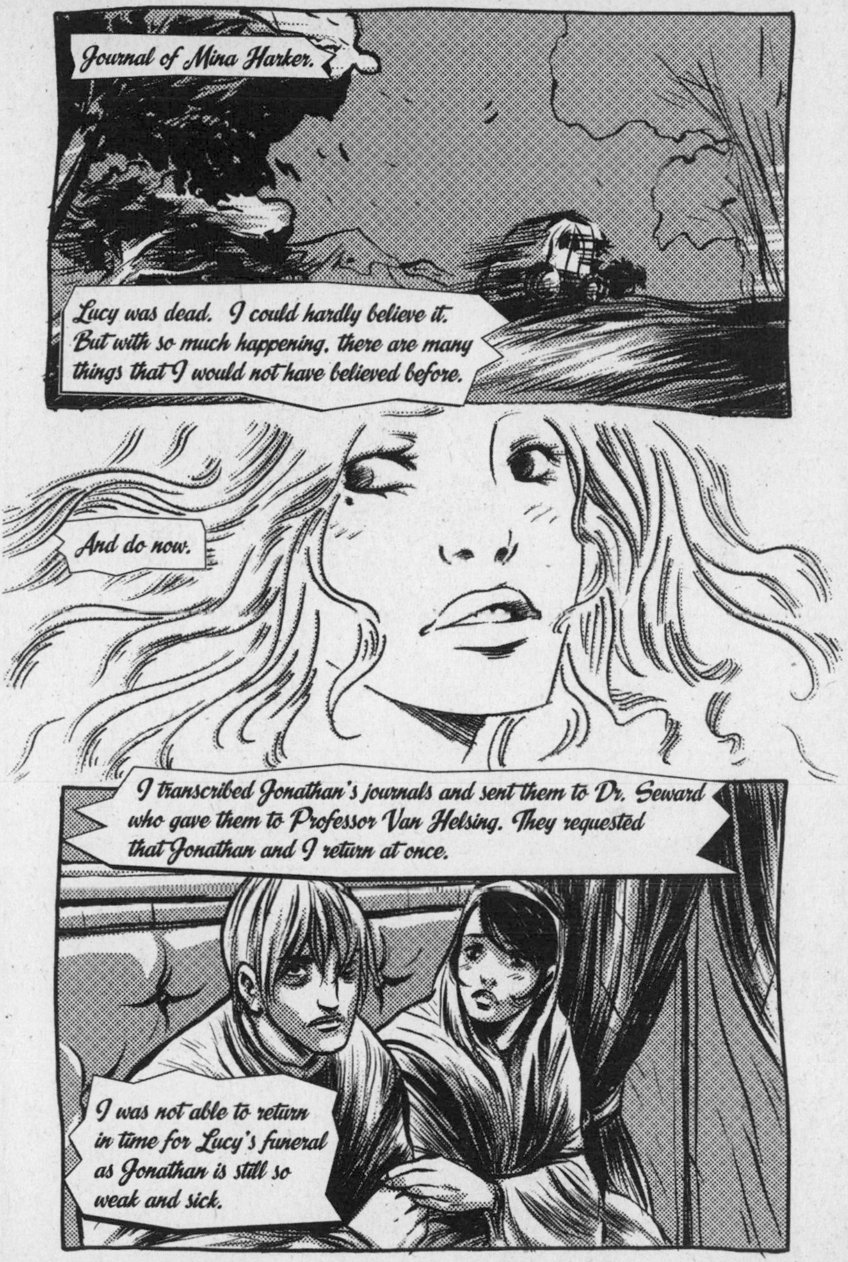
Journal of Mina Harker.
Lucy was dead. I could hardly believe it. But with so much happening, there are many things that I would not have believed before.
And do now.
I transcribed Jonathan's journals and sent them to Dr. Seward who gave them to Professor Van Helsing. They requested that Jonathan and I return at once.
I was not able to return in time for Lucy's funeral as Jonathan is still so weak and sick.

His horrible experience with the Count has left him tired and unable to travel for long periods of time.
His hair has turned white and his eyes have lost their cheerfulness. I only hope that he can gain his strength back soon.
Jonathan still has nightmares and he even said he saw the Count in London, but somehow the Count was now younger.
I fear for his sanity sometimes. But the Count is now in his past and can't threaten him any more.

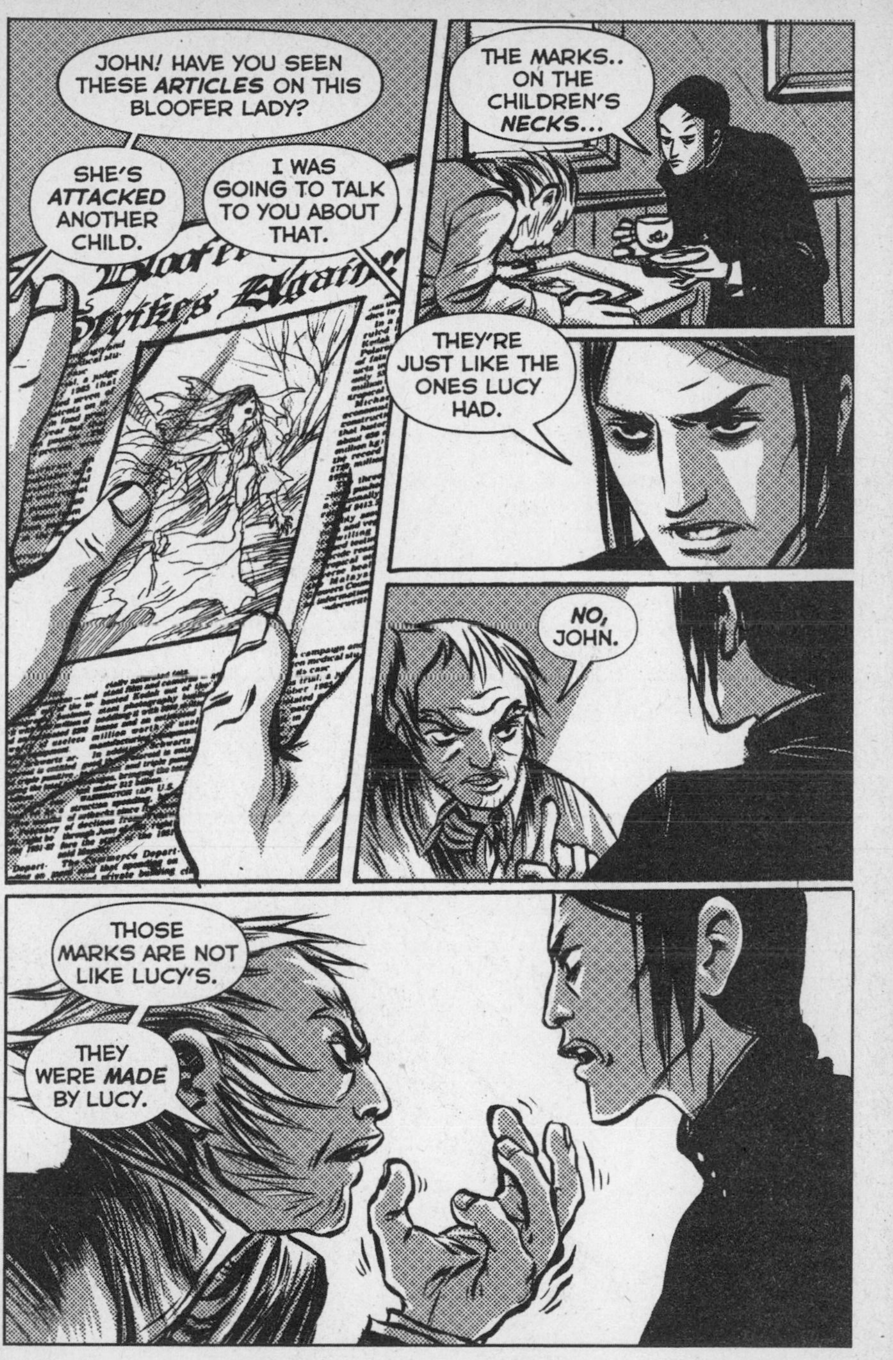
JOHN! HAVE YOU SEEN THESE *ARTICLES* ON THIS BLOOFER LADY?
SHE'S *ATTACKED* ANOTHER CHILD.
I WAS GOING TO TALK TO YOU ABOUT THAT.
THE MARKS.. ON THE CHILDREN'S *NECKS*...
THEY'RE JUST LIKE THE ONES LUCY HAD.
NO, JOHN.
THOSE MARKS ARE NOT LIKE LUCY'S.
THEY WERE *MADE* BY LUCY.

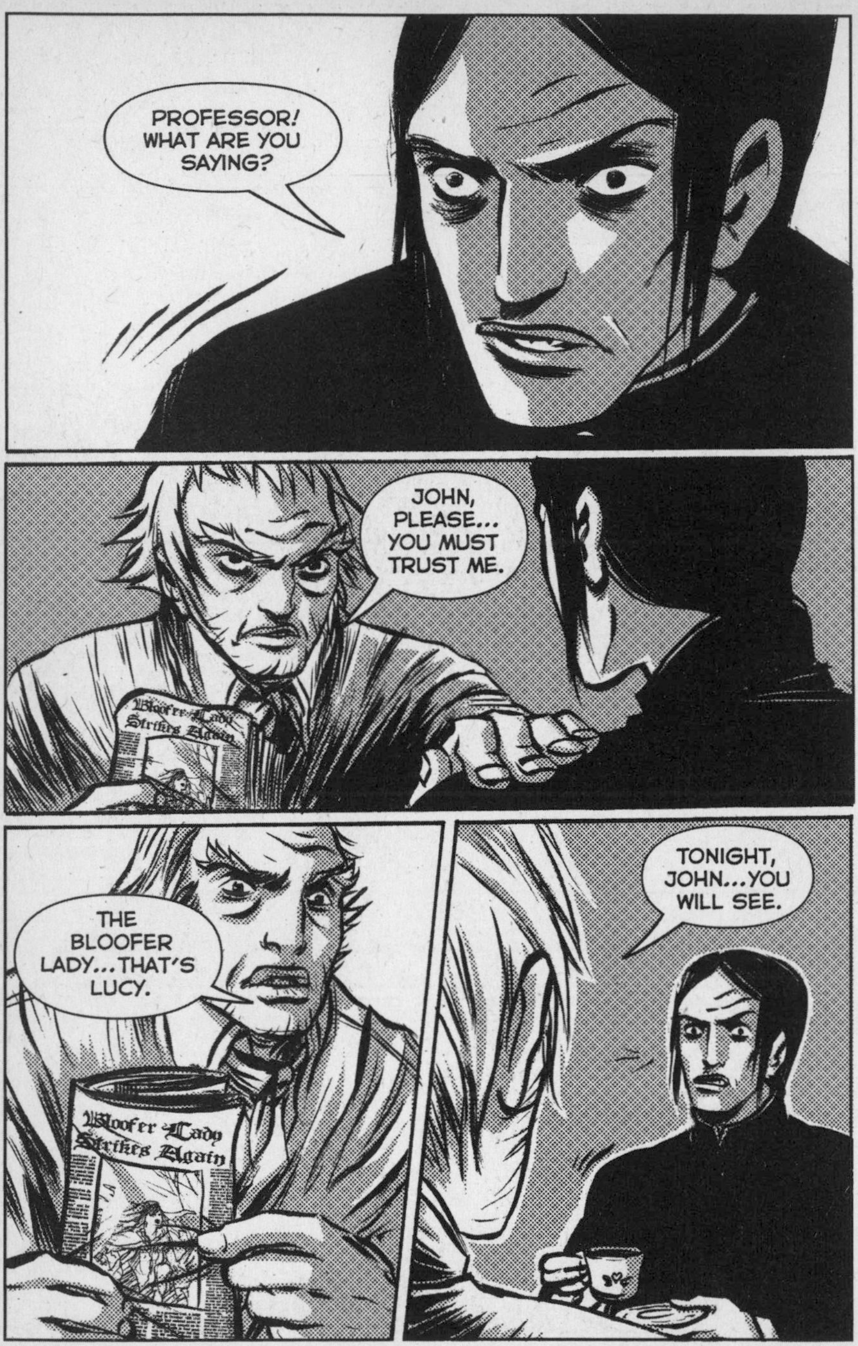
PROFESSOR! WHAT ARE YOU SAYING?
JOHN, PLEASE... YOU MUST TRUST ME.
Bloofer Lady Strikes Again
THE BLOOFER LADY... THAT'S LUCY.
TONIGHT, JOHN... YOU WILL SEE.

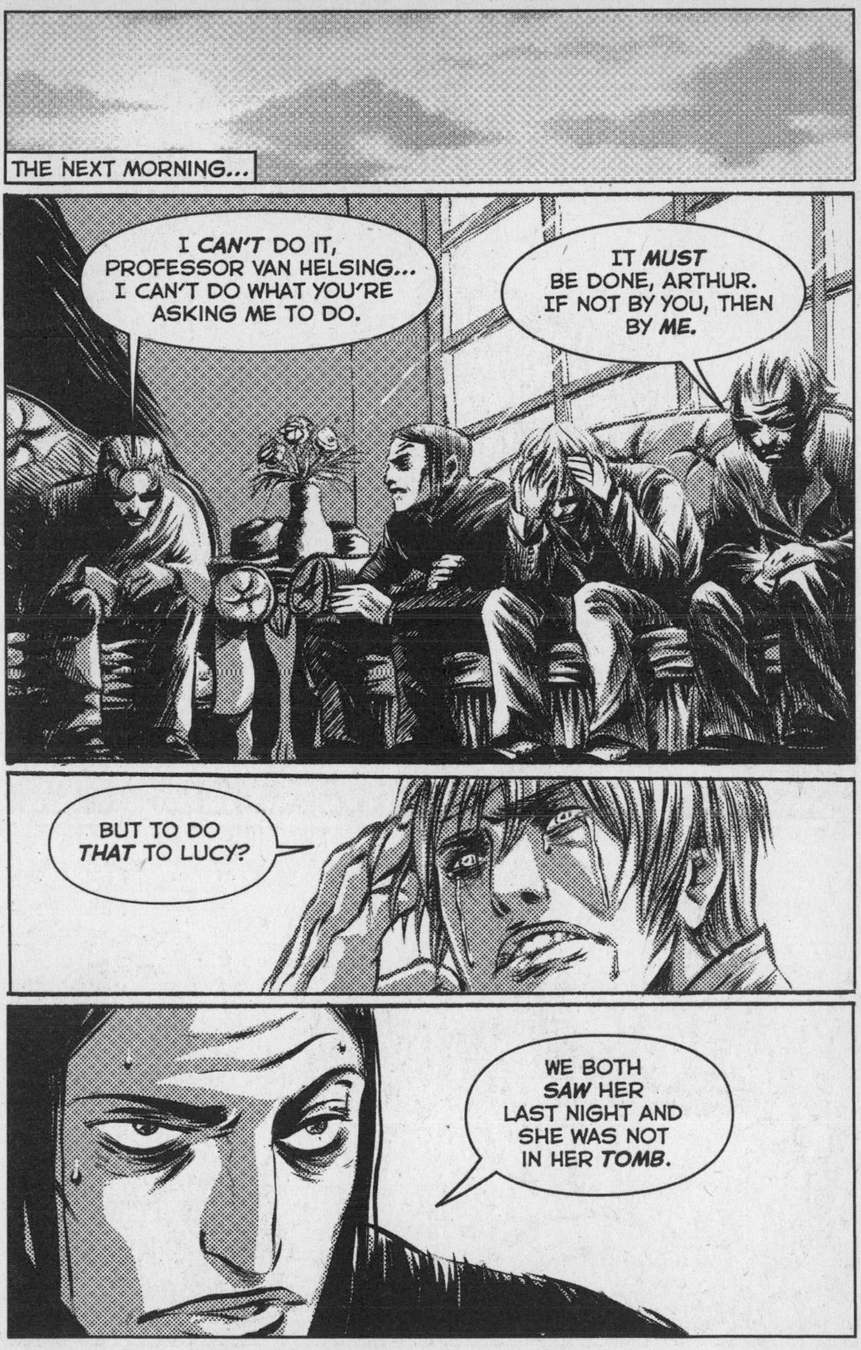
THE NEXT MORNING...
I CAN'T DO IT, PROFESSOR VAN HELSING... I CAN'T DO WHAT YOU'RE ASKING ME TO DO.
IT MUST BE DONE, ARTHUR. IF NOT BY YOU, THEN BY ME.
BUT TO DO THAT TO LUCY?
WE BOTH SAW HER LAST NIGHT AND SHE WAS NOT IN HER TOMB.

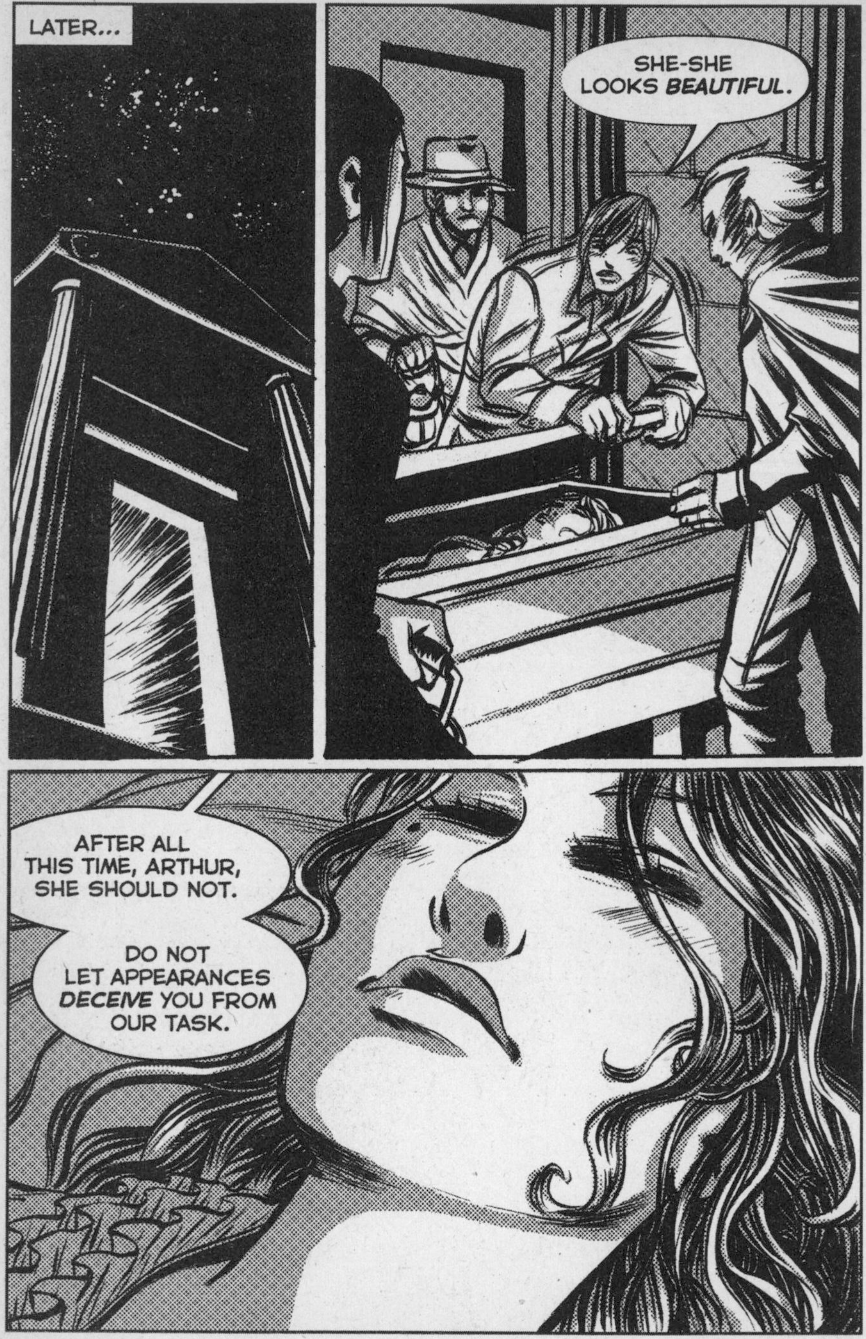
LATER...
SHE-SHE LOOKS BEAUTIFUL.
AFTER ALL THIS TIME, ARTHUR, SHE SHOULD NOT.
DO NOT LET APPEARANCES DECEIVE YOU FROM OUR TASK.

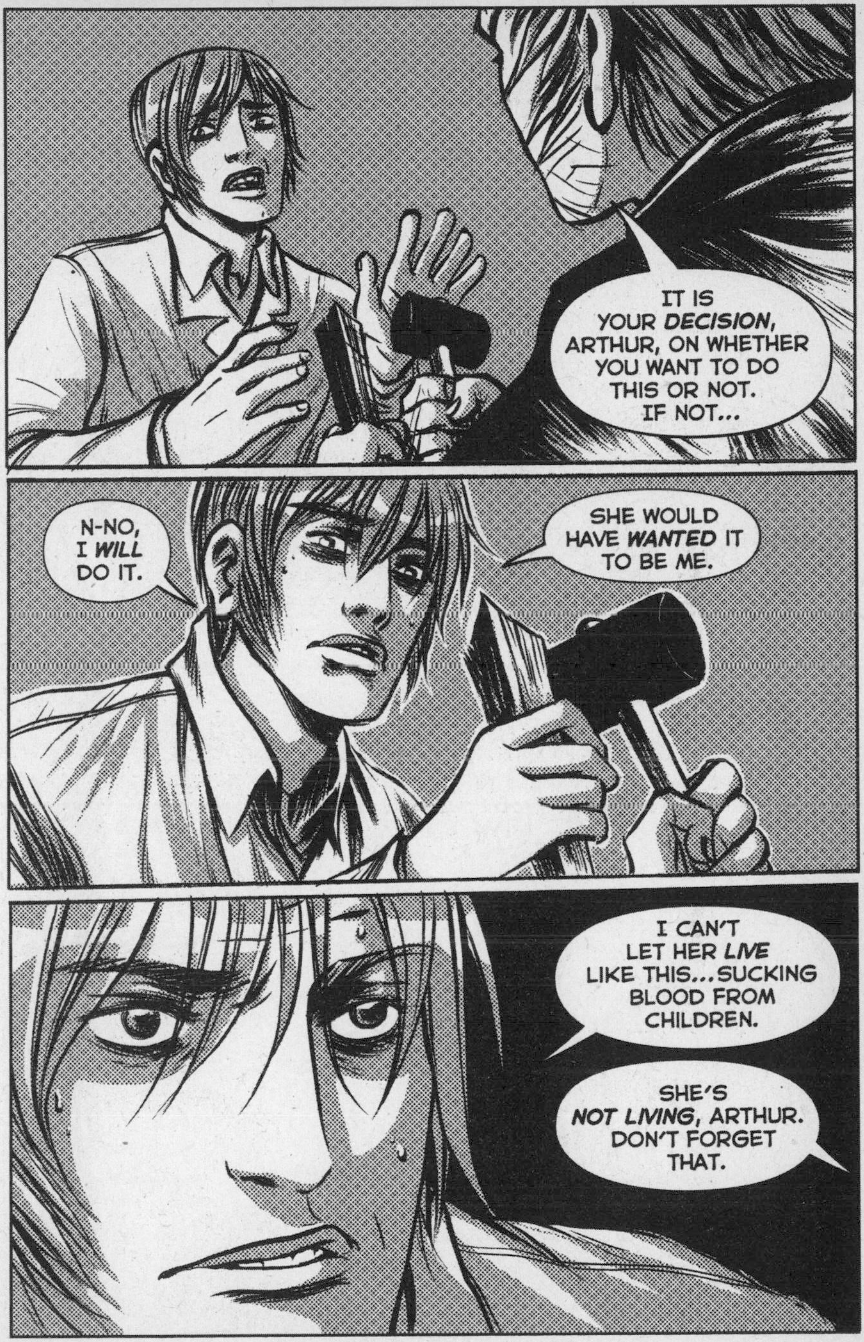
IT IS YOUR DECISION, ARTHUR, ON WHETHER YOU WANT TO DO THIS OR NOT. IF NOT...
N-NO, I WILL DO IT.
SHE WOULD HAVE WANTED IT TO BE ME.
I CAN'T LET HER LIVE LIKE THIS...SUCKING BLOOD FROM CHILDREN.
SHE'S NOT LIVING, ARTHUR. DON'T FORGET THAT.

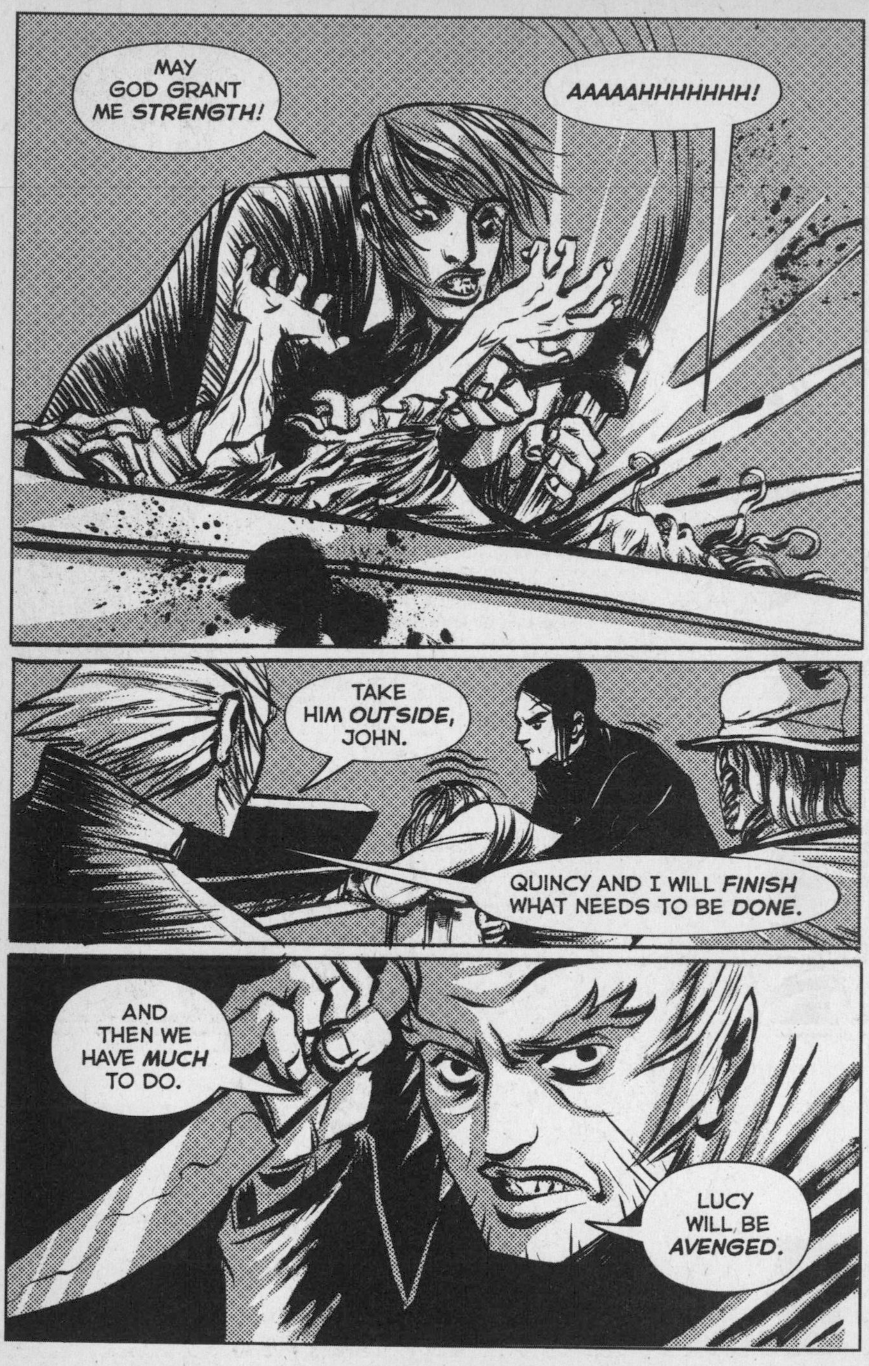
MAY GOD GRANT ME STRENGTH!
AAAAAHHHHHHH!
TAKE HIM OUTSIDE, JOHN.
QUINCY AND I WILL FINISH WHAT NEEDS TO BE DONE.
AND THEN WE HAVE MUCH TO DO.
LUCY WILL BE AVENGED.

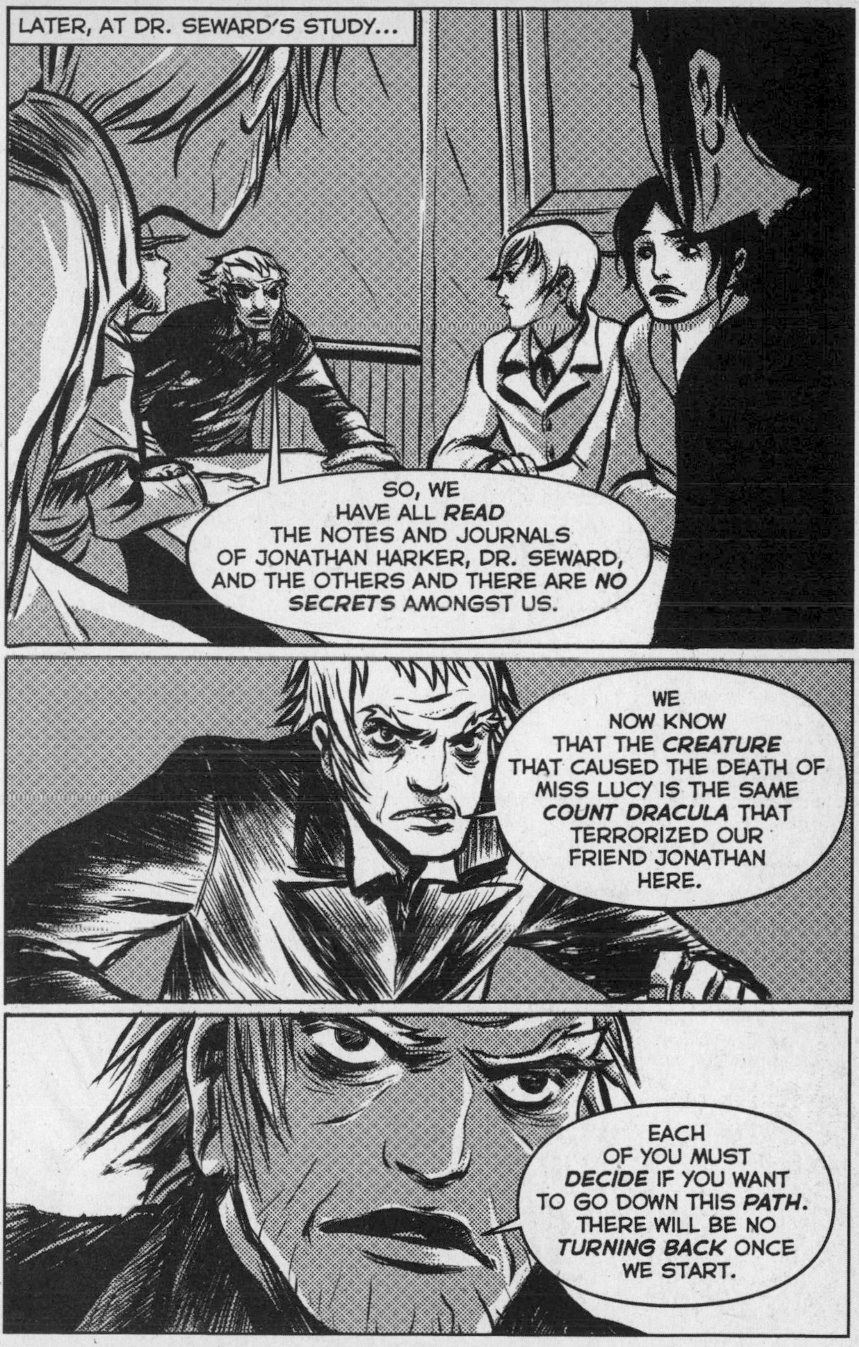
LATER, AT DR. SEWARD'S STUDY...
SO, WE HAVE ALL *READ* THE NOTES AND JOURNALS OF JONATHAN HARKER, DR. SEWARD, AND THE OTHERS AND THERE ARE *NO SECRETS* AMONGST US.
WE NOW KNOW THAT THE *CREATURE* THAT CAUSED THE DEATH OF MISS LUCY IS THE SAME *COUNT DRACULA* THAT TERRORIZED OUR FRIEND JONATHAN HERE.
EACH OF YOU MUST *DECIDE* IF YOU WANT TO GO DOWN THIS *PATH*. THERE WILL BE NO *TURNING BACK* ONCE WE START.

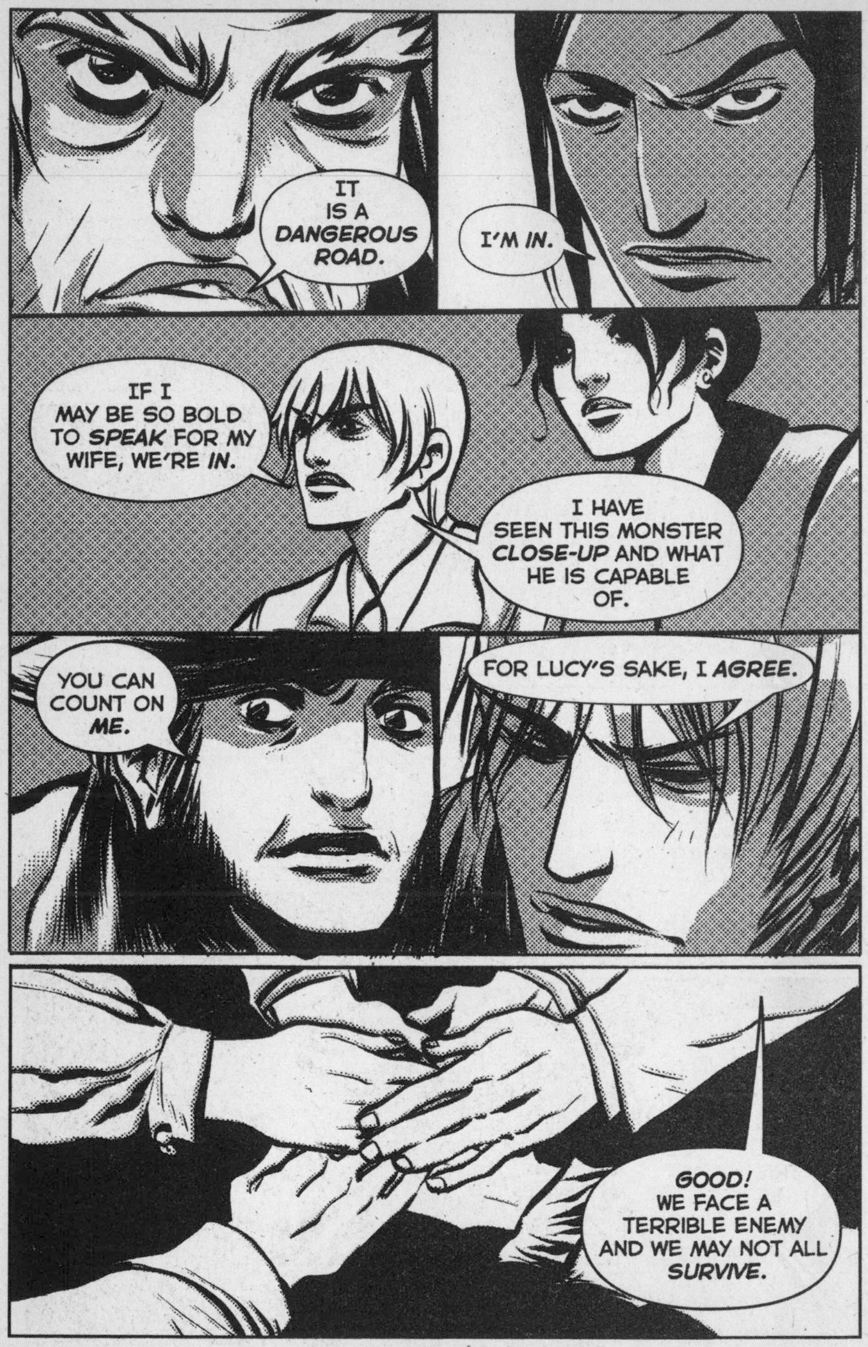
IT IS A DANGEROUS ROAD.
I'M IN.
IF I MAY BE SO BOLD TO SPEAK FOR MY WIFE, WE'RE IN.
I HAVE SEEN THIS MONSTER CLOSE-UP AND WHAT HE IS CAPABLE OF.
YOU CAN COUNT ON ME.
FOR LUCY'S SAKE, I AGREE.
GOOD! WE FACE A TERRIBLE ENEMY AND WE MAY NOT ALL SURVIVE.

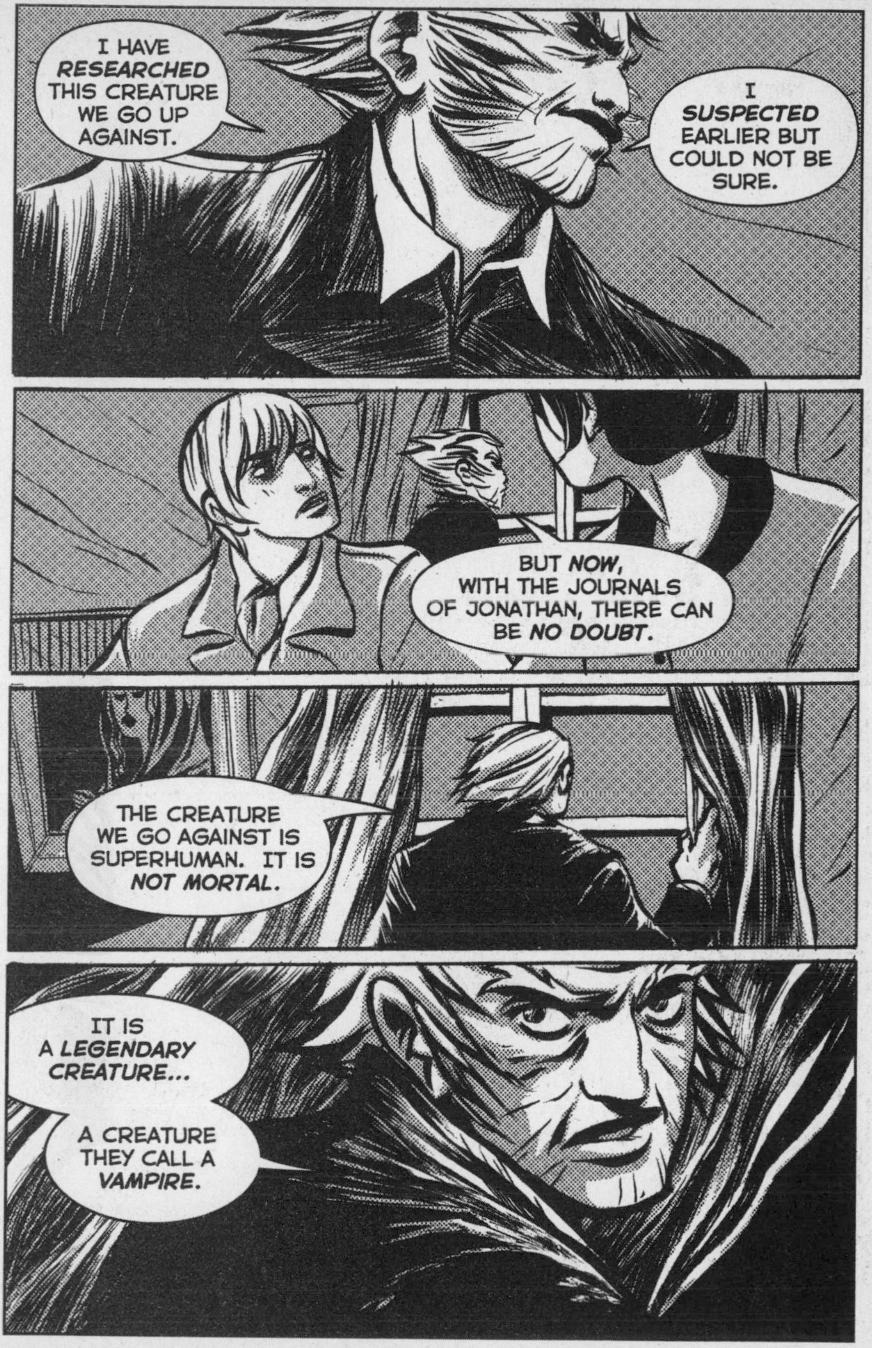
I HAVE RESEARCHED THIS CREATURE WE GO UP AGAINST.
I SUSPECTED EARLIER BUT COULD NOT BE SURE.
BUT NOW, WITH THE JOURNALS OF JONATHAN, THERE CAN BE NO DOUBT.
THE CREATURE WE GO AGAINST IS SUPERHUMAN. IT IS NOT MORTAL.
IT IS A LEGENDARY CREATURE...
A CREATURE THEY CALL A VAMPIRE.

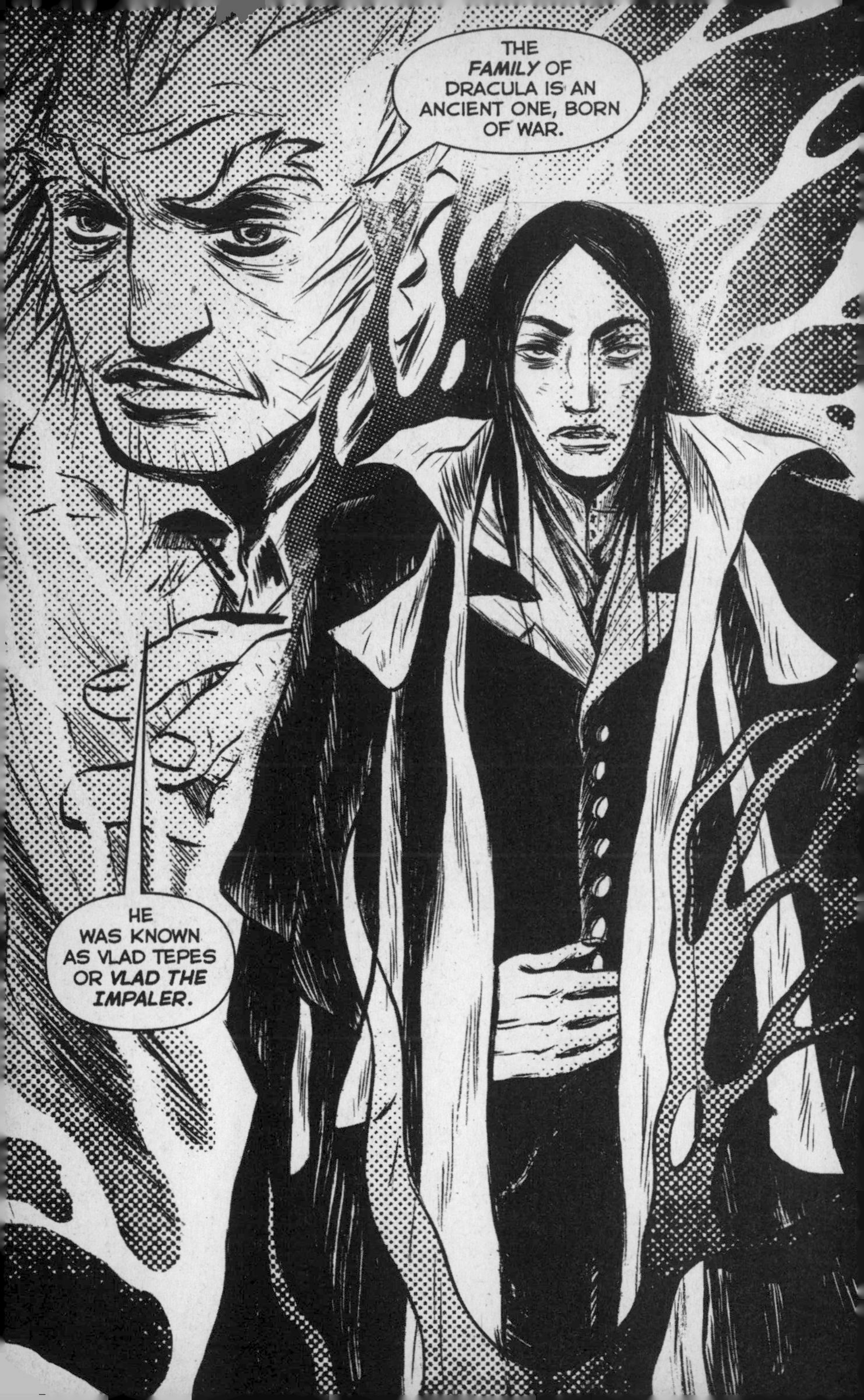
THE FAMILY OF DRACULA IS AN ANCIENT ONE, BORN OF WAR.
HE WAS KNOWN AS VLAD TEPES OR VLAD THE IMPALER.

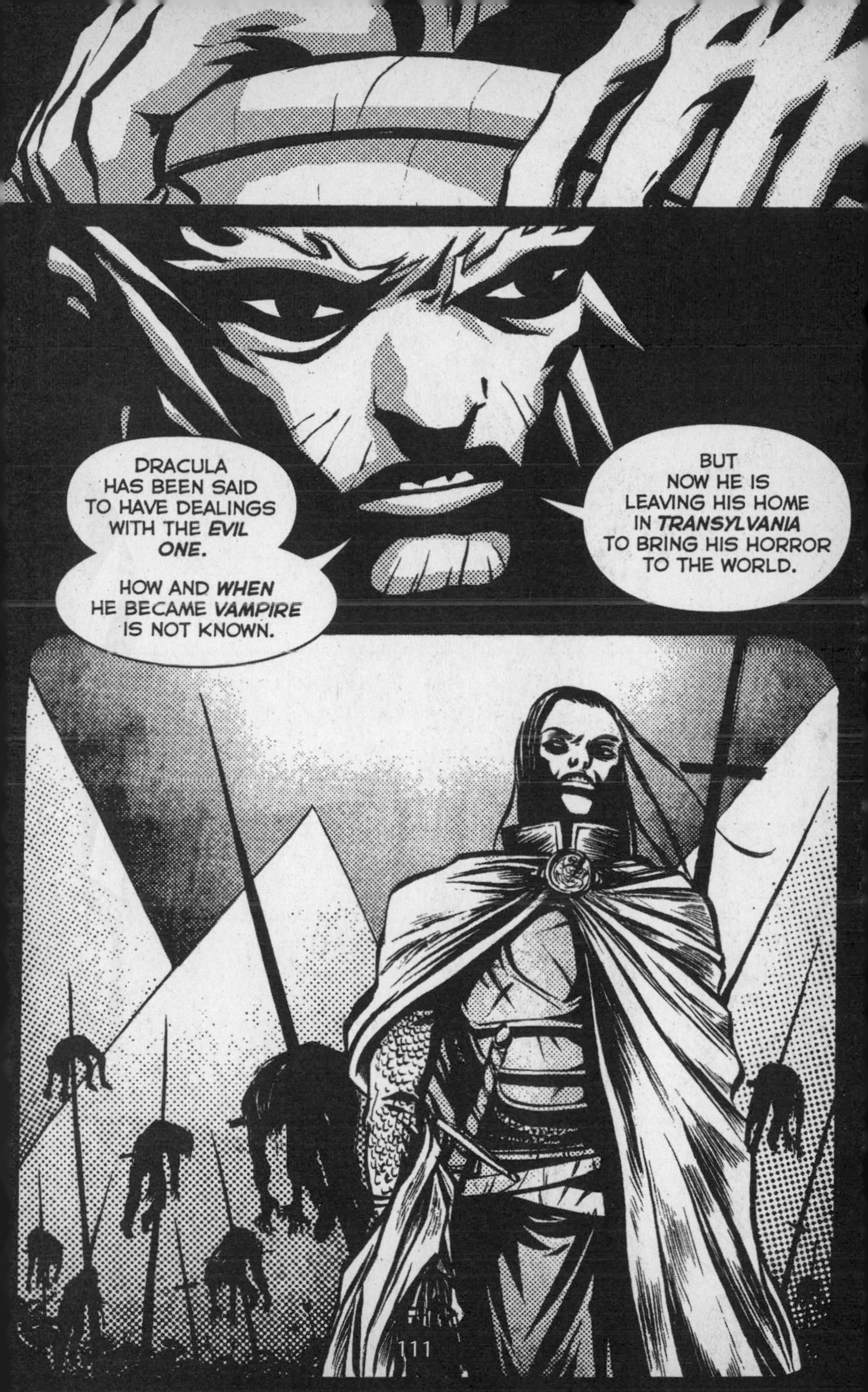
DRACULA HAS BEEN SAID TO HAVE DEALINGS WITH THE *EVIL ONE.*
HOW AND *WHEN* HE BECAME *VAMPIRE* IS NOT KNOWN.
BUT NOW HE IS LEAVING HIS HOME IN *TRANSYLVANIA* TO BRING HIS HORROR TO THE WORLD.

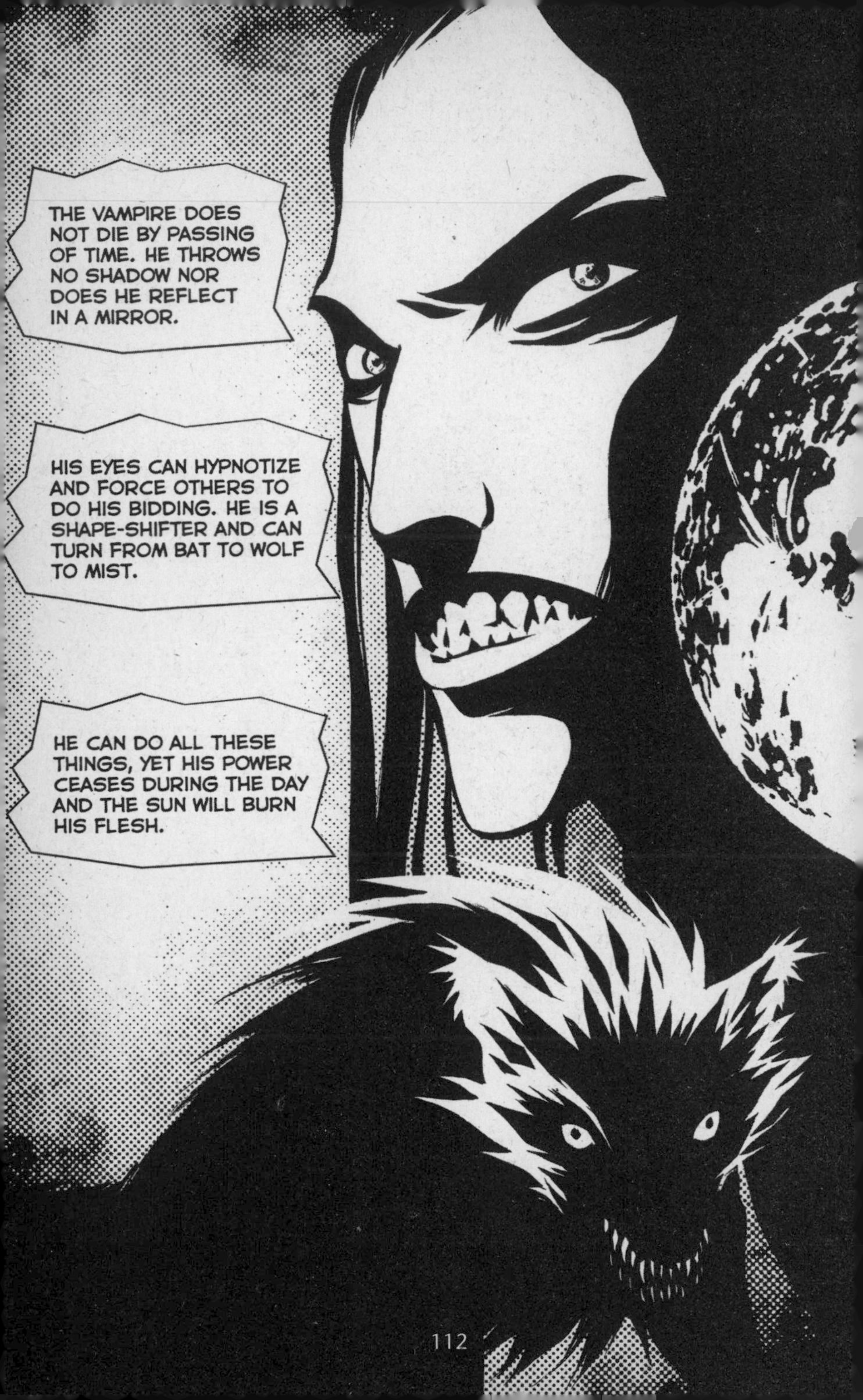
THE VAMPIRE DOES NOT DIE BY PASSING OF TIME. HE THROWS NO SHADOW NOR DOES HE REFLECT IN A MIRROR.
HIS EYES CAN HYPNOTIZE AND FORCE OTHERS TO DO HIS BIDDING. HE IS A SHAPE-SHIFTER AND CAN TURN FROM BAT TO WOLF TO MIST.
HE CAN DO ALL THESE THINGS, YET HIS POWER CEASES DURING THE DAY AND THE SUN WILL BURN HIS FLESH.

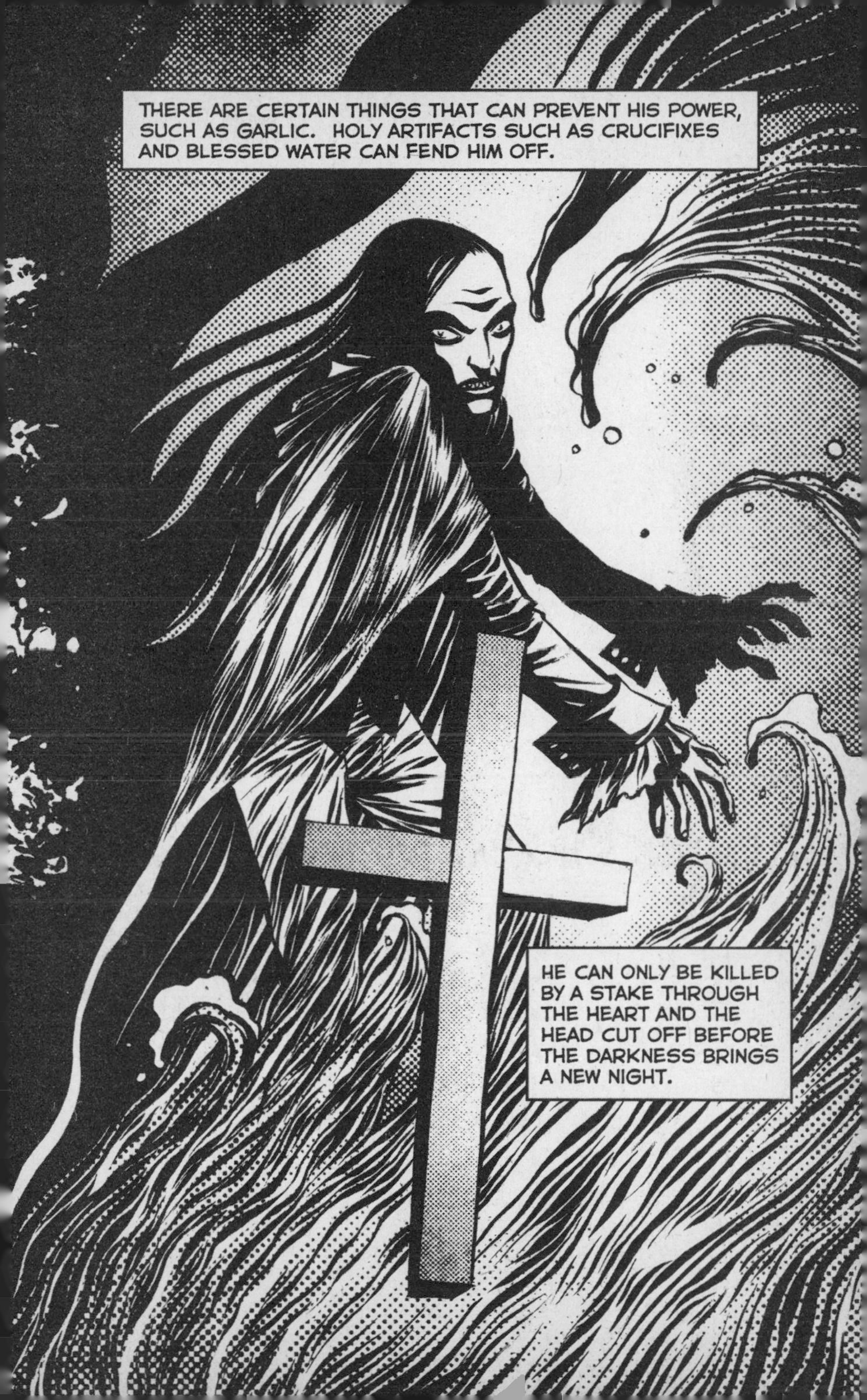
THERE ARE CERTAIN THINGS THAT CAN PREVENT HIS POWER, SUCH AS GARLIC. HOLY ARTIFACTS SUCH AS CRUCIFIXES AND BLESSED WATER CAN FEND HIM OFF.
HE CAN ONLY BE KILLED BY A STAKE THROUGH THE HEART AND THE HEAD CUT OFF BEFORE THE DARKNESS BRINGS A NEW NIGHT.

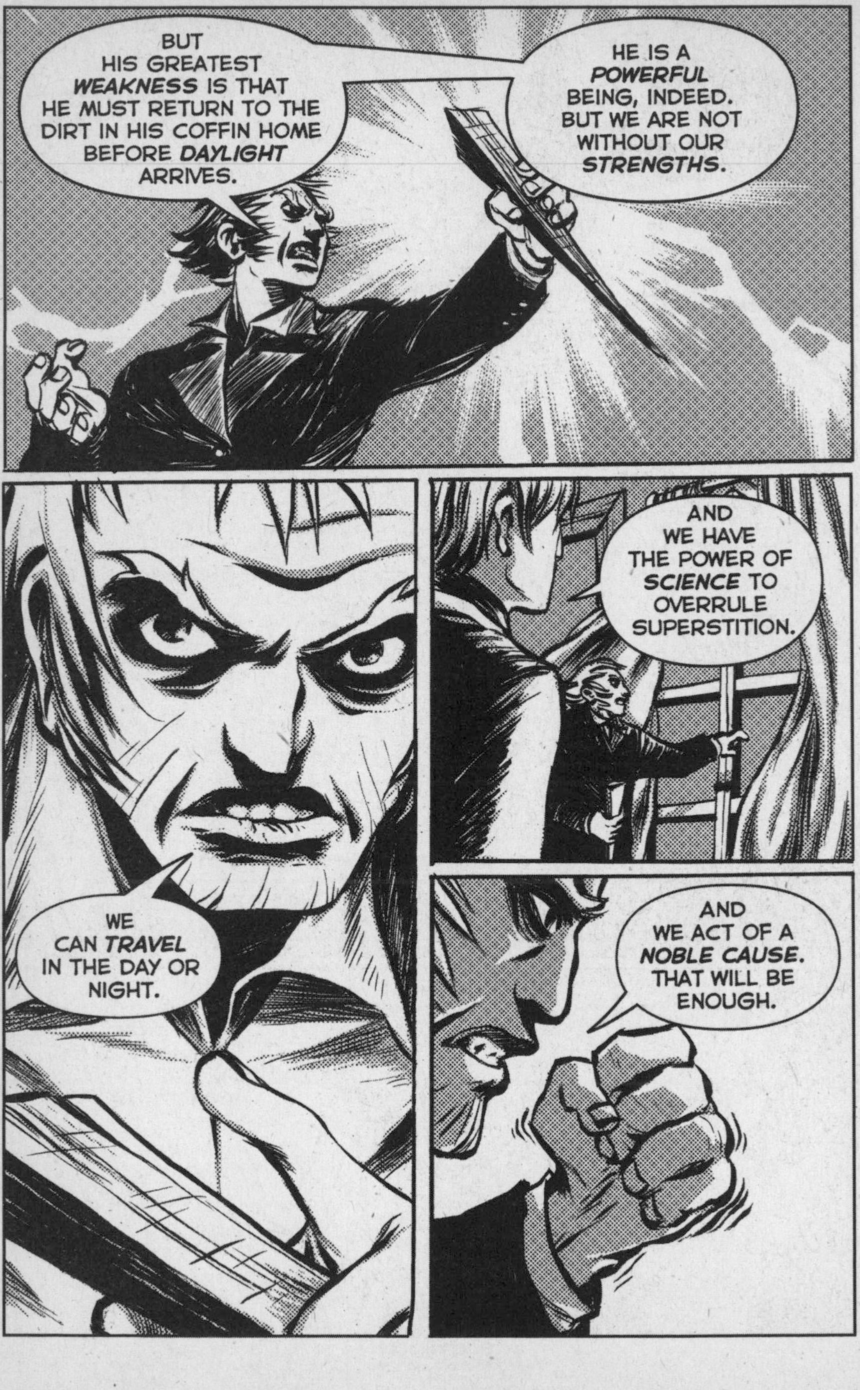
BUT HIS GREATEST WEAKNESS IS THAT HE MUST RETURN TO THE DIRT IN HIS COFFIN HOME BEFORE DAYLIGHT ARRIVES.
HE IS A POWERFUL BEING, INDEED. BUT WE ARE NOT WITHOUT OUR STRENGTHS.
WE CAN TRAVEL IN THE DAY OR NIGHT.
AND WE HAVE THE POWER OF SCIENCE TO OVERRULE SUPERSTITION.
AND WE ACT OF A NOBLE CAUSE. THAT WILL BE ENOUGH.

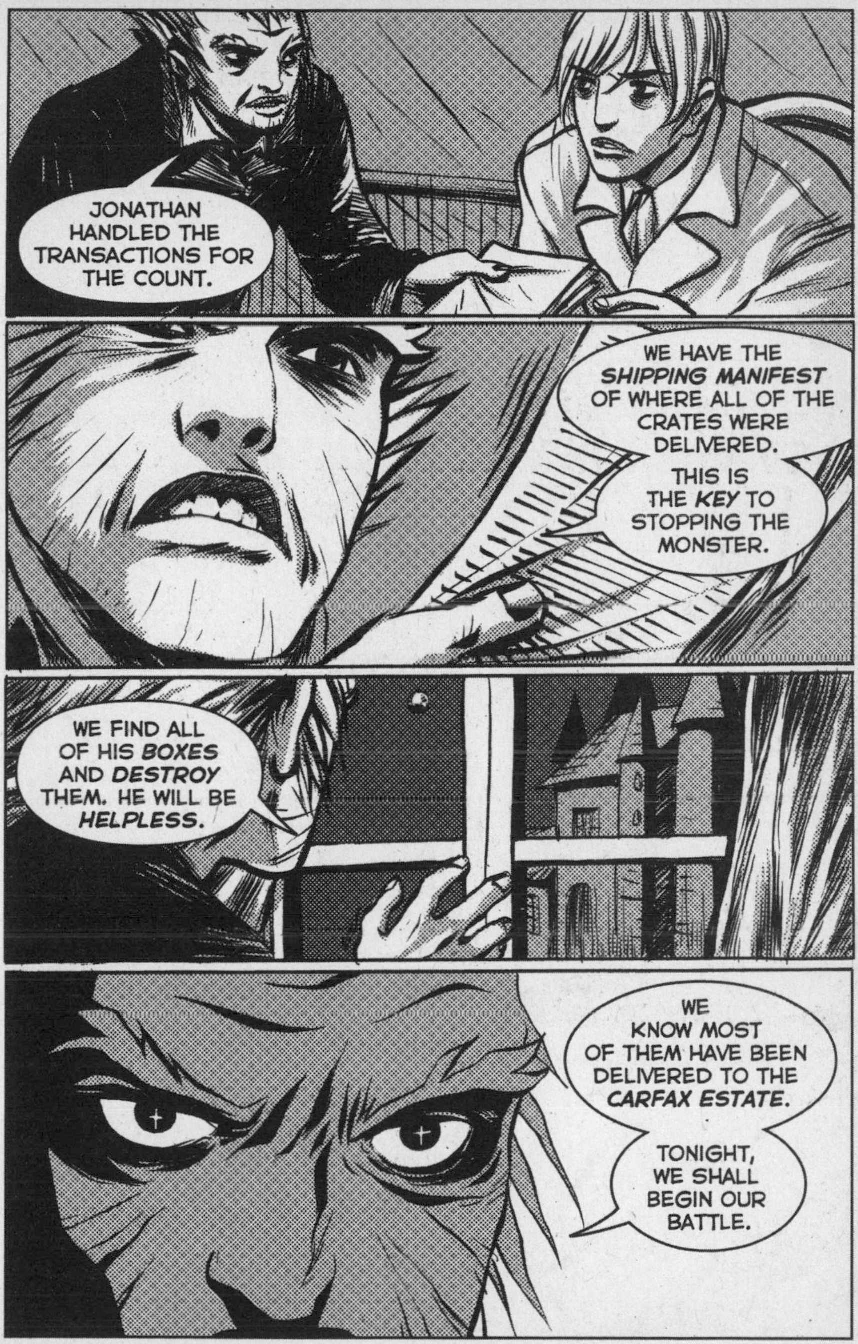
JONATHAN HANDLED THE TRANSACTIONS FOR THE COUNT.
WE HAVE THE SHIPPING MANIFEST OF WHERE ALL OF THE CRATES WERE DELIVERED.
THIS IS THE KEY TO STOPPING THE MONSTER.
WE FIND ALL OF HIS BOXES AND DESTROY THEM. HE WILL BE HELPLESS.
WE KNOW MOST OF THEM HAVE BEEN DELIVERED TO THE CARFAX ESTATE.
TONIGHT, WE SHALL BEGIN OUR BATTLE.

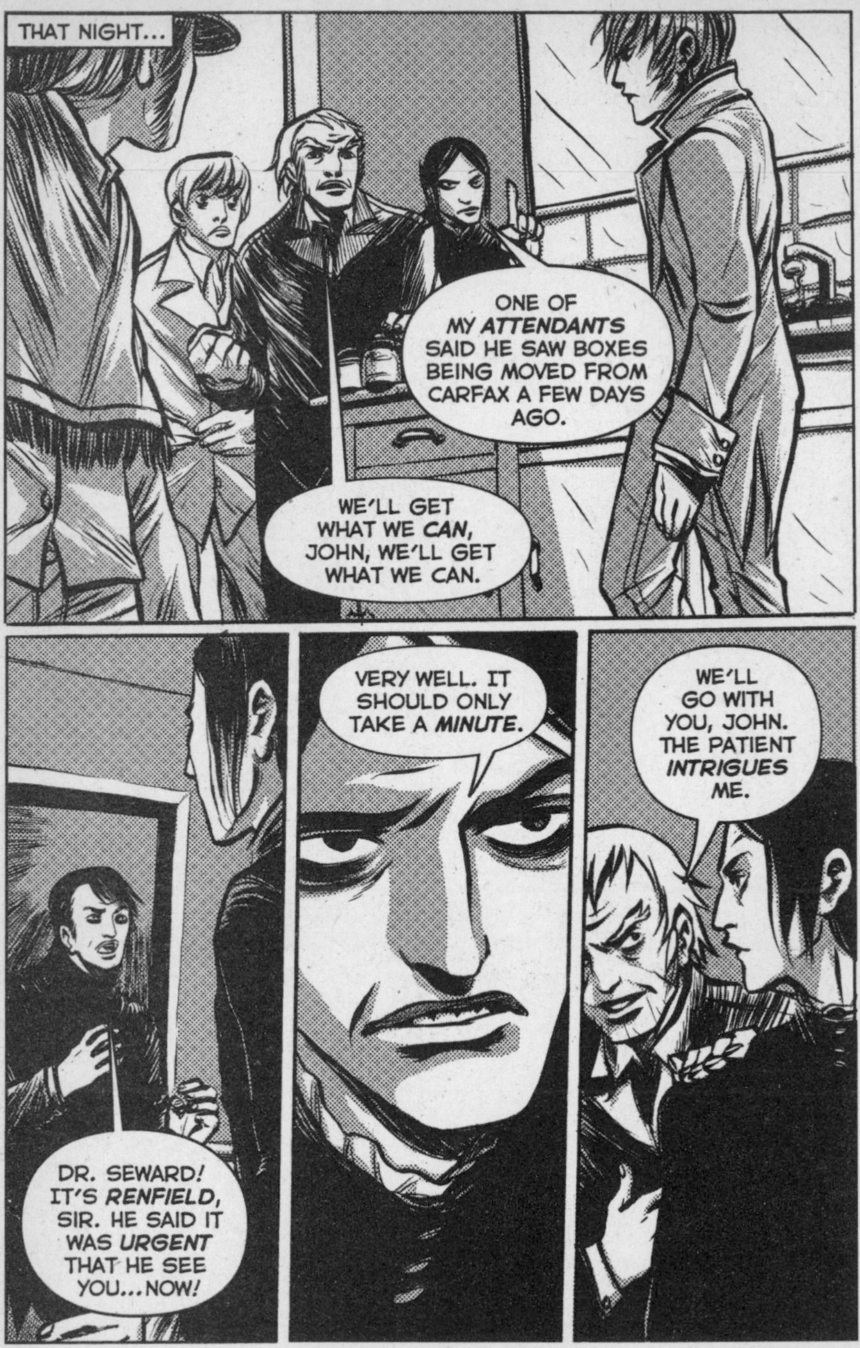
THAT NIGHT...
ONE OF MY ATTENDANTS SAID HE SAW BOXES BEING MOVED FROM CARFAX A FEW DAYS AGO.
WE'LL GET WHAT WE CAN, JOHN, WE'LL GET WHAT WE CAN.
DR. SEWARD! IT'S RENFIELD, SIR. HE SAID IT WAS URGENT THAT HE SEE YOU...NOW!
VERY WELL. IT SHOULD ONLY TAKE A MINUTE.
WE'LL GO WITH YOU, JOHN. THE PATIENT INTRIGUES ME.

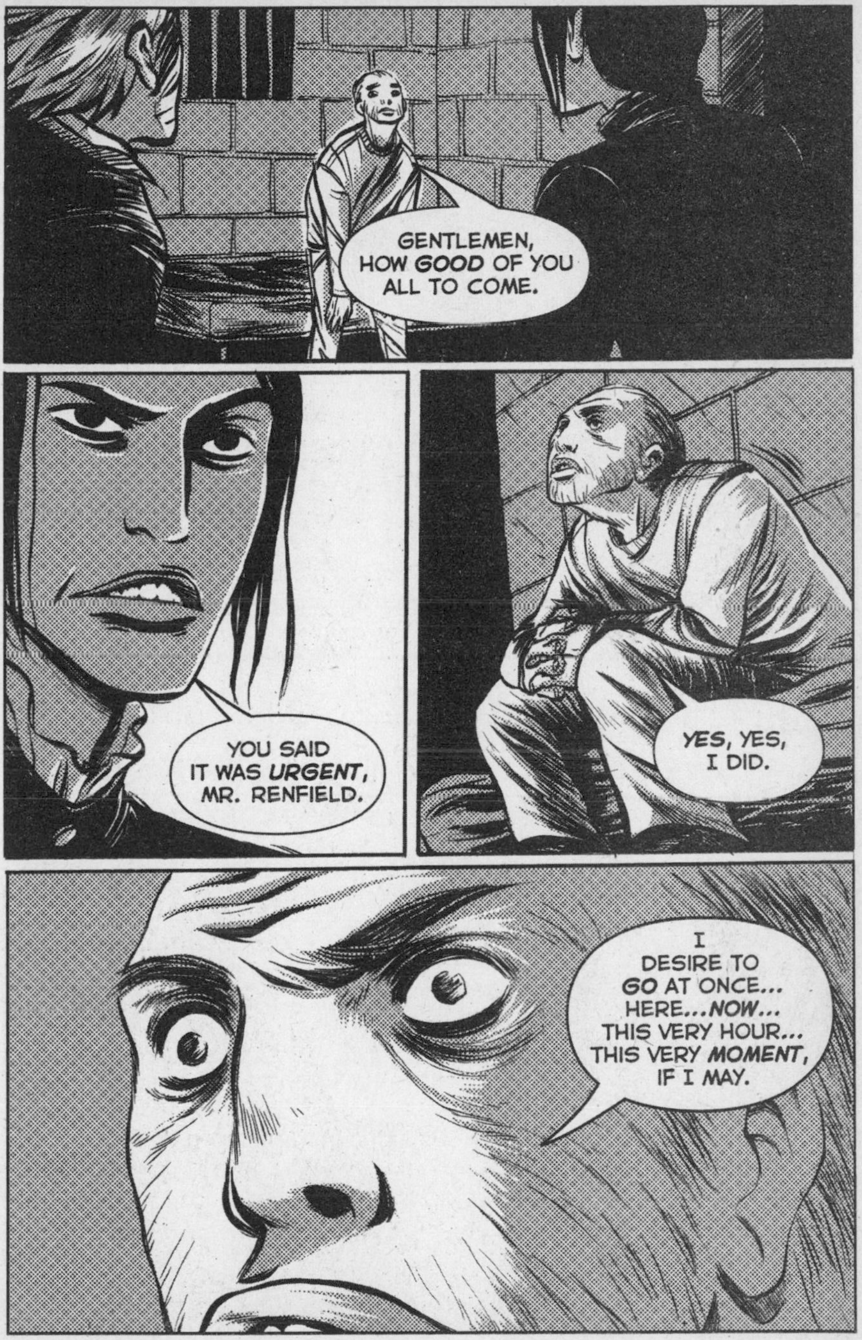
GENTLEMEN, HOW GOOD OF YOU ALL TO COME.
YOU SAID IT WAS URGENT, MR. RENFIELD.
YES, YES, I DID.
I DESIRE TO GO AT ONCE... HERE...NOW... THIS VERY HOUR... THIS VERY MOMENT, IF I MAY.

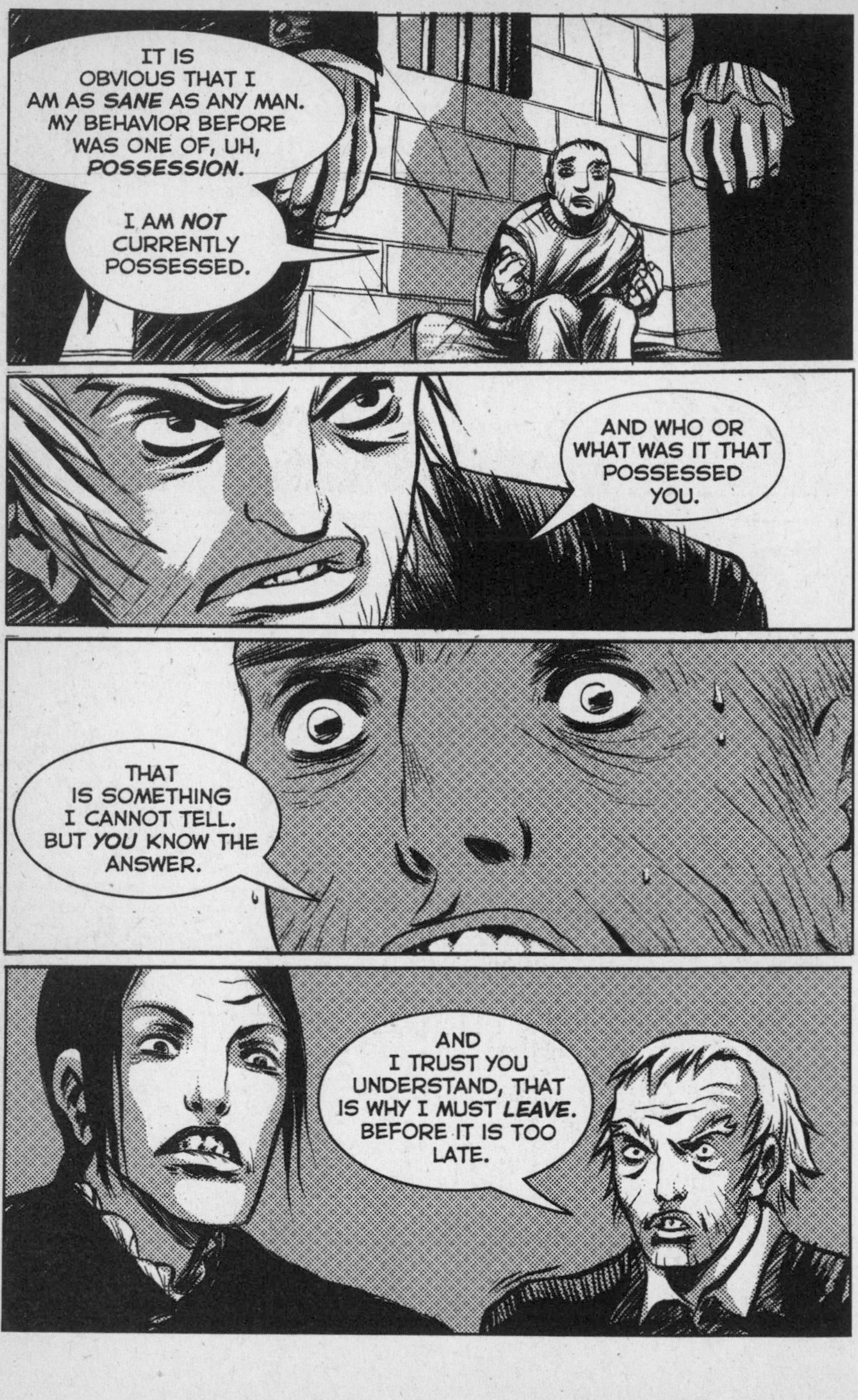
IT IS OBVIOUS THAT I AM AS *SANE* AS ANY MAN. MY BEHAVIOR BEFORE WAS ONE OF, UH, *POSSESSION*.
I AM *NOT* CURRENTLY POSSESSED.
AND WHO OR WHAT WAS IT THAT POSSESSED YOU.
THAT IS SOMETHING I CANNOT TELL. BUT *YOU* KNOW THE ANSWER.
AND I TRUST YOU UNDERSTAND, THAT IS WHY I MUST *LEAVE*. BEFORE IT IS TOO LATE.

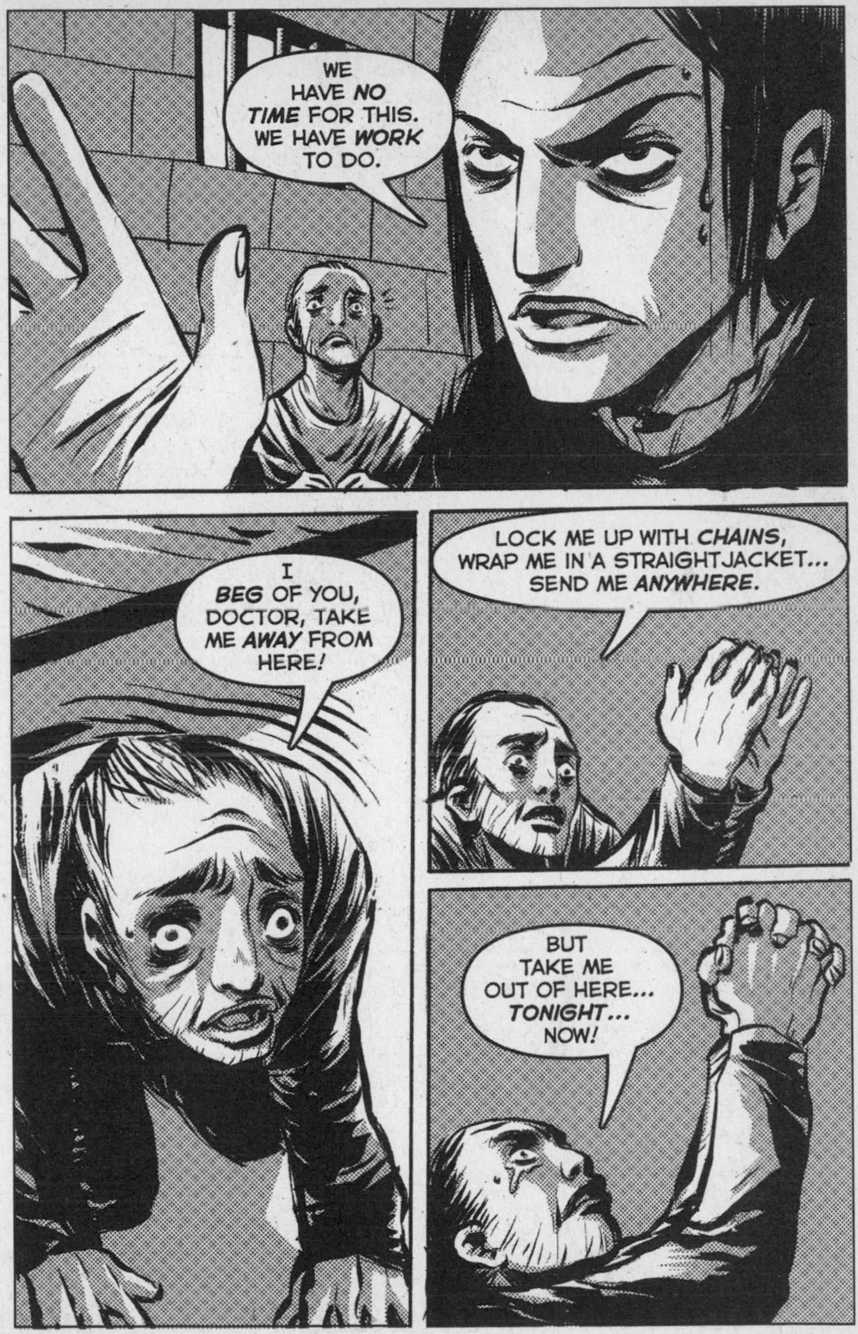
WE HAVE NO TIME FOR THIS. WE HAVE WORK TO DO.
I BEG OF YOU, DOCTOR, TAKE ME AWAY FROM HERE!
LOCK ME UP WITH CHAINS, WRAP ME IN A STRAIGHTJACKET... SEND ME ANYWHERE.
BUT TAKE ME OUT OF HERE... TONIGHT... NOW!

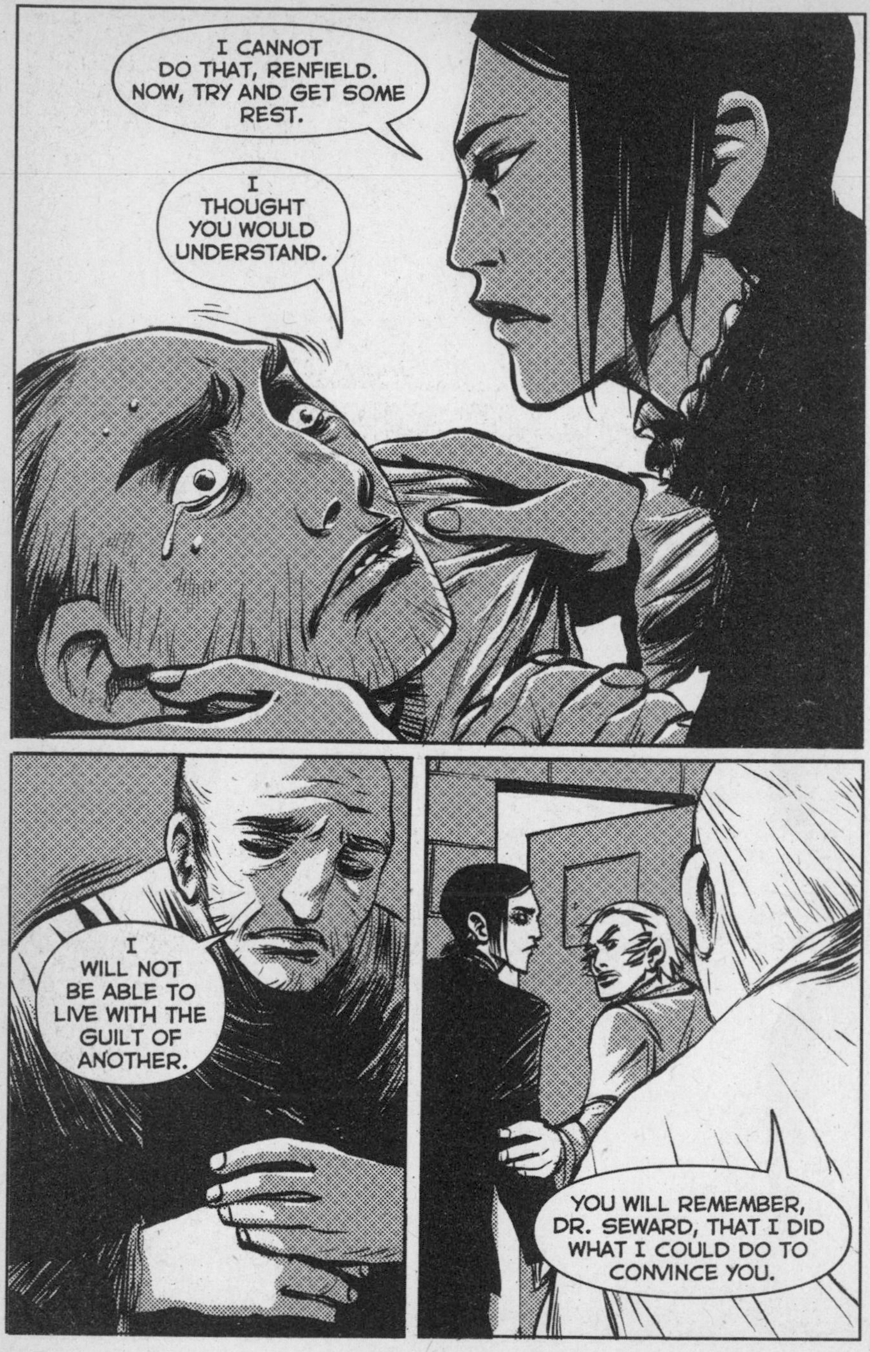
I CANNOT DO THAT, RENFIELD. NOW, TRY AND GET SOME REST.
I THOUGHT YOU WOULD UNDERSTAND.
I WILL NOT BE ABLE TO LIVE WITH THE GUILT OF ANOTHER.
YOU WILL REMEMBER, DR. SEWARD, THAT I DID WHAT I COULD DO TO CONVINCE YOU.

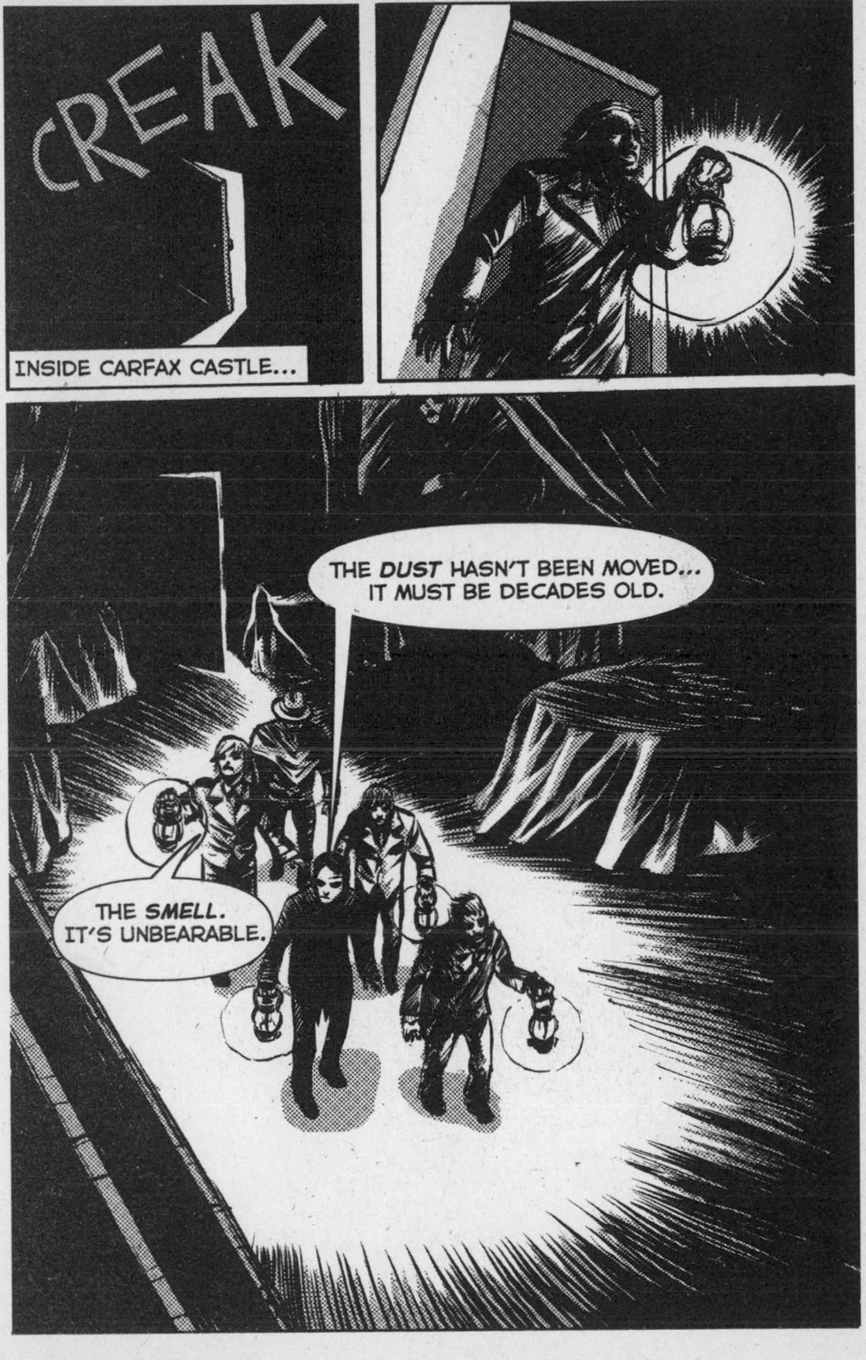
CREAK
INSIDE CARFAX CASTLE...
THE DUST HASN'T BEEN MOVED... IT MUST BE DECADES OLD.
THE SMELL. IT'S UNBEARABLE.

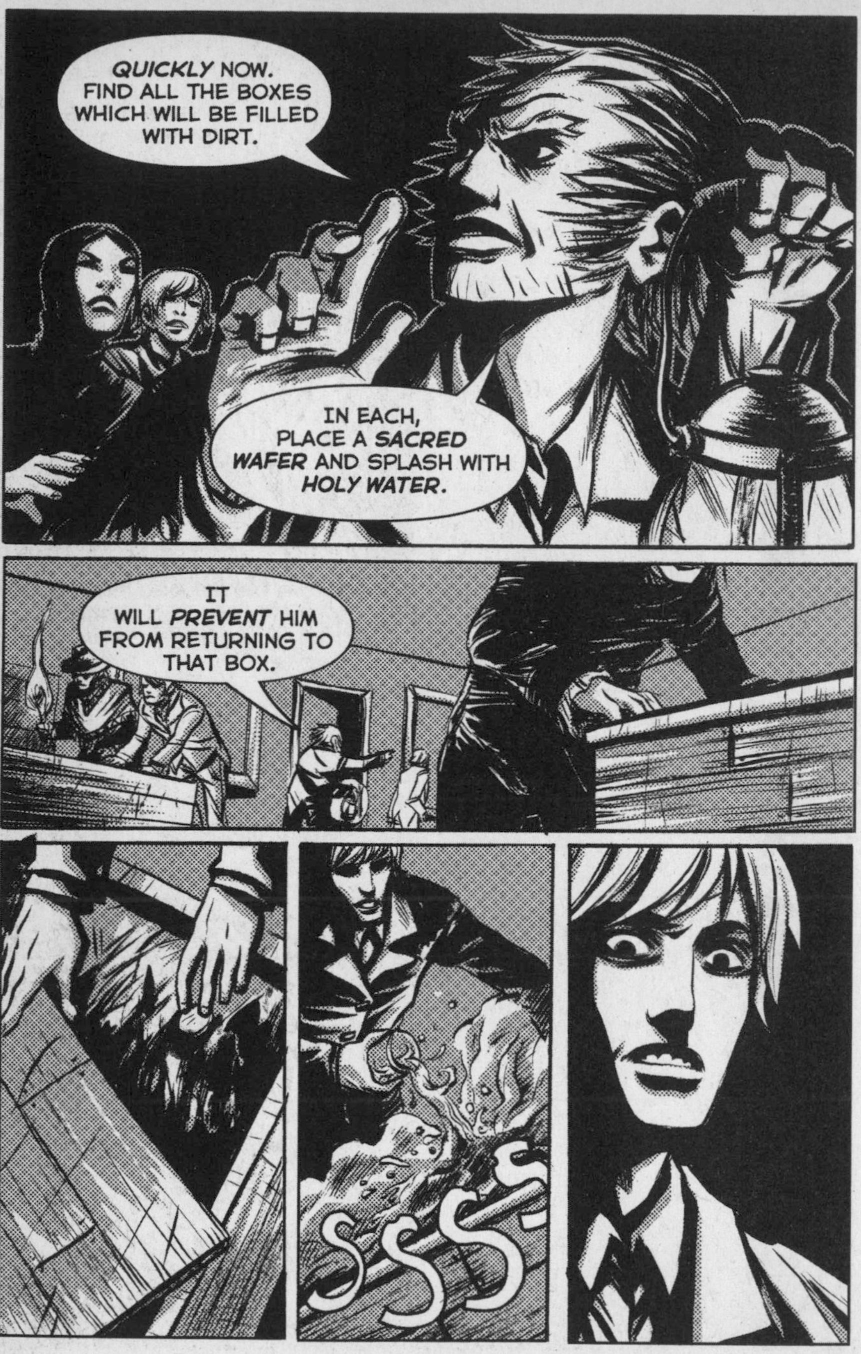
QUICKLY NOW. FIND ALL THE BOXES WHICH WILL BE FILLED WITH DIRT.
IN EACH, PLACE A SACRED WAFER AND SPLASH WITH HOLY WATER.
IT WILL PREVENT HIM FROM RETURNING TO THAT BOX.
SSSS

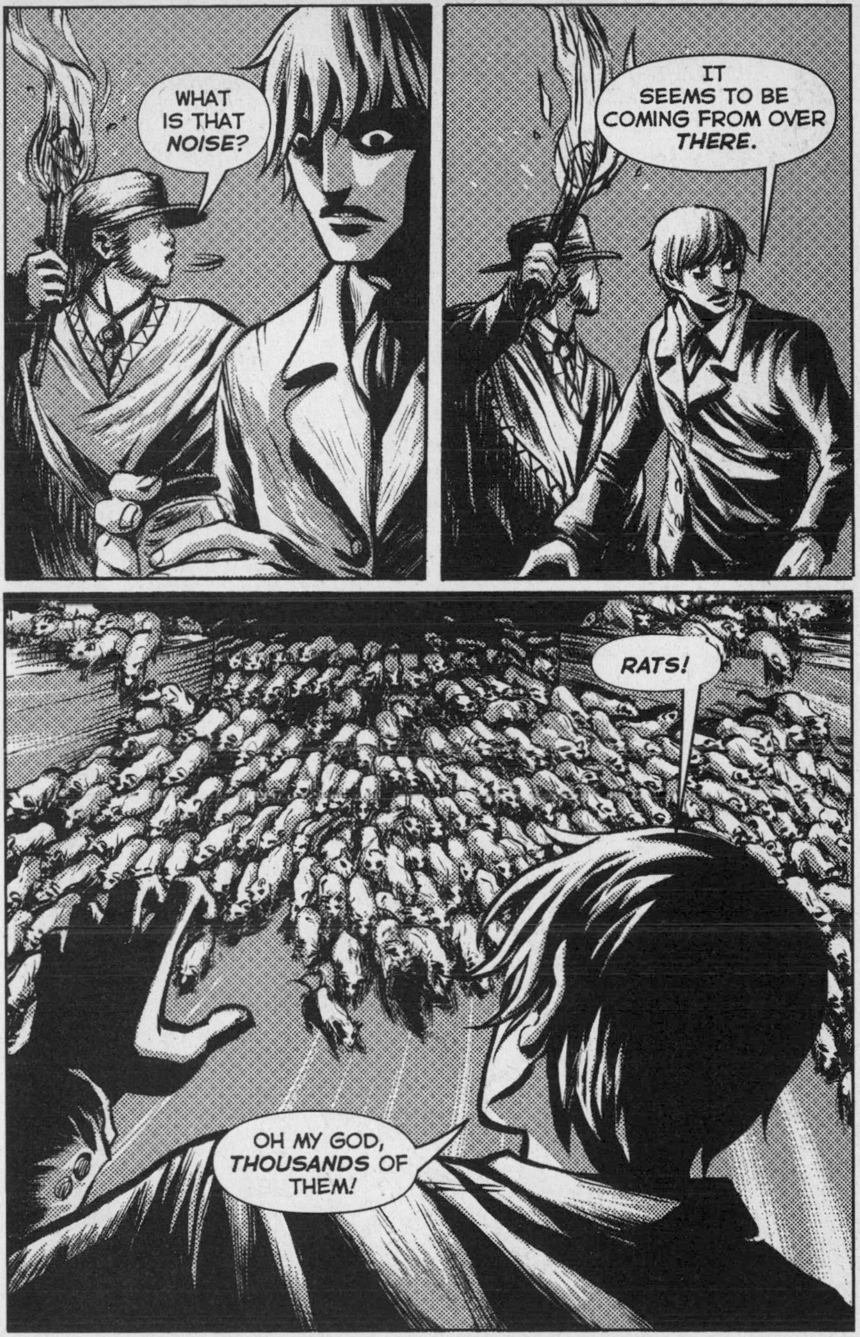
WHAT IS THAT *NOISE?*
IT SEEMS TO BE COMING FROM OVER *THERE.*
RATS!
OH MY GOD, *THOUSANDS* OF THEM!

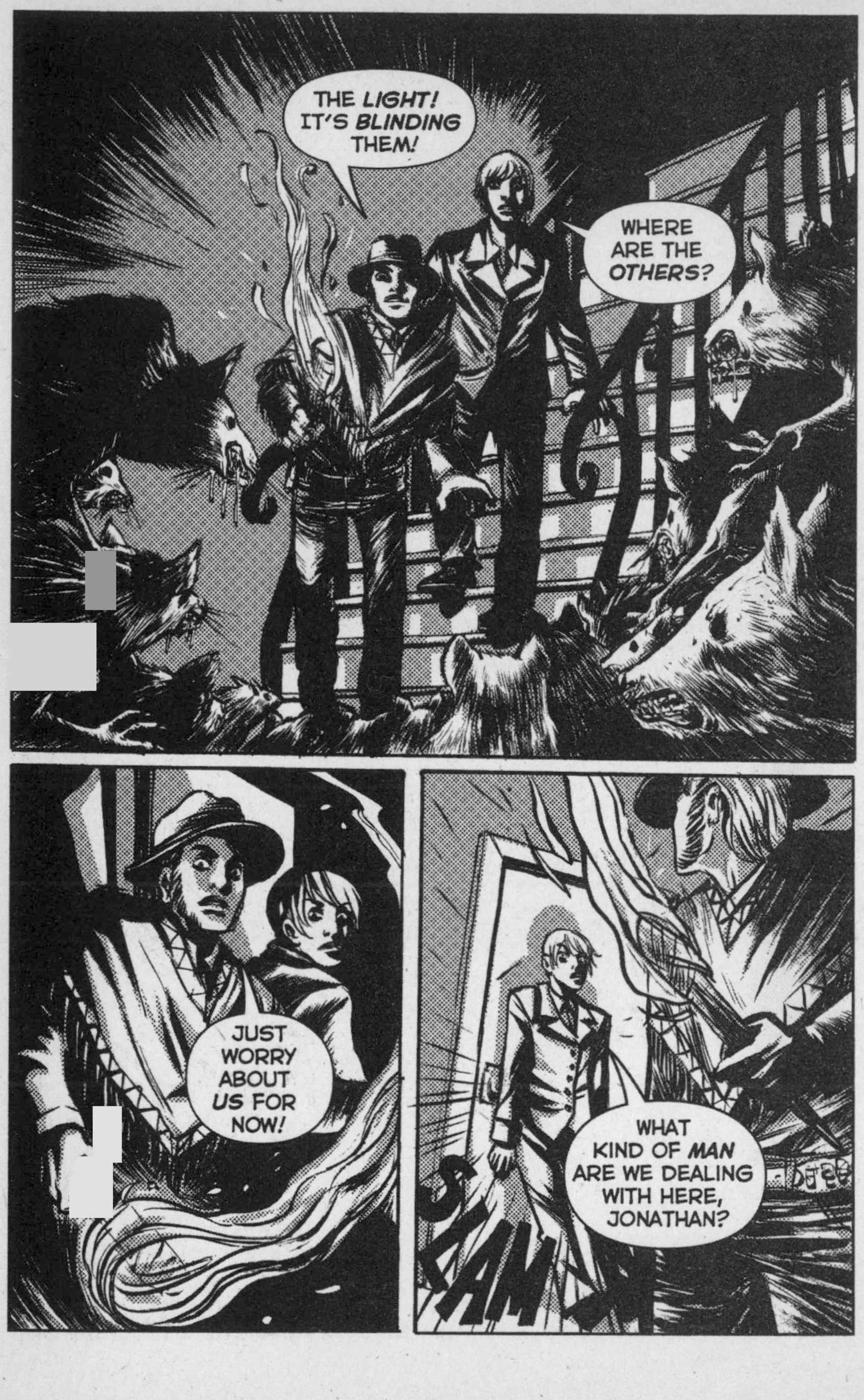
THE *LIGHT!* IT'S *BLINDING* THEM!
WHERE ARE THE *OTHERS?*
JUST WORRY ABOUT *US* FOR NOW!
SLAM
WHAT KIND OF *MAN* ARE WE DEALING WITH HERE, JONATHAN?

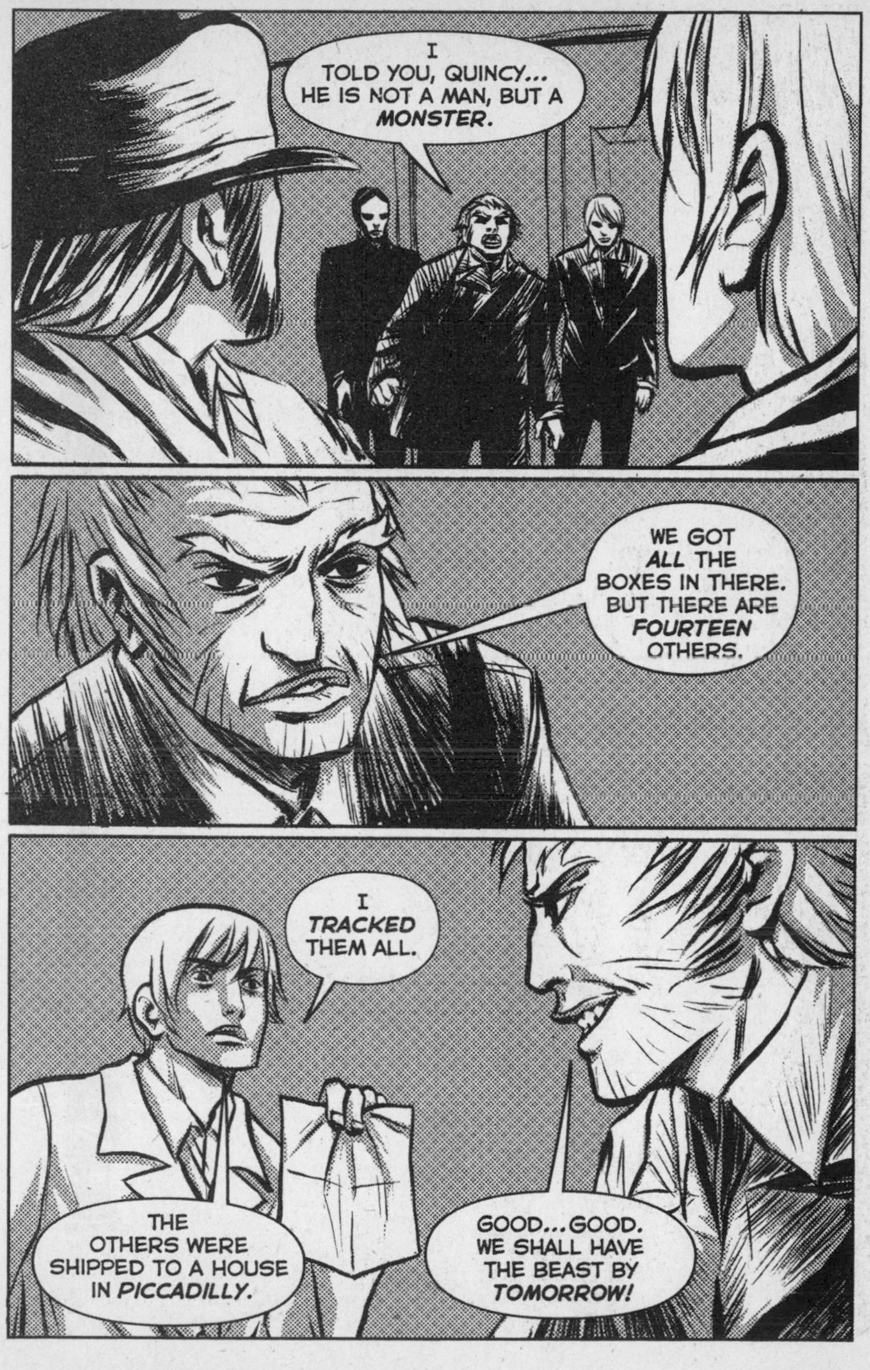
I TOLD YOU, QUINCY... HE IS NOT A MAN, BUT A MONSTER.
WE GOT ALL THE BOXES IN THERE. BUT THERE ARE FOURTEEN OTHERS.
I TRACKED THEM ALL.
THE OTHERS WERE SHIPPED TO A HOUSE IN PICCADILLY.
GOOD...GOOD. WE SHALL HAVE THE BEAST BY TOMORROW!

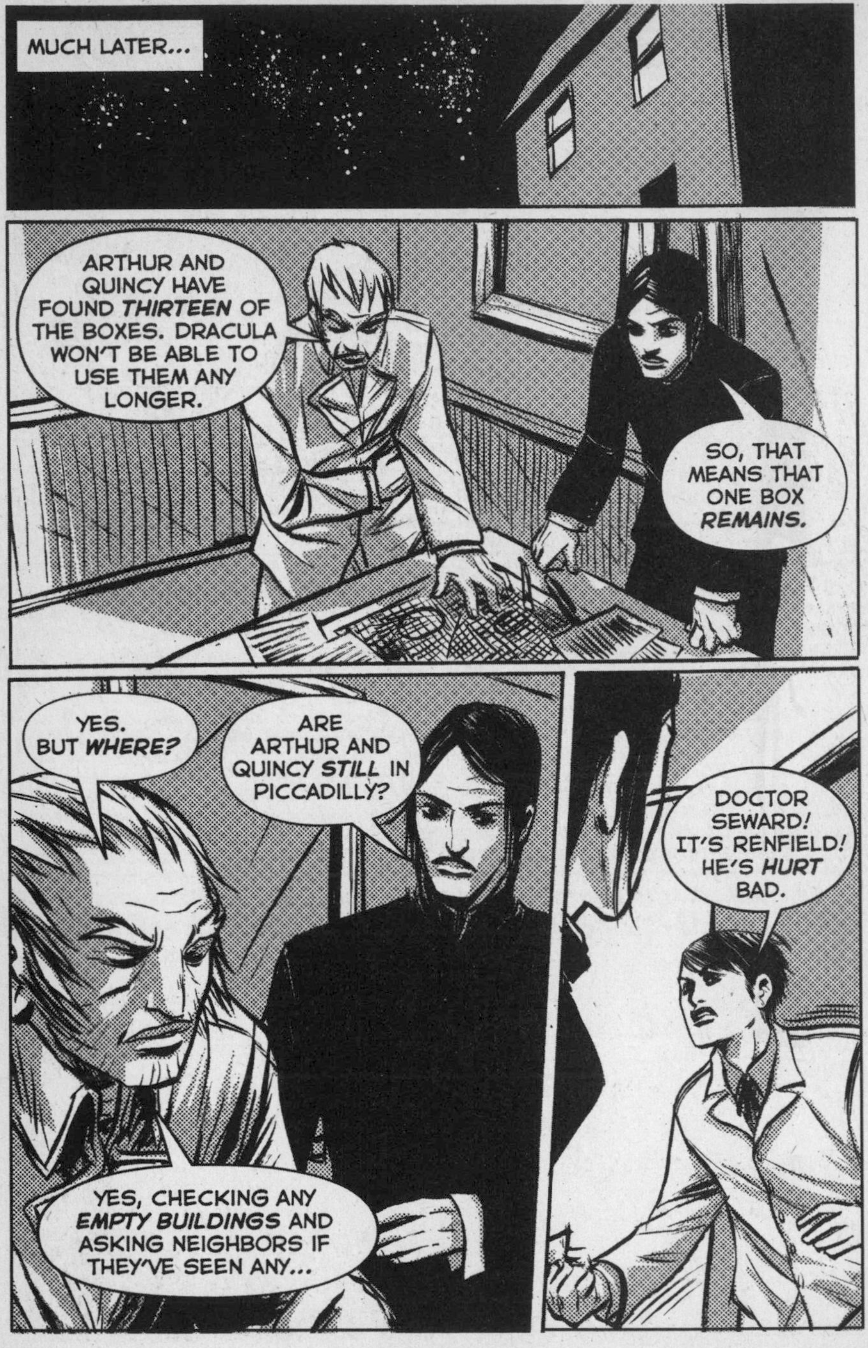
MUCH LATER...
ARTHUR AND QUINCY HAVE FOUND *THIRTEEN* OF THE BOXES. DRACULA WON'T BE ABLE TO USE THEM ANY LONGER.
SO, THAT MEANS THAT ONE BOX *REMAINS.*
YES. BUT *WHERE?*
ARE ARTHUR AND QUINCY *STILL* IN PICCADILLY?
YES, CHECKING ANY *EMPTY BUILDINGS* AND ASKING NEIGHBORS IF THEY'VE SEEN ANY...
DOCTOR SEWARD! IT'S RENFIELD! HE'S *HURT* BAD.

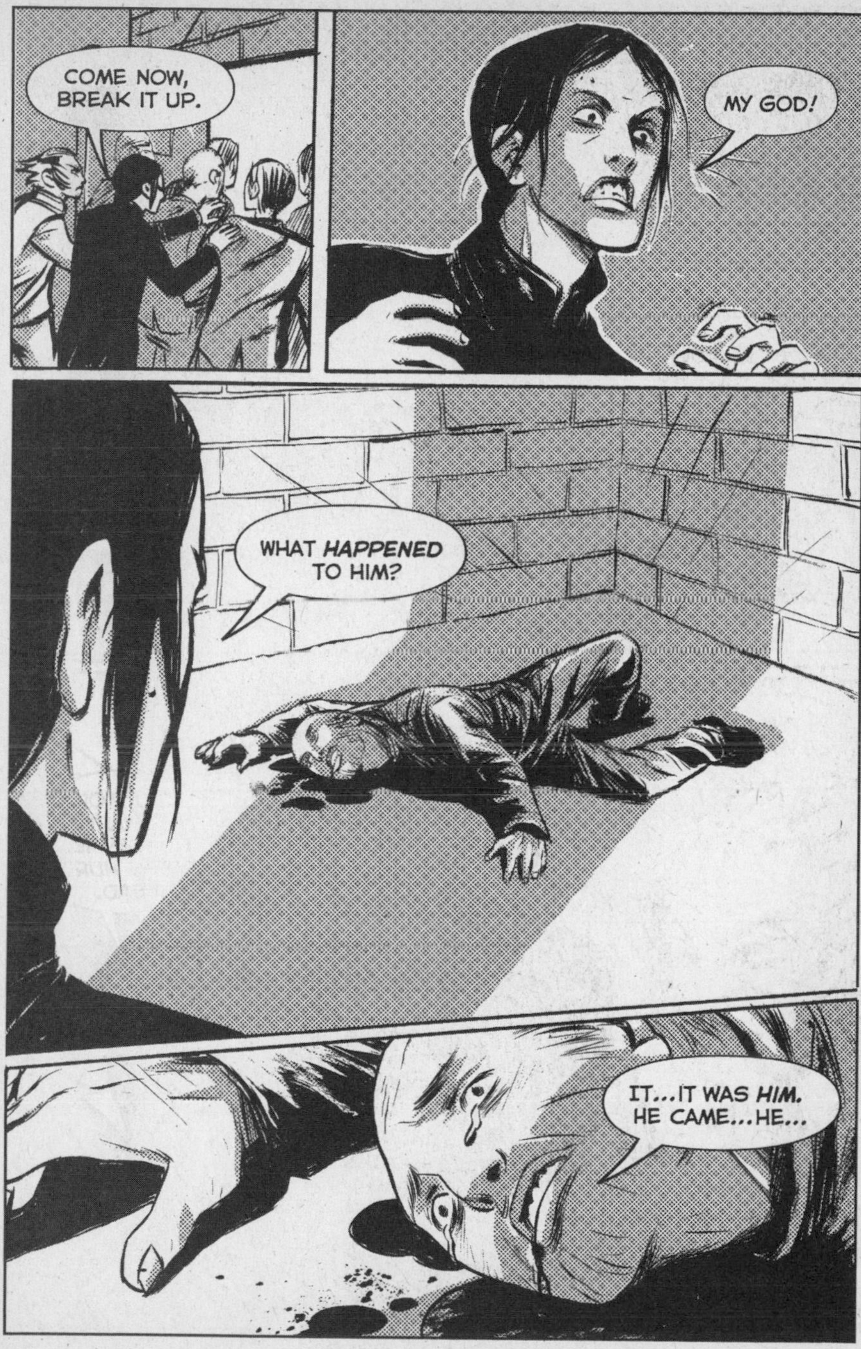
COME NOW, BREAK IT UP.
MY GOD!
WHAT *HAPPENED* TO HIM?
IT...IT WAS *HIM.* HE CAME...HE...

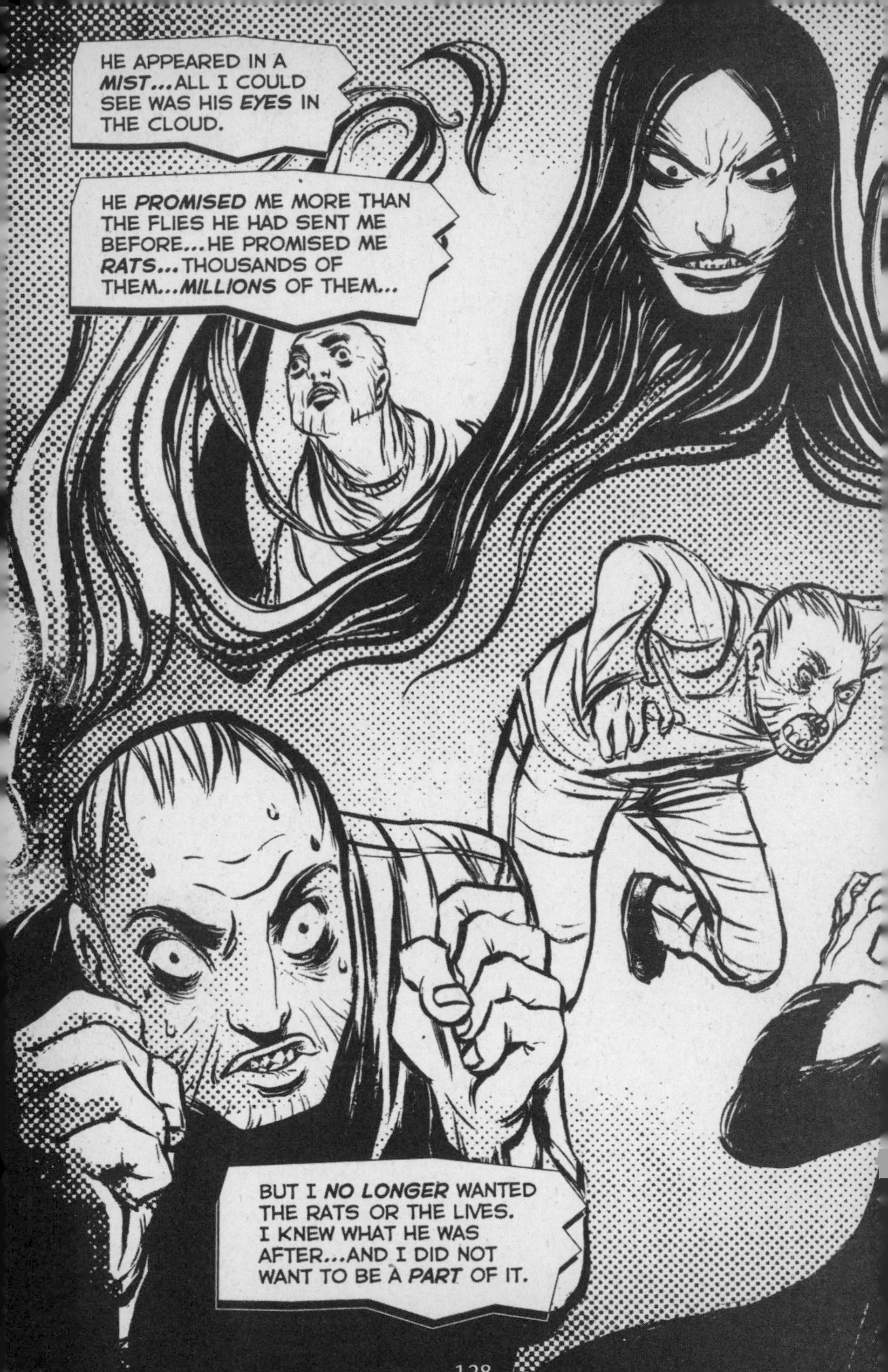
HE APPEARED IN A MIST...ALL I COULD SEE WAS HIS EYES IN THE CLOUD.
HE PROMISED ME MORE THAN THE FLIES HE HAD SENT ME BEFORE...HE PROMISED ME RATS...THOUSANDS OF THEM...MILLIONS OF THEM...
BUT I NO LONGER WANTED THE RATS OR THE LIVES. I KNEW WHAT HE WAS AFTER...AND I DID NOT WANT TO BE A PART OF IT.

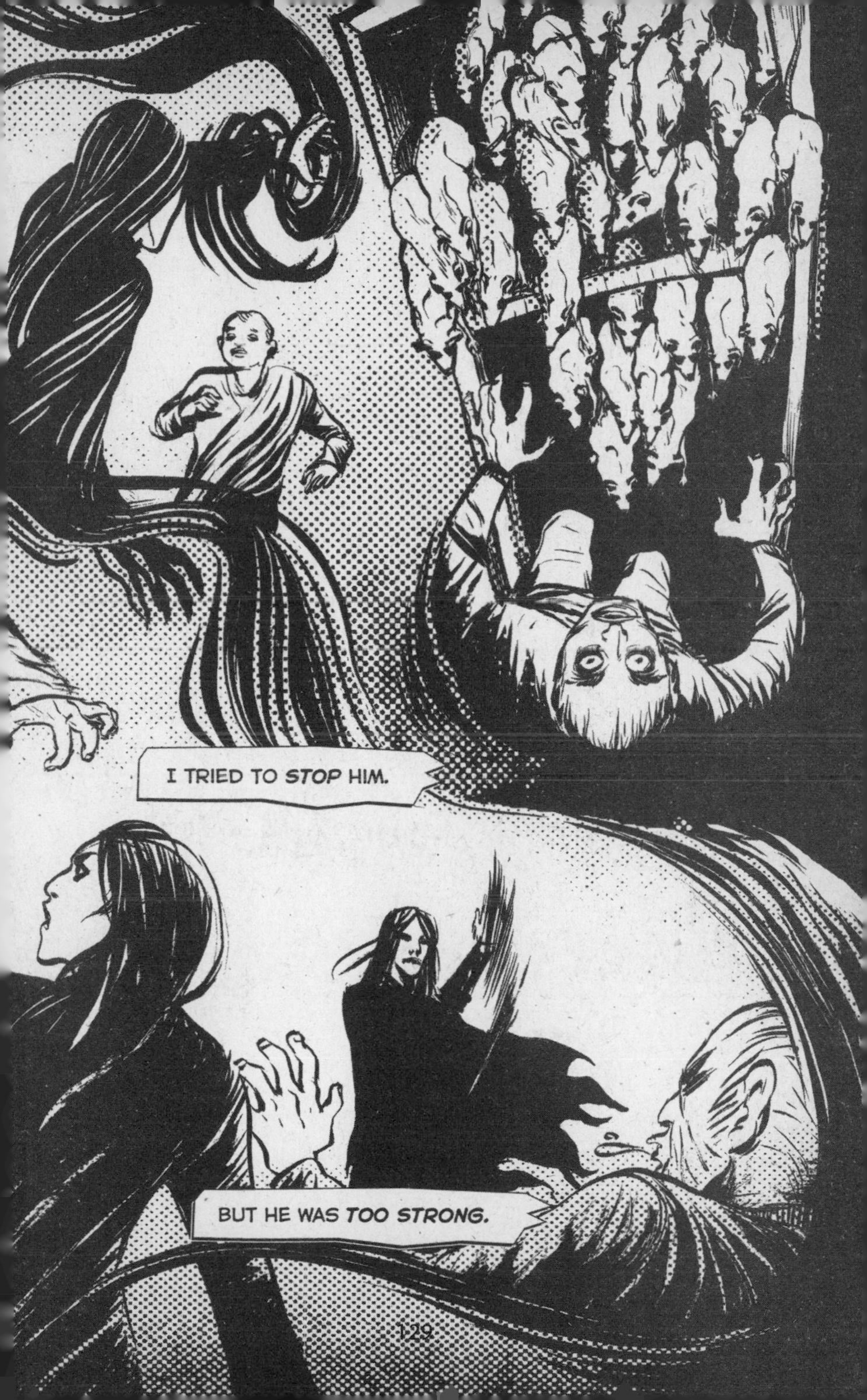
I TRIED TO STOP HIM.
BUT HE WAS TOO STRONG.

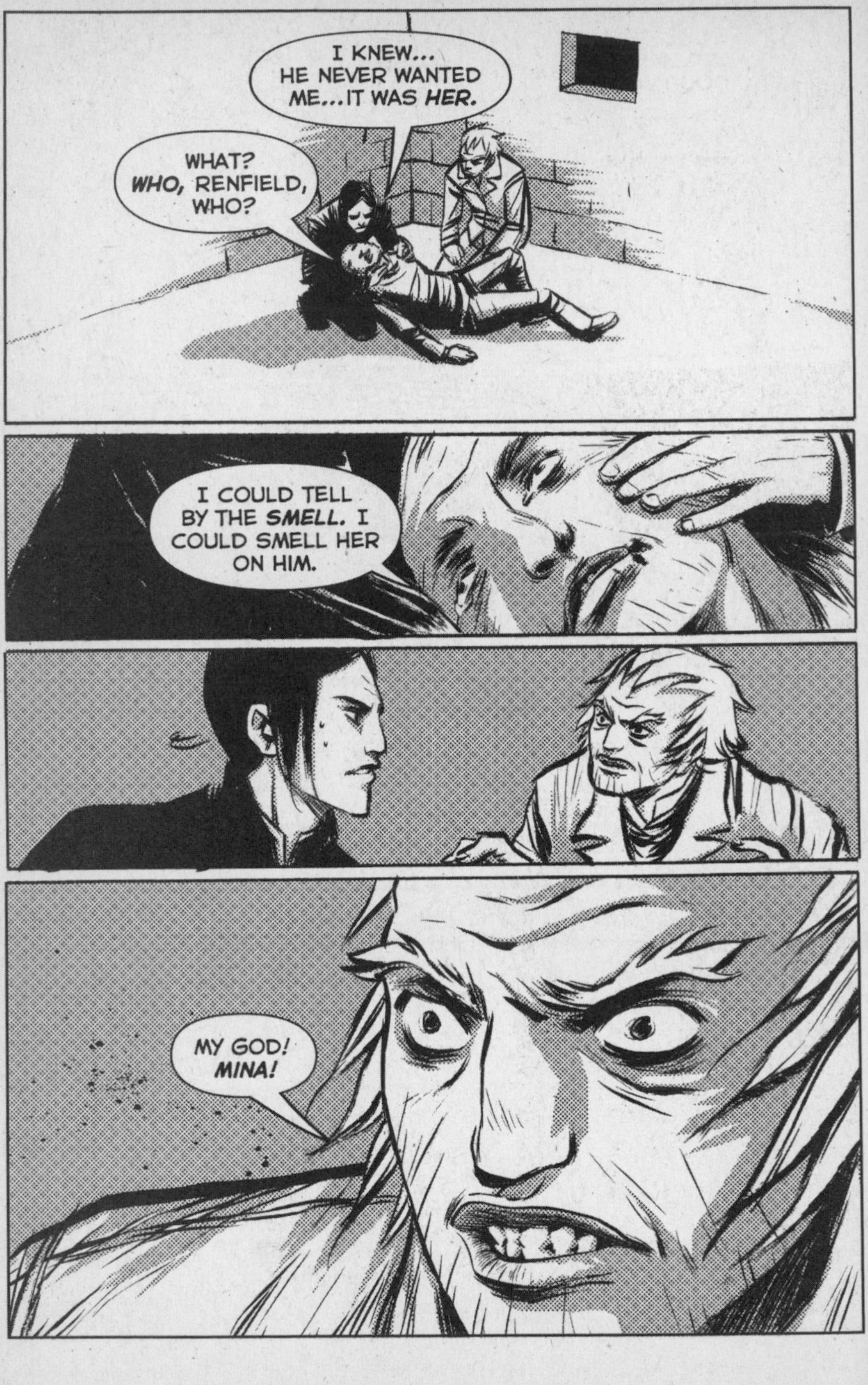
I KNEW...
HE NEVER WANTED
ME...IT WAS HER.
WHAT?
WHO, RENFIELD,
WHO?
I COULD TELL
BY THE SMELL. I
COULD SMELL HER
ON HIM.
MY GOD!
MINA!

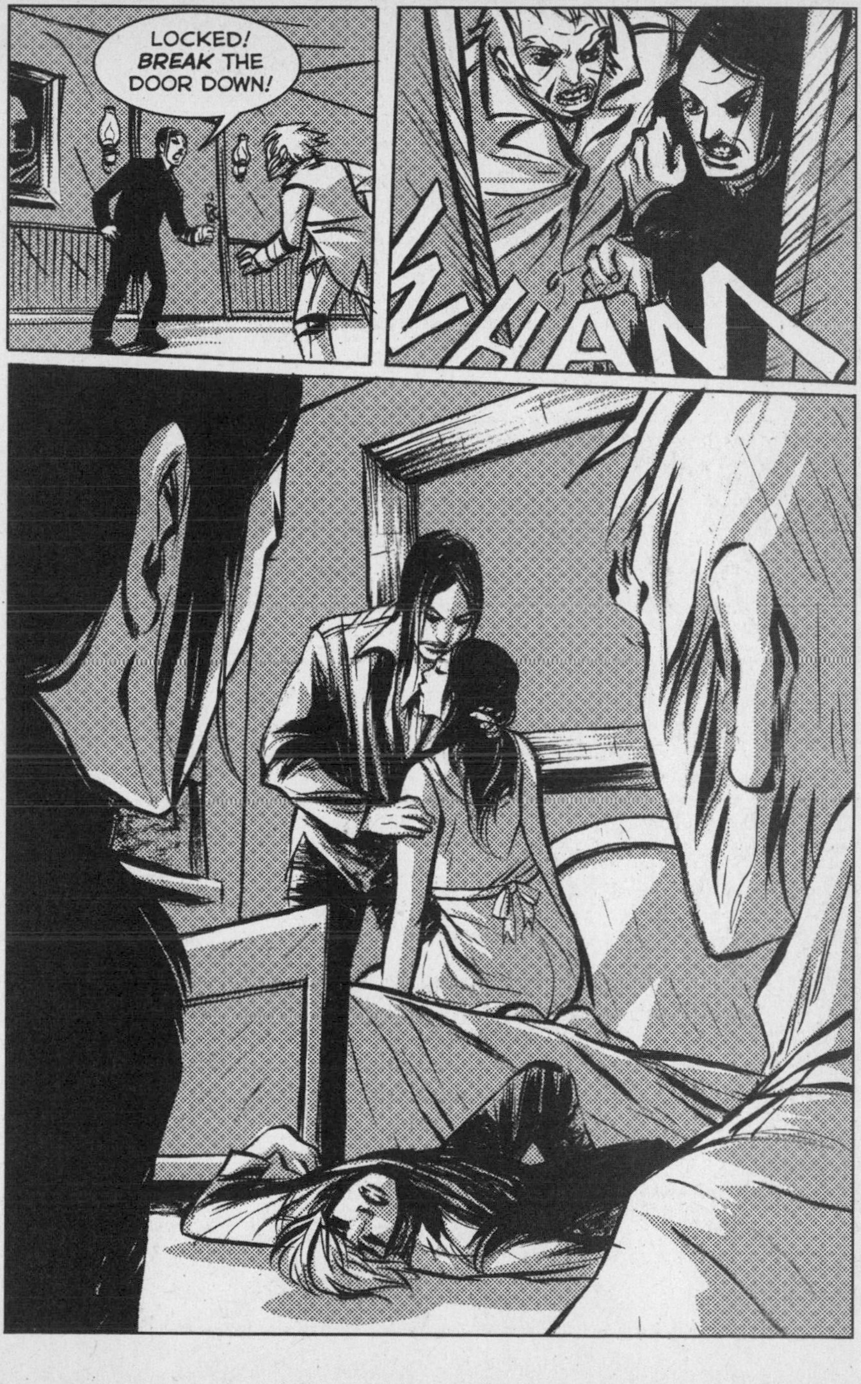
LOCKED! BREAK THE DOOR DOWN!
WHAM

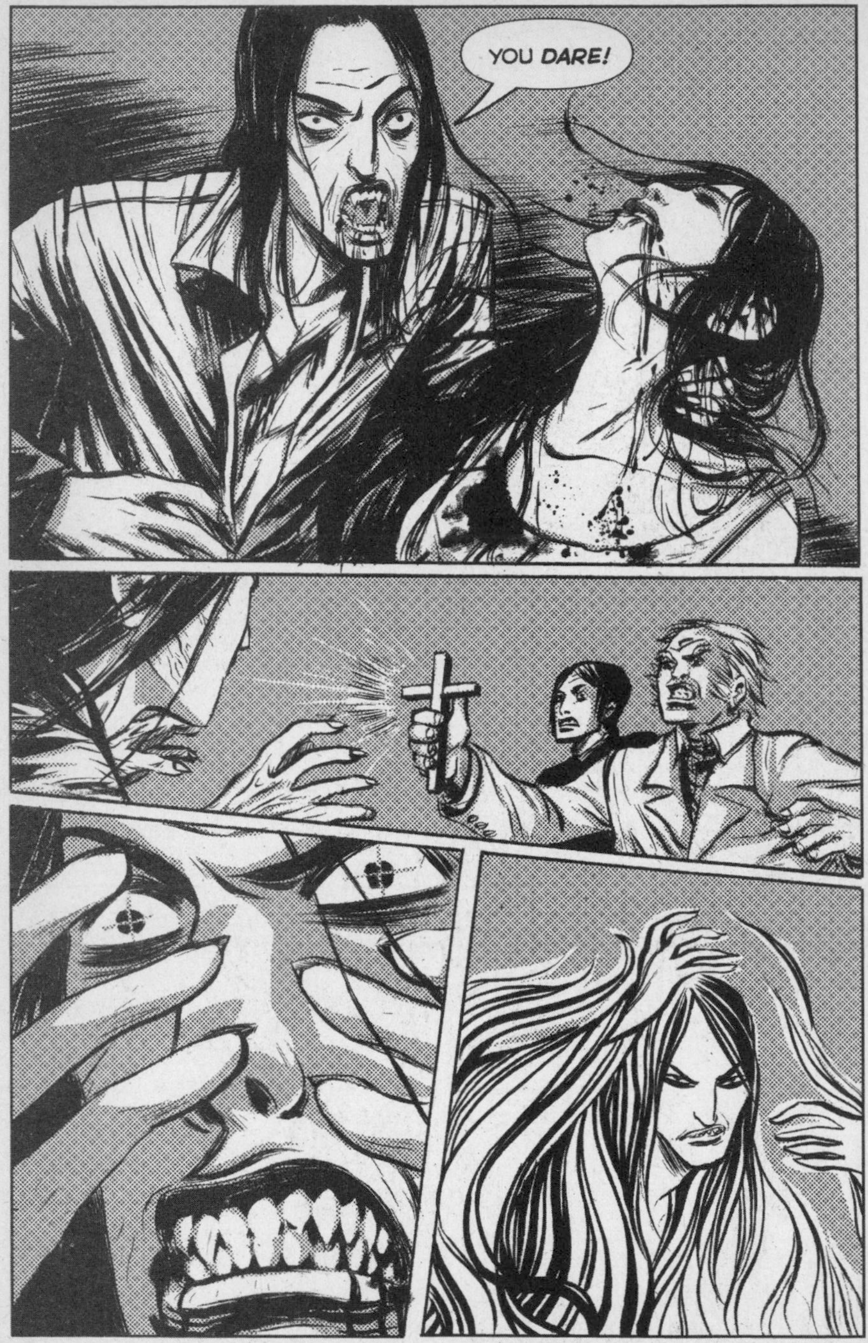
YOU DARE!

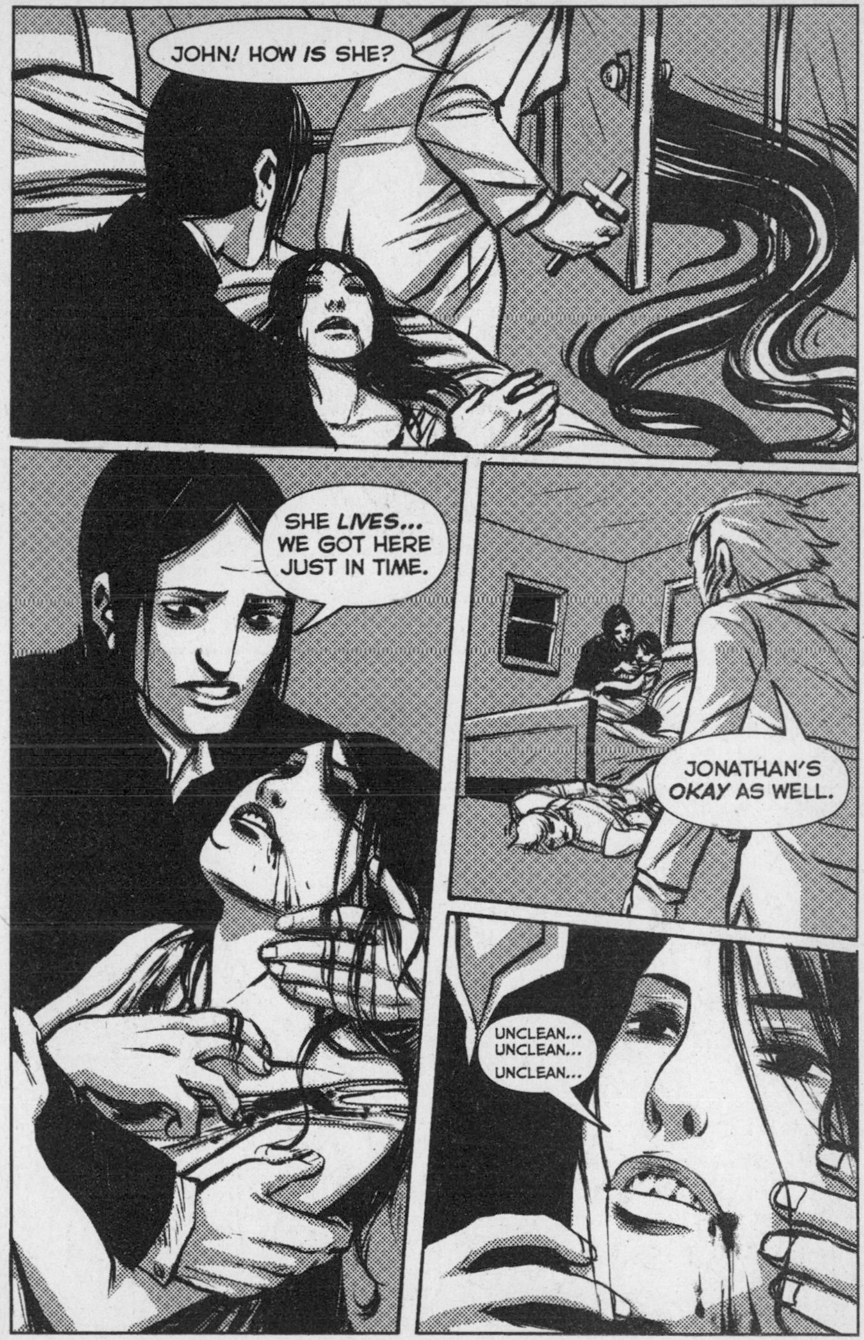
JOHN! HOW IS SHE?
SHE LIVES... WE GOT HERE JUST IN TIME.
JONATHAN'S OKAY AS WELL.
UNCLEAN... UNCLEAN... UNCLEAN...

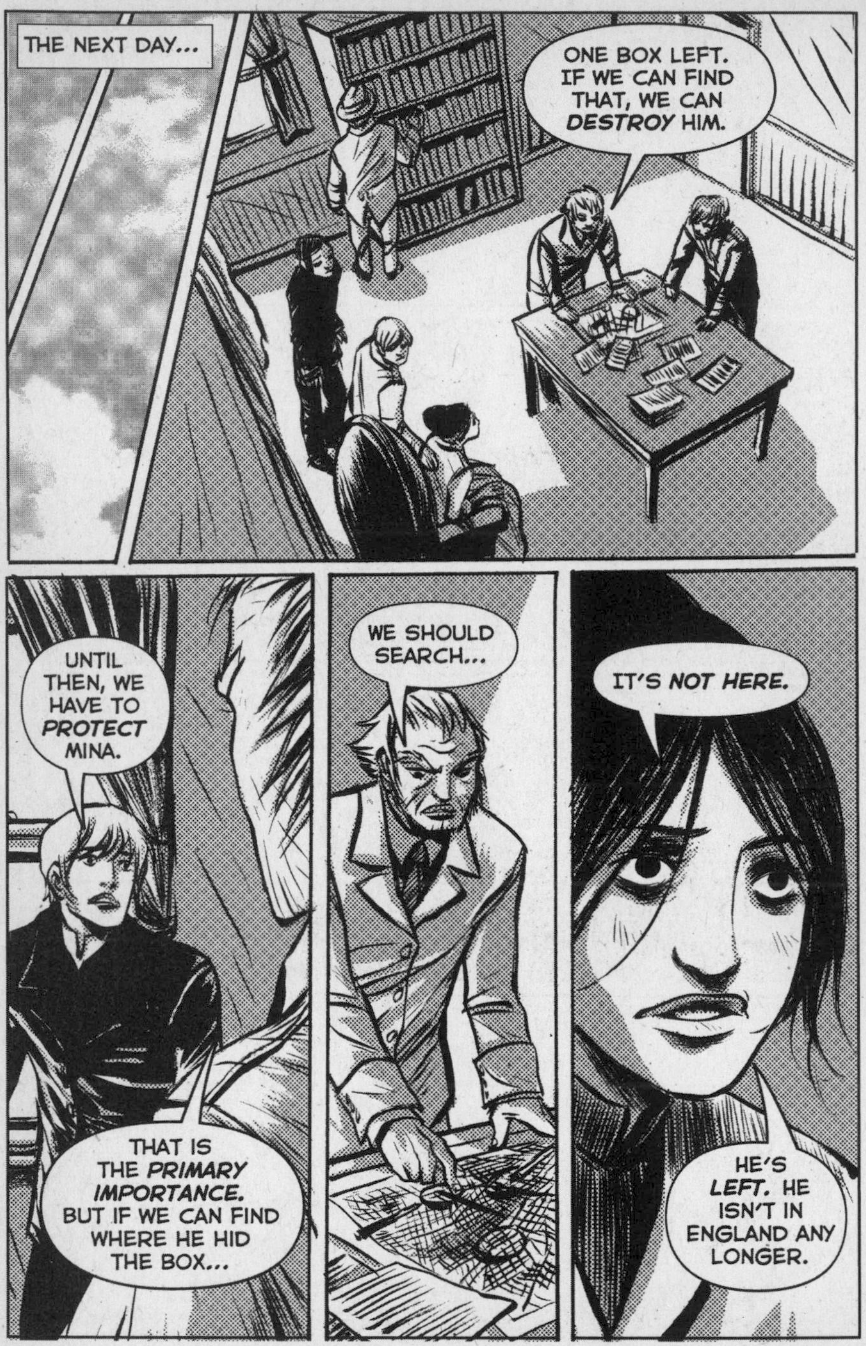
THE NEXT DAY...
ONE BOX LEFT. IF WE CAN FIND THAT, WE CAN DESTROY HIM.
UNTIL THEN, WE HAVE TO PROTECT MINA.
THAT IS THE PRIMARY IMPORTANCE. BUT IF WE CAN FIND WHERE HE HID THE BOX...
WE SHOULD SEARCH...
IT'S NOT HERE.
HE'S LEFT. HE ISN'T IN ENGLAND ANY LONGER.

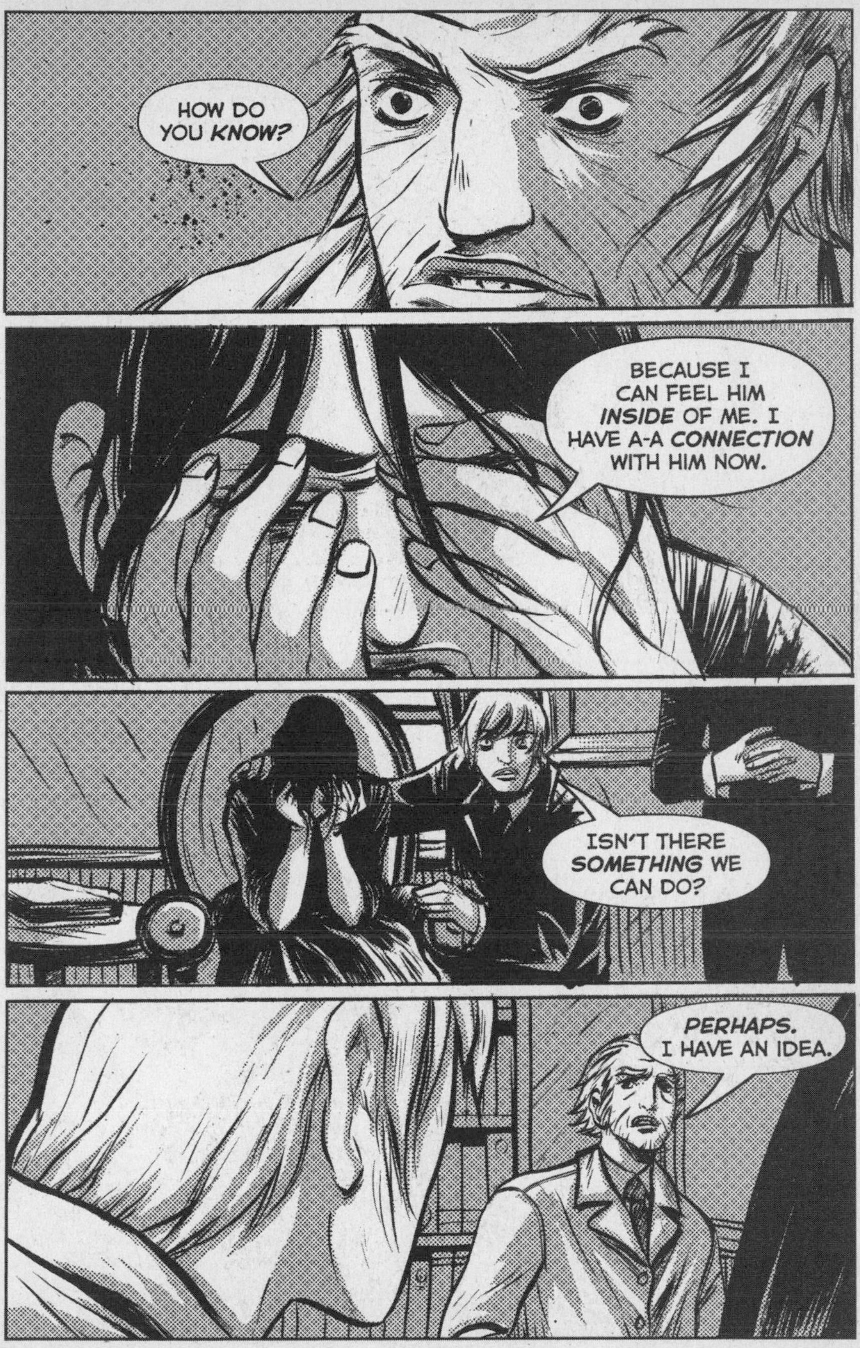
HOW DO YOU *KNOW?*
BECAUSE I CAN FEEL HIM *INSIDE* OF ME. I HAVE A-A *CONNECTION* WITH HIM NOW.
ISN'T THERE *SOMETHING* WE CAN DO?
PERHAPS. I HAVE AN IDEA.

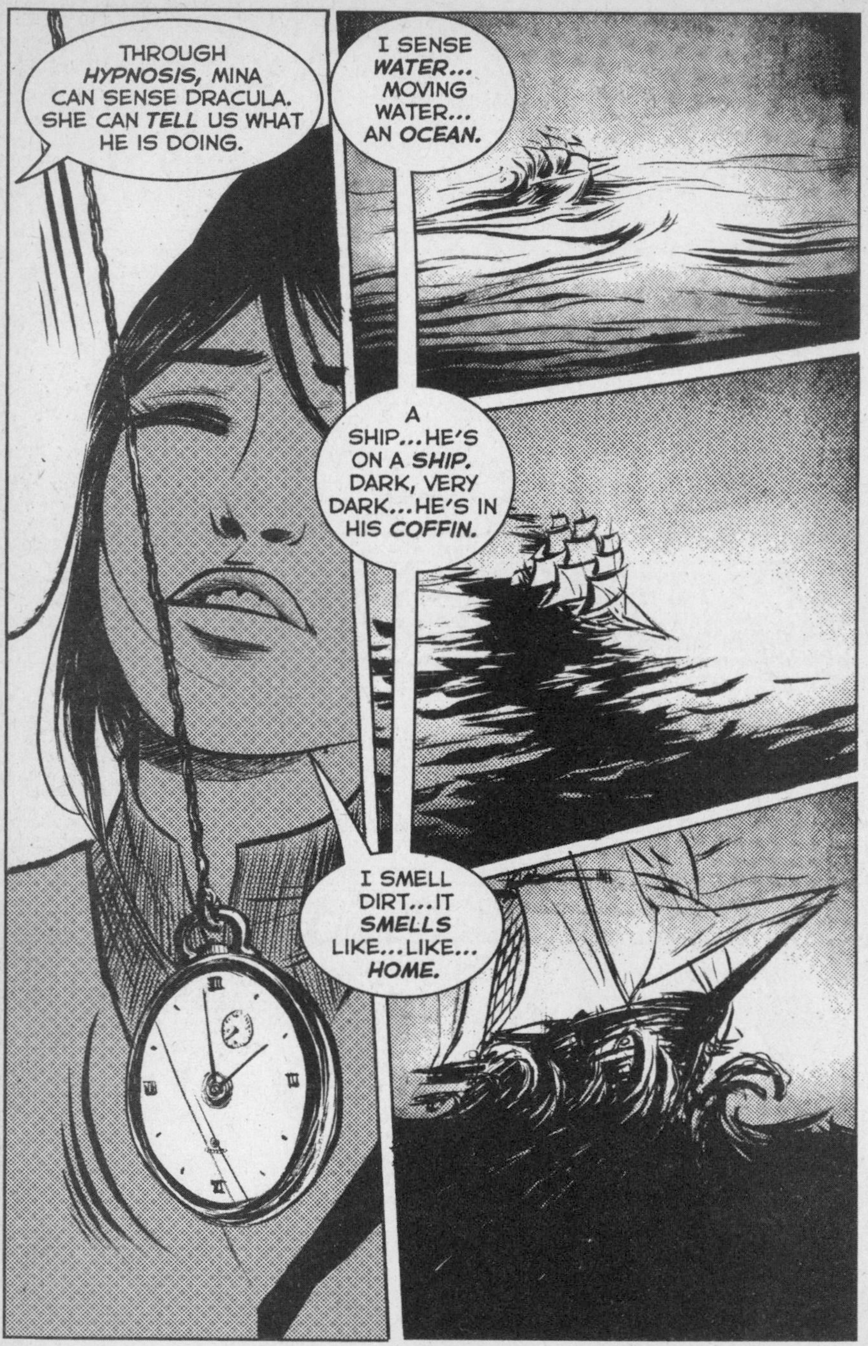
THROUGH HYPNOSIS, MINA CAN SENSE DRACULA. SHE CAN TELL US WHAT HE IS DOING.
I SENSE WATER... MOVING WATER... AN OCEAN.
A SHIP...HE'S ON A SHIP. DARK, VERY DARK...HE'S IN HIS COFFIN.
I SMELL DIRT...IT SMELLS LIKE...LIKE... HOME.

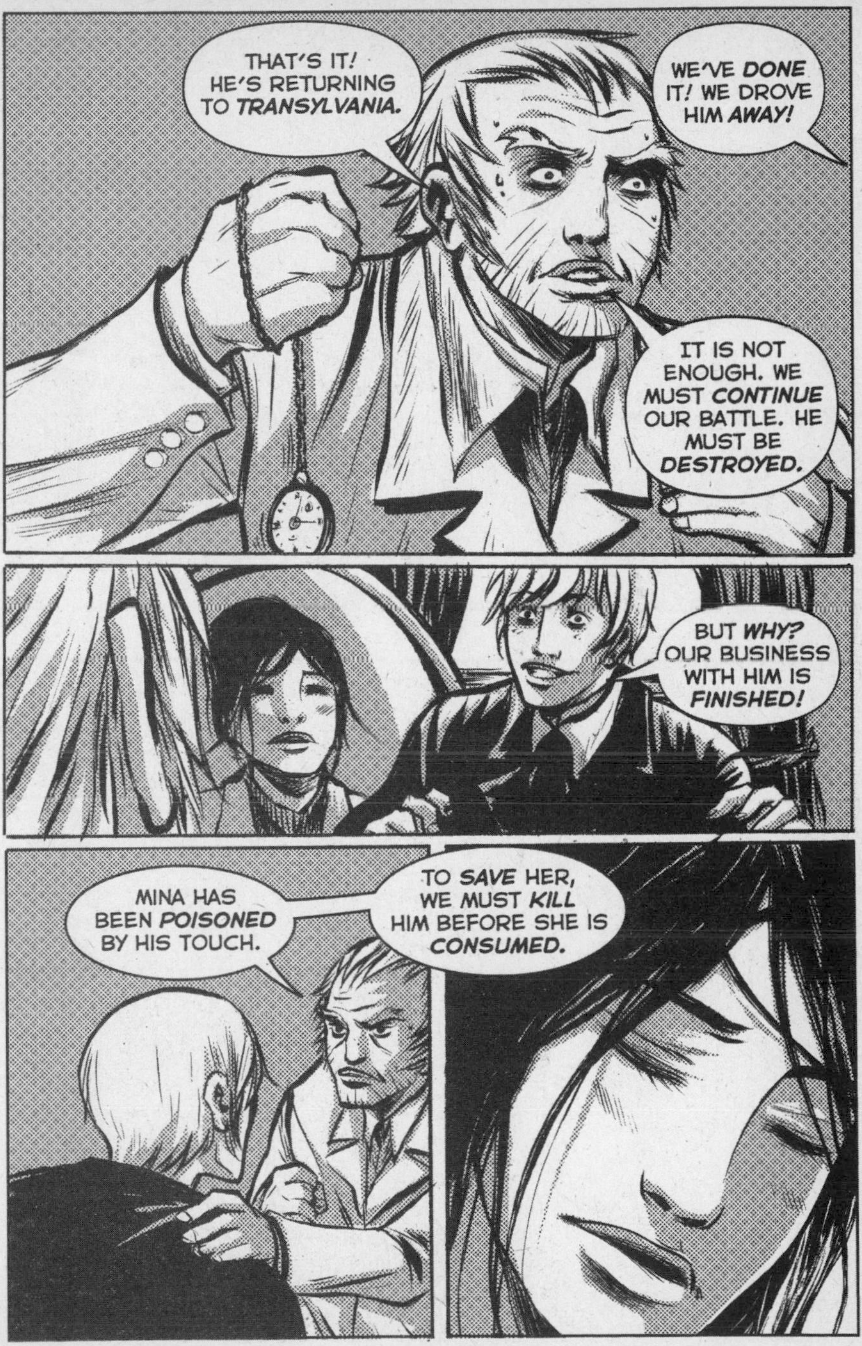
THAT'S IT! HE'S RETURNING TO TRANSYLVANIA.
WE'VE DONE IT! WE DROVE HIM AWAY!
IT IS NOT ENOUGH. WE MUST CONTINUE OUR BATTLE. HE MUST BE DESTROYED.
BUT WHY? OUR BUSINESS WITH HIM IS FINISHED!
MINA HAS BEEN POISONED BY HIS TOUCH.
TO SAVE HER, WE MUST KILL HIM BEFORE SHE IS CONSUMED.

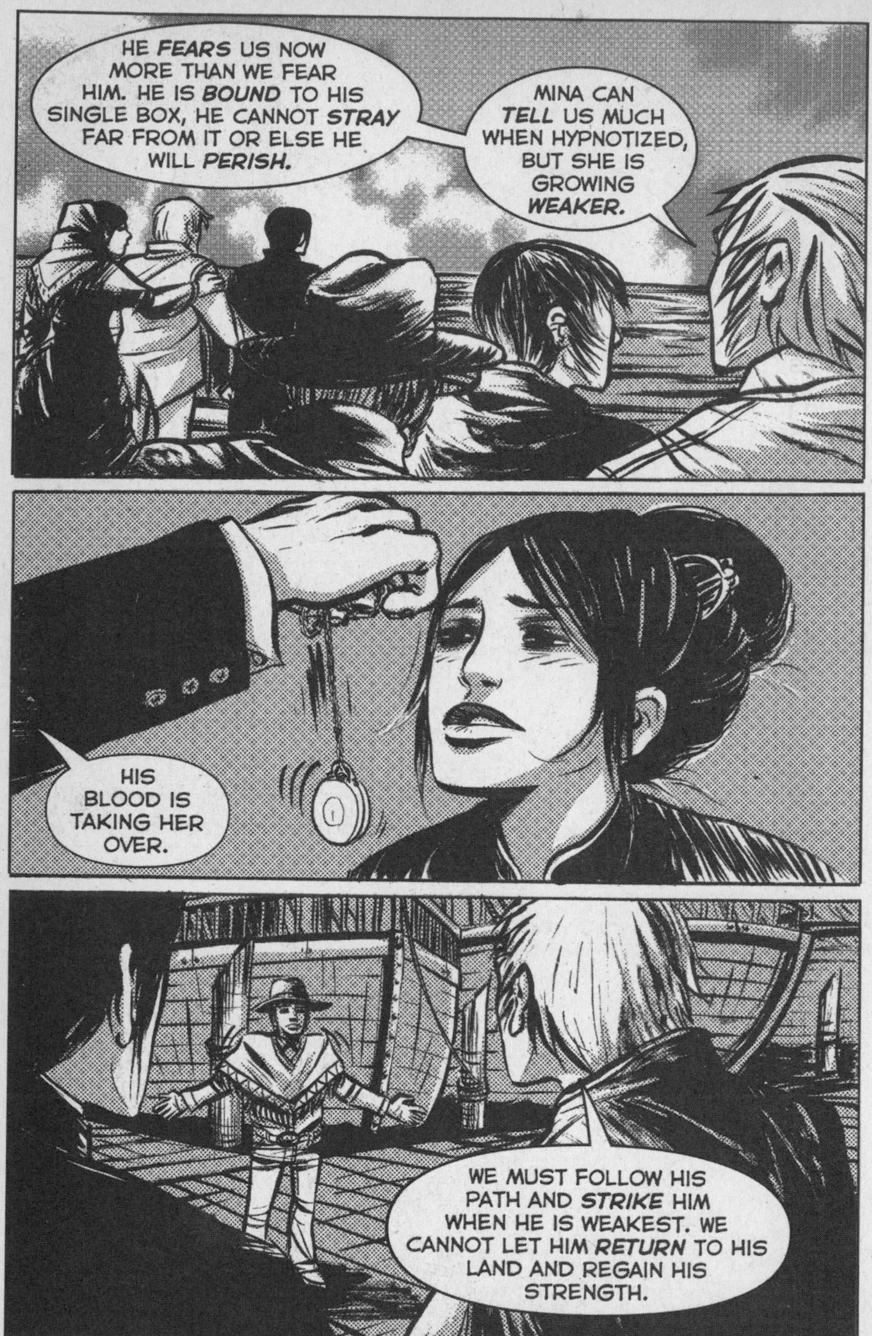
HE FEARS US NOW MORE THAN WE FEAR HIM. HE IS BOUND TO HIS SINGLE BOX, HE CANNOT STRAY FAR FROM IT OR ELSE HE WILL PERISH.
MINA CAN TELL US MUCH WHEN HYPNOTIZED, BUT SHE IS GROWING WEAKER.
HIS BLOOD IS TAKING HER OVER.
WE MUST FOLLOW HIS PATH AND STRIKE HIM WHEN HE IS WEAKEST. WE CANNOT LET HIM RETURN TO HIS LAND AND REGAIN HIS STRENGTH.

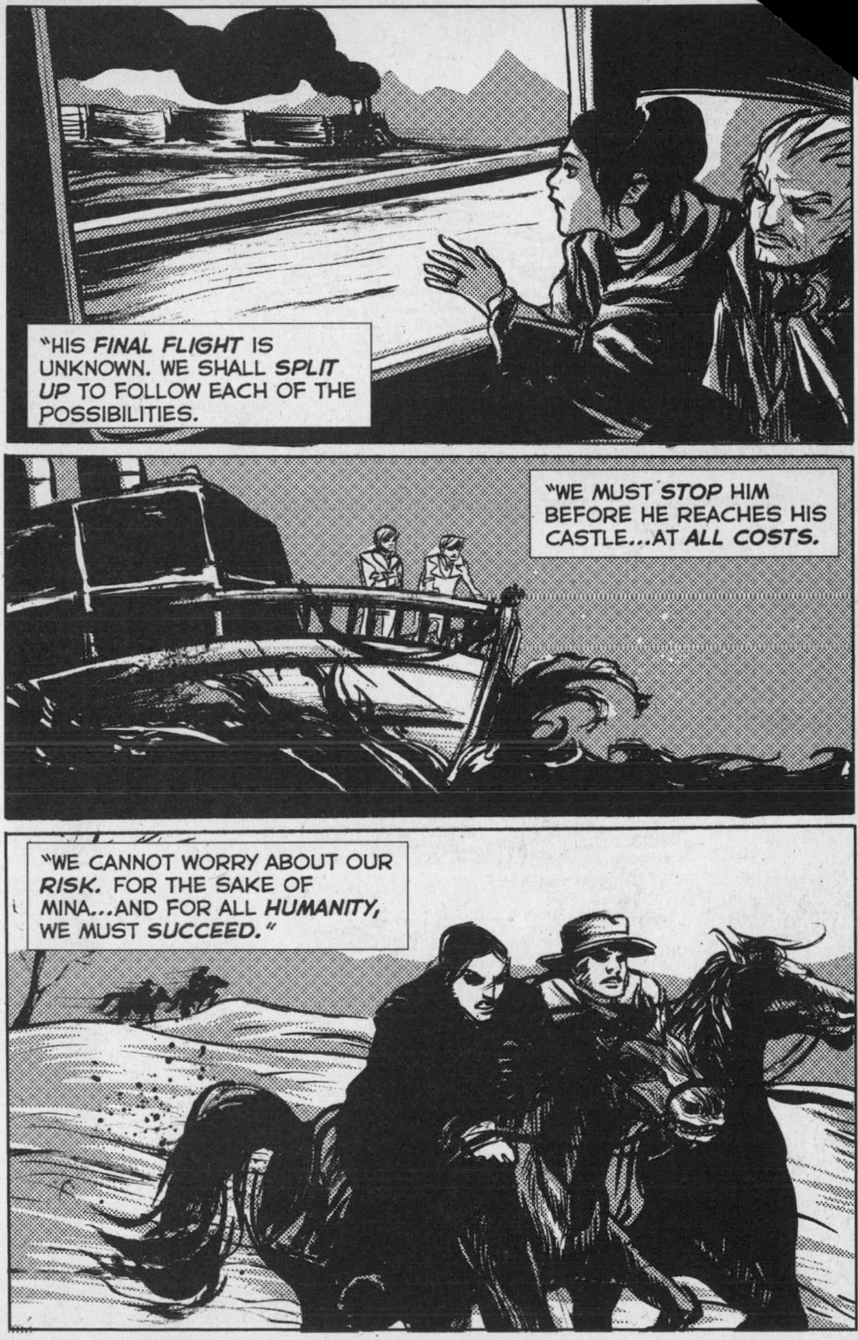
"HIS FINAL FLIGHT IS UNKNOWN. WE SHALL SPLIT UP TO FOLLOW EACH OF THE POSSIBILITIES.
"WE MUST STOP HIM BEFORE HE REACHES HIS CASTLE...AT ALL COSTS.
"WE CANNOT WORRY ABOUT OUR RISK. FOR THE SAKE OF MINA...AND FOR ALL HUMANITY, WE MUST SUCCEED."

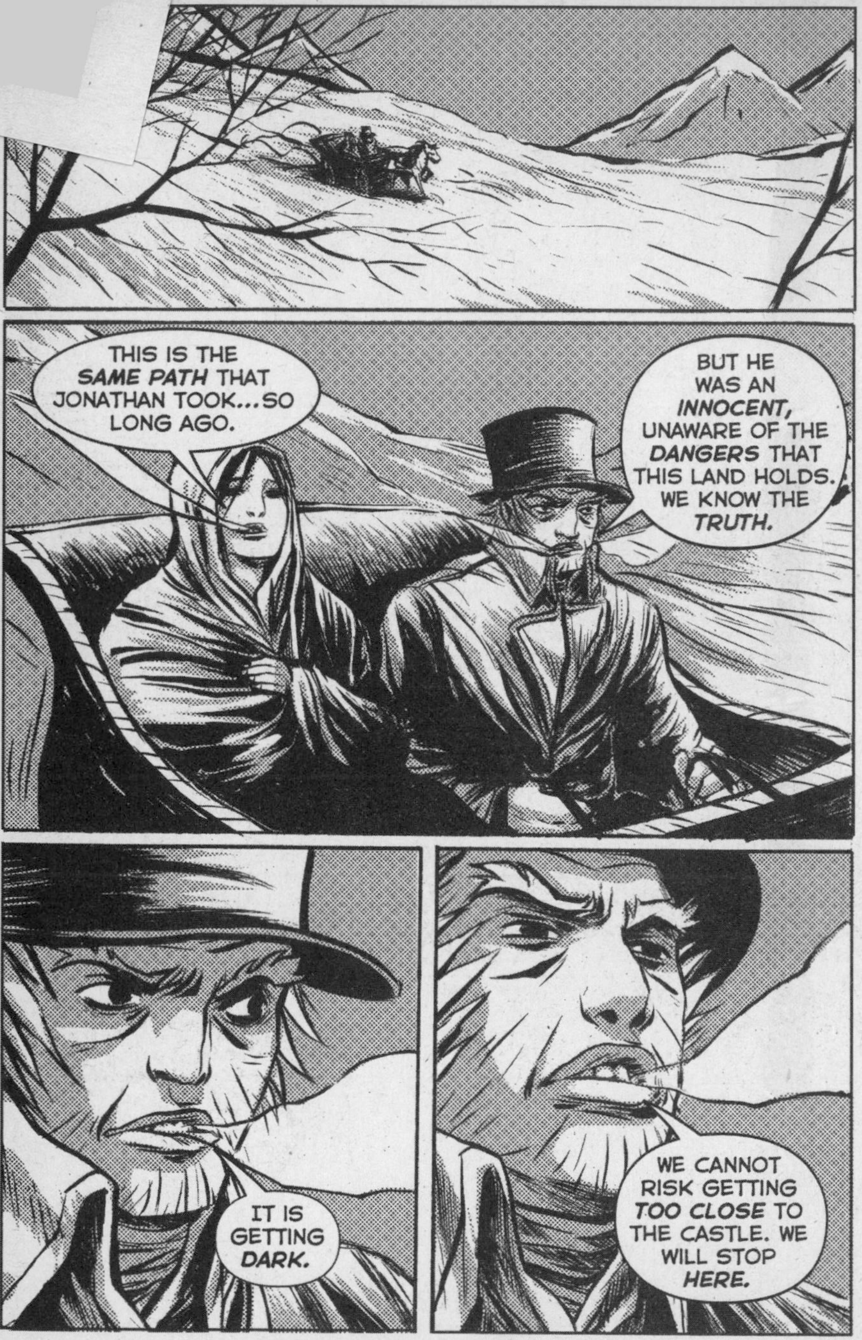

THIS IS THE SAME PATH THAT JONATHAN TOOK...SO LONG AGO.
BUT HE WAS AN INNOCENT, UNAWARE OF THE DANGERS THAT THIS LAND HOLDS. WE KNOW THE TRUTH.
IT IS GETTING DARK.
WE CANNOT RISK GETTING TOO CLOSE TO THE CASTLE. WE WILL STOP HERE.

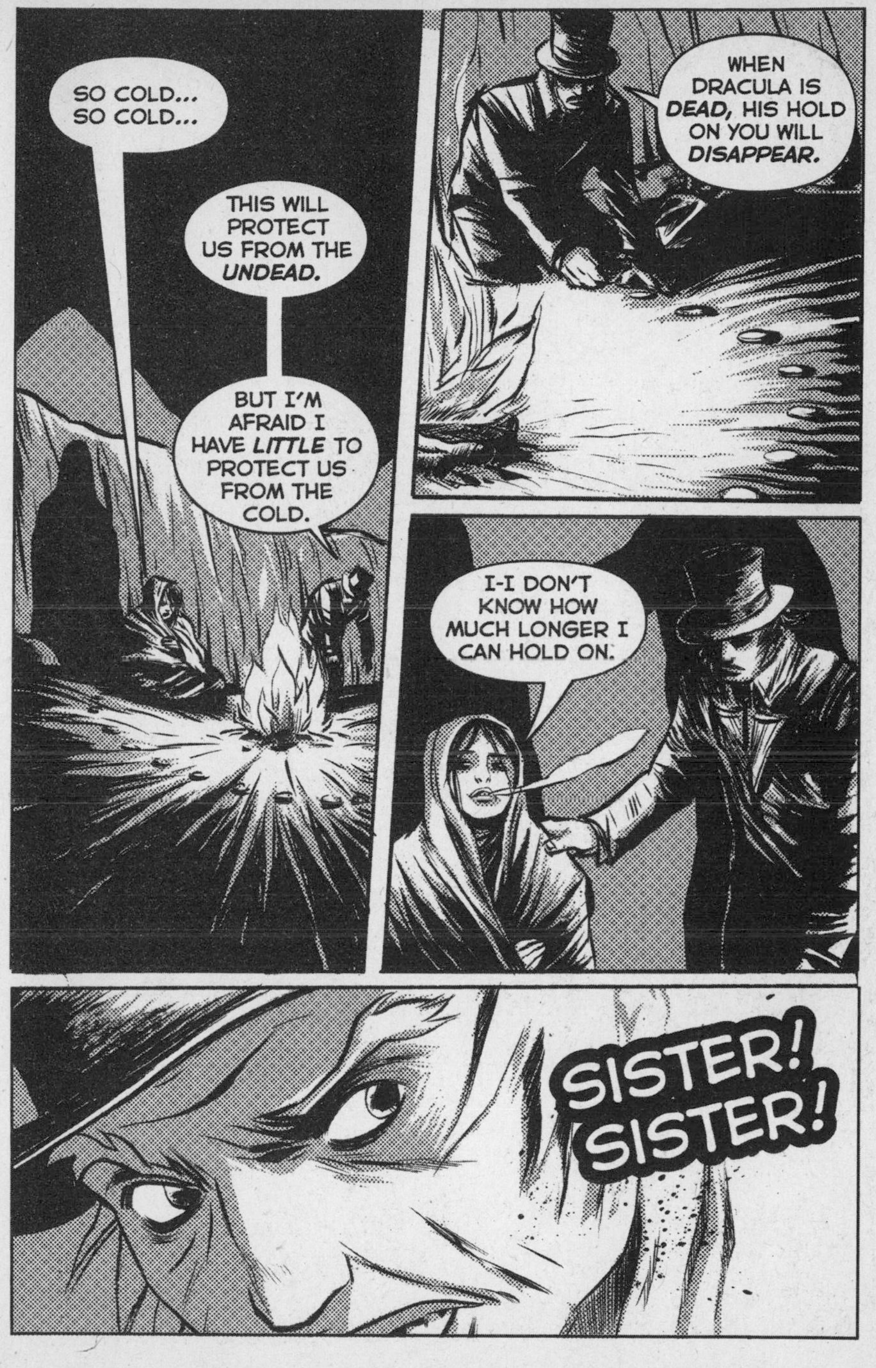
SO COLD... SO COLD...
THIS WILL PROTECT US FROM THE UNDEAD.
BUT I'M AFRAID I HAVE LITTLE TO PROTECT US FROM THE COLD.
WHEN DRACULA IS DEAD, HIS HOLD ON YOU WILL DISAPPEAR.
I-I DON'T KNOW HOW MUCH LONGER I CAN HOLD ON.
SISTER! SISTER!

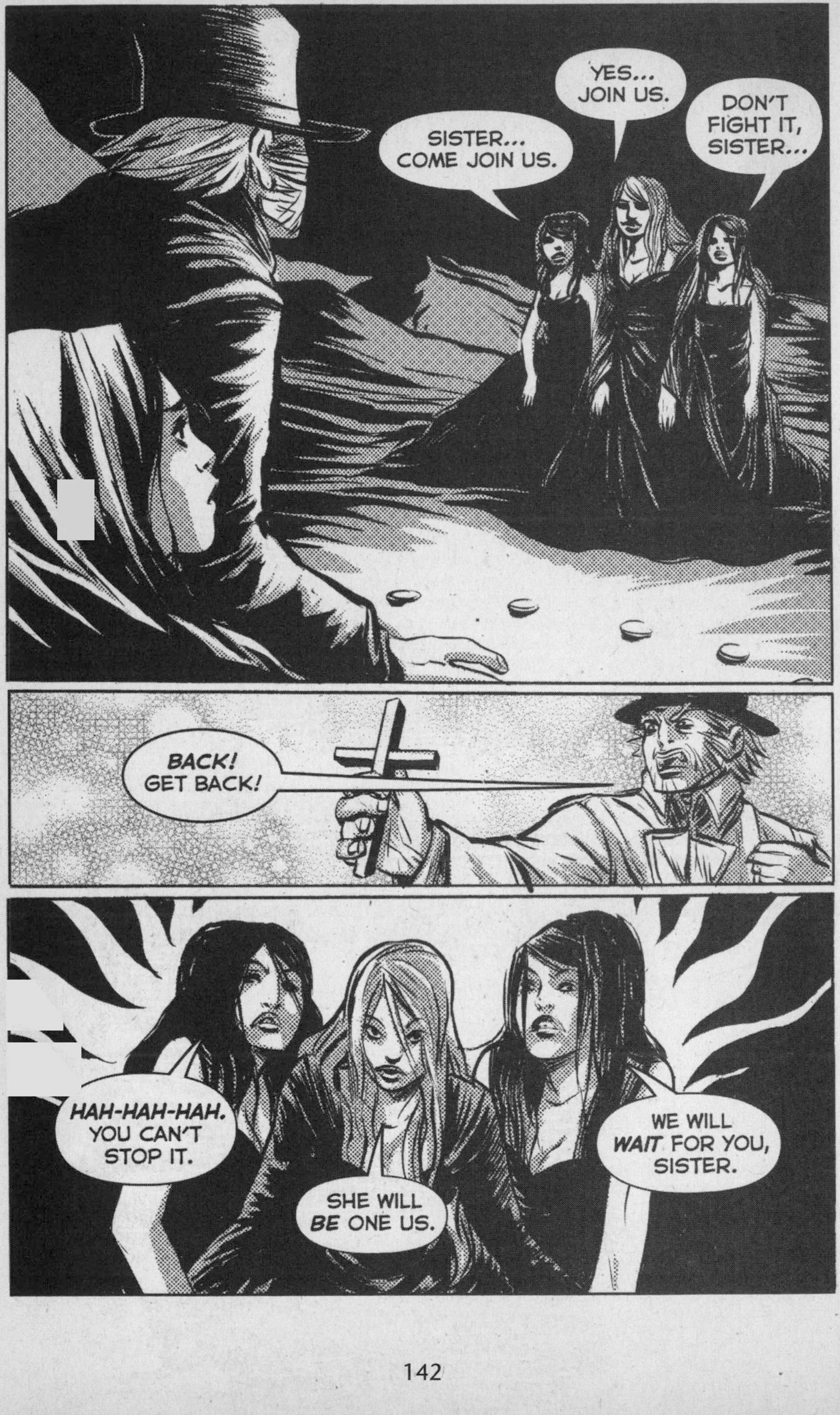
SISTER... COME JOIN US.
YES... JOIN US.
DON'T FIGHT IT, SISTER...
BACK! GET BACK!
HAH-HAH-HAH. YOU CAN'T STOP IT.
SHE WILL BE ONE US.
WE WILL WAIT FOR YOU, SISTER.

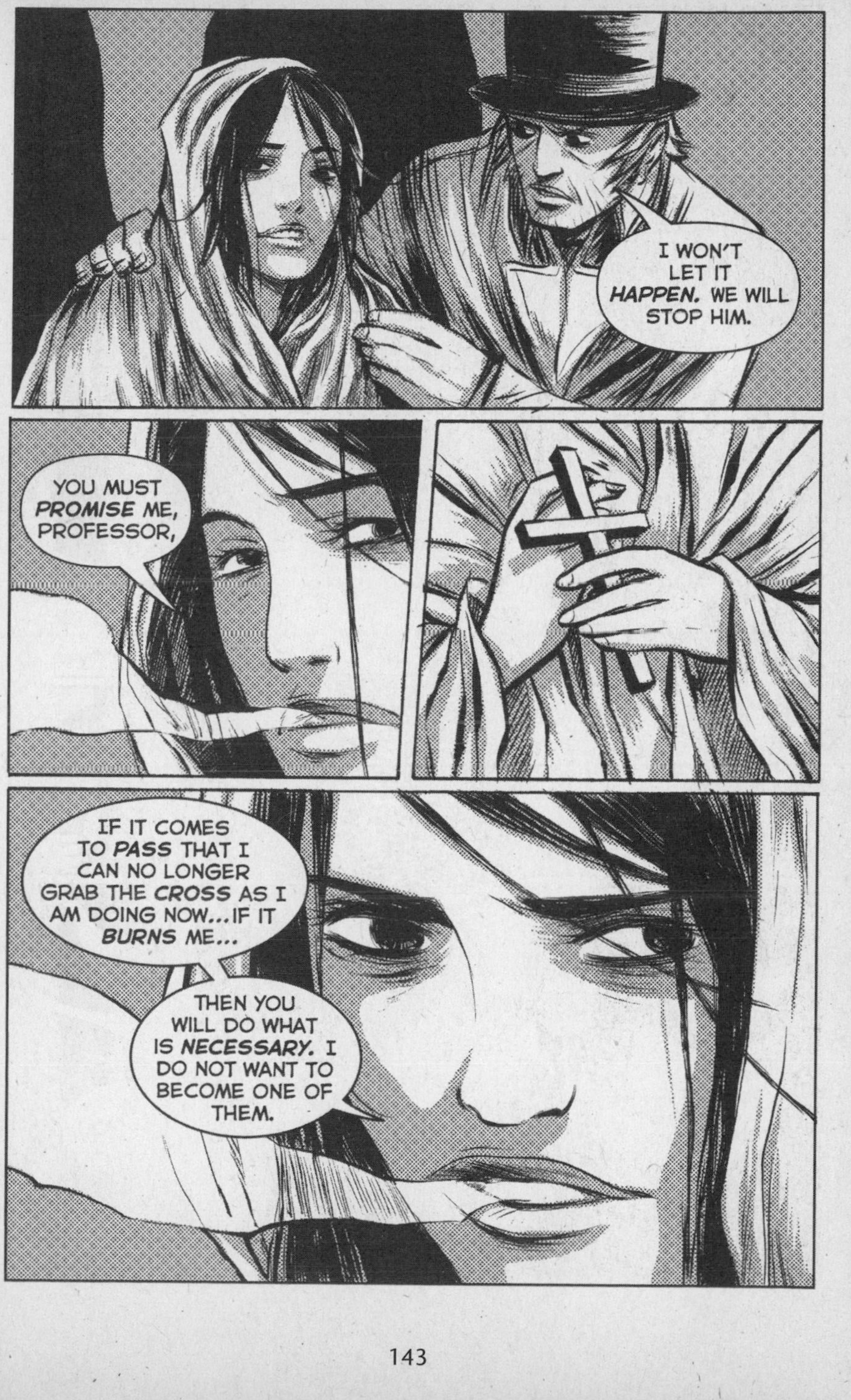
I WON'T LET IT HAPPEN. WE WILL STOP HIM.
YOU MUST PROMISE ME, PROFESSOR,
IF IT COMES TO PASS THAT I CAN NO LONGER GRAB THE CROSS AS I AM DOING NOW...IF IT BURNS ME...
THEN YOU WILL DO WHAT IS NECESSARY. I DO NOT WANT TO BECOME ONE OF THEM.

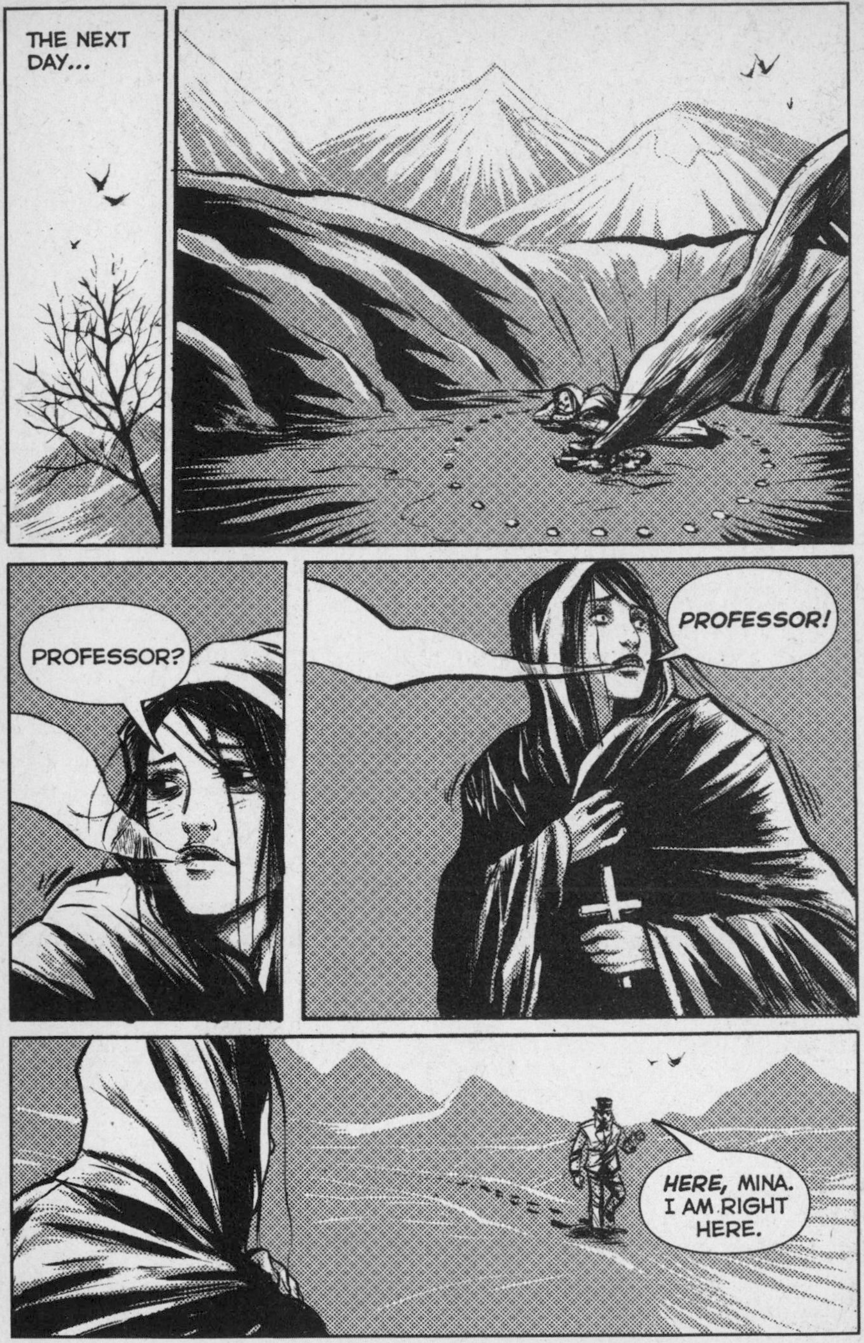
THE NEXT DAY...
PROFESSOR?
PROFESSOR!
HERE, MINA. I AM RIGHT HERE.

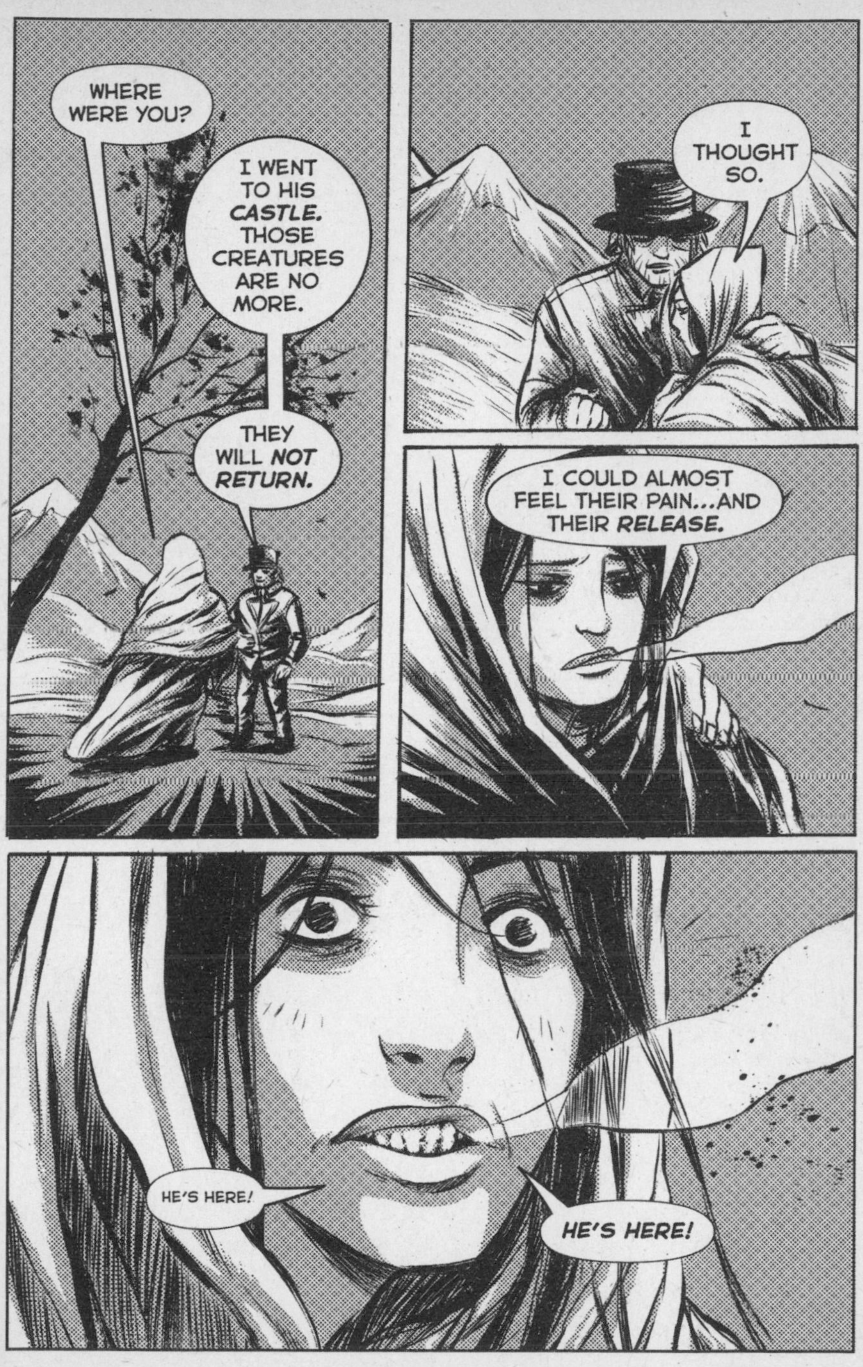
WHERE WERE YOU?
I WENT TO HIS *CASTLE.* THOSE CREATURES ARE NO MORE.
THEY WILL *NOT RETURN.*
I THOUGHT SO.
I COULD ALMOST FEEL THEIR PAIN...AND THEIR *RELEASE.*
HE'S HERE!
HE'S HERE!

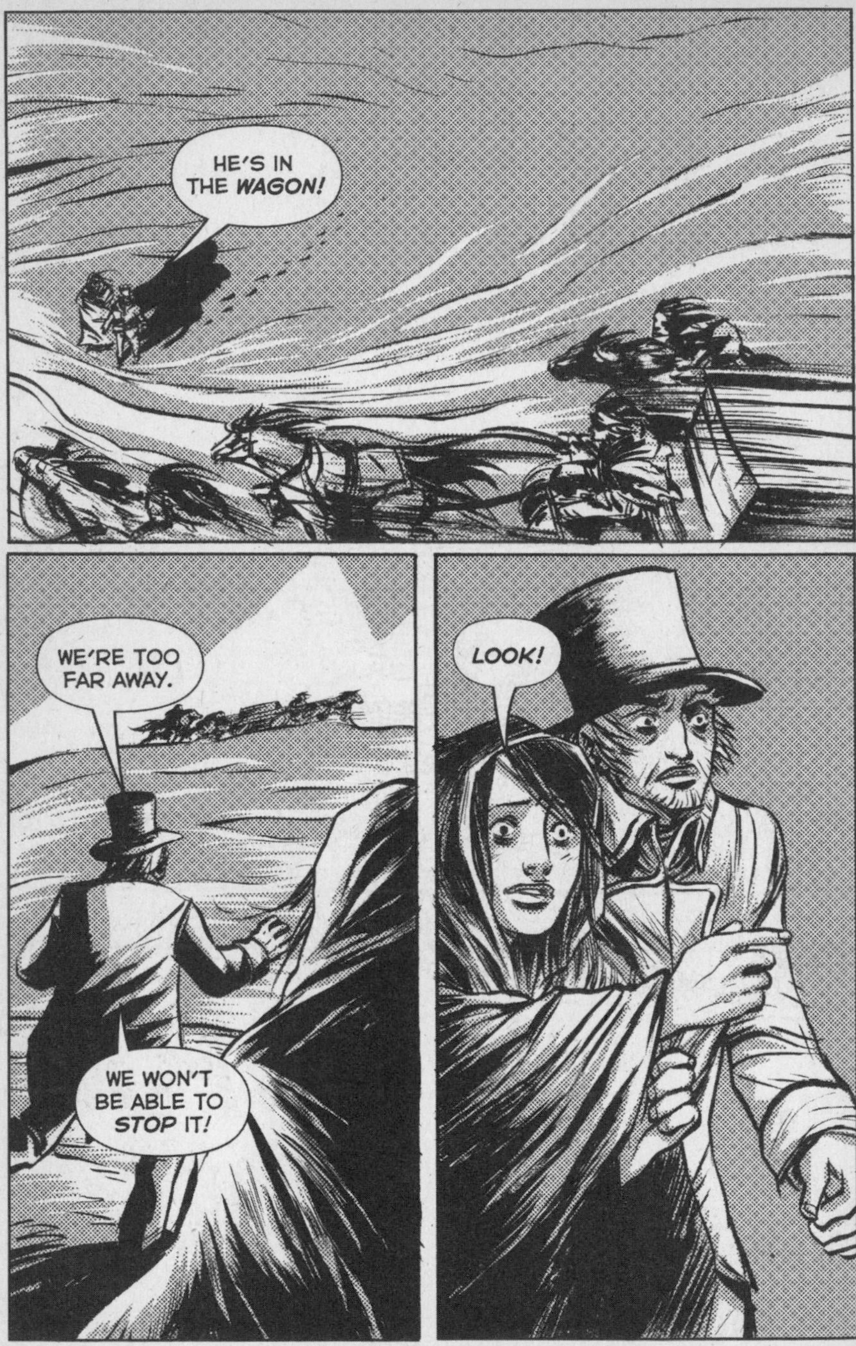
HE'S IN THE WAGON!
WE'RE TOO FAR AWAY.
WE WON'T BE ABLE TO STOP IT!
LOOK!

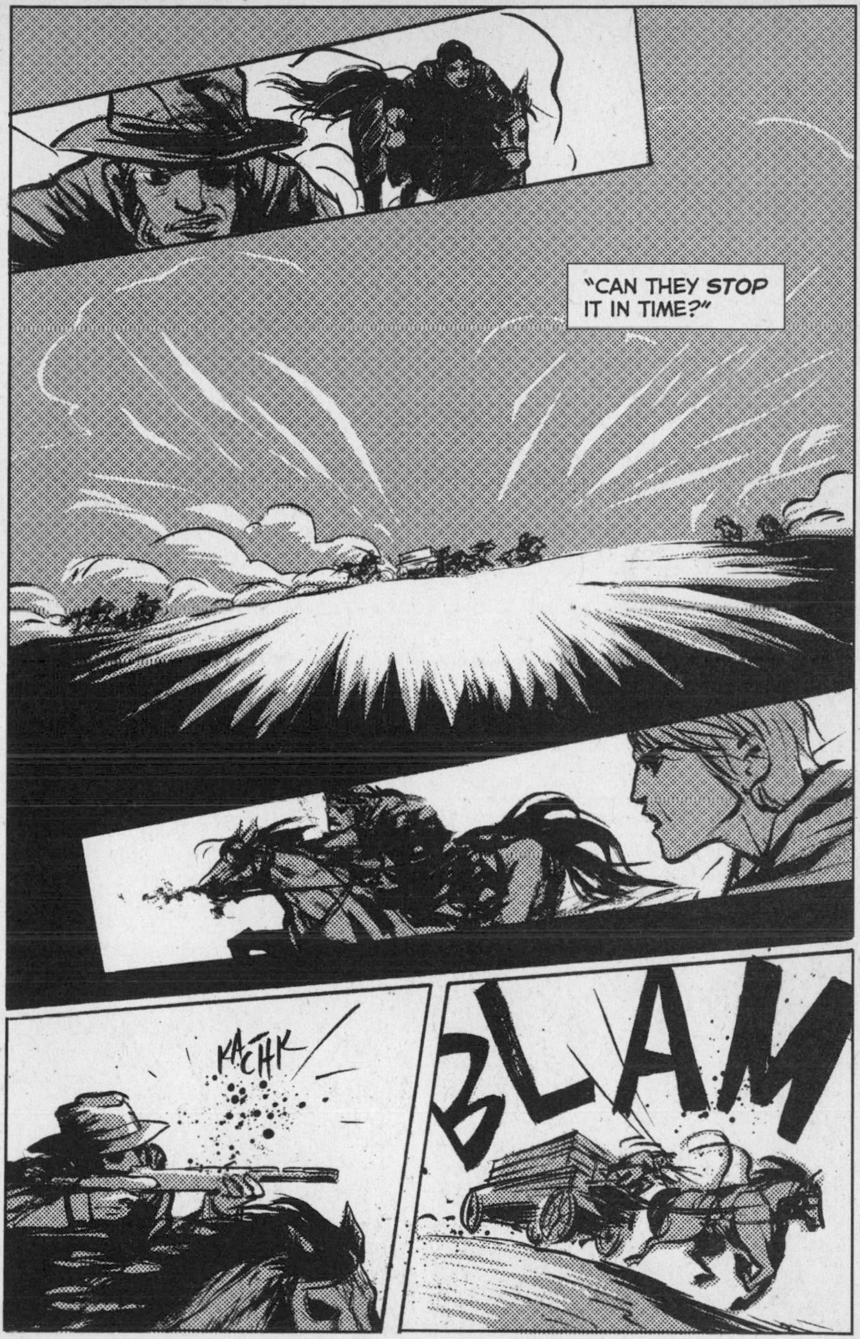
"CAN THEY STOP IT IN TIME?"
KACHK
BLAM

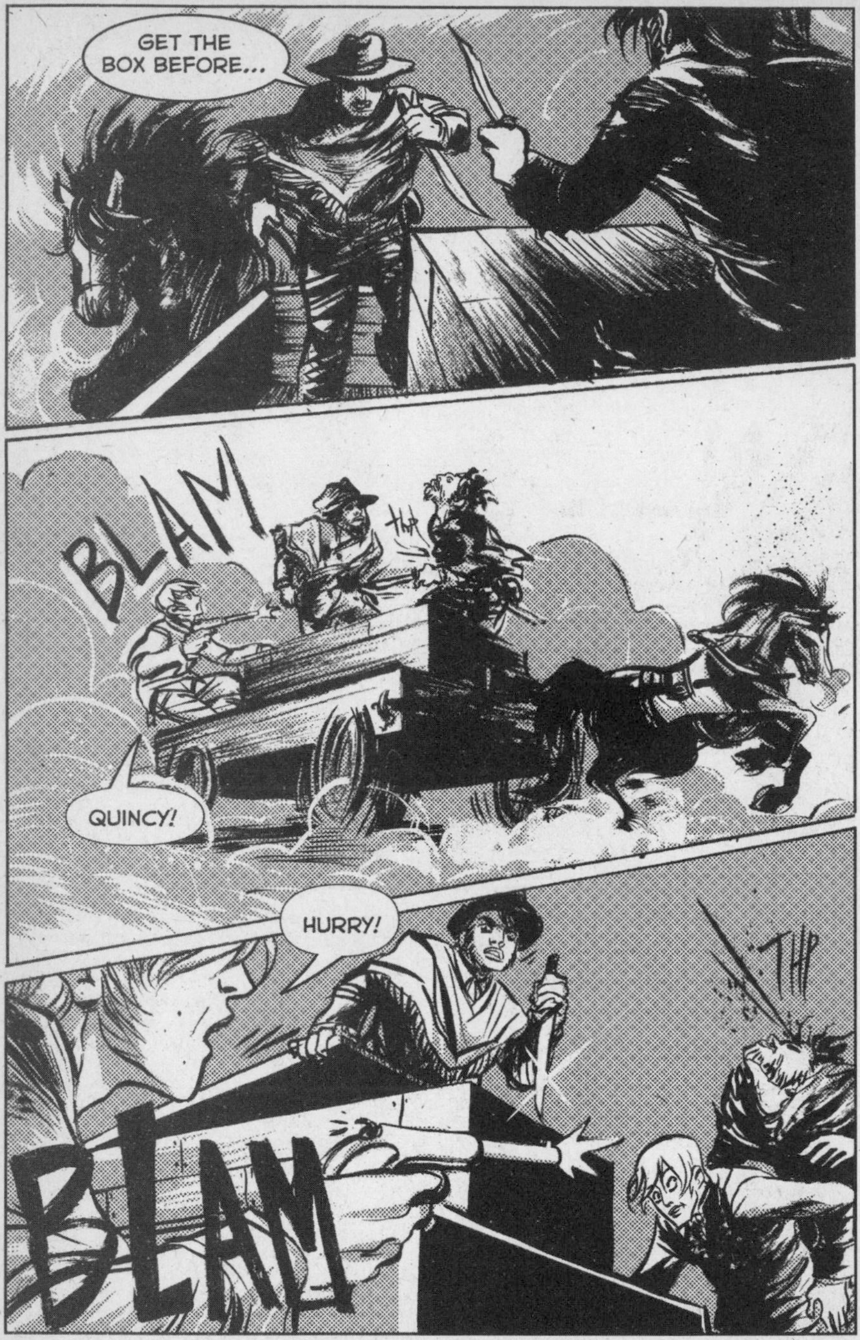
GET THE BOX BEFORE...
BLAM
THP
QUINCY!
HURRY!
THP
BLAM

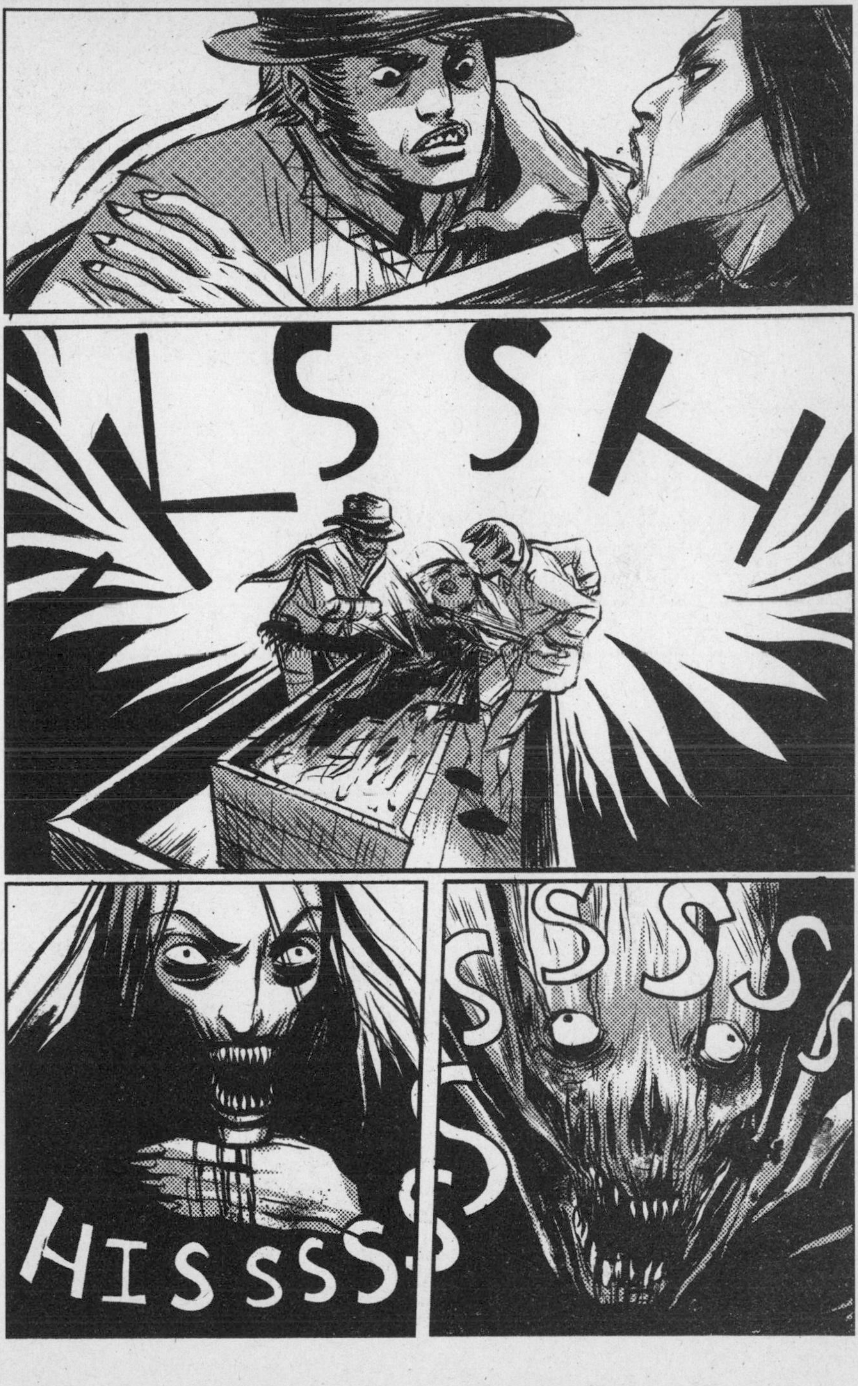
KSSH
HISSSS
SSSSSSS

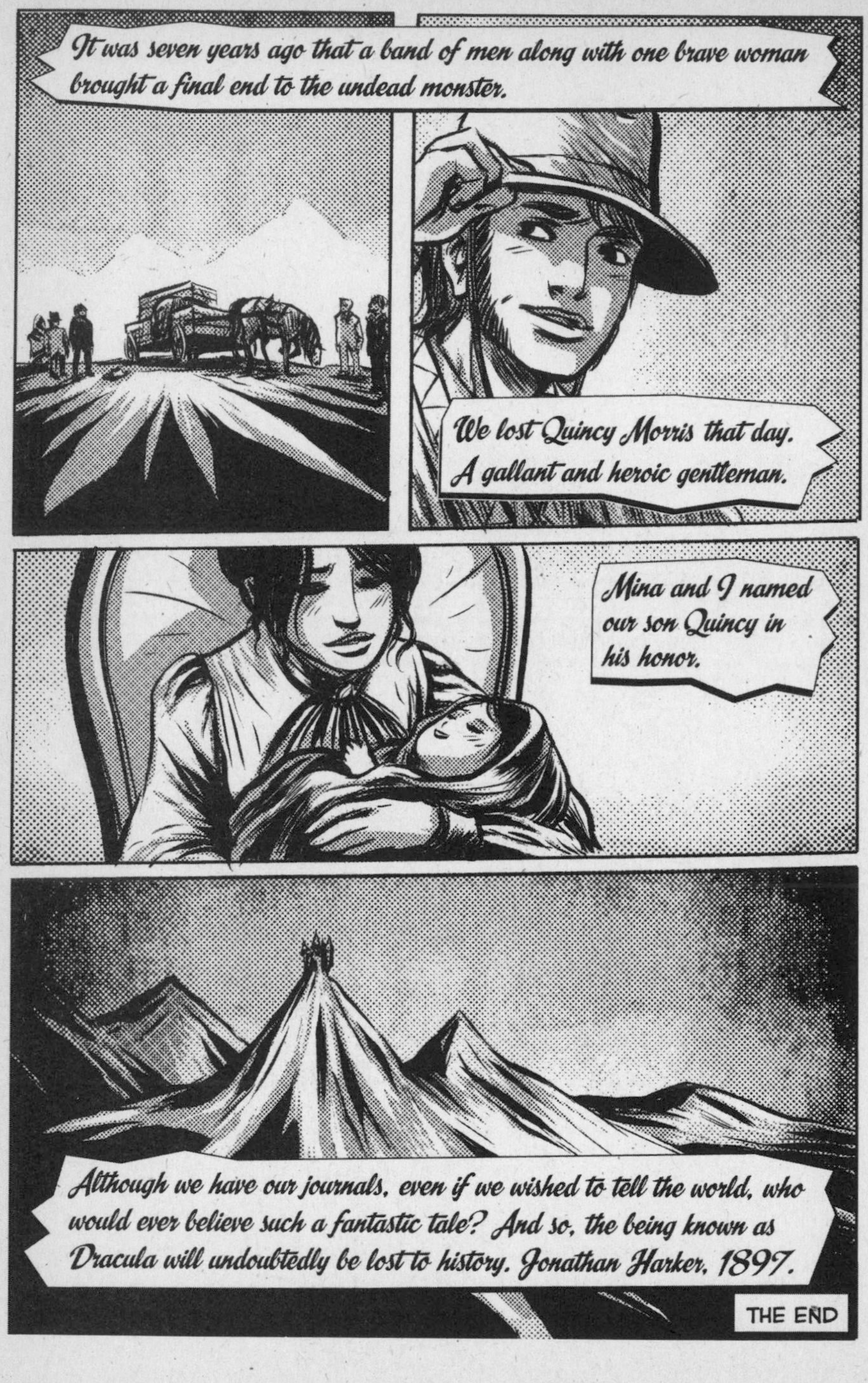
It was seven years ago that a band of men along with one brave woman brought a final end to the undead monster.
We lost Quincy Morris that day. A gallant and heroic gentleman.
Mina and I named our son Quincy in his honor.
Although we have our journals, even if we wished to tell the world, who would ever believe such a fantastic tale? And so, the being known as Dracula will undoubtedly be lost to history. Jonathan Harker, 1897.
THE END

THE MAKING OF

BRAM STOKER'S

Dracula

"I hope this adaptation will introduce new readers to Stoker's great novel." —Gary Reed

"It was a treat to draw this book. I'm really glad I got the chance to take a stab at Dracula." —Becky Cloonan

GARY REED
TALKS ABOUT HIS ADAPTATION OF

BRAM STOKER'S
Dracula

One of the hardest tasks for a writer is an adaptation. When the original work is a classic of literature, the task can seem overwhelming. Readers want something that stays true to the original yet is also fresh enough to make a new version of the book worthwhile.

I was familiar with *Dracula*, not only from reading it but also from a previous graphic novel I had written called *Renfield*. Notably, with *Renfield*, I was creating my own world, filling in the story that Stoker didn't include about Renfield.

To most people, *Dracula* is a straight horror story that introduced the world to the lore of vampires. But, even more than that, *Dracula* was a sign of how the world was changing as science replaced old superstitions; Victorian values were swept away in a sea of technology, nationalism, and a new sense of morality.

I concentrated primarily on the horror aspect of the novel, as that is the crux of what continues to make *Dracula* compelling. I kept the story sequential to Stoker's original and moved within the parameters that he so ably created. The format limited excursions into some areas, but the adaptation is faithful in terms of scenes and events. The dialogue is abbreviated, yet still captures the essence of the original.

Bram Stoker was never considered a great writer, but in *Dracula*, he wrote a great novel. My hope is that I can introduce new readers via the adaptation and entice them to savor Stoker's original work.

BECKY CLOONAN
TALKS ABOUT HER ART FOR

BRAM STOKER'S
Dracula

One of the biggest challenges was to portray the material in a way suitable for all ages. I also tried to update the look of it enough so that when kids pick it up, it would pique their interest and not feel dated.

To get inspiration, I watched F. W. Murnau's film *Nosferatu*, and Robert Wiene's film *The Cabinet of Dr. Caligari*, two excellent expressionist films that I think captured a feeling I hoped to get across with my representation of the book. I was listening to a lot of metal, too, which helped (heh heh).

One thing I tried to portray clearly was the different environments. I think the stronger the environment is, the stronger the characters will appear against it. I also wanted to really accent the different moods of the story. Additionally, I was paying very close attention to the acting of the characters, giving them different expressions and gestures.

This was probably one of the hardest comics I've ever drawn. Just the fact that it is based on such a notorious novel is enough to put the pressure on!

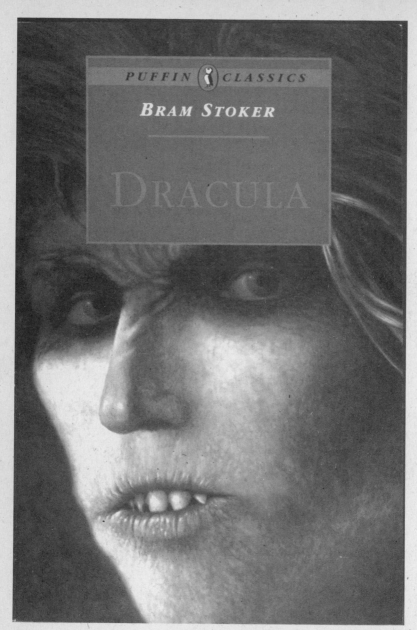

PUFFIN CLASSICS

BRAM STOKER

DRACULA

Gary and Becky used for their reference the Puffiin Classics edition of *Dracula*.

DENNIS CALERO'S COVER SKETCH GALLERY

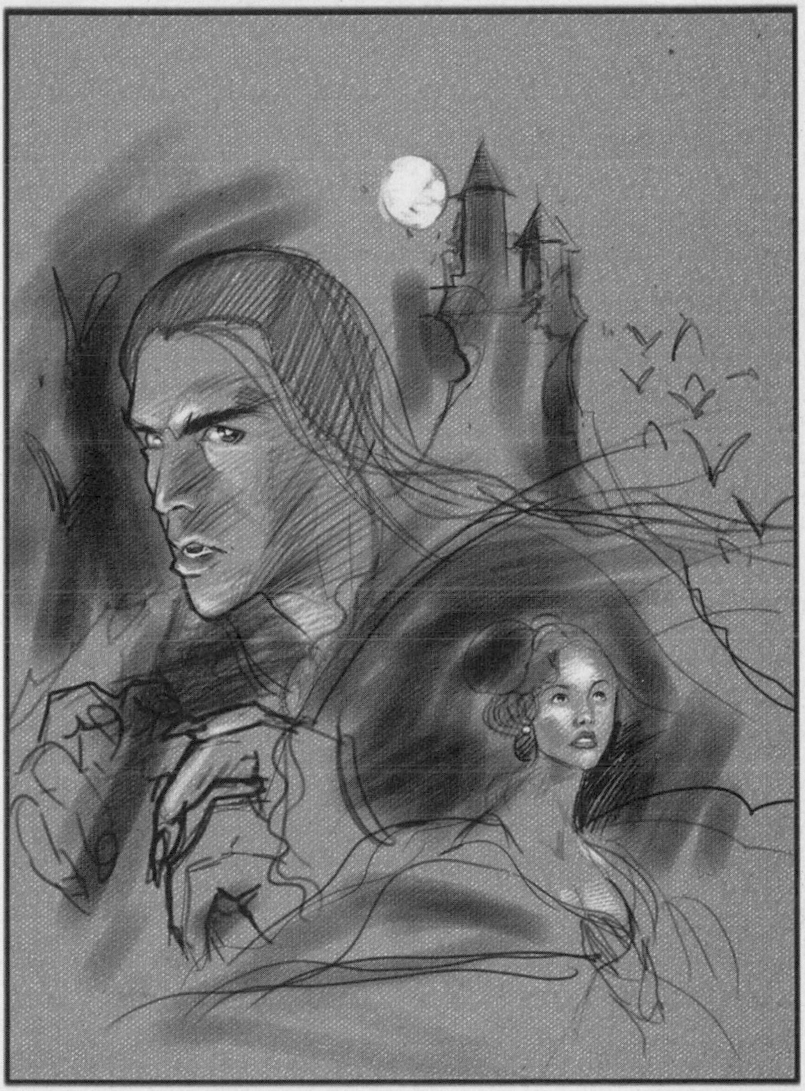

Dennis Calero did a number of sketches for the cover to *Bram Stoker's Dracula.* This is his first version.

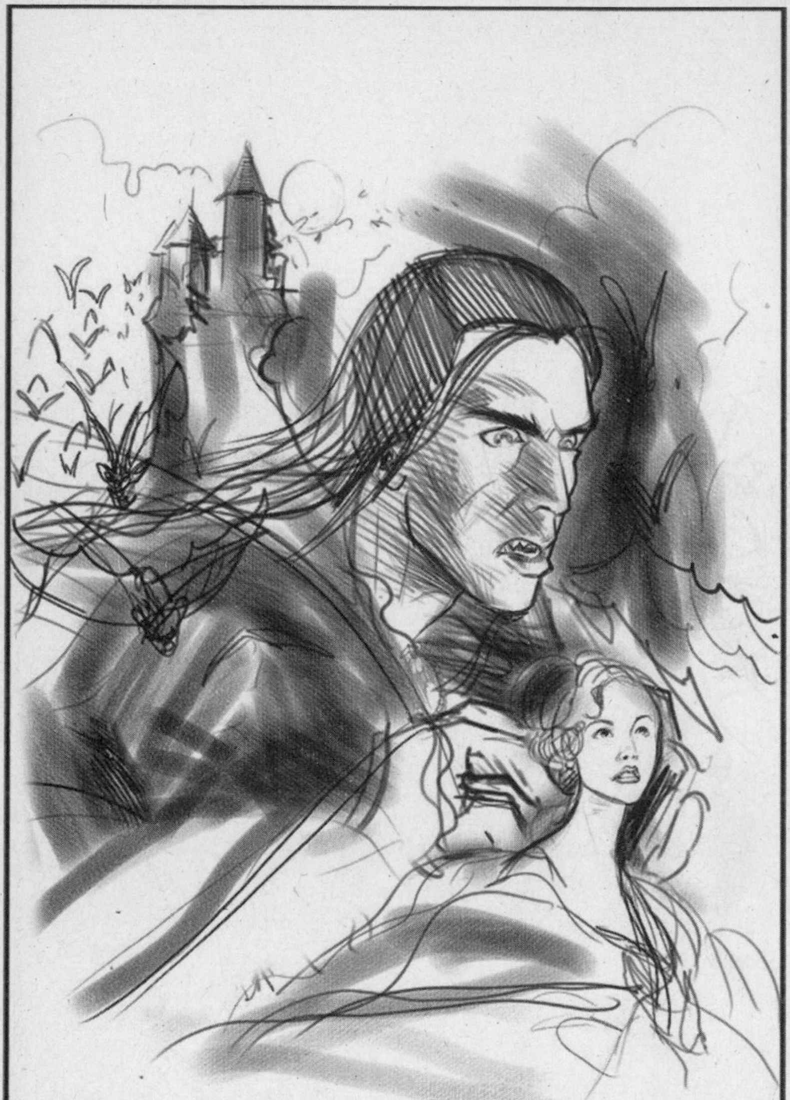

In this version, note that Dracula's head is turned to look at Mina.

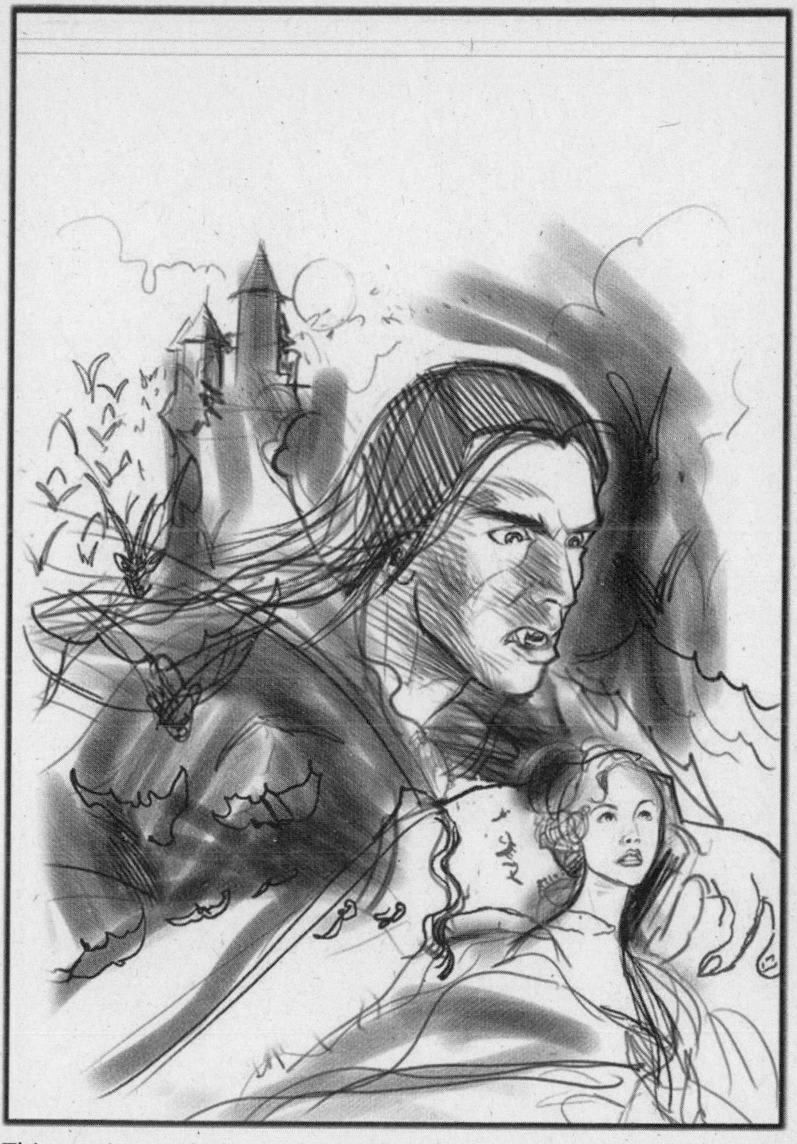

This version includes Dracula's hands appearing to reach out for Mina, adding more menace to the cover. Also note the larger swarm of bats.

BECKY CLOONAN'S SKETCHBOOK

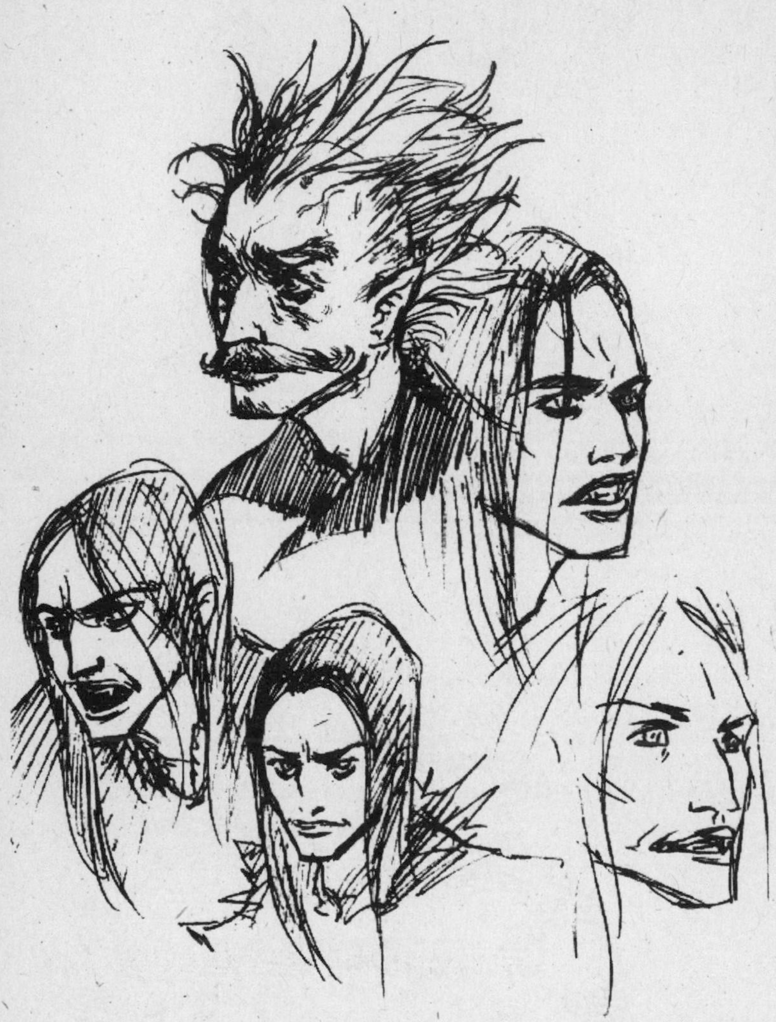

Becky did a number of sketches of the characters for the story. Here are a variety of **Dracula** faces and expressions.

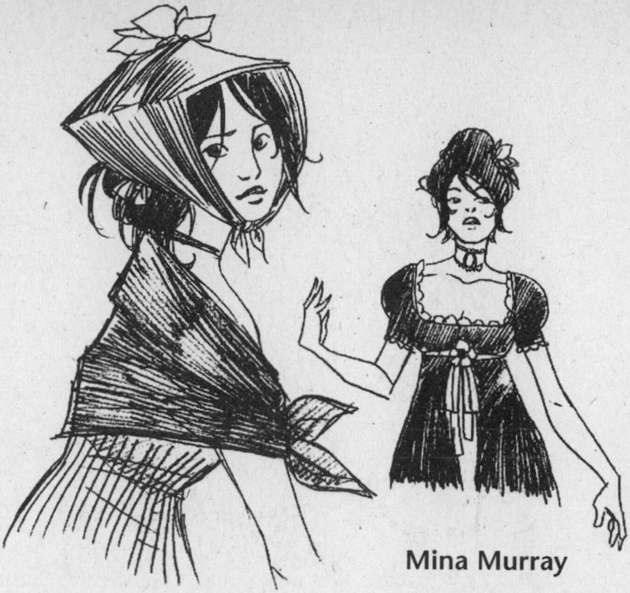

Mina Murray

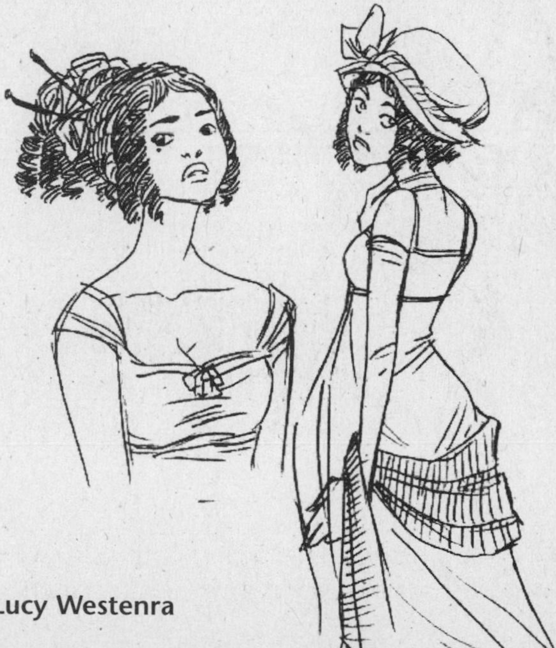

Lucy Westenra

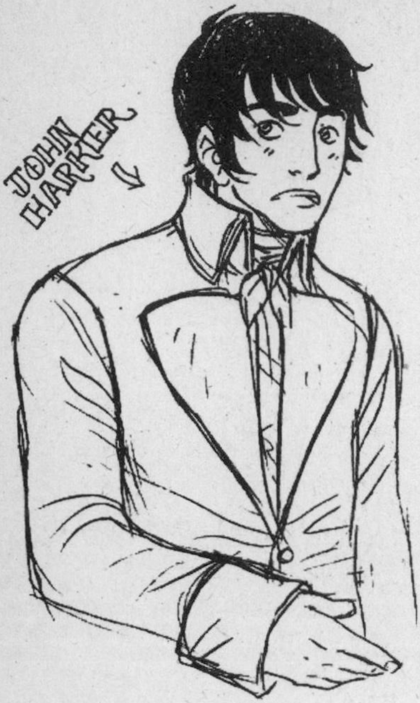
JOHN
HARKER

Jonathan Harker

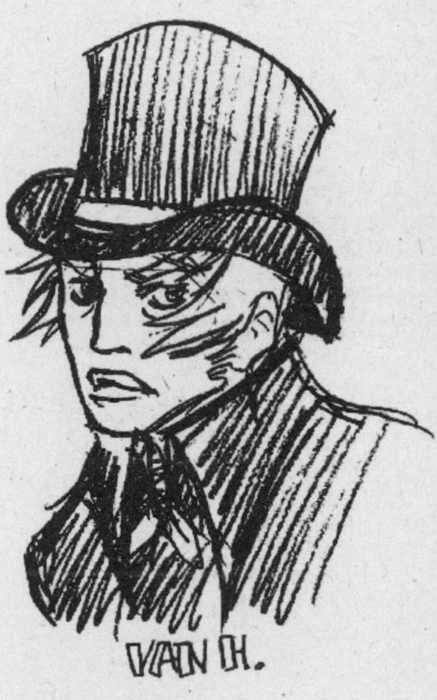
VAN H.

Dr. Abraham Van Helsing

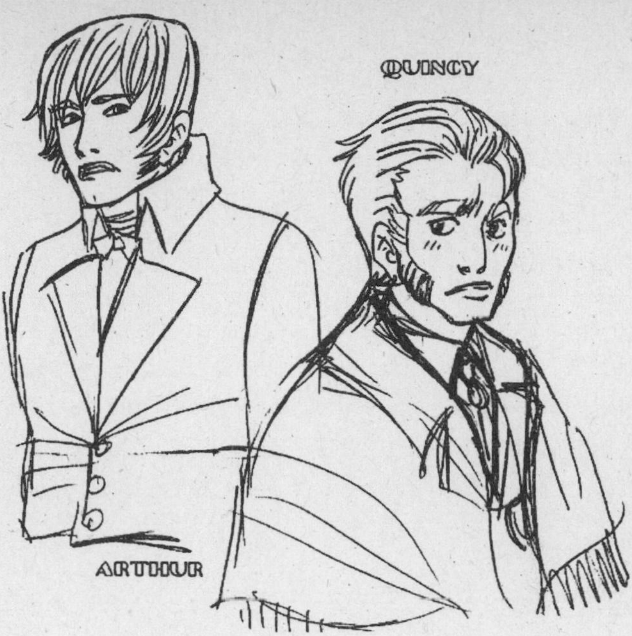
QUINCY
ARTHUR

Arthur Holmwood (left)
Quincy P. Morris (right)

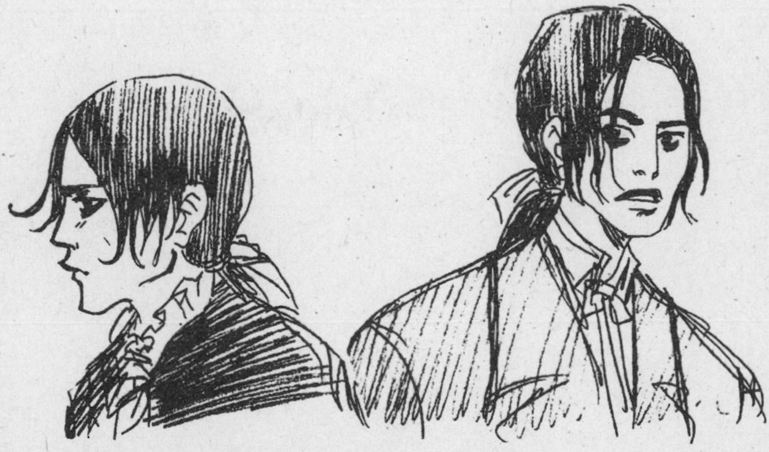

Dr. John Seward

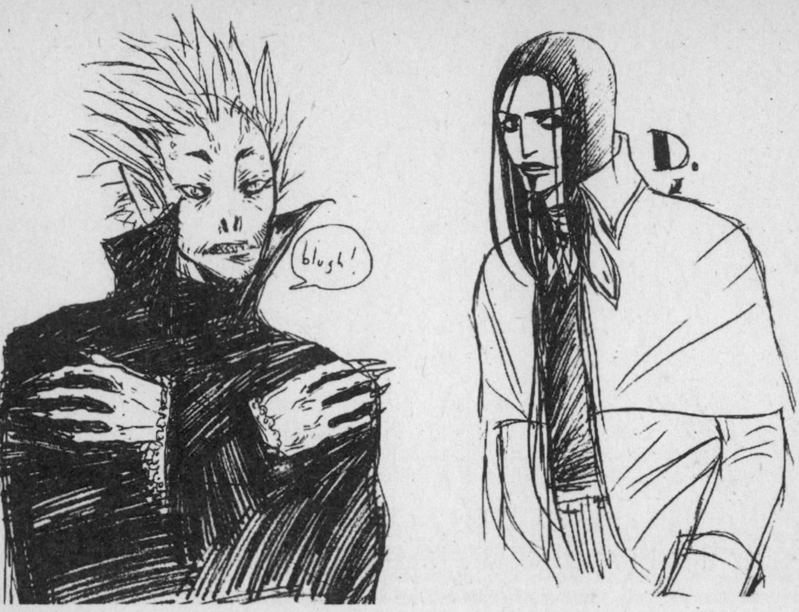
blugh!
D.

Two versions of Dracula

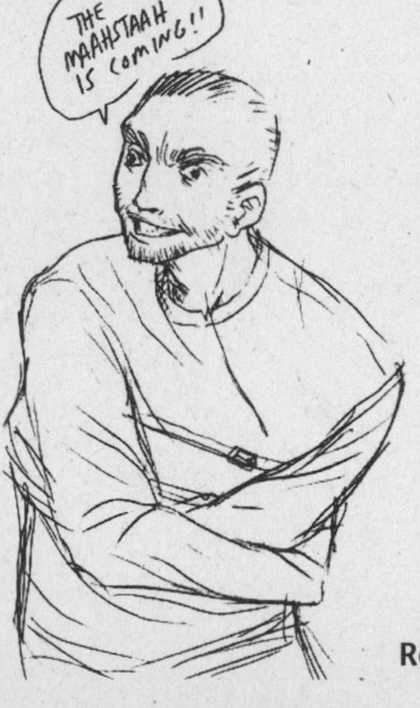
THE MAAHSTAAH IS COMING!!

Renfield

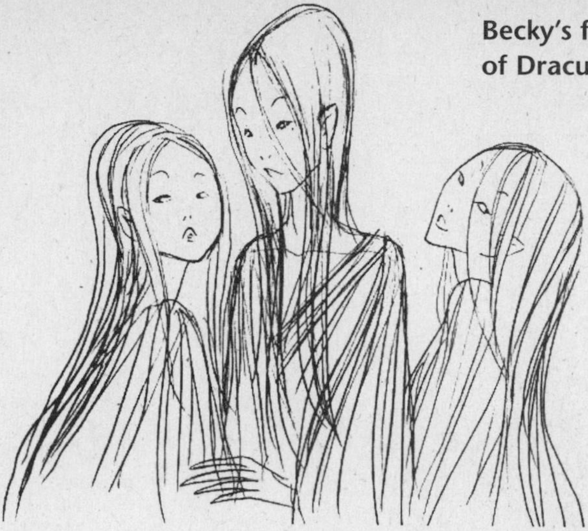

Becky's first version of Dracula's brides

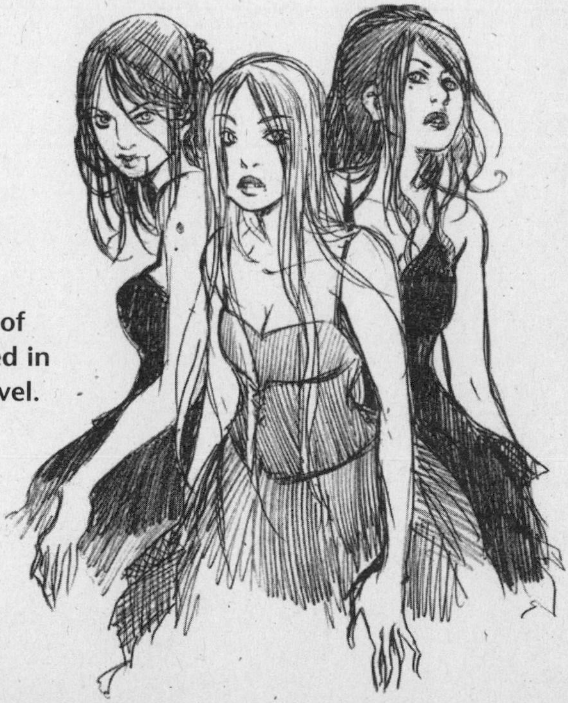

An early study of the version used in the graphic novel.

HOW BECKY DRAWS

Since every comic is different, I approach each comic differently. On this particular book, after I got the script I drew thumbnail sketches in chunks of five or ten pages. Then I would draw more detailed pencil art pages that would be sent to the editors for approval. After I got approval, I would ink and tone them. For inking, I prefer to use a brush and Sumi ink. Tones are done in Photoshop with the help of Deleter's Comic Works program. Doing tones on computer is pretty standard nowadays.

When the pages were complete, I uploaded computer files of the art to the publisher via their ftp server. This is much easier than sending disks or art boards via FedEx, since I can further tweak pages how I see best.

On the following pages are a selection of Becky's pencil art breakdowns. The first eight pages are from a scene early in the story, when Jonathan Harker first meets Count Dracula. The last two pages are from a scene featuring Mina Murray and Lucy Westenra. Compare these pages with the finished art and note the changes.

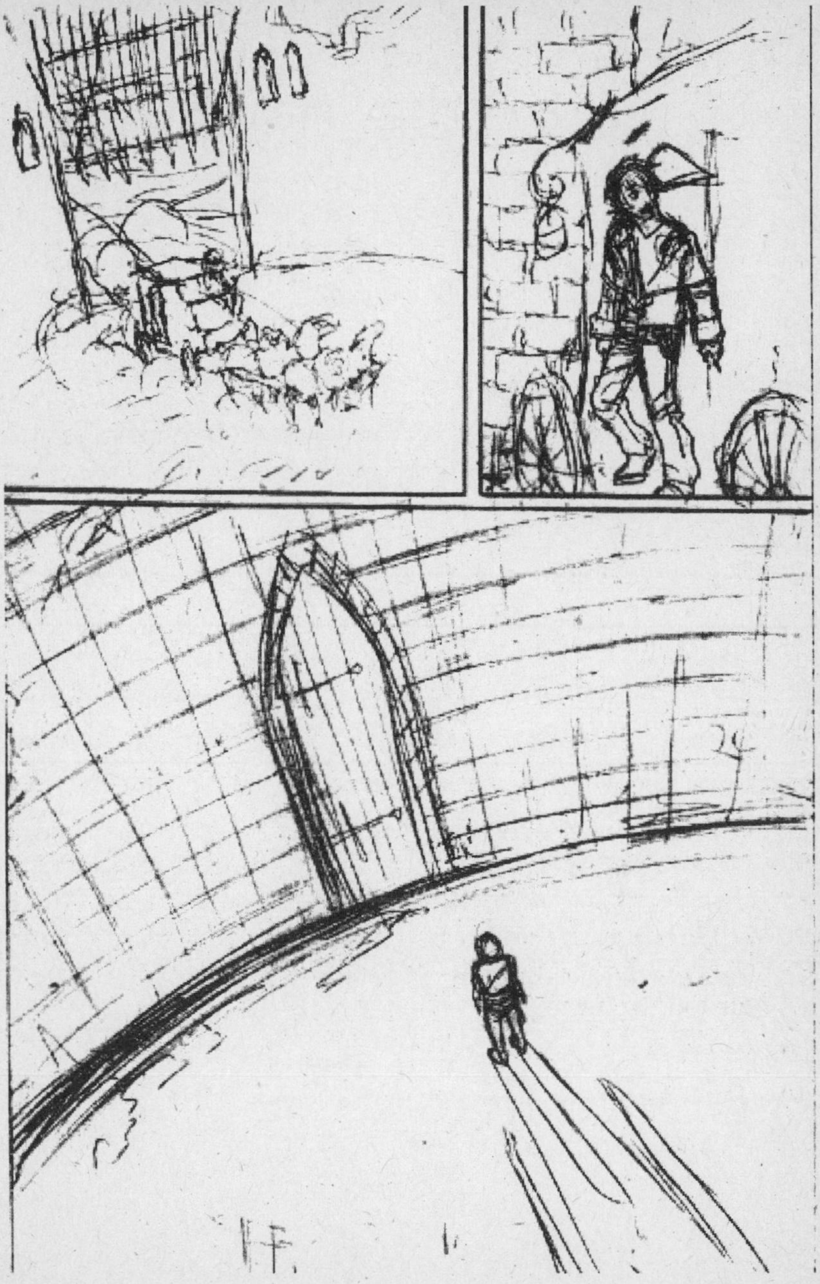

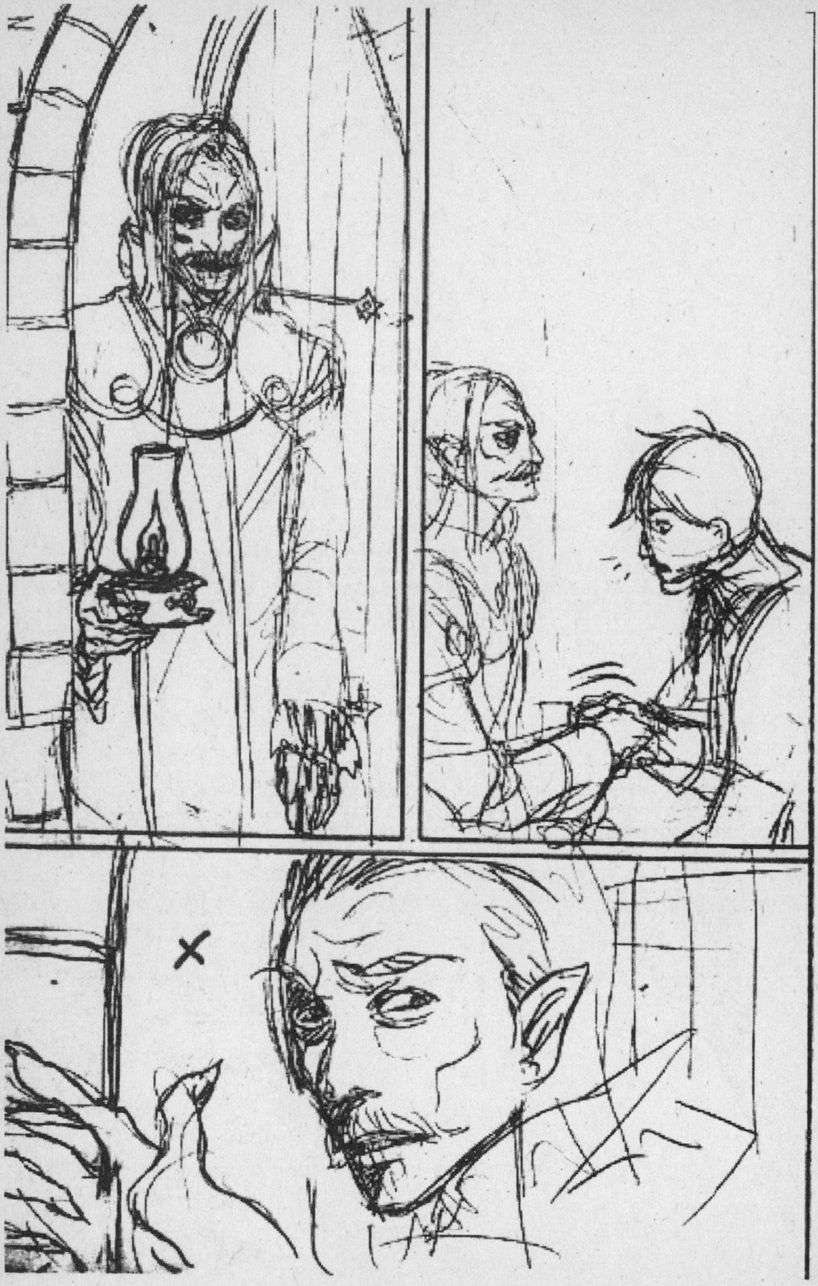

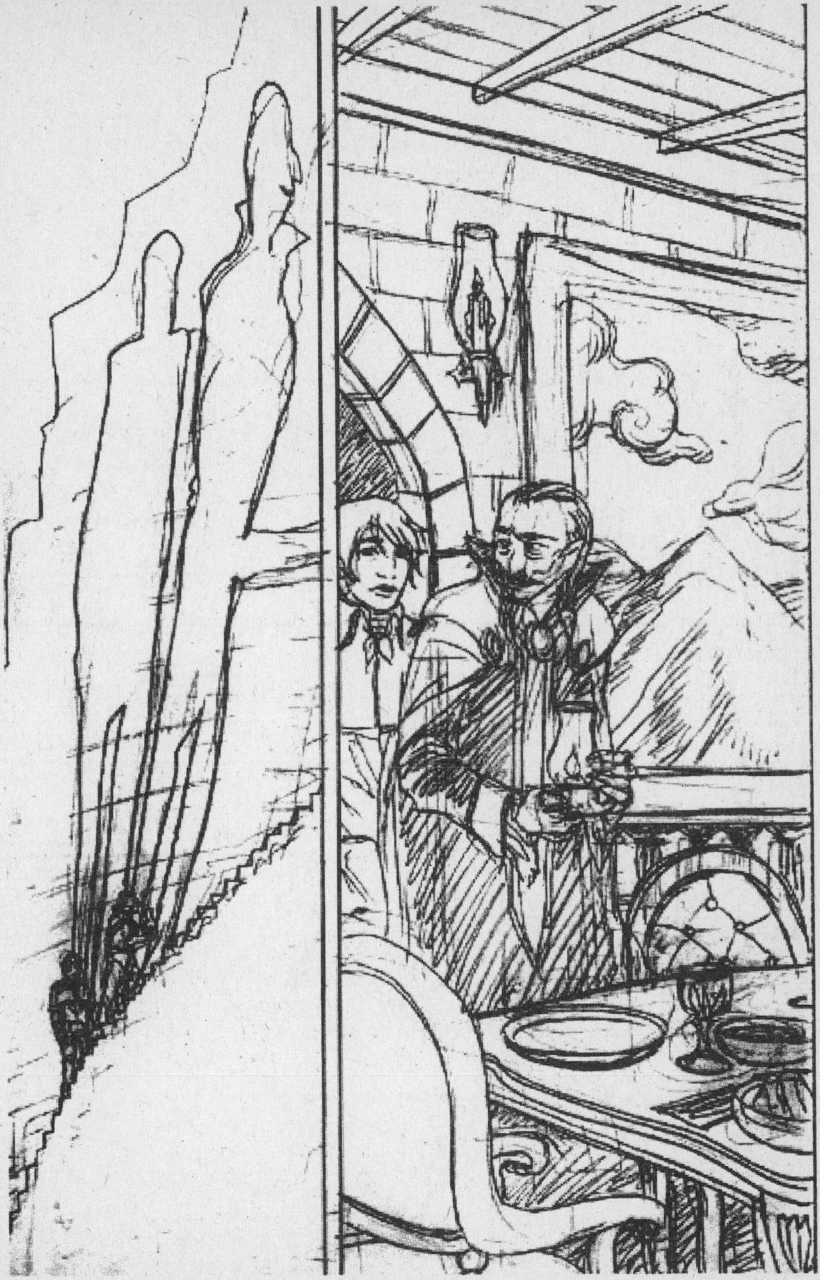

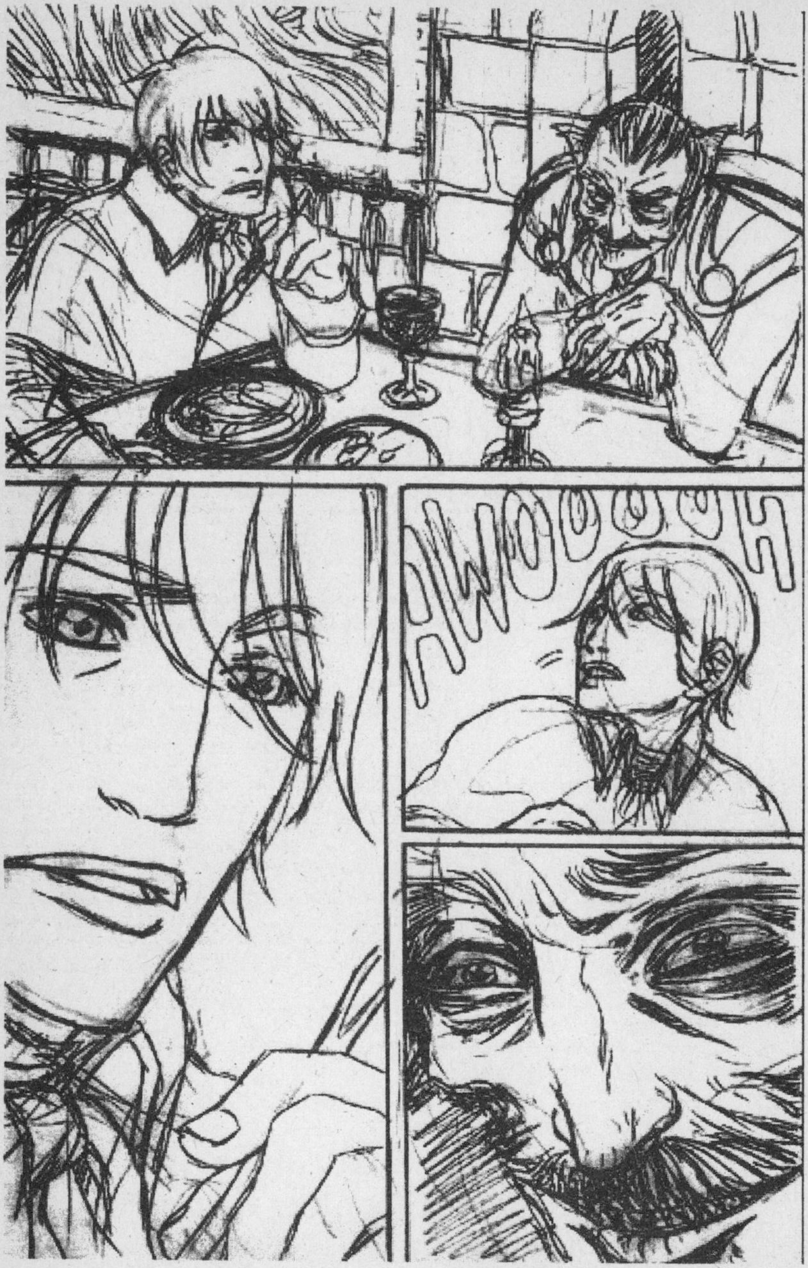
AWOOOOH

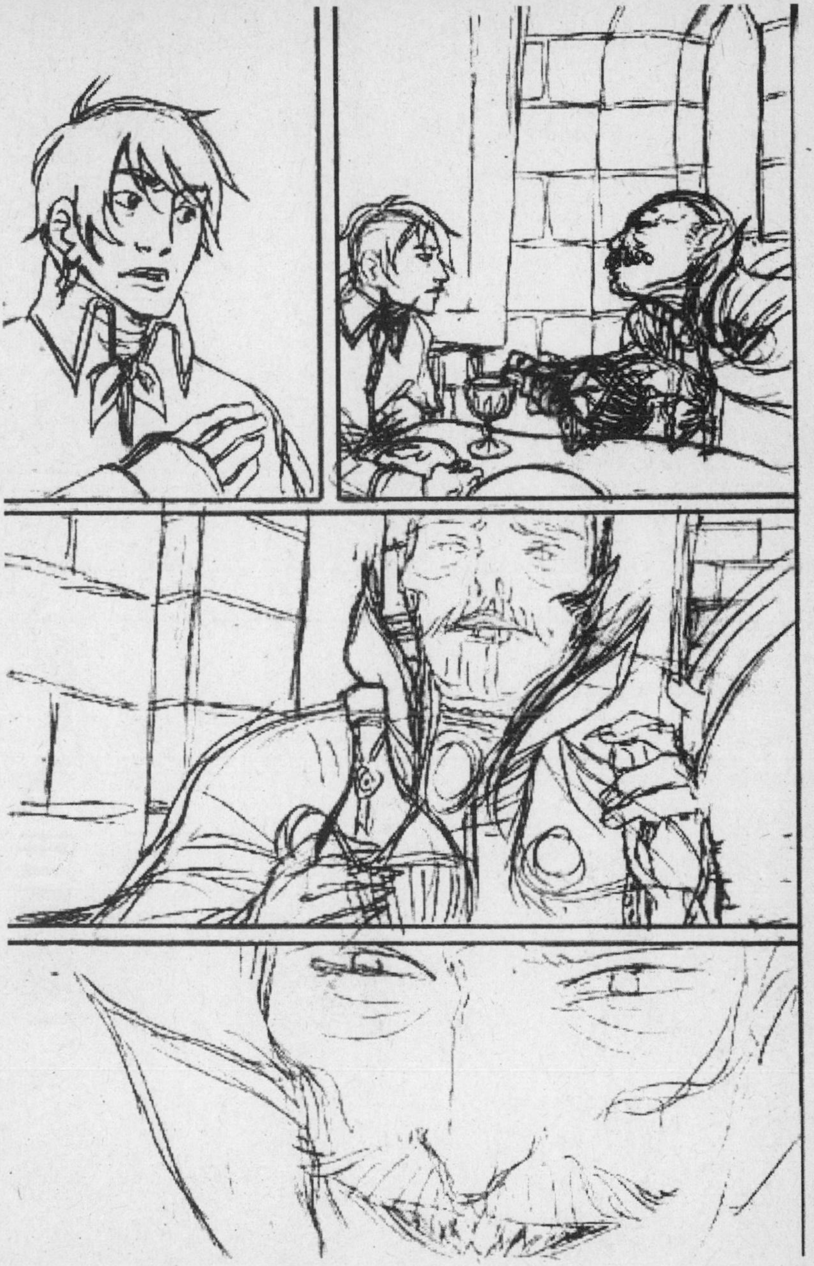

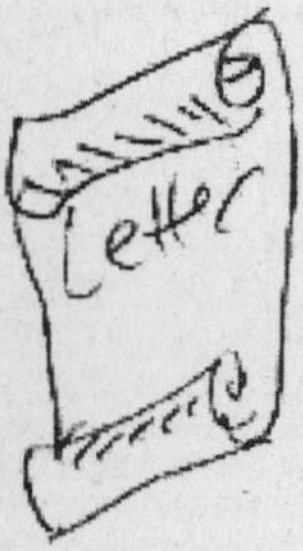
Letter

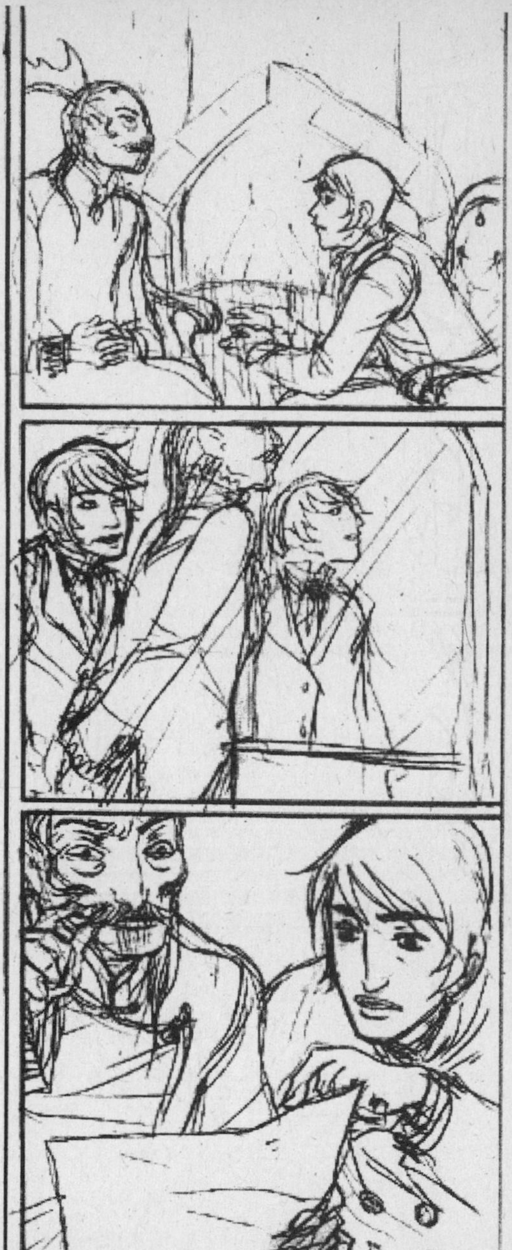

This is the original art design for page 20. The page was redesigned to allow enough space for the text.

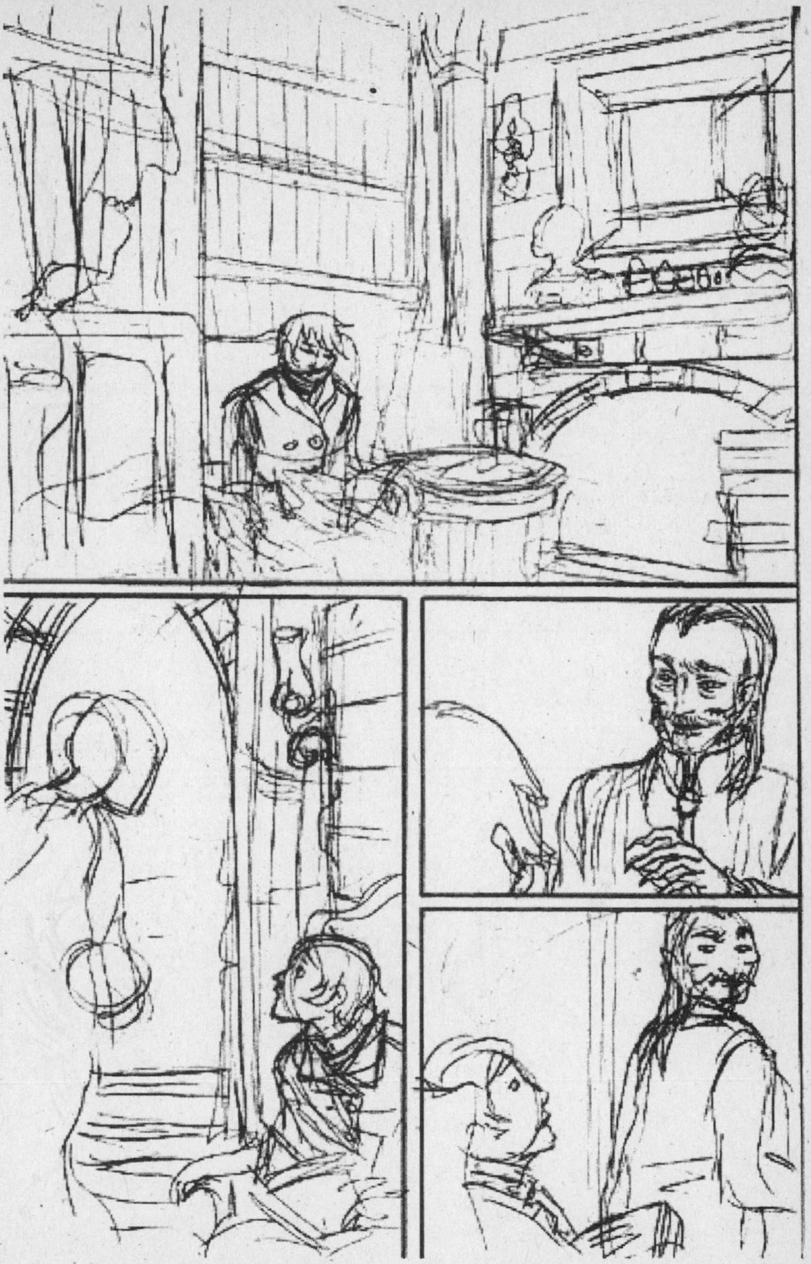

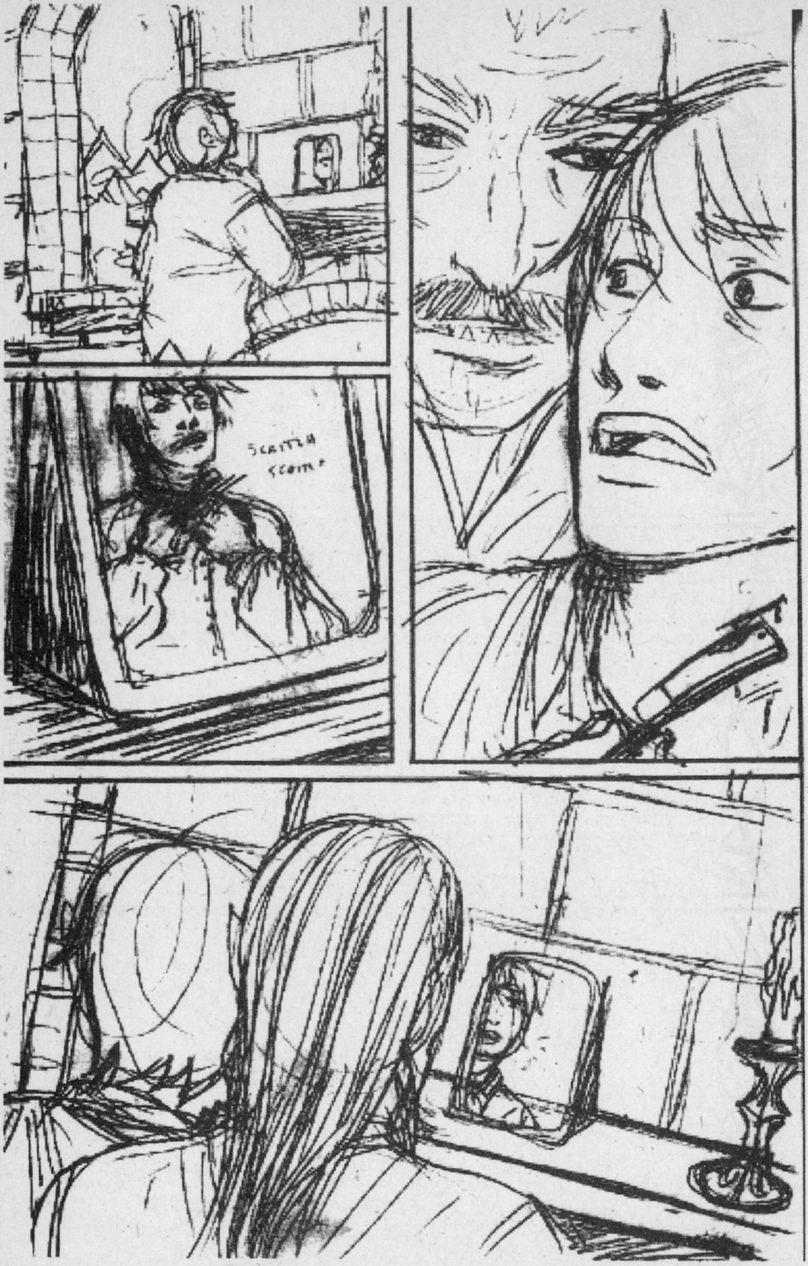
SCRITCH

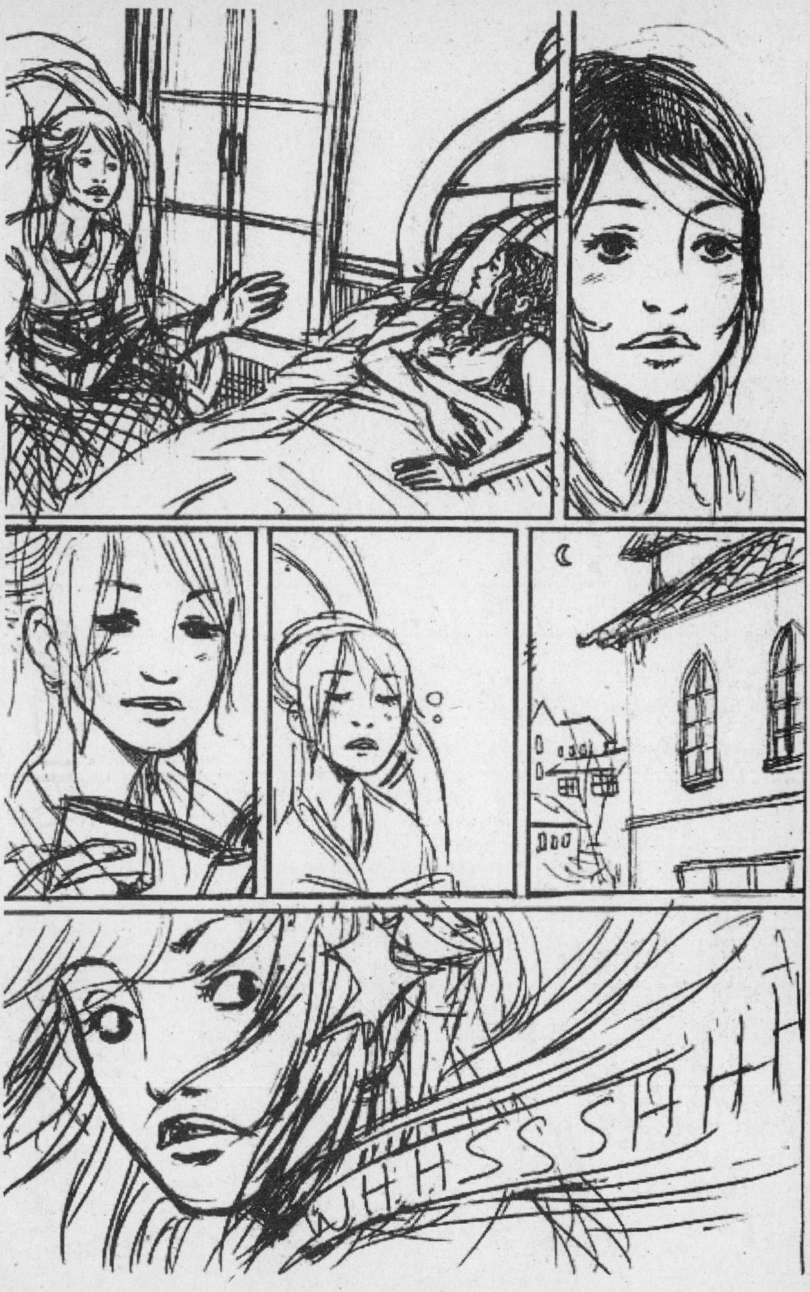
WHHSSSAHH

The two-page section featuring Mina and Lucy.

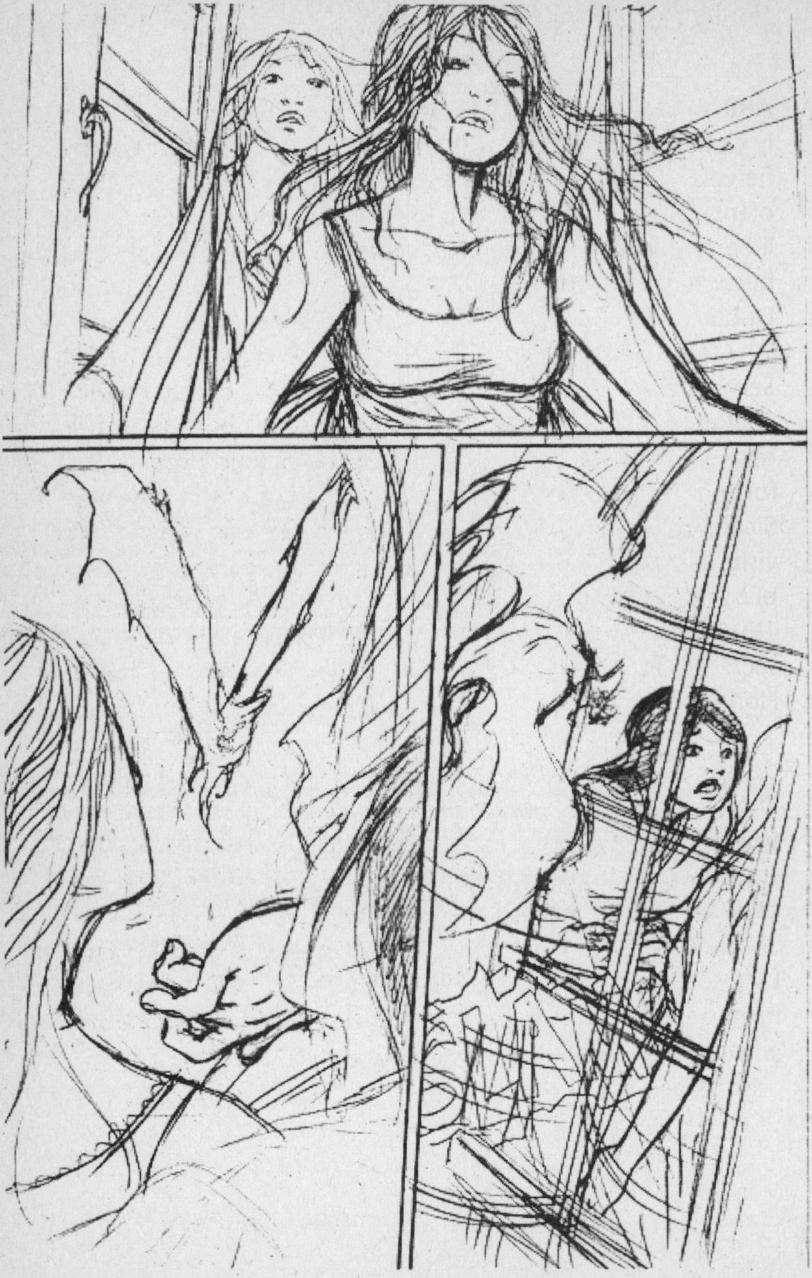

ABRAHAM "BRAM" STOKER (1847–1912) was such a sickly child that he could hardly stand on his own two feet until he was seven years old. As with many sickly children, he had plenty of time to read and developed an abiding passion for literature. He made up for his early weakness, however, and became the champion athlete of his year at Trinity College, Dublin.

After university, he followed his father into the Irish Civil Service in his native Dublin, but soon became bored and disenchanted with this career. He enjoyed the theater, and to give his life some variety, he became an unpaid drama critic for the Dublin *Mail.* The most famous actor of the time was Sir Henry Irving, and in 1876 Stoker helped advertise Irving's visit to Dublin. Naturally enough, the two men met. They became firm friends, and from 1878 until Irving's death in 1905 Bram Stoker's main job was as Irving's manager and secretary. In 1878 he married Oscar Wilde's former girlfriend, Florence Balcombe.

He was also pursuing a literary career. He wrote about a dozen books, but is today remembered for only one— *Dracula,* which was first published in 1897. The book is a true masterpiece of the macabre; with its parade of evil monsters and its compelling storyline, it was an immediate success, and has remained so ever since.

The definitive film version was made in 1931 with Bela Lugosi in the title role. Since then, dozens of Dracula films have been made, a recognition of the enduring fascination with one of the great villains in literature.

GARY REED was the publisher of Caliber Press, a specialty publisher of comics and books that released over 1,500 issues in the 1990s. In addition to serving as president of Caliber, he was also publisher of Stabur Graphics and vice president of McFarlane Toys during their inaugural launch. Gary has written over 200 comics and books, including *Baker Street, Renfield, Saint Germain,* and *Raven Chronicles.* Gary also wrote the Puffin Graphics adaptation of *Mary Shelley's Frankenstein.*

BECKY CLOONAN was born in 1980, in Pisa, Italy. She attended the School of Visual Arts in Manhattan, majoring in animation. She left after three years to pursue a career in comics. Her best-known works, both written by Brian Wood, include the graphic novel *Jennie One* and the critically acclaimed twelve-issue series *Demo,* which *Entertainment Weekly* praised as "touching" and *Variety* called "more human than mainstream comics dare to be." She also contributes to *Meathaus* and *Flight* anthologies. Her next book is *East Coast Rising.*